Advance Praise for *Mohamed's Moon*

Blending the suspense a̶̶̶̶̶̶̶̶̶̶ *Blink,*
Mohamed's Moon is a b̶̶̶̶̶̶̶̶̶̶ storytelling and thought-prov̶̶̶̶̶̶̶̶̶

ILSON

THOR

OF *FIREPROOF* AND *FIELD OF BLOOD*

Marvelous! Clemons has a gift for creating characters you'll come to call friends, twists that keep you gulping and guessing, and insights that will have you talking and thinking. I was turning pages so fast I have a paper cut to prove it.

—PHIL CALLAWAY
SPEAKER AND AUTHOR OF *LAUGHING MATTERS*

A stirring story of culture clash, love, and sacrifice, *Mohamed's Moon* is a sensitive and beautifully written tale about the Truth. From the harsh sands of Egypt to the busy streets of California, from the bondage of Islam to the freedom of Christianity, this story rings true in every way possible. Keith Clemons has got himself a winner here...and has established himself as an author to keep your eye on!

—MIKE DELLOSSO
AUTHOR OF *THE HUNTED* AND *SCREAM*

Rarely do I read a book with such riveting action, great character development, and powerful insights. Clemons has given us a realistic glimpse into a culture that's alien to most Americans while confirming our Christian beliefs. A wonderful read packed with intrigues and suspense. I recommend it for everyone!

—LARRY CARPENTER
PRESIDENT OF STANDARD PUBLISHING

Keith Clemons has done it again with an exciting tale of love, sacrifice, and redemption. A wonderful read, *Mohamed's Moon* is sure to expand Clemons' growing fan base.

—LARRY J. LEECH II
PRESIDENT OF WORD WEAVERS WRITING GROUP

Clemons ties lavish description, complex characters, and an intriguing plot together with an eye-opening, yet compassionate, message about the differences between Christianity and Islam. Ultimately, *Mohamed's Moon* asks the age-old question: can love defeat hatred, or will the world continue to be plunged into devastating wars?

—N. J. LINDQUIST
MOTIVATIONAL SPEAKER,
FOUNDER OF THE WORD GUILD,
AND AWARD-WINNING AUTHOR OF *GLITTER OF DIAMONDS*

MOHAMED'S
MOON

MOHAMED'S MOON

KEITH CLEMONS

REALMS
A STRANG COMPANY

Most STRANG COMMUNICATIONS BOOK GROUP products are available at special quantity discounts for bulk purchase for sales promotions, premiums, fund-raising, and educational needs. For details, write Strang Communications Book Group, 600 Rinehart Road, Lake Mary, Florida 32746, or telephone (407) 333-0600.

MOHAMED's MOON by Keith Clemons
Published by Realms
A Strang Company
600 Rinehart Road
Lake Mary, Florida 32746
www.strangbookgroup.com

Quotations from the Bible are from the New King James Version of the Bible. Copyright © 1979, 1980, 1982 by Thomas Nelson, Inc., publishers. Used by permission.

Quotations from the Quran are taken from *The Quran Translation*, 7th edition, translated by Abdullah Yusef Ali (Elmhurst, NY: Tahrike Tarsile Quran, Inc., 2001).

The characters portrayed in this book are fictitious unless they are historical figures explicitly named. Otherwise, any resemblance to actual people, whether living or dead, is coincidental.

Design Director: Bill Johnson
Cover design by Justin Evans

Library of Congress Cataloging-in-Publication Data
Clemons, Keith.
   Mohamed's moon / Keith Clemons. -- 1st ed.
      p. cm.
   ISBN 978-1-59979-525-6
   I. Title.
   PS3603.L473M85 2009
   813'.6--dc22

                                    2009002441

First Edition

09 10 11 12 13 — 987654321
Printed in the United States of America

ACKNOWLEDGMENTS

I WANT TO THANK THOSE who, whether knowingly or unknowingly, participated in the development of this story. First and foremost I want to thank my friends Mohamed and Sally Mohamed for their careful review of the manuscript, ensuring its accuracy. Their personal story is a book in itself. Born and raised in Egypt, they were devout Muslims when they met Jesus and were called into His service. Their account is a chapter right out of the Book of Acts—one miracle upon another. May God continue to bless their ministry to Arabic-speaking people around the world.

My wife, Kathryn, and my sister, Kathleen, also read the manuscript, providing me with words of encouragement as well as valuable critique. Thank you, ladies. I love you both.

I am also grateful to the ministry of Brother Andrew and to his book *Secret Believers*, which opened my eyes to much of what happens when a Muslim embraces Christ, and to the Voice of the Martyrs ministry, which faithfully speaks out for the persecuted church worldwide.

The sermon given in chapter 16 was originally delivered to the congregation of Good Friends Fellowship by Pastor Don Fitchett. I want to express my sincere thanks to Pastor Don for allowing me to use an adaptation of his words in this book. Readers, please take note: the description given of the pastor who delivers the sermon in the book is not that of Pastor Don. I borrowed only his words, not his appearance or personality. My heartfelt thanks also go to the senior pastor of Good Friends, Rod Hembree, who constantly encourages us to lift our persecuted brothers and sisters up in prayer.

In fine-tuning this manuscript, I had the privilege of working with two of the finest editors in the business, Lori Vanden Bosch, who meticulously trimmed the unnecessary fat and made suggestions that led to an improved plot, and Anne Severance, whom I've had the pleasure of working with on several earlier novels and was thrilled to be working with again. Ladies, I sincerely appreciate your patience with me and your careful polishing of these pages. If this work has any merit at all, my readers have you to thank.

Finally, I want to mention my good friends, John and Beth Ellis, without whom this manuscript might still be on my desk instead of in print. Upon reading one of my previous novels, *Angel in the Alley,* they took it upon themselves to send the book to a friend of theirs at Strang Communications. That gesture resulted in imprint editor Debbie Marrie contacting me, which opened discussions that led to the publication of this work. John, Beth, I know you say you only did what you felt God was leading you to do. All I can say is thank you for responding to *His* voice.

Solo Dei gloria—to God alone the glory!

He who has the Son has life; he who does not
have the Son of God does not have life.

—1 John 5:12

PROLOGUE

ACROSS THE SOUTHERN SWEEP *of Egypt, mounds of sand change their shape and location, following the direction of the wind. The dunes rise two and three stories high, curling at the crest like waves tossed on the sea. The sand spits and furls and undulates like a maelstrom born of the deep, but there's no water here. This sea is yellow, and its spray is limestone abrasion. And it's hot. Unbearably hot. The sun shimmers on the sand, blurring the eyes.*

The wind blew incessantly, painting the sky a dirty brown. It had come up suddenly, a desert storm, whipping the sand into a froth, tearing at clothes, twisting hair, and scouring lungs. The man hid behind his camel with his head buried in the animal's thick fur, using it as a wall against the assault. Smelly matted hair, like old rugs, soiled and musty and full of ticks, but the insulation kept him alive. The beast knelt with its eyes closed, its legs folded underneath, hunkered down to ride out the storm.

Khalaf coughed, clearing his throat, and reached under his scarf to wipe grit from his nose. He pulled the scarf tight again, careful to protect his eyes. All men are born to die. He would die too, *soon*, just not here and not now. Allah be praised, his death would be glorious, the kind of death befitting a soldier.

He watched the tracks of his camel filling in, big as tambourines, being swept away as though they were never there—*just like man*—here one day, gone the next. If he did die, they wouldn't find him. He'd be buried by the hand of Allah. Only the rack of his bones, bleached by the sun, would remain. His camel would wander free, carrying its water on its back until found by someone smarter, or better prepared to cross the desert, than he.

Enough!

Allah had not brought him here to die. The wind had to stop—*eventually.* His camel would lead him out of this...*this hell.* He slapped the animal's thigh. The mountain of fur began to shift, turning its head. *Don't...awww— curse you and the mother that weaned you—beast!* Khalaf swept a viscous mix of slobber and sand from his shoulder. He had wanted a horse, the mount of warriors and kings, but they'd given him this cursed ungulate. "A Bedouin crossing the desert will not be of interest to American satellites," they'd said. *Can those Western devils really see from the sky? Are they gods?* He imagined himself being buried, one grain of sand at a time, until nothing remained. *They must be laughing.*

The sun too was relentless, like a sponge sucking moisture from the air. He could feel the heat burning his skin even though he wore several layers of clothing—*sun?* His camel was getting anxious. It snorted, trying to stand. Khalaf slipped his scarf down just enough to peek, blinking the sand from scratched, watery eyes. The sky looked blurry, but it was blue, not brown. The wind had ceased.

Scooping handfuls of sand from his lap, he struggled to his feet. He coughed more sand from his throat and spat, rolled his tongue around his mouth and spat again, the grit grinding against his teeth. *Al hamdullah, I survived!* Sand poured like rain from the folds of his *abaya* as he dusted himself off. He stretched, working the kinks out of muscles that hurt from sitting in one place too long. He'd passed the test, even if no one was there to see it. When the time came, he would not fail.

CHAPTER 1

S UN SPARKLES ON THE *Nile in flecks of gold, shimmering like the mask of Tutankhamen. The decaying wood boat—a felucca—is as ancient as the flow that passes beneath its hull, its sail a quilt-work of patches struggling to catch the wind. The craft creaks with the prodding of the rudder, bringing it about to tack across the current, cutting toward land with wind and water breaking against its bow. All along the shore a pattern emerges: villages sandwiched between checker-board squares of cornfields, sugarcane, and cotton bolls. In the distance a barefoot girl herds sheep, goading them with a stick. At the sound of their bleating, a water buffalo foraging in the marsh lifts its head, causing the birds on its back to take flight. A dark-robed woman stoops to wash her dishes in the canal. Purple lilies clog the water in which a small boy also swims.*

The cluster of yellow mud-brick homes erupts out of the ground like an accident of nature, a blemish marring the earth's smooth surface. There are fewer than a hundred, each composed of mud and straw—the same kind of brick the children of Israel made for their Egyptian taskmasters. Four thousand years later, little has changed.

Those living here are the poorest of the poor, indigent souls gathered from Egypt's overpopulated metropolitan centers and relocated to work small parcels of land as part of a government-sponsored program to stem the growth of poverty. It's the dearth that catches your eye, an abject sense of hopelessness that has sent most of the young men back into the cities to find work and thrust those who stayed behind into deeper and more odious schools of fundamentalist Islam.

• • • ☽ • • •

Zainab crouched at the stove, holding back the black *tarha* that covered her hair. She reached down and shoveled a handful of dung into the arched opening, stoking the fire. The stove, like a giant clay egg cut in half, was set against the outside wall of the dwelling. She blew the smoldering tinder until it erupted into flame, fanning the fumes away from her watering eyes while lifting the hem of her black *galabia* as she stepped back, hoping to keep the smoke from saturating her freshly washed garment.

She had bathed and, in the custom of Saidi women, darkened her eyes and hennaed her hair just as Nefertiti once did, though it was hard to look beautiful draped in a shroud of black. She fingered her earrings and necklace, pleased at the way the glossy dark stones shone in the light. Mere baubles perhaps, but Khalaf had given them to her, so their value was intrinsic.

He had been away more than a month, attending school. She hadn't been able to talk to him, but at least his brother, Sayyid—she cringed, then checked herself—had been kind enough to send word that today would be a day of celebration. It had to mean Khalaf was coming home. She brought a hand up, feeling the scarf at the back of her head. She wanted him to see her with her hair down, her raven-dark tresses lustrous and full, but that would have to wait.

She went inside to prepare a meal of lettuce and tomatoes with chicken and a dish called *molohaya* made of greens served with rice. It was an extravagance. Most days they drank milk for breakfast and in the evening ate eggs or beans. She'd saved every extra piaster while her husband was away, walking fifteen miles in the hot Egyptian sun to sell half of the beans she'd grown just so they'd be able to dine on chicken tonight. Khalaf would be pleased.

She turned toward the door. A beam of yellow light streamed into the room, revealing specks of cosmic dust floating through the air. She brought her hands to her hips, nodding. Everything was ready. She'd swept the straw mat and the hard dirt floor. The few unfinished boards that composed the low table where they would recline were set with ceramic dishware and cups. Even the cushion of their only other piece of furniture, the long low bench that rested against the wall, had been taken outside and the dust beaten from its seams.

Not counting the latrine, which was just a stall surrounding a hole in the ground that fed into a communal septic system, the house boasted only three rooms. One room served as the kitchen, living room, and dining room. The other two were small bedrooms. The one she shared with her husband, Khalaf, was barely wide enough for the dingy mattress that lay on the dirt floor leaking tufts of cotton. The other was for their son, who slept on a straw mat with only a frayed wool blanket to keep him warm.

She wiped her hands on her robe, satisfied that everything was in order. If Sayyid was right and Khalaf had news to celebrate, he would be in good spirits, and with a special dinner to complete the mood, perhaps she would have a chance to tell him.

She thought of the letter hidden safely under her mattress. Maybe she'd get to visit her friend in America *and*...best not to think about that. *Please, Isa, make it so.*

She reached for the clay pitcher on the table and poured water into a metal pot. Returning to the stove outside, she slipped the pot into the arched opening where it could boil. Khalaf liked his *shai* dark and sweet, and for that, the water had to be hot.

The boy danced around the palm with his arms flailing, balancing the ball on his toe. He flipped it into the air and spun around to catch it on his heel and then kicked it back over his shoulder and caught it on his elbow, keeping it in artful motion without letting it touch the ground. He could continue with the ball suspended in air for hours by bouncing it off various limbs of his body. Soccer was his game. If only they would take him seriously, but that wouldn't happen until he turned thirteen and became a man, and that was still two years away. It didn't matter. One day he would be a champion, with a real ball, running down the field with the crowds chanting his name.

He let the ball drop to the ground, feigning left and right, and scooping the ball under his toes, kicked it against the palm's trunk. *Score!* His hands flew into the air as he did a victory dance and leaned over to snatch his ball from the ground—not a ball really, just an old sock filled with rags and enough sand to give it weight—but someday he would have a real ball and then...

A cloud of blackbirds burst from the field of cane. There was a rustling, then movement. He crept to the edge of the growth, curious, but whatever, or whoever, it was remained veiled behind the curtain of green.

He pushed the cane aside. "What are you doing?" he said, staring at Layla. The shadow of the leafy stalks made her face a puzzle of light.

"Come here," she whispered, drawing him toward her with a motion of her hand.

"No. Why are you hiding?"

"Come here and I'll tell you." Her voice was subdued but also tense, like the strings of a lute stretched to the point of breaking.

"I don't want to play games. You come out. Father's not here to see you."

"We're leaving."

"What?"

"Come here. We have to talk."

"Talk? Why? What's there to talk about?" The boy let his ball drop to the ground. He stepped forward and, sweeping the cane aside and pushing it behind him, held it back with his thigh.

"We have to move. They're packing right now. We have to leave within the hour." Layla's eyes glistened and filled with moisture.

The boy blinked, once, slowly, but didn't respond. He knew. His mother had overheard friends talking. He shook his head. "Then I guess you'd better go."

"My father came here because he wanted to help, but now he says we can't stay. He says we're going to Minya where there are many Christians."

"Then I won't see you again?"

"I don't know. Maybe you will. Father says he can't abandon his patients. He may come to visit, but Mother's afraid. Why do they hate us?"

The boy shook his head, his lower lip curling in a pout.

"Do you think we will marry someday?"

His eyes narrowed. *Where had that come from?* "Marry? We could never be married. You...you're a Christian."

"I know. But that doesn't mean..."

"Yes, it does mean! My father says you're an infidel, a blasphemer. If your father wasn't a doctor, they would've driven him out long ago. Father would never let us marry. He hates it when he sees us together."

"That's why I've been thinking..." She paused, adding emphasis to her words. "You and your whole family must become Christians. Then we can be married."

"You're talking like a fool, Layla. My family is Saidi. We will never be Christian."

"But your mother's a Christian."

"No, she's not!"

"Is too. I heard—"

"Liar!" The boy clenched his fists. "My dad says all Christians are liars. My mother would never become a Christian. They would kill her."

Layla reached out, took the boy by the collar, and pulled him in, kissing him on the lips. Then she pushed him back, her eyes big as saucers against her olive skin, her eyebrows raised. She shrank back into the foliage. "Sorry, I...I didn't...I just...excuse me. I have to go. I'll pray for you," she said and, turning away, disappeared into the dry stalks of cane.

CHAPTER 2

K HALAF WORMED HIS WAY through the crowd. He had made it, crossing the desert by camel, fighting wind and burning sand. He had slipped into Sudan undetected, conveying weapons for the jihad. His instructor had been right. No one noticed a lone desert traveler passing from one country into another where there were no roads or fences.

Khalaf was received as a hero with a celebration of shouts and dancing. The Russian Kalashnikovs spat casings on the ground as bullets were fired recklessly into the air, wasting the ammunition he had just risked his life to bring. The men acted more like drunks at a wedding than soldiers receiving a delivery of supplies.

They fed him beans and rice and put him on a truck that took him east to the Red Sea, where they ferried him across into Saudi Arabia, passing him from one contact point to the next with the efficiency of a greased machine. From his drop-off in Saudi, he was taxied by Land Rover north to Jordan, crossing into the neighboring Arab nation with papers labeling him a courier on a diplomatic mission. Guards on both sides of the border seemed oblivious to the fact that his scraggly beard, soiled *abaya,* and scuffed sandals weren't the trimmings of a diplomat.

At the border to Israel, he was given a new identity. He was handed the passport of a Palestinian, a former resident of Tel Aviv who had journeyed outside the country to pay last respects to a dying relative. Khalaf's photo now graced the document. He had traveled fifteen hundred miles, farther than he'd been in his entire life, but he was finally here.

No, not quite. His final destination was paradise.

The sun shone on the stalls of the city's bustling outdoor market. He reached up, rubbing scabs where the wind had scoured his face. Overhead, the sky looked metallic—like brass clouds welded to a sheet of aluminum. Two young boys chasing each other jostled his arm. He brought his hand down and slipped it into his pocket. The narrow alley was crowded with Jews, Arabs, and Christians haggling over the value of trinkets. A bearded man in gray slacks and blue shirt with a small beanie perched on his head held up a long spiraled *shofar*, the ram's horn used by Israel as a call to arms. The Christian was offering too little; the Jew wanted too much.

Khalaf smiled. No alarm would be sounded today and many would die, praise be to Allah.

Two Palestinian brothers smelling of the Mediterranean were peddling fish packed in salt from the back of a truck, their long bony arms brown and hairy. Fruits and vegetables laid out on carts were being inspected by overzealous hands, and spices scooped from wooden barrels sent plumes of red and yellow powder into the air. Khalaf wiped his sleeve across his forehead, his heart thumping against the bands that were wrapped around his chest.

He slipped his hand into his pocket, letting his fingers play with the switch, a small button that would deliver him into the arms of Allah. He did not want to die—he was scared to death of dying—but there was no other way. He'd been an unfaithful servant, destined for hellfire. He'd embraced a reckless life in the city, not necessarily an unbeliever, but not a fanatic like his brother, either. The only solution—the will of Allah, *blessed be his name*—would benefit all concerned. His debt to Sayyid would be covered, his wife and son provided for, and he would receive an everlasting reward—all with one push of a button.

He felt moisture building on his forehead, his heart hammering his chest—*tha-thump, tha-thump, tha-thump*. A bead of sweat rolled down his forehead and clung to the end of his nose.

In a few minutes he would be no more. Free from the debt owed on that worthless piece of land. Free from the shame of not being able to provide for his family. There had better be a paradise as Sayyid promised. He tried to imagine the hereafter. Cool breezes and quiet waters, far from the frenzied crowds.

Someone bumped his elbow. He jerked his thumb off the button, avoiding a premature launch into paradise. *A Jew!* The man was staring at him. Did he suspect something? People must wonder why he wore a coat in this weather. His heart's thumping ached against his chest. He turned, fearing the sweat pouring down his face might give him away—*tha-thump, tha-thump, tha-thump.* He slipped his finger back over the button, just in case.

Think calming thoughts. He saw the ripples of a pure crystalline river pouring over rocks and flat stones with wide, shallow falls. Seventy beautiful women veiled in semitransparent lingerie beckoned him to a tent surrounded by palms and lush green ferns. Pulling the flaps back, the ladies motioned him inside, bidding him to lie on a feathered bed covered in cool white linen. He tasted dates dripping with honey.

That miserable piece of squalor he called a farm hadn't produced one decent crop in all the years he'd worked it. *Inshallah*—as God wills. His brother, Sayyid, owned a large parcel of land and had horses and people working for him. His brother was a man of means—but this was no time for regret. Man chooses his path and must follow where it leads. He'd wanted to see the world—drink the wine, dance to the music, and taste the honey of passion's lips.

When his father died, he and Sayyid had received an equal share of the inheritance, but Khalaf had sold his portion to his brother. He got as far as Cairo and within a year spent everything he had on blurry nights so vaporous and inconsequential that he had nothing to remember save a steady routine of waking up to a glaring sun with a cymbal crashing in his head and questions about how he'd fallen asleep in another pool of vomit. With eyes burning and his tongue dry as sand, he'd stumbled into the Salwa bakery looking for relief and found Zainab—the most beautiful girl he'd ever seen—but by then it was too late. He'd squandered his fortune chasing the wind. He could barely afford the few spinach rolls he purchased each day just to have her bless him with a few moments of conversation.

When he could stand it no longer, he went home to beg his brother for enough to pay her dowry and a little extra so he could purchase the five squat acres he now owned, but they'd had to move upriver and take advantage of government handouts to afford even that. And five acres just didn't yield enough crops to pay the growing number of bills.

The farm where he'd grown up under the shade of palm trees with the fragrance of incense, olive oil, dates, and pomegranates in abundance was just outside Assyut, a center of radical Islam. It was there Omar Abdel-Rahman issued a fatwa for the assassination of Anwar al-Sadat. His father labeled the killing an act of patriotism and later, when Omar was convicted by a U.S. court for his role in the World Trade Center bombing, called the man virtuous. Father would have disowned Khalaf before letting him inherit part of his estate and squander it the way he had.

Sayyid, the eldest, was the blessed son. While Khalaf was out frittering his birthright away, Sayyid was nurturing his. He established ties with the Muslim Brotherhood and began recruiting young men to defend Islam, bringing the hopelessly disenfranchised into the fold with the promise of paradise. The brokering of their lives proved lucrative and provided him with a supplemental income that continually allowed him to increase the borders of his land.

Khalaf now realized his brother was right. You either serve Allah in life or by death. There was nothing to be gained by remaining on this earth and everything to be gained by moving on.

Khalaf stood to the side to let a wooden cart loaded with bundles of flax clomp by. The driver had long curly earlocks and wore a flat-rimmed black hat, a long black coat, and white socks. The wagon creaked as the donkey struggled under the weight of the load. He caught the trader's eye. He had half a mind to do it right then, send the impatient merchant to a place in hell reserved for Jews, but he had no desire to destroy a dumb animal. Khalaf turned and slipped into the crowd, hoping the man hadn't noticed the abnormal amount of perspiration soaking through his coat. He wiped a sleeve across his brow.

His only regret was his family. If things were different, he would have asked Zainab to join him in paradise. She was his best friend, the only one he could talk to without feeling patronized. Seventy pretenders, like the girls he'd known in Cairo, would be a poor substitute, but for reasons no one was able to explain, paradise was the domain of virgins, not wives. The smell of flax wafting off the trader's cart took his thoughts home…

He was standing in his garden, the heads of lettuce small and limp, the sugarcane stunted in its growth. Zainab wiped her hands and came out to stand beside her husband. "I think we'll see a good crop this year," she said. "The cane is short, but it seems strong."

"Perhaps, but we will not see a good crop. The land is not good to me, Zainab."

Khalaf's father had often spoken of life before the Aswan Dam. During the monsoons, when the river ran high, the crops were destroyed by floods, but during the dry season, when the Nile was low, water was scarce and crops withered in the heat. There was only enough sun and rain to produce one harvest a year. But the dam changed all that. The Aswan and the two-hundred-mile lake it created provided control of the water so the river flowed at predetermined levels all year round, allowing farmers to increase the number of annual harvests from one to three. Khalaf's father had prospered.

But as his imam said, every blessing comes with a curse, maintaining the balance of good and evil. The Aswan brought a steady flow of water, making year-round irrigation possible, but most of the nutrients carried by the river from the mountains of Ethiopia to the Egyptian plain were trapped behind the dam, so the soil was never replenished. And the increased farming stripped the soil further still. Now it had to be supplemented with chemical fertilizers, which for rich landowners like Sayyid was feasible, but for poor farmers like Khalaf it added an unbearable cost. Each succeeding year robbed the earth of more nourishment, and each succeeding year brought a harvest that was more pitiful than the one before.

Khalaf stared at the rows of paltry sugarcane and wilting lettuce. It was pointless to continue. He turned and took the hands of his wife, her eyes dark and piercing, her long hair framing smooth flat cheeks with

13

lips full and red. The face of an Egyptian queen, strong enough to make him change his mind—almost. "There's nothing for me here," he said. "I've decided to do something for my family..."

He hadn't lied when he'd told her he was going to school—he couldn't lie to those eyes—but he'd purposely withheld what school he planned to attend and the fact that he wouldn't be earning a diploma. He simply said he wanted to study engineering and left it at that. She had embraced the idea with enthusiasm; that's all that mattered. His brother promised his wife and son would be cared for.

Khalaf brought his hand up, feeling the explosives taped to his chest. His coat was moist. If he didn't do it soon, someone was bound to notice— *tha-thump, tha-thump, tha-thump.*

An attractive Jewess, wearing a dark business suit and sunglasses, her brunette hair pinned in a bun, picked up a basket of eggs and handed it to the young man at her side. Khalaf watched as she leaned in and selected a loaf of bread—much like his own wife and son. He hesitated, relaxing his finger on the trigger, succumbing to a moment of regret, but then corrected himself. These were not humans; they were vermin. They were enemies of God, and enemies of God did not deserve to live.

Two uniformed Israeli soldiers stepped out from behind a vegetable cart, each pausing to light a cigarette. Khalaf's heart pounded like a jackhammer. The throngs were bustling around him. A good crowd. He felt the button, smooth as ivory, slick under his thumb. He looked up and saw the sun shining, surrounded by lacy clouds with gilded edges. He smiled—*a good day to die.*

With his eyes fixed on the heavens, he screamed, *"Allah Akbar!"* and pressed the trigger. There was a flash of light (which he never saw) and a deafening sound (which he never heard) as his body shredded. What he did see, seconds before he was thrust from this life into the next, were the clouds closing in to block the sun's light.

CHAPTER 3

THE CLATTER OF HOOFBEATS woke her from her thoughts. Zainab rushed to the door, then stopped, blinded by the sun. Placing one hand on the door frame, she brought the other up to shade her eyes.

A pure white Arabian stallion was kicking up dust in her front yard. The animal pitched forward, snorting, lowering and shaking its head. Her brother-in-law, Sayyid, was mounted in the saddle holding on to a harness as bejeweled as King Tut's crown.

Where is Khalaf?

Sayyid brought his leg around to dismount, his feet thudding as he hit the ground. He handed the reins to his nephew. "Tether him," he said.

The boy took the halter and tugged on the leather strap, leading the horse while looking back at his uncle.

Zainab's eyes narrowed. Sayyid's spotless white robe disguised his portly stomach...and the billowy turban? A man of wealth, yes, but how could he afford a horse such as this? How could anyone?

She pulled her *tarha* up to cover her mouth and, lowering her eyes, took a step back. Sayyid swept into the room, his corpulent body pressing her against the wall. His beard was neatly trimmed and his long flowing white *jalabiya,* with its gold-embroidered trim, regal as the robes of a sheikh. He stood for a moment and glanced around the room, taking inventory.

Zainab's stomach tightened. The table was set with her welcome-home feast, but the meager surroundings, the paucity that engulfed the room, made her uneasy. Khalaf was doing all he could, but as far as Sayyid was concerned, it was never enough.

Sayyid folded his arms and turned to face Zainab. "Allah be praised. I raced over to tell you as soon as I heard. My brother, your husband, has proved himself worthy. He is a man of honor!"

"What?"

Sayyid paused, then blurted out, "I heard it on the radio. Thirty-two people were killed by our beloved in Jerusalem's Old City."

Zainab stood unmoving, her face growing pale. She felt the prickle of goose bumps forming on her neck and arms. *Nooooooo!* She brought a hand up to cover her mouth, her eyes burning. Out the door she caught a glimpse of her son walking toward the house. She blinked back her tears, dabbing her cheeks with her palms, and turned away, keeping her expression veiled behind her *tarha*.

Her son entered but stopped when he saw his mother pacing. He looked at his uncle, then at his mother again. She reached out to take hold of his shoulder and fold him into the dark cloak of her *galabia*. Her hand was trembling as she stroked his hair.

Sayyid stepped forward, encompassing both the boy and mother in his arms. "Tears, Zainab? Why tears? You should be happy. Khalaf did this for you. He has glorified Allah. He has provided for you in the only way he knew how. You will never go hungry again."

Zainab stiffened and turned away, breaking free.

He nodded, backing up to take a seat on the long bench that rested against the wall, the narrow cushion wheezing at the settling of his weight. Folds of his flesh draped over the side as he looked up at Zainab. "Now that Khalaf is dead, you are, of course, free to marry me."

Her son glanced up sharply, his eyes wide and alarmed. She reached for the wall and exhaled, fighting to keep from passing out. She shook her head, her voice faltering, barely a whisper. "Marry you? No, I can't. I...I couldn't possibly. What about Fatma?"

"Fatma is barren." Sayyid raised his hand dismissively. "She can't give me sons, but that does not concern you. She will welcome you as a sister.

In fact, her face lit up with joy when I told her. She's past her prime and no longer able to provide what I need. She's delighted to share me with you."

Khalaf would never...he wouldn't kill himself, not for any reason...impossible!

Zainab turned to face Sayyid, her eyes red and veined. He was trying to look compassionate, but his lust betrayed him. He was there to claim his prize.

She looked down at her son, squeezing him to assure herself he was still there. He squirmed, wrestling free, and fled out the door. Her hand fell back to her side, empty. She glared at Sayyid.

"I'm not a chattel! You can't walk in here and tell me my husband is dead and expect me to follow you home. We haven't even had time to mourn."

Sayyid leaned forward, placing his hands on his knees to push himself up. "Of course. How impudent of me. I thought only that you'd want to leave all this behind as quickly as possible"—he made a faint wave around the room—"but you're right; we must respect my brother, may Allah grant him peace. I personally will attend to his memorial. He will be held in high esteem and long be remembered.

"But know this—it was Khalaf's wish that you become my wife. I'm not doing this to shame Fatma. I could have four wives, but I've never asked for another until now, though I can well afford it. Of course, you have the right to refuse, but not the boy. Our law requires I take my brother's son and raise him as my own."

"You're threatening to steal my son?"

"No, of course not. I'm just saying if you choose not to marry me, then I have no obligation to take care of you, and...how do I say this...when Khalaf came to me asking for my help, I gave him my word. He had the compensation you're entitled to directed to me, so your well-being is now in my hands. He still owed me for the land, you see, and for your dowry. That debt has now been paid." Sayyid extended a pudgy palm toward the door. "See that horse out there? That's the finest animal I've ever owned, but it cost a princely fortune."

Zainab began slowly shaking her head. "What have you done?"

17

"Done?"

"You...you traded my husband's life—*for a horse!*"

"I did no such thing. Khalaf chose to die for the glory of Allah. He died so you could have a better life. From now on, I will care for you...and *I* will raise the boy!"

"But...you can't." Zainab's lips quivered.

Sayyid's eyes narrowed and then relaxed. He brought a hand up, stroking his beard, his crows' feet smoothing as he glanced around the room. "When was the last time you owned an electric appliance or drew a hot bath? Once you are settled in and enjoying the comforts you have missed all these years, you will see the wisdom of Khalaf's decision and love him all the more for it. You will have a new home and a better life."

"At the cost of my husband's." Zainab wiped her cheek and pointed to the door. "Get out! Now!"

Sayyid backed up, raising his hands defensively, the smile gone. "As Allah is merciful, I will overlook your ingratitude. You are not thinking clearly, but once you come to your senses, you will know I am right. Allah be praised. For now, I will go, but I'll be back tomorrow for the boy, and for you, *if* you promise to behave."

Sayyid lumbered from the room, leaving Zainab reeling in confusion. She shook it off. *Murderer.* This wasn't about some stupid intifada; it was about Sayyid's unquenchable lust. He wanted her. He couldn't stand his brother having something he himself was denied. Poor Fatma. She wasn't that old, only a few years older than Zainab herself, and already put out to pasture. *She has to have noticed the way Sayyid leers at me.*

The hoofbeats faded into the distance. Zainab moved to the door. Across the lane two men were playing backgammon at a table in front of a small café, making moves between sips of tea. A merchant rode by, cages of clucking chickens strapped to the rattling fenders of his bicycle. Further in the distance men in white diapers were working in the marsh, their purple backs bowed toward the sun as though worshiping Amun-Ra.

Zainab glanced around, hoping to see her son. Once before she had prevented a child from falling into Sayyid's hands, and not a day went by that it didn't make her cry. She had to find the boy.

She picked up the hem of her *galabia* and marched outside. *Let the fool come tomorrow. We're leaving tonight.*

CHAPTER 4

Twelve years later...

CREPE PAPER ROPES STREAMED from the chandeliers, twists of white decorating a room resounding with toasts and cheers. The vice president of the United States, Mike Baden, and his fiancée, Alexandria Rodashan, stood in front of a huge screen filled with images of their courtship—a nonstop loop of photographs depicting their riding a tandem bike, holding hands at a "Find a Cure for Cancer" fund-raiser, and waltzing the night away at a Washington social ball.

Two newsroom anchors, Chet Macy and Christy Williams, were stationed in a soundproof booth away from the noisy crowd, a place from which they commented on the event. Their roving reporter, Steve, walked the floor, soliciting interviews with statesmen, power brokers, and members of the family—a time used by Christy to fluff her hair and by Chet to grab a quick cigarette.

The floor manager held up his hand, rolling his fingers down one at a time—*five...four...*Chet snuffed out his cigarette...*three...two...*Christy put on her best smile...*one*—the red light over the camera came on.

"Wow! I've got to tell you, Christy, this is one fantastic party!"

"Yes, it is, Chet. Listen to that excitement. Such energy! You can almost feel the goodwill pulsating through the walls. The vice president sure seems to have touched the heart of the people."

"Yes, he has. It's a story that resonates with the American public: the death of his wife and the pit of depression he fell into, followed by a year of heavy drinking and his subsequent victory over the bottle. Then his recent efforts to raise money for the American Cancer Society and falling in love

21

all over again. I think everyone's just happy to see him getting on with his life."

"I agree. And it certainly looks as though he's achieved that end. Allie Rodashan is one terrific girl. And the fact that she comes from a Muslim background will bode well in international politics. Never hurts to have a beautiful wife at your side who understands the way 'the other guys' think when you're negotiating peace in the Middle East."

The room was swirling with senators and congressmen, bankers and lawyers—a stable full of the kind of people Mohamed needed to know if he wanted to further his career. Being invited to attend the vice president's official engagement party was a great honor, though it didn't escape him that many of these men would soon be dead.

He watched the milling masses stumbling across the floor, drinks in hand. The lineup for the bar seemed never ending. The decadence bothered Mohamed, but tonight it would be overlooked. This was a night for celebration, not judgment. America's rush to sobriety would happen soon enough. He held up a glass filled with the bubbling effervescence of sparkling water. He didn't need an artificial high to feel good. His eyes wandered over the rim to the giant television screen. He raised the glass higher, toasting the future of America, and took a sip.

His uncle would be proud to see him mingling with America's elite, as long as he remained aloof and impervious to the bacchanalia of the occasion. He brought his napkin up to wipe his mouth, smoothing the sides of his black goatee, his eyes dark and foreboding as they pierced the crowd.

Beside him stood his mentor, Dr. Omar Muhsin. They were dressed to the nines in black tuxedos with full cummerbunds, wing collars, and black bow ties, though Omar's rented outfit hung on his thin frame like tar paper stapled to a prairie post. No matter how many shirt studs, cuff links, and other accessories he wore, with his gray beard hanging down to his waist and beaded cap on his head, he seemed out of place.

Mohamed took another sip of bubbly water and set his glass down. He leaned toward Omar's ear. "So when do I get to meet the vice president?" he whispered.

Omar stroked his beard and nodded. "Now is as good a time as any." He led the way across the room toward the receiving line, spreading his hands in greeting, Mohamed hovering close behind. The bride-to-be smiled as they approached. No one could say Allie didn't look ravishing standing beside her future husband. This assignment was going to be a pleasure.

Mohamed had to admire Omar's nerve. Neither of them had ever met Vice President Mike or his fiancée, but that didn't stop Omar from stepping up and boldly putting out his hand.

"Mr. Vice President, Allie, there's someone I'd like you to meet." His air of familiarity implied that they were old friends.

If Allie realized she didn't know the man speaking to her, she didn't let on. She smiled as Omar turned toward Mohamed. "This is Mohamed El Taher. You may have heard your parents speak of him."

Allie's face conveyed puzzlement. "No, don't believe I have, or if I did, it's slipped my mind." She gave a short, self-deprecating laugh. "You'll have to forgive me. I meet so many people these days, I'm having trouble remembering all their names."

Dr. Muhsin waved her off. "Don't give it another thought. Your mother knows Mohamed's family back in Egypt. She's asked him to assist you with the wedding." Omar brought up his hand, cupping his mouth as though divulging a secret. "Actually, he's studying to be a lawyer." Omar dropped his hand. "But don't hold that against him. Mohamed is a fabulous administrator. He'll be taking care of all the details so you can relax and enjoy the big day without added pressure. Tonight, however, we're here as guests of your family. I just wanted to take the opportunity to make an early introduction."

Allie took Mohamed's hand in her own. "Well, Mr. Taher, I guess we'll be seeing a lot of each other. I look forward to hearing what you have to say."

Mohamed felt the warmth of her fingers. "The vice president's a lucky man to have found someone so gracious and beautiful." Mohamed shifted his gaze to Mike. The vice president's face was tanned and wrinkle-free, but his neatly trimmed hair held just enough gray over the ears to suggest maturity. "My best wishes to you both," he said. "May you have a long and happy marriage."

Mike and Allie nodded cordially and then turned to greet another group of well-wishers who were patiently waiting their turn.

Omar and Mohamed politely stepped back and moved away. "That went well, I think," Omar said, keeping his voice below the din of the crowd. Mohamed had to lean close to hear. "Now you must gain the lady's confidence. Having her influence in the Oval Office will enable us to achieve what has never been done before."

Mohamed pursed his lips and nodded. He folded his hands behind his back as he walked. The prophet Muhammad had said, "Unbelief is one nation." Those who loved and served Allah were governed by his laws, not those of a political system. That was the truth he needed to get his head around—either that, or bow out before it was too late.

CHAPTER 5

MATTHEW FELT THE HEAT rising from his back as he stood on the turf, leaning over with his hands on his knees to catch his breath. He was panting, blood pumping though his veins, his heart pounding, his lungs on fire. He stood again, wiping the back of his hand across his forehead, a trickle of sweat rolling down his chest. Too warm for September.

He glanced at the clock. He had but seconds to turn a tie into a victory. The whistle screeched. The ball popped out of the corner into play. His left defender drove it to the left forward. Matthew stayed to the right. He grimaced, his fists tightening into knots. *Come on, guys, bring it over.*

The pass went to the center. Matthew moved into position as his teammate kicked the ball, launching it into the air. He clenched his teeth. *Augggh, he's going for the goal!* From the corner of his eye, Matthew saw the keeper preparing to block. The man went right, his feet leaving the ground as he dove with arms extended. No time to consider the risk. The clock was a second away from the end of the game.

As the ball passed overhead, Matthew did a backward flip, landing on his hands. With his feet in the air, he kicked the ball back to the left into an empty net as the keeper crashed to the ground on the right.

The horn blared. People in the stands exploded out of their seats. Matthew scrambled to his feet, first making sure the ball had struck home, and then raised his hands with his fists clenched in a victory salute as he turned to face the crowd. His girl was out there somewhere, one of the faceless throng cheering from the bleachers.

This was what he lived for, his moment, his time, when all the grueling, sweat-filled hours of training paid off. Nothing could beat the feeling. His back took a thumping as he was mobbed by his teammates, throwing their arms around his shoulders. The Bruins had just defeated the Huskies by a narrow one-point margin, setting the stage for a great season.

· · · ☽ · · ·

The locker room was in pandemonium with metal doors slamming, water running, steam rising above the showers, and voices raised above the chaotic confusion. Matthew wiped his face on a towel and tossed it aside. He tugged the wet jersey from his skin, pulling it over his head and dropping it into his sports bag.

Ouch! He smarted from a slap on his shoulder and looked up.

"You just love them airborne acrobatics, don't you? You realize if you'd missed, it would have cost us the game." Dustin grabbed Matthew around the neck and gave his scalp a knuckle rub. "I'm proud of you, boy."

Matthew ducked out from under his friend's elbow and snatched his towel from the bench, snapping it menacingly. "I sure wasn't going to wait for you. Last time I looked, you were in the stands signing autographs."

The room erupted in whistles and catcalls. "Hey, hey, Lusty Dusty! Any of 'em give you their number?"

Dustin turned, took a bow, and raised his arms, flexing his biceps. "My friends, them purty l'il things were climbing all over me, but out of respect for my formidable talents, they respectfully refrained from trying to pick me up." He flexed again, showing off his sinewy physique, and cocked his head to the side with an exaggerated wink. "Now looky here, I plan to buy the first round at Mulrooney's, and Matthew, my man, I plan to buy *you* a double."

Art McGreeley approached, his ever-present whistle dangling from his neck. "OK, knock off the sweet talk. I gotta tell you, Matt, I didn't like what you did. Much too risky. Georgie's kick might have made goal. But it was a good effort and we won, so I'm not going to make a big deal of it. Just play by the book next time. As for you"—the coach turned to Dustin—"that's the last I want to hear about any drinking and partying. We're up against the Cardinal next week, and I want everyone in top shape, and that means lots of practice…with no hangovers."

Matthew was feeling woozy; a light-headed faintness had overtaken him—*again*. He braced himself against the locker, waiting for it to pass.

The buzzing in his head caused him to miss most of McGreeley's spiel, *yada, yada, yada, yaawwwn*, but when the coach pointed at him and said, "Got it?" he shrugged and nodded.

"Took the words right out of my mouth, Coach. No parties. Besides, I have a date tonight with a special lady, and this is one date I plan to keep."

Matthew checked his watch as he pulled his Volkswagen into the empty parking space in front of Layla's dorm. She'd been waiting half an hour, but he couldn't help it if Artful Dodger made them go through a complete postgame analysis. No big deal. She was used to waiting.

He tweaked the mirror to adjust his hair. *Perfect!* He blinked, his chocolate eyes with their thick brows staring back. Then he pulled his lanky frame from the car.

Whammm! The sound of a hammer on tin reverberated in his ears as he slammed the door. *Bucket of bolts. Rusty too.* He reached through the open window to remove the new tan corduroy jacket he'd purchased at the "Factory Warehouse Clearance Event." Good thing she loved him for his looks, not his fancy clothes—or his car.

The front door opened, and Layla stepped outside into the warm California evening. Resplendent! *That's my girl.*

She wore a lace wrap over her sleeveless arms, her petite figure accentuated by the long slinky outfit he'd bought her for her birthday—*just her way of saying, "I love it; thank you."* Spiked heels gave her an extra two inches, adding height to her lithe form. Her hair was lustrous, pulled into a vertical roll and pinned at the back of her head. Her olive complexion seemed to shine in the waning light, her dark eyes bright as obsidian and her mouth glossed in red. *Perfect.* This was Layla at her best, just the way he liked. And all for him. Tonight was going to be perfect.

He gave a low wolf whistle and offered her his arm, escorting her to the car. He opened the door and helped her in, then hopped around back—*crudola! Didn't matter how many times he washed and waxed the oxidized yellow paint, it wasn't going to shine*—and eased himself behind the steering wheel. He was nearly six feet tall, too tall to sit comfortably in a car with an interior smaller than the desk in his apartment. Not the kind of vehicle he would have picked for himself, but it was great on gas. Attending UCLA on a partial scholarship and living on the salary of a part-time grocery clerk, he couldn't afford better. Especially since he was on his own. His parents had died in an automobile accident when he was seventeen, leaving only enough life insurance to cover his tuition.

He pulled up in front of the restaurant. A man in a white jacket rushed over, opened the passenger door, and helped Layla out. Matthew handed the man his key, wishing he could park the car himself, though the sign clearly read: "Valet Parking Only." The little bug looked like a dab of mustard against the silver backdrop of BMWs and Mercedes-Benzes. The name of the establishment, *Le Chateau*, radiated off the brick wall in scrolling, two-foot-high letters of neon pink.

The restaurant's interior was a quiet retreat of dark walnut paneling and candlelight. Silver-haired men sat in embroidered chairs entertaining women in fur wraps as they spoke in library-hushed tones. The volume of conversation was so low, the sound of cutlery scraping against fragile china and the occasional ringing of a crystal glass seemed amplified.

"Well, what do you think?" Matthew asked as soon as they were seated. A penguin-suited waiter stood to the side, waiting to hand him the wine list.

"About the restaurant?"

"Sure, I guess." Matthew took the list from the waiter and opened it to scan the prices. To his dismay, there weren't any.

Layla picked up her table knife and rubbed her thumb along the heavy scrolling. "Well," she said, "I think I should withhold comment until I've had a chance to taste the food."

The waiter stood obediently to the side. "Can I get you anything to drink?" he inquired.

Matthew shook his head, folded the wine list, and passed it back to the waiter. "Two coffees will be fine."

There was a glint in Layla's eye as she tilted her head, letting her wrap slide down to expose her bare shoulders. She was onto him. It *was* the anniversary of their first date, an excuse he'd used to ward off questions about why he was being so extravagant. It was going to cost him a week's paycheck, but it was worth every penny.

His thoughts were interrupted by the quiet rattling of a coffee cart as it bumped up to the table. The little silver pot in the center glowed in the flame of a tiny candle. Matthew occupied himself by sliding the silver ring off his fan-folded linen and spreading the napkin in his lap.

The waiter poured and returned the coffeepot to its stand. He picked up two menus, handing one to Matthew and the other to Layla. "If I may, the cassoulet is excellent, and the mushroom-capped escargot in garlic butter makes a superb hors d'oeuvre. I'll be back to take your order in a few minutes." He bowed lightly and turned to take his leave.

Matthew stared at his cup. The waiter had filled it to the brim. The petite handle of the fine china was barely big enough to loop one finger through. He wondered how he was going to get the coffee to his lips without spilling. It was too hot to drink anyway.

Music from a string ensemble wafted across the room, filling the small gaps in their conversation. A candle in a glass vase flickered in the center of the table. Matthew opened his menu as the waiter returned, a linen towel draped neatly over his arm, and stood awaiting instructions.

Layla patted her napkin smooth in her lap and then looked up, smiling. "I'm sorry," she said, "I need another minute."

Matthew gave his menu a quick glance. He couldn't read a word. He knew only two things: it was all in French, and the prices weren't listed. "I'll have what you recommended," he ventured.

"The cassoulet? An excellent choice. Would you also like the hors d'oeuvre?"

"Yes, uh…whatever. That will be fine." He wasn't about to embarrass himself by asking the man to interpret the menu.

The waiter turned toward Layla. "*Et pour vous, mademoiselle?*"

"Could I just have a garden salad with oil and vinegar?" She held the menu up so the waiter could retrieve it.

"*Merci,*" he said, taking their menus and tucking them under his arm as he turned to go.

Matthew slipped his finger through the cup's tiny handle and tried to pick it up. The liquid sloshed around the rim, steam rising. He set it back on the saucer awkwardly and began fiddling with his spoon.

The china clinked as Layla set her own cup down, her forehead furrowed. "I know it's our anniversary, but you really can't afford this."

Matthew leaned forward. "You want to know why we're here?"

"Of course."

Matthew reached out to take her hand, smiling as he gently squeezed her fingers. He'd been planning this night for weeks. The mood was perfect— his winning goal, the soft music, her warm touch—all coming together in a tapestry of romance, letting him know the time was right.

He pulled his hand back to slide a velveteen box from the inside pocket of his blazer. He snapped the lid open to expose a ring that reflected rainbows of color in the light.

Layla's eyes narrowed, a look of uncertainty clouding her face. "Oh, Matthew, what is that?"

"It's an engagement ring. I want you, Layla Adjulah, to be my wife."

"I thought we agreed not to talk about this until after graduation."

"We did…I know. And I'm not saying we have to get married right away. I just want to know we have a plan. I mean, we could get married now…if you wanted to. Please, say you'll make me the happiest man on earth. Say 'yes.'"

"You can't afford a wife…"

"They say two can live as cheaply as one."

She shifted in her seat, looking around for the waiter as if needing someone to come to her rescue.

"What's the matter? You're not...I mean, hey, I thought you loved me."

Layla returned her gaze to Matthew, the small furrow still creasing her smooth brow. "I...I do."

"Then what's the problem? I thought you'd be overjoyed."

"Matthew, you know what it is. I'm still struggling with who you are. I know you say you're Matthew Mulberry, that your parents moved here from Egypt when you were a child, but I can't help thinking you're someone I knew when I lived there, and every time you say you're not..."

Layla flinched as Matthew snapped the ring box closed. "Are we back to that again?" He took his napkin from his lap and tossed it on the table.

"Please, Matthew, this is important to me. I understand your wanting to remain incognito, especially if your family fled to avoid persecution. But I can't marry someone who isn't totally honest with me."

"This is so ridiculous, Layla. What's it going to take?"

She shook her head. "It's not that I don't love you, but we've only been together a year. My heart's still searching for the man I know is inside you, but something's missing."

"What! For Pete's sake, what? Tell me what it is, Layla. You're looking for a ghost of the past." Matthew's face was pinched, his eyes narrowing. "This is the here and now, Layla. It's time to leave the past behind and move on."

"Don't be angry."

Matthew inhaled deeply. He grabbed his napkin, wadding it into a ball, and let his fist fall on the table with a thud. His coffee splashed in its cup, sloshing over the side. "I'm not angry!"

"Matthew, please. I fell for you the day we met. That hasn't changed. Just give me time to get used to the idea. Marriage is a big step. We need to know it's the right thing for both of us. Come here." She reached for his hand, but he jerked it back. "You're not being fair. We both agreed we wouldn't talk about marriage until after graduation." Layla leaned back in her seat, her shoulders folding in resignation. "This isn't like you, Matthew. You're better than this. If you're half the man I think you are, you'll wait as long as it takes."

"And...exactly how long is that?"

The waiter approached with the hors d'oeuvre, picked up Matthew's napkin, and placed it in his lap as he set the dish in front of his guest. Matthew stared at the steaming plate. He didn't know he had ordered snails.

CHAPTER 6

MOHAMED STOOD ON THE porch and rang the bell, breathing in the fragrance of the lush cascades of bougainvillea that flowed from a trellised archway in front of the door. This was his fourth visit to the home of Allie Rodashan, but in spite of becoming more familiar with the area, parking wasn't any easier to find. This time he'd had to leave his car four blocks away and hoof it up the steep incline of Powell Street. He'd looked over his shoulder several times, hoping to hitch a ride on one of San Francisco's famous cable cars, but though he could hear the trolley bell clanging in the distance, one never passed by.

Perched on Nob Hill and overlooking the bay and Marin County beyond, the house was an upscale symbol of status situated in an area with a well-deserved reputation for snobbery. Mohamed had read a travel brochure alleging the district's wealth dated back to the California Gold Rush. Early bankers, railroad magnates, and strike-it-rich tycoons had labored to make the hilltop accessible by cable car so they could build their mansions to take in the panoramic view.

Mohamed looked over his shoulder admiring the vista, the city of San Francisco shining in the sun with its shell-pink, coral, and pearl-white buildings stretching to the brink of the ocean. The day was blue and the air crisp. He shifted the book he was carrying to his other hand as he reached up to knock, just in case they hadn't heard the bell. The solid walnut door had an oval insert of beveled glass etched with flowers. He hadn't asked where Allie's father got his money, but Omar said they were well off, and the neighborhood attested to the fact. But if the family was old money, their wealth had to have come out of Egypt because Allie had told him her parents were immigrants.

Allie opened the door and stepped back so he could enter. "Good afternoon, Mohamed; it's good to see you again." She turned and led him inside. The stained glass from the parlor windows painted rainbows of light on the wall. "How'd you make out with the caterer?" she said over her shoulder.

"Uh, that's what I wanted to talk to you about. Unfortunately, they're fully booked. Apparently you have to request their services up to a year in advance, and even then, they select whom they work for. The gentleman I spoke to said they reject more clients than they take on." Mohamed followed Allie down the hall, taking note of her svelte figure. She was every bit as gorgeous in casual dress as she had been the night of her engagement party when she'd dazzled everyone in her sequined evening gown. But his admiration went beyond her good looks. As a Vassar graduate with a degree in political science, she was as conversant in the diplomatic arena as her fiancé. And while committed to her Islamic faith, she was modern and prone to wearing Western fashions. Subtle highlights streaked her hair, and she wore understated makeup and clothing, right down to the two-inch heel of her shoes.

"I have, however, found someone I'm sure will do an excellent job, a first-rate concern with an incredible client list, and, owing to a recent cancellation, they just happen to have the weekend of the twenty-ninth open. I've taken the liberty of booking them to get your name on their calendar before the date gets taken. I've also brought along a photograph album of past events they've put on so you can see the kind of work they do and hopefully give your approval."

The living room smelled musty and old, though the handwoven Arabian carpets and French provincial furniture so popular among Egypt's upper class were decidedly new. Mohamed sat in a chair with gold gooseneck arms and embroidered padding. The windows were draped in a heavy gold material that hampered the light in spite of being drawn back and secured with braided cords.

Allie sat on the adjacent loveseat, her hands folded in her lap. She wore a brown pantsuit with an orange top that complemented the reddish tint of her hair. Mohamed leaned in and handed her the book, but she placed it beside her on the couch without looking inside.

"I'm disappointed," she said. "So far there hasn't been a thing I've wanted that you couldn't supply, but I guess some things just aren't meant to be." She smiled and sat up straighter. "May I offer you a beverage—tea, coffee, or something cold to drink?"

Mohamed shook his head. "No, I really can't stay. I just wanted to drop off the book. I promised to have it back by the end of the week."

Allie sighed, her lips forming a pout. "Now there's my second disappointment. Last time you were here we talked for hours. Are you sure you can't stay? I really enjoyed hearing about what's going on back in Egypt from someone who's been there recently."

She looked down, her fingers sweeping the book's silver embossed cover. "You know, it's funny really. I asked my mom how she knew your family, and she couldn't answer." She paused, bringing her eyes up to search his again. "She just said you were related to some distant cousin somewhere. Not that it matters. Frankly, I'm thrilled she found you. I wouldn't have wanted to work with a commercial wedding planner. I don't think they'd listen the way you do. You seem to really care. I guess that's why I'm disappointed you have to leave. There's...uh, something I wanted to ask you...but there's no point in getting started if you have to go."

"What?"

"Nothing...really nothing." She paused again as if weighing her words, then continued. "It's just that my parents are acting strange, but...I'm sure they're just under a lot of pressure...with the wedding, I mean."

Mohamed looked at his watch. "Parents acting strange, *hmmm*. You're right, that's a topic that would take us from now until midnight, and we still wouldn't cover it. But unfortunately, I have to get back to the university or I'll miss practice. How 'bout we agree to discuss it next time?" He stood and held out his hand. "It was good seeing you again, Allie. And don't worry...everything's going to work out fine."

He'd meant it as a farewell, but Allie latched on to his hand and pulled herself up. "Uh-uh. You're not getting off that easy. Come on, I'll show you to the door." She slipped her arm into his, and with shoulders pressed together they strolled back to the vestibule.

"I really can't stay," he said.

"I know, but I'm starved for conversation. With the Secret Service watching the house, my friends feel scrutinized. They rarely come around anymore. And with his busy schedule, I hardly ever get a chance to see Mike."

Mohamed patted her hand. "The price of fame. I suppose running a country, even as vice president, takes a lot of time. I read the press release explaining how you were getting married next month because it was the only weekend Mike had open, but a two-month engagement? It's enough to make anyone's head spin. How did you two meet anyway?" Mohamed pulled his arm back, and they turned to face each other.

"Just one of those serendipitous things. As part of my curriculum at Vassar, we were encouraged to take part in the election. I became involved with Mike's campaign and ended up being his assistant, which is really a glorified word for gopher, but we got along really well, not romantically, mind you; he was married. But after his wife died and he came out of recovery, he gave me a call. He had a social event to attend and said I would be doing him a favor if I would be his escort. One thing led to another, and voilà, here we are."

Allie opened the door, letting the smell of bougainvillea blend with the marine salt sweeping in off the ocean. Mohamed paused for a moment to think about how fittingly her parents had named her: Alexandria, a beautiful Egyptian woman named after a beautiful Egyptian city.

"Mike's a lucky guy. Now, if I don't get going, I'll end up running laps for the rest on my life, and I've got better things to do. Don't forget to look at the caterer's book. They come highly recommended, and I'm sure they'll do an excellent job, but I'll need to give them a confirmation ASAP."

Allie smiled and nodded, then reached out and took his hand, squeezing it as she leaned in to kiss him on the cheek. "If you say so, I'm sure they'll be fine."

He let go and stepped off the porch, looking at his watch. His manager was going to be peeved. He picked up his pace as he dashed back to his car. At least this time the route was downhill.

CHAPTER 7

NORMALLY THE WEEKS FLEW by so fast they left Matthew wondering if in his hurry to get everything done, he'd accomplished anything at all. But the week since he'd proposed to Layla had passed slowly. It was like the minutes, hours, and days were gummed together, clogging the gears of time. It stood to reason. If time raced by when you were having fun, it should grind to a halt when the fun was taken away.

It was another warm day, the hazy sun hidden behind a dirty veil of smog. Matthew squinted to clear his burning eyes as he scanned the stands. He didn't see Layla anywhere. He needed to keep his mind on the match, but his thoughts kept getting in the way. She hadn't called, nor had she returned his calls. He hadn't seen her on campus or off—she'd simply slipped off the radar. She was avoiding him. His heart felt like a hot coal smoldering in his chest. He shouldn't have proposed. People want what they can't have. He'd made himself too have-able.

He scanned the crowd again. It was too early in the season for the bleachers to be packed. She had to be out there somewhere, *had to be*; she wouldn't miss a game. Then again, if she really was trying to avoid him, she might.

The ball was down at the far post. Two Bruin defensemen were putting pressure on the striker, trying to frustrate him into making a mistake. All Matthew could do was stand his ground and wait for a pass.

His mind kept wandering back to Layla, making it hard to focus on the game. She'd been acting strange for months, going on about his being someone else. What had begun as mild curiosity had grown into a serious inquiry and finally developed into an obsession. It was crazy. Now she was threatening not to marry him until she knew who he was. How was he supposed to remedy that? He was Matthew Mulberry. She either loved him or she didn't. The problem was, it was beginning to look like she didn't.

●　●　●　☽　●　●　●

Layla wasn't in the stands; she was at ground level, hovering around the team. It was something the manager didn't normally allow but for the moment seemed willing to ignore.

The Bruins' fans raised a cheer as their defensemen captured the ball.

Layla pumped her fist. "*Yes!*" A thin layer of perspiration built as she fidgeted, twisting her purse strap in her fingers. She *did* love him, or at least she thought she did. She didn't understand why she was so reluctant to accept his proposal. What did it matter if he was, or was not, the man she thought he was? She had fallen in love with him, not some ghost from the past.

But the resemblance was uncanny: they looked the same, they had the same gestures and mannerisms, the same tilting of the head when trying to comprehend something they didn't understand, and they both loved soccer. It was almost inconceivable to think he wasn't the grown-up version of the boy she'd known in Egypt, yet Matthew claimed it was impossible.

Hearing a moan from the crowd, she looked up. The ball was back in Cardinal possession. "Cut him off at the knees!" someone screamed from the bleachers. The sun was beating down on the backs of the fans. They were becoming hostile.

Matthew stood with his hands on his hips looking peeved. His lean athletic body and smooth skin, his dark wavy hair, the perfect mouth, the firm jaw—all combined to make Layla the envy of her roommates. She loved the way they ogled him when he arrived to pick her up for a date. What was she waiting for? Every human being on Earth was supposed to have a double somewhere. She just had to accept that and let it go. But God forbid she find out later his family had come to America and changed their name just to leave the past behind. She could never be happy with someone she didn't fully trust.

Another cheer rose from the stands. The Bruins had possession of the ball again.

There was one other possibility, but it was one she discounted because it was just too bizarre. Still, what if he *was* the boy she had known back home, only he suffered from amnesia and couldn't remember? No, she'd rather believe he was hiding his identity than that. No memory lapse would prevent him from recognizing her. They were soul mates. She was convinced God Himself had brought them together. What else could account for her parents moving all the way from Minya to Arizona and then sending her to a university in California where she just happened to run into a boy she knew back in Egypt? Coincidences like that just didn't happen.

The ball swept by Matthew, catching him off guard. He heard the murmur of discontent from the stands. He had to stay focused. Fortunately his center raced over and covered him so the Bruins still had possession.

Matthew launched himself across the field, his feet pounding the turf. He was back in the zone. His feet padded the grass with the loping footfalls of a cheetah, *thump, thump, thump, thump, thump.* It was a sound he loved, the rhythm and flow of the game. The post was just ahead. The ball was passed to him, but a Cardinal defenseman was already there. He dribbled the ball around his feet, keeping it out of reach as he spun around looking for someone to pass to. The left forward was open downfield. He kicked the ball. The forward took it off his knee, bouncing it into the air, a volley shot at the net, but an opponent was there to block.

Once again the ball was traveling in the wrong direction. Matthew moved to intercept, determined not to let the other team score. He'd faced this player before. He knew his weakness. His opponent feigned to the left but turned right—*silly freshman trick.* Matthew stayed on him. The man tried to drag the ball back with his heel but left part of it exposed. Matthew stepped in, pinching it with his toe, popping it out from beneath his opponent's feet. He spun around, turning a one-eighty. He tried to move forward, but the Cardinal defenseman was on him again. Looking for an open teammate, he swung the other way and—*WHAM!*—felt a jersey in his face, tasted sweat, heard the screech of a whistle, saw a flash of white, then red, then everything went black.

Layla was abandoned to her thoughts, too distracted to watch the game. The collective gasp from the crowd brought her head up sharp. She heard the shrill piercing of the referee's whistle. Her eyes locked on Matthew. He seemed dazed, wavering on his feet, then his eyes closed and he slumped to the ground. Layla didn't think about it; she flew across the chalk line onto the field.

She was panting as she squeezed through the circle of teammates. A medical technician was already there, holding salts to Matthew's nose. His eyes popped open. The man said something in Matthew's ear and he nodded. Layla sucked in her breath. The medic stood and reached out a hand to help Matthew to his feet.

Seeing the linesman hadn't called charging against the Stanford team, the players stepped back and began drifting toward their positions to resume play. All except the man with whom Matthew had collided.

"Sorry, didn't mean to knock you down, sport." A conciliatory hand was extended. Matthew looked at the man, smiled weakly, but then drew back as his expression froze. Shock registered on the other man's face as well.

Layla glanced from one to the other. Except that one wore a mustache and goatee, they were identical...twins?

CHAPTER 8

THERE ARE TIMES IN a person's life when past and present converge into a single moment. Times when you can stand back and view your life like a painting with no beginning and no end, only a collage of events compressed into one frame. These moments are called *déjà vu*—the sense that you exist in the present while simultaneously standing in the past.

Layla recoiled, her long dark hair shining like a raven's feather as she jerked her head back and brought a hand to her mouth. "Mo...Mohamed?"

Mohamed glanced to the side. It took a second, but he squinted ever so slightly. "Layla?"

What is this? Matthew's eyes darted from his look-alike to his girlfriend and back to the look-alike again.

The coach stared at Mohamed, his forehead furrowed with questions, but he swung around and stepped in front of Matthew, placing a hand on his shoulder. "You OK?" He ducked his head slightly, trying to catch Matthew's eye, then took hold of his arm. "Come on, I think you should sit this one out."

Matthew turned away, shooting a look at the clock, and shrugged him off. "With two minutes left? No way, Coach. I'm fine. Let's play."

McGreeley's lower lip jutted out, but his gaze followed Matthew's to the scoreboard. He nodded and took Layla by the elbow to escort her off the field. The referee blew his whistle, sending the players back to their positions.

Layla staggered along after the coach, rotating her head around for another look. *It can't be…* Her foot caught a tuft of grass and she stumbled.

"Get off the field," McGreeley huffed. "We'll sort it out later."

The players lined up at the center circle. A ball was dropped into a fury of dancing feet and came out in Cardinal possession. Layla leaned out. She could see Matthew but not the other player. She stepped forward to get a better view, but Coach McGreeley held her arm. She shook him off. Maybe she'd imagined it—*but no, he'd said her name.*

She spotted the man down by the net—Matthew…with a beard? He was staring at her. She raised her hand to her shoulder and waggled her fingers, but he didn't acknowledge her. She pulled her hand down and glanced around, hoping no one noticed. From this distance, she couldn't even be positive he looked like Matthew.

The rest of the game passed in a blur. When the final whistle blew, Layla couldn't say who had won or lost. Her focus had been leveled at one man. She started onto the field, but McGreeley caught her arm and spun her around. "That way," he said, gesturing with his chin. She pursed her lips but complied. She knew the rules: no fans on the field. She pushed her way into the exiting masses, squeezing through a glut of elbows and arms.

"Hey, slow down, sister, take it easy!"

She wasn't about to slow down or take it easy. *And I'm not your sister!* Feathers fluttered in her chest, but she pressed on. "Excuse me, excuse me, coming through, excuse me." She finally reached the fringe where the crowds were thinning and paused, her hand to her throat, waiting to catch her breath.

It had taken too long. The players were nowhere to be seen. She headed in the direction of the locker room but at a slower pace. A man in gray slacks and a white polo shirt with a red Stanford *S* passed by. She hurried to catch up with him. "Excuse me," she said, reaching out to take his arm.

The man stopped, frowning. "What?"

"I'm looking for Mohamed." It was all she could think to say.

"Sorry, no interviews." He turned to walk away.

"Wait!"

Just outside the men's locker room, he halted again, his face fraught with irritation.

"I really need to speak to him. It's important."

"Sorry, can't help you." He swung the door open so hard it slammed against the wall, then disappeared inside, letting the door close behind him with a *bang*.

"There you are. I've been looking for you."

Layla's heart caught in her throat. That voice—*wind off the desert, cranes winging over the Nile, gold glinting on the water*—so many memories. She'd know that voice anywhere. She took a deep breath and spun around.

He stood facing her with his back to the sun, a silhouette with hair ringed in droplets of sweat, glistening, his skin brown as desert sand, but when he stepped away from the light—it was Matthew.

Matthew's budget didn't justify eating out again, but when Layla volunteered to wait until he finished his shower so they could grab a bite, there was no way he was about to refuse. At least it was cheap—*in a way*. Westwood wasn't known for its low-budget eateries, but Manoly's, a dinky hole in the wall with stacks of magazines strewn about, was as close as it came. The place was noisy, cluttered, and always crowded. He wolfed down his chimichanga as Layla picked at a plate of chips and cheese.

She was excited, effusive, her eyes sparkling as she bantered nonstop. This was the Layla he knew and loved. She'd apologized half a dozen times for having doubted him. She was wrong and admitted it, but now she was insisting that this Mohamed character must be his brother, and that was a bus he didn't want to take.

Steam rose from the back of the establishment to the clatter of dishes and flatware being washed. Voices speaking Spanish were raised above the din.

Layla dabbed her lips with a napkin. "Do you really know everything about your parents? I mean, isn't it at least possible that before they came to America, your mother had another child that somehow got left behind? I know it's far-fetched but...what about cousins? Do you have any of those? Too bad your mother isn't...well...isn't here to ask."

Matthew twisted in his seat, his fingers kneading a paper napkin. He leaned forward to take a sip of water, stalling as he mulled over how to respond. "I'll concede anything's possible, so what? What's the big deal?" Matthew wiped his hands on the napkin, crunched it into a ball, and tossed it on the table. He sat back, crossing his legs, trying to appear nonchalant.

Layla smiled. "Don't you see? I've been accusing you of pretending to be someone else. I've always said you remind me of a friend I knew back home, and then—news flash!—he shows up right here, playing soccer with you! Don't you find that the least bit curious?"

Matthew gripped his ankle, pulling his foot in closer as he picked at his sock. "You might be wrong about that too. He might not be who you think *he* is either. And even if he is, all I see is my girlfriend getting all starry-eyed over someone she hasn't seen in more than a decade. What am I supposed to make of that?"

"Am not!"

"Yes, you are. You weren't waiting for *me,* were you? You were looking for *him.*"

Layla leaned across the table to reach for Matthew's hands. "Don't be silly," she said, her fingers tugging at his arm.

But Matthew kept his eyes down and his hands wrapped around his ankle, out of reach.

"Matthew, don't be that way." Layla tugged again.

He let go of his foot, uncrossed his legs, and leaned forward, flopping one hand over so she could take it, though it remained stiff.

"Matthew, it doesn't change anything between us." She squeezed his hand, rolling his palm over as she stroked his fingers. "I fell in love with *you,* not someone from my past. If I *seem* excited, it's just that it answers so many questions. The main thing is, now I see you've been telling the truth. I don't want to be married to someone with a secret past, someone who's not completely honest with me, but now..."

Matthew leaned forward, taking both Layla's hands in his own—*so soft and warm.* "Does that mean you're saying yes?"

"Matthew, I..."

He pulled back, tilting his head as he crossed his arms. "You...what? What is it? If you really love me, just say yes."

"I will, I think...I just need time. Marriage isn't something you rush into. We both need to make sure this is what the Lord wants."

Matthew let his breath out in a puff. He reached out to pick up the check, avoiding her eyes. "Just don't take too long, Layla. I can't wait forever." Sliding his wallet from his pocket, he took out a few bills, tossed them on the table, and stood.

"Come on, Layla, let's go."

CHAPTER 9

MOHAMED SAT AT THE desk in his apartment, staring out the window. In front of him his laptop burned with high-definition images of the search he'd just completed. Matthew Mulberry: American father, Egyptian mother, honors program at UCLA School of Medicine, men's soccer team, active involvement in InterVarsity Christian Fellowship.

He got up and went to the window, looking down upon the tops of the trees and the heads of the children at play. Half a dozen young boys kicked a soccer ball back and forth as they ran across the lawn—boys being boys—the same everywhere around the world. The sun, magnified through the glass, felt warm on his face. He reached for the pull cord and closed the blinds. The glare was washing out the image on his computer screen.

He sat down again and googled the Department of Motor Vehicles, hoping to find out who owned the car that was following him. He tapped his fingers on the table. That is, *if* they were following him. He couldn't be sure, but it did seem odd to see the same dark blue sedan in his rearview mirror everywhere he went.

Changing the direction of his thoughts, he googled another site. Now he was staring at an online phone directory. He typed in a name, *Layla Adjulah*. It was more difficult without an address, but assuming she was a student at UCLA, he typed "Westwood" as the city and "California" as the state, and then clicked the search button. A few seconds later, he had her number.

He glanced at the phone but, instead of picking it up, pushed himself back from the table and went to the window, opening the blinds again to slide back the glass. A breeze swept in, carrying with it the smell of newly mown grass and the sound of giggling children. *Layla Adjulah.*

Village of Mohamed's youth, twelve years earlier

A pile of rocks formed the wall of the canal. The water flowing down the sluice was a dirty brown, pumped from the banks of the Nile and channeled through a network of waterways to irrigate the crops. He picked up a large stone, hefted it a moment, feeling its weight, and then slammed it into the drink. *Wathunk!* He picked up another, *wathunk!* Then another, *wathunk.* And another, *wathunk.* He turned around. The flames were reflected in the tears washing down his cheeks. The sun had set only a few hours ago, but Layla's house burned with such intensity it rivaled the coming of dawn.

What made them so angry? *Laylaaaaaa!*

He picked up another stone, this time heaving it at the burning house, though he was much too far away to hit anything. A dozen men and boys shared the darkness, their robes bathed in the fire's yellow light. They took turns throwing twigs and branches on the flames, making sure the house and everything in it burned to the ground. Fathers and sons, purging the world of infidels.

Mohamed wiped a sleeve across his eyes to clear the blurring. Had his father been there, he would have been required to join in. But his father was dead and…and Layla was gone.

He heard his mother's voice calling.

"Mohaaamed! Mohhhaaamed!"

He glanced around for a place to hide, but it was too late. She had already seen him. She was waving, the folds of her robe outstretched like the feathers of a huge black bird. Behind him stood the canal, cutting off his retreat. Light from the fire exposed him. There was no place to run. Her arms were open, but he did not want to be held. He wanted to disappear.

"Mohamed, I've been searching everywhere for you." She reached out, pulling him to her. "Don't look," she said, turning him away from the inferno. "They're safe. I saw them leave." She wrapped him in her *galabia* and began leading him along the bank of the canal, the flames of the fire reflected in the dark water.

The cool night enveloped them as they moved away from the blaze. The canal ended in a T with one sluice going right and the other left. Two logs, covered with sheets of plywood, were extended over the waterway, providing a bridge. Zainab took his hand and led him across, turning left on the side opposite the village. Now the air felt cold. Zainab tucked him under her shawl, and for once he was glad to have the warmth of his mother beside him.

Mohamed's mind harbored a thousand questions—*What happened to Father? Why do they hate Layla? Where are we going?*—but he refused to give them words. He wasn't ready to hear the answers. He felt a new surge of tears streaming down his face. His body trembled.

Zainab stopped. Taking her son by the shoulders, she stooped to face him eye to eye. "Your father was a good man, Mohamed...but even good men sometimes do foolish things." Then she wrapped him in her arms, and all his fear, anger, and pain poured from his soul in sobs.

She waited until his quivering stopped and his tears went dry before taking his hand and leading him deeper into the night, farther from their home. A full moon, bright enough to paint shadows on the ground, accompanied them, lighting the way. The golden orb had been low on the horizon at the start of their journey but was now high in the sky. Mohamed struggled to keep up, but his mother trudged on like she was on some kind of *hajj*.

The moon rose to its zenith and fell as Zainab led her son past several small villages not unlike their own, slipping through unobserved, the only noise the sound of night insects and the far-off *whoo, whoo, whooooooo* of an owl. Zainab looked out across the darkness for signs of life, but there were no discernible lights in the distance.

"We need to reach Minya. We'll be safe there."

"Safe from what?"

She ignored the question. "I think your friend Layla is there. You'd like that, wouldn't you?"

The saline streaks of Mohamed's tears, though dry, still reflected the sheen of the moon. He looked at his mother, his eyes red, his head slightly skewed to the side.

Zainab felt a rumbling and turned to see two white beams cutting through the night. She grabbed Mohamed and started to run—a jackal panicked by the sudden appearance of a car. It didn't occur to her to get off the road. The lights pinned their backs. A horn *beeeep, beeeeeped*, warning them to get out of the way.

She grabbed Mohamed, tucking him in close as she turned to face the wheezing monster that had come to a stop behind them. She raised her hands to shield her eyes, dust diffusing the rays of light. The door opened and someone stepped out. *Sayyid?* She could barely make out the black silhouette.

"Why are you walking the road at this hour?"

The voice gurgled like pebbles poured into a glass of water. Not Sayyid's voice. Zainab didn't answer.

"You are many kilometers from the village. Please, allow me to give you a ride." The man approached. The car lights shining on the side of his face revealed a stubby white beard and eyes scored deeply with wrinkles. A silver tooth glinted when he spoke. "Come. Come. It is cold out."

They squeezed onto the seat of a rickety flatbed truck carrying a load of melons to market, but it was a chariot to them. The old man explained how he traveled by night because the cool air kept his produce from spoiling. "Melons don't like the hot Egyptian sun," he said.

They rode along in silence, though the driver occasionally broke the quiet by humming an unfamiliar tune. Mohamed, lulled by the rumbling of the wheels, leaned against his mother's shoulder and fell asleep.

Zainab couldn't say how far they'd traveled, only that it seemed like hours before the driver pointed to their destination looming ahead, a distance she now realized they would not have been able to reach on foot. The town looked like blocks of ice under the light of the blue Egyptian moon. Its walls ascended out of the desert in vertical slabs. Off in the distance she could hear the bleating of sheep and the jingling of a cowbell. The truck continued to piff and sputter as it lumbered along.

"Are you from Minya?" she ventured to ask.

The man turned his cheek, smiling. "Yes, all my life I have lived in this place."

The truck bounced down the road, the battery of bumps bruising much of the fruit it carried. So much for worrying about what the sun might do.

Zainab had heard there were many churches in Minya. She had been told Christians there were left alone as long as they refrained from sharing their beliefs with anyone else. She needed to solicit their help. People at a mosque would take her in, but they would send her back to Sayyid. Still, the idea of asking to be left at a Christian church caught in her throat. It was not a question she would dare ask in her own village. She closed her eyes, hoping the Christian God would give her strength.

"I need you to take me to a church," she said.

"Ah, you are Christian. This is good. Yes, yes, there are many churches here. Which one do you seek?"

"We're not from here. Any church will do. Are you Christian too?"

"Me? *Na'am*, yes, a very good Christian. And a good Muslim. It is better, I think, if I venerate both gods. This way I receive a double blessing. Am I not wise?"

The truck wheezed and hissed as it rolled to a stop. The driver pulled up in front of a building with an arched roof and conical spires. The spires looked like inverted teardrops with crosses mounted at their uppermost points.

Zainab nudged Mohamed to awaken him, pulling him with her as she climbed out of the truck. She leaned in. "*Shokran. Rabema y'khalik.* Thank you. May God keep you."

"Out from my eyes for you," the driver responded. The door closed and the truck sputtered and rattled as it pulled away.

Zainab hesitated for a moment, looking around as Mohamed rubbed the sleep from his eyes. They stood in an arched portico, a chill wind seeping through the columns. She held her breath and raised her hand; with her fist clenched, she pounded on the door three times. She pulled her son closer, sheltering him from the breeze as they stood back waiting. She let a minute pass, then raised her hand and knocked again. This time she heard a muffled voice from the other side.

"Yes, yes, be patient. I'm coming. I'm coming." The door opened, allowing a thin curtain of light to escape. "What do you want?"

"*Momken te'sa'edni? Mehtaga doctor!* Can you help me? I need a doctor."

The door opened a bit wider. The man was plump and bearded and wore a white muslin sleeping gown. "Are you sick?"

"No, no, we are in good health, thank you. I'm looking for a doctor from the Adjulah family. He is my friend. We need to find him."

"I'm sorry...I do not know this man. Come back in the morning. Maybe I can ask around."

The door started to close, but Zainab raised her hand, holding it open. "Please, you must help us."

The man on the other side paused, sucking in his cheeks. "What is so important that you must knock on my door before the sun rises and wake everyone in the house?"

Zainab glanced over her shoulder, peering into the darkness. Then, covering her son's ear with one hand, she leaned in and whispered, "Please, I am Christian. The doctor is the one who told me of Isa. This doctor also told me of this place. I know he is here. Please. They burned his house. I know they will come for me."

The door closed in her face, leaving a crack through which she could see only one of the man's eyes and part of his nose. But even in the dim light she could tell he was shaking his head. "I'm sorry, there's nothing I can do." The door shut with a thud.

What? Zainab stepped back, confused. Had not Doctor Adjulah said the reason he helped people was because Isa loved him so much he felt compelled to show the same love to others? It was this love that first attracted Zainab to Isa, but this man showed no such kindness.

She looked down the street. There wasn't a light to be seen anywhere. She stepped off the portico and began walking. A cat yowled and raced down an alley. Zainab froze, pulling Mohamed in tightly. Just a…a…cat. She released her son and took him by the hand.

They'd traveled several blocks but had yet to see light seeping from a window or to find anyone they could talk to. The city was asleep. An ever-so-slight illumination, almost imperceptible, was hugging the horizon. She could make out the shadow of several towering minarets. Soon the imams would be calling people to prayer. The town would awaken then.

Something on the side of a cinderblock wall caught her attention. It was a large red cross painted on a sheet of wood with words that bespoke affiliation. She didn't know one church from another, only that the cross was a symbol of the Christian faith. She approached the front of the building and began pounding on a door with a glass window.

Mohamed sagged against her, his heavily lidded eyes only half open. Zainab grabbed his arm, propping him up as she continued pounding on the door.

Finally a light inside snapped on, and a man appeared behind the glass. He opened the door a crack. "What?"

"Please. Do you know a doctor of the family line of Adjulah?"

The man shook his head, yawning. He raised his arms to stretch, shivered in the cold, and folded his arms in front of him.

"Please, can you help us? I am Christian. My husband is dead. His family wants me to live with them, but they are Muslim, so…I…I felt I had to leave, but if they find us, I fear my brother-in-law will kill me. Please, my son and I need a place to stay."

The man waited for a second as if searching for the right words. Behind him, a woman wrapped in a tunic appeared in the doorway that led to an adjoining room.

"Who is it, Peter?"

"No one. Go back to bed. I'll be there in a minute." He turned back to Zainab. "I'm sorry...there is no room for you here."

"But I am Christian. Do not Christians help other Christians?" Zainab turned around, pointing down the street. "*He* would not help me either."

The man stepped outside, his eyes following her finger. "Father Botros? Yes, I know him. We disagree on many things, but he is a good man. You must understand, there is nothing anyone can do for you. It is against the law to convert. If I let you in, they will burn my church and throw me in jail, maybe even kill me. We cannot change what is. Go home. Keep Isa in your heart, but keep Him to yourself. To do otherwise will only bring pain."

Zainab pulled Mohamed in front of her, as if fearful that someone might snatch him away. "But...but I can't..."

"You must. Do you think you are the only one? Isa has come to many in dreams and visions, but we cannot help. Only last month a girl came to me saying Isa had appeared to her. She begged me to teach her more. I did what I could, but I urged her to keep it quiet. She would not listen. When she told her family, they locked her in her room and threatened to beat her, trying to force her to change her mind. She escaped and came back here. I tried to hide her, but she ignored my warning about not going outside..." He hesitated, more guarded now. "Last week, they found her body...." He drew a finger across his throat. "I do not believe she betrayed me, or I would not be standing here now. But...please...for both our sakes, I advise you to keep your conversion a secret."

"But what can I do? I have nowhere to go."

The man gave a short jerk of his head toward the back of the building. "I have a shed. You can rest there. But if anyone finds you, you must tell them you stumbled upon the place yourself."

Zainab held Mohamed's hand as they made their way down a narrow alley between two buildings. The crude shed was little more than four poles stuck in the ground with a piece of corrugated tin for a roof, but the wall of the church provided protection from the wind. Zainab took several cloth sacks from a pile and spread them out like a mattress to lie on. The moon was still bright and the shadows long on the ground as she snuggled up against Mohamed, rolled her shawl up over their shoulders, and fell asleep.

She awoke with a start. A hot, white sun blinded her as she opened her eyes. Her head was pounding. What was that noise? *Beep, beep, beeeeeeeeep!* Zainab sat up, pulling her shawl around her shoulders. *Beeeep, beeeeeeeeep!* She felt her heart thudding. She climbed to her feet, looking around for Mohamed, but the boy wasn't there. Then she heard a voice. She inched toward the alley and tried to peek around the corner.

"Zainab! Zainnnnaaaab! I know you are here. Did you think to escape so easily? I have your letter, the one from your friend in America. You have blasphemed Allah Most High. This is your last chance. If you come out now and confess, as Allah is merciful, I will show you mercy. But if you do not, my servants will search every corner of this town until you are found."

Behind the corpulent body of Sayyid, she saw the truck of the man who had given them a ride. Every melon in the back had been smashed. A mash of rinds and pulp dripped over the side. The old man was sitting on the ground leaning against a tire, rocking back and forth. He appeared to be crying.

Zainab's heart was pounding in her chest. Then she saw Mohamed standing in the shadows at the other end of the alley. He raised his hand and stepped into the light.

"We are here, Uncle. Over here."

CHAPTER 10

THE LAST STAND OF summer came with a vengeance. The September sun beat down on red tile rooftops as though it knew, with the ever-shortening days, that the season was drawing to a close. The remaining fall flowers bowed their heads in woeful submission as waves of corrugated heat spiraled up from the asphalt, baking people in their cars.

The trio relaxed on the outdoor patio where they could take advantage of a cooling ocean breeze, though they still had to fan themselves to keep the air moving in front of their faces. The terrace overlooked the Pacific with its undulating waves crashing on the white sand below. Rows of palms waved in the wind against a royal blue sky.

When Mohamed had asked Layla her favorite food, she'd immediately replied, "Mexican!" so he'd reserved them a table at Las Brisas. The elegant setting was once known as the Victor Hugo Inn, a first-class restaurant catering to the rich and famous. Built on a cliff above Main Beach in 1938, it was purchased from its original owner in the late seventies and remodeled to serve the traditional cuisine of the Mexican Riviera.

Matthew would not have brought Layla here. It was too pricey, and he'd already spent a week's salary on his failed engagement. Besides, there was nothing wrong with Manoly's. At least they'd agreed to a Tuesday lunch. Dinner on Saturday would probably be twice as expensive—*and more intimate.* He ordered nachos, one of the cheapest items on the menu.

The lunch had been the idea of his look-alike, who was relaxing in a cool-looking white cotton suit with an open-collared black shirt, nibbling on a halibut filet. *"Ohhh, that sounds good. I'll have that too,"* Layla had gushed, like fish was something special. She looked positively goo-goo-eyed.

Layla had introduced the interloper as Mohamed. The two men shook hands, friendly enough, before sitting down, but the other man had been giving him the evil eye ever since. Matthew determined on the spot to dub him "Moped."

He took another bite, careful not to let the crumbs fall into his lap. He was still miffed that he'd ordered before Moped offered to pay, but at least Layla had invited him along. It was a sure bet Mohamed, or whatever his name was, wouldn't have extended an invitation. He leaned back, feeling awkward. He'd been hunched over his plate, jamming chips into his mouth. It was as good an excuse as any for not entering a conversation he could neither relate to nor comment on. Those two were reliving the past.

The only redeeming thing about the lunch so far was that Layla had introduced him as her fiancé. He'd shot her a sidelong glance, but she shrugged it off and picked up her napkin, smoothing it in her lap. It didn't take a brain surgeon to figure out she'd only said it to keep Moped from hitting on her. At least Layla hadn't tried to sneak off and meet him alone; he had to give her credit for that.

"So how did you find me?" Layla asked. "I mean, if you're living all the way up there in Palo Alto, you wouldn't have an LA phone book."

"Quite simple really; you can find anyone on the Internet. All I did was type your name into an online phone directory, and there you were."

Layla's eyes were locked on Mohamed even as she chewed. She hadn't taken them off the man since they arrived. He was playing the part of the gentleman, holding her chair while she was seated—*get real*—and pausing to wait until she'd opened her menu before looking at his own. Matthew saw right through the ruse. So he wore a suit, *so what*? Matthew had a suit, or at least a blazer. He'd just bought it brand-new. He could've worn it if he'd wanted to. That's what niggled him. He'd purchased it to impress Layla but left it at home because it was too hot. Besides, they were only going to lunch, or so he *thought*. The jerk was showing off. Matthew looked down at his plaid button-down shirt, faded Levi's, and tennis shoes. They suited him just fine. He glanced up when Layla started giggling.

"Oh, I do remember that, Mohamed! You were so funny. I remember my mother telling me to be careful about you, you were such a little brat. I don't think she ever forgot what you did to her flowers."

"But it was your birthday and I didn't have anything else. They were so pretty, I knew they were meant for you." Mohamed's teeth gleamed white and perfect, bright against his olive complexion. Matthew had to admit, if it weren't for that silly goatee, he'd be one good-lookin' dude, but then...*hey*, they were a matched set, identical, so it figured. It's just that the brute looked so cool and relaxed sitting there in his suave Armani suit, though his forehead *was* glistening with perspiration. The breeze did little to compensate for the sun, which seemed to grow warmer by the minute.

Matthew finally caught Layla's eye and received a tacit apology for leaving him out of the conversation. Her gaze went back to Moped. "I just don't get it," she said. "You two look so much alike, I can't believe you're not brothers."

Moped's head tipped to the side as he examined Matthew. Then, suddenly, his nose wrinkled, and he sneezed.

Layla reached in her purse and found a handkerchief. "Here," she said.

Mohamed took it. "Sorry, I don't know what happened. Must be something in the air." He sniffed, dabbed his nose, and folded the cloth loosely as he continued the conversation, looking from Matthew and then back to Layla. "The resemblance *is* striking, like looking in a mirror, but you yourself know I'm an only child. Besides, there's more to being brothers than DNA."

"What do you mean?"

Matthew bent his head over his plate but felt Mohamed's scrutiny. He grabbed for another tortilla chip and used it to scoop up more guacamole.

"Even if you told me this man and I have the same mother, he would still not be my brother. I am of Egyptian birth and heritage. When I look at him, I see America. No, we are too different."

"But he was born in Egypt. So was I. America is just where we choose to live." Layla took a bite and glanced at Matthew, who was pretending to ignore the conversation, letting them talk about him in the third person as though he wasn't there.

"Yes, but I know your heart, Layla. He's not like you. I'll bet he wakes up singing the 'Star-Spangled Banner' and then goes to work and pays taxes to his Uncle Sam, who hands the money over to Israel so they can kill more of our people."

"Mohamed!"

Mohamed fixed his gaze on Matthew. "Isn't that right? You're an American through and through."

Matthew glanced up at Mohamed before looking down to scoop salsa onto another chip. He stuffed it into his mouth and looked up smiling, refusing to take the bait.

Layla shook her head. "What are you talking about? What's wrong with America? It's a beautiful country. *You're* here, going to school, getting a good education. I'm proud to be here. It's the land of plenty."

Mohamed set Layla's handkerchief on the table, the smiles in the conversation having dissipated with the breeze. "Yes, but at least I have not forsaken my people. Look around you. Don't you see the hypocrisy? All these rich people sitting here eating fifty-dollar lunches, while in the town where you and I grew up, families can't afford boiled beans."

A man of obvious Mexican descent was washing the deck with a hose. Every so often, he shot a spray of water at the squalling seagulls to keep them from bothering the guests. Matthew gave a discreet shake of his head. *That man came to America to find work and feed his family, and I bet they eat more than beans,* he thought, but he didn't join the conversation. He kept his face expressionless, feigning interest. Moped's true colors were starting to show. *Give the man a millstone and he'll drown himself in the sea.*

The man with the hose raised it to nail another seagull, then brought it down to resume watering a potted bougainvillea. An onshore breeze caught the spray and showered the table with a light mist. Mohamed looked over his shoulder, annoyed.

Layla picked up her napkin and began wiping the table. "The fact that people are starving in Egypt isn't the fault of the United States," she said without looking up. "You can't blame us for being prosperous and enjoying the blessings of God."

Mohamed dusted droplets of water from the lapel of his coat. "*Bahhh*, America won't see true blessing until it submits to the will of Allah."

Matthew patted the side of his head.

Layla stopped, her fingers pinching the wet linen as she squinted at Mohamed. "So you're still a Muslim. I'm disappointed. I was hoping your mother had taught you to become a Christian."

Mohamed's lips thinned, his features growing hard. For a minute he didn't say anything. Then he blurted out, "My mother betrayed our family. I could never be Christian. Look around you, Layla; all this is deception. Satan keeps these people blinded by their wealth so they can't see the truth."

A server came to their table and began wiping it with a cloth as she'd done for several tables around them. The trio sat back, staying out of her way until she was finished. "And what truth would that be?" Layla continued as soon as the girl was gone.

"That which you call 'freedom' is just an excuse to engage in immorality. Only a fool would serve a God who sits by and does nothing to stop evil." Mohamed paused and shot Matthew a glance as though suddenly realizing winning this contest might cost him the prize. Matthew smiled and nodded, encouraging him to continue.

"I'm not ignorant of what you believe, but little of it is carried out in practice. So far, all I've seen is people who sit and listen, and then go out and ignore the words of their teacher. Isa said feed the poor, but look around you—all these people do is stuff their pockets and spend their money on themselves. You call it the land of plenty. I call it the land of gluttony. Everyone eats in restaurants, lives in a big house, drives a fancy car—"

"Oh, give me a break," Matthew interjected. "We're only eating here because this is where *you* wanted to meet. Talk about hypocrisy, I saw your car, a big shiny Lexus LS 460. Did you see what I'm driving? I'm in a 1972 Volkswagen Beetle, and it's falling apart. If the Quran tells you to give to the poor, then maybe you can start by giving your car to me!"

Mohamed glared at Matthew. "Have you read the Quran?"

"The Quran? No, I—"

"You need to read it before you accuse me of not living up to its principles."

"Maybe, but I bet you've never read the Bible either."

"We of Islam respect your holy book just as we revere our own. The words of Jesus and the other prophets are sacred when taken as they were before they were changed to suit your Christian propaganda."

"What?" Matthew shook his head, slanting it to the right.

"One reason we know the Quran is superior is that it is the latest and final revelation of God. The original Bible was good, but it became corrupted. Early Christians changed the words to—"

"Oh, get a life!" Matthew wiped his fingers and threw his napkin on the table. "They disproved that bunk years ago. The fact is there are more early copies of the Bible than any other book of antiquity, including the Quran. They've got hundreds of early codices, including fragments that go back almost to the time of Christ, and they all say the same thing. There haven't been *any* changes, and anyone who says otherwise is either just plain ignorant or a liar—"

"Matthew, please!" Layla intervened. Her face was flushed, eyes wide with dismay. The two men were glaring at each other but simultaneously turned in her direction. She took a breath. "Please, let's just agree to disagree and drop it. Neither of you has read the other's holy book, so it's pointless to argue."

Matthew shook his head, his impatience growing. "I don't have to read the Quran. Christ said no one comes to the Father except through Him. If the Quran doesn't say that, it isn't worth reading."

"You Christians added that to suit your own religion. Muhammad came to—"

"There you go with that garbage again. The Bible hasn't changed—"

"Stop it! Please! We're here to enjoy lunch, not to argue. You both need to take a breath and calm down. Matthew, you need to read the Quran to speak intelligently about what it does or does not say. And you, Mohamed, need to read the Bible. That's the only way to have a valid discussion. I want you to promise me you'll do that. Both of you. And, Mohamed, I'd like to invite you to our church. It's not fair to say Christians go to church but don't live out what they believe. I think if you see our congregation, you'll get a whole different perspective."

Layla looked at Mohamed, then at Matthew, and sighed. The two men glared at each other. So much for feigned goodwill. Neither man put out his hand to shake the other's when they parted company.

CHAPTER 11

DOWN BY THE OCEAN, while dining on the patio at Las Brisas, the onshore breeze had cleared the air, leaving the sky blue. But as they inched their way up the San Diego Freeway at the northern end of LA, they became buried in brown smog. With no air conditioning in the tiny Volkswagen, the combination of stifling heat, smog, and traffic was enough to frazzle anyone's nerves. Layla was already in a sour mood, so Matthew was relieved when she climbed into the car, laid her head back, closed her eyes, and fell asleep, or at least pretended to. She hadn't said a word the entire drive.

Matthew kept the car radio tuned to a station playing contemporary Christian music, a subtle reminder of why she should reserve her affections for him and not Mr. Moped. Even an idiot could see the creep was some kind of Islamofascist. A definite bad choice. But Matthew had to be careful not to push the point. People don't like being told they're wrong. He flipped his blinker on and squeezed to the right.

Layla began to stir. Matthew tried stretching his arm across the back of her seat but removed it when she stiffened.

"I was thinking maybe we could go to a movie tonight. We haven't done that in a while. What do you think?" He winced as he said it. He couldn't afford a movie, but he had to do something to compete with Moped's lavish lunch and to make up for the way things had ended.

Layla didn't respond. He glanced over and saw her eyes fixed straight ahead, examining the line of cars like it was a chrome caterpillar with warning lights.

"You're still angry? Don't let him upset you. The guy's a jerk." Matthew leaned forward and fiddled with the radio dial.

Layla glanced over, unsmiling. "*You're* the jerk. He was trying to be nice, and you insulted him. You ruined the entire lunch."

"Me? What'd I do?"

"You practically told him he worships a false god."

"He does!"

"It's not what you said; it's how you said it." Layla struggled to straighten herself.

Matthew slipped his arm out the window, catching the jet stream in his palm. Some of that dirty brown air was bound to stick. He pulled his hand back inside. "And you told him you hoped he'd become a Christian. That's the same thing as saying his beliefs are wrong."

"Is not!"

Matthew looked at Layla, shaking his head. "Is so. How come if *you* say something, it's right, but if I use different words to say the same thing, it's wrong?"

"Huh! You know what your problem is? All you want to do is argue."

"I'm not arguing. I'm just saying it like it is."

Layla shook her head. "You two are alike in more ways than your looks. You push, and he pushes back."

"Now that's where you're wrong. We're *nothing* alike." Matthew glanced back at the road and slammed on his brakes, realizing the traffic had stopped.

Layla flew forward against her seat belt. She looked at him with eyes darkened and lips pursed as she loosened the belt from her collar. "See? All you want to do is argue. I'm not up for this. I refuse to talk about it anymore."

"Don't be upset at me just 'cause you found out your old boyfriend's a terrorist."

Layla shot him another one of those "you're crossing the line, buster" looks. "I'm really tired," she said. "If you don't mind, I'd like it if you just took me home."

Matthew stumbled into his apartment, tense to the point of exhaustion, his mind racing with questions. Was she putting the skids on their relationship? He dropped into the only comfortable piece of living room furniture he had. The threadbare padded armchair had been purchased at Sally Anne and smelled of mothballs and sweat.

He reached for the ring box on the table beside the chair. His world was spiraling out of control. He popped the lid open, holding the ring up to the window. The light bounced off the facets, creating rainbows on the wall. It was one fine gem, but he couldn't keep it—not if she wasn't going to be his wife. He snapped the lid shut and tried to shake off the pounding in his head. Too much heat and smog.

His bottle of aspirin was in the bathroom. He pushed himself up, determined not to let the headache become a migraine, but the room started to spin and he heard a droning in his ears. The light in the room began to fade. He reached for the back of a chair, trying to keep from passing out. His head fizzed like television snow.

When he finally opened his eyes, he was surprised to find he was still standing, but the ring was no longer in his hand. He took several deep breaths—*inhale, exhale, inhale, exhale*—until his head cleared. The ring box had bounced under the table. He stooped over to pick it up.

It didn't happen often but enough to raise concern. Only a few days ago it happened on the soccer field—of course, he'd been broadsided, so it wasn't quite the same thing. Still, the occurrences seemed to be increasing in both frequency and duration. It was time to admit that something was wrong.

He was a medical student. He should be able to diagnose himself, but every idea he had for what might be causing the spasms, he rejected out of hand. As far as he knew, he was in perfect health. It was time to admit he needed to see a doctor. He hesitated. Using the school's medical facility might result in word getting back to the coach, which could get him tossed off the team. It wasn't that he expected them to find anything wrong, but there was no point in taking chances.

He had nothing to fear. He was a child of God. There were, in fact, only four things he loved: God, Layla, soccer, and medicine, and in that order. God had blessed him, and God wasn't going to take the blessing away, was He?

Matthew went to the kitchen, opened a cupboard, and removed the telephone directory. It was two inches thick and covered most of LA. He began flipping through the book, looking for the number of a friend, a doctor he knew from his church. He wasn't one of the doctor's regular patients, but discretion was required. If there *was* a problem, he didn't want it getting back to his coach—*or to Layla*. God forbid she hear something was wrong with him. She didn't need another reason to turn him away.

He picked up the phone to dial.

"Michaels' residence."

"Hey, John, it's Matthew, from church."

"Hey, Matthew, what's up?"

CHAPTER 12

THE TRACT OF HOMES was classic suburbia, a cookie-cutter row of buildings that all looked the same, with only slight variations made to the façade. The street angled up along a bluff that overlooked the wildlife refuge at the lower portion of San Francisco Bay. The last house on the street had the advantage of being highest in elevation and free of the encumbrance of neighbors. It was separate unto itself, with the grandest view that took full advantage of the sun-speckled waters and pelican-filled sky. Mohamed parked at the curb and stormed up the sidewalk.

He could hear the screeching birds and a boat sounding its horn out on the bay as he approached the front door. He could still feel the anger churning like electricity through his veins. He'd given himself a day to calm down, but the more he thought about it, the more resentful he became. Layla, his girl, the only girl he'd ever been able to share his innermost thoughts with, was engaged to an impostor. He chided himself for not waiting until Friday. With no game scheduled on the weekend, they'd arranged to meet and update each other, but he couldn't help it; he needed spiritual guidance now. All he'd wanted was a little time to renew a relationship with an old friend, but this guy Matthew had sabotaged their reunion.

He pushed through a door inlaid with tiles, a decorative application that let those who entered know they were stepping into another world. Inside, the room had the appearance of a mosque. The ceiling overhead had been cut away and a large blue glass dome constructed to transmit light. Pot lights on dimmers were embedded around its circumference to create various moods in the evening when the dome was dark. Pillars stood floor to ceiling in each of the four corners, lending a feeling of solemn antiquity. Perhaps of even greater importance, the windows had been covered with tapestries to prevent the curious from peering in.

Mohamed's gaze swept the room. The banners were embroidered with the words of the Messenger and the *shahadah*—"There is no God but Allah and Muhammad is his prophet"—scrolled in Arabic. Interspersed among the tapestries were flags from Muslim nations, especially one that always caught Mohamed's eye: the red, white, and black flag of Egypt with the eagle of Saladin in its center.

But this wasn't a mosque, at least not in the canonic sense; it was a large room inside a modern home. The rest of the house contained contemporary furniture, Western art, computers, and a multispeaker surround sound entertainment system with a fifty-two-inch flat-screen HDTV.

The house was owned by Omar Muhsin. To his growing flock he was known as Sheikh Omar, or simply, El Sheikh, but his role as imam was confidential, known only by the select few who needed private instruction. To everyone else he was Professor Muhsin. Omar had come to the United States several years before Mohamed and had established tenure at the university where he led studies in Eastern history, culture, and literature.

He was a thin man with bladelike features and a beard that dangled to his waist. His association as a longtime spiritual mentor and friend went all the way back to Mohamed's youth when he'd been commissioned by the boy's uncle, Sayyid, to facilitate his education throughout his formative years. Even today he continued as a professor at the same university where Mohamed studied law.

Sheikh Omar rose to his feet and greeted Mohamed as he entered. In the role of professor, he wore slacks and a turtleneck, but now, dressed for his part as an imam, he wore a tightly wrapped turban and a muslin robe with billowy sleeves that slid back on his thin forearms. His hawkish nose hooked forward like a beak.

As was customary, they settled on pillows across from each other. El Sheikh recited in Arabic from the Quran: "'Only those are Believers who have believed in Allah and His Messenger, and have never since doubted, but have striven with their belongings and their persons in the Cause of Allah: such are the sincere ones. Say: "What! Will you instruct Allah about your religion? But Allah knows all that is in the heavens and in the earth: He has full knowledge of all things." They impress on you as a favor that they have embraced Islam. Say, "Do not count your Islam as a favor upon me: Nay, Allah has conferred a favor upon you that He has guided you to the Faith, if you be true and sincere. Verily Allah knows the secrets of the heavens and the earth: and Allah sees well all that you do.'" Surah 49:15–18.'"

Mohamed accepted the pronouncement with a nod. His mentor blinked and closed the Quran, setting it aside. Pushing himself up, he stood on the hem of the pillow. "I'm glad you stopped by," he said. "Wait here; I have something for you." He left the room and returned a moment later carrying a leather satchel. He sat again and made himself comfortable before flopping the satchel open to remove an envelope.

"I think we need to discuss this privately, though the others already know," Sheikh Omar said, handing the envelope to Mohamed. "We're not questioning your loyalty. Your progress with Miss Rodashan is commendable, and I'm confident you will do well, but..."

Mohamed raised the flap and removed a printout of an e-mail. The page was filled with pictures. He scanned them one by one, slowly shaking his head. "Where did you get this?"

"You need to be careful about the company you keep, my brother. Those who dance with the devil are doomed to fall."

Mohamed brought his eyes up and locked them on the imam. He had never challenged his mentor before, never had a reason to, *but this—and the blue car*? "Are you having me followed?"

"You have many friends in the Brotherhood, many who are willing to lay down their lives for Allah. Do not waste precious time making new friends—especially with those who serve the infidel."

Mohamed shuffled a photo from the top to the bottom of the stack. They were pictures of himself at Las Brisas in Laguna Beach with Layla and her friend Matthew. "I want to know who took these." He raised his eyes again, meeting those of the imam.

"That is not your concern."

"I don't like being followed."

"We are all under observation." His eyes narrowed, his finger tapping the cover of the Quran enigmatically. "Not to be caught doing wrong but for our protection. Now... tell me about these new friends of yours."

Mohamed stared at the pictures again. "Hardly new friends. The girl is someone I knew in Egypt. She now goes to UCLA. She was at my last soccer match and we connected, but we didn't get a chance to talk. She knew I was on the Stanford team. She looked me up and suggested we get together. End of story." He stared at a picture of Layla, smiling at him with her fork raised to make a point, her hair shining in the light. "We were friends when we were growing up, quite close. As a matter of fact, we were inseparable. It would have seemed more suspicious if I'd tried to avoid her."

Sheikh Omar raised his hand to hold up one last picture. "And the young man? It's hard to tell from the back, regrettably the only angle the photographer could get and remain discreet, but I'm given to understand he looks just like you."

Mohamed shook his head. "I don't think we look anything alike, but Layla, the girl in the picture, said the same thing. Anyway, I don't know him. She brought him along. What's it got to do with me?"

Omar nodded. His thin lips were veiled behind his beard, making it hard to know if his mouth held a smile or a frown. "You would do well not to see them again. You need to distance yourself from relationships that might result in your being compromised. Our mission is too important. You must be vigilant. Be on your guard at all times. The devil is out to destroy you. It's my job to see he doesn't succeed."

Mohamed pressed his lips together, denying himself the right to object. Why he was being followed and photographed he couldn't guess. Aside from his own private thoughts, which they knew nothing of, they had no reason to doubt him. He folded his arms. There was much he could say, but it was better left unsaid—at least for now.

CHAPTER 13

MATTHEW WAS IN A war zone. He was supposed to take the exit for the Santa Monica Freeway, but he was so wrapped up in his emotional drama that he passed the turnoff and was at the Marina Freeway before he realized he'd gone too far. Pulling onto the ramp he found himself in a confusion of roads that looped like tangles of spaghetti, causing him to lose all sense of direction. The sign said he was on Slauson, heading east. Traffic was light for a Saturday and, at the time, moving freely. He opted to keep going. He had to hit Western sooner or later, and moving forward had to be easier than turning back.

On the seat beside him was a two-inch-square velveteen box containing his unfulfilled dream. All week he'd wrestled with whether or not to return it. Taking the diamond back was akin to saying he was giving up, *but he wasn't giving up*; it's just that she'd said no. She hadn't even bothered to look at the ring, and he needed the money.

The sun was broiling the inside of the car, attesting to another unseasonably warm weekend. Matthew kept his windows down to circulate the air as he drove, but it wasn't *fresh* air. It was the same muddy brown smog, recycled over and over again.

He looked to the right and left—block after block of neon signs advertising liquor stores, dry cleaners, pawn shops, and cheap hotels with iron bars guarding their windows and graffiti masking the bullet holes in their walls.

Matthew pulled his yellow Volkswagen to a stop at the light. Three black kids with bandanas wrapped around their ears and baseball caps turned sideways on their heads stood on the other side of the intersection, bebopping around a car with its stereo playing rap music at a volume that rumbled the street. Another car pulled to the side. One of the youths ducked his head through the window on the passenger side and came out with a fistful of dollars. He reached into his vest pocket, produced a small bag of white powder, and dipped back into the car to hand it to the driver—dealing drugs in broad daylight.

The light turned green. Matthew pulled around the car, glancing over to see the driver sniffing a line of cocaine. Where were the police?

He leaned over, grabbed his jewelry case off the seat, and stretched out to stuff it into his pocket. He didn't particularly want to take the ring back, but it would be worse to have it stolen. He'd put twenty dollars away every week since meeting Layla, knowing from the first time he saw her that he'd one day need the money for a ring. But no matter how hard he saved, it seemed it was never enough. Every jewelry store he walked into wanted at least three thousand dollars for a diamond big enough to see without a magnifying glass, and they only went up from there. But that was in Westwood, and Westwood was rich man's land.

In relating his dilemma to his lab partner, he was told to try a pawnshop and was given the name of a place with "excellent" deals. Some of the rings were brand-new, sold by ladies who had broken up with their boyfriends and then pawned the rings they'd received as compensation for emotional damage. His friend said his thousand dollars would have double, if not triple, their worth in a store like that.

He pulled to another stop. Two young blacks crossed the street looking at him like he'd forgotten to put his clothes on before leaving. "Yo, dude, check it out. I wouldn't let my grandma jack that set o' wheels."

Matthew cringed, feeling a bit like a mouse being scrutinized by an owl. He rolled up his windows and locked his doors, prepared to sacrifice comfort for the sake of security. The light for cross traffic changed to yellow. He started to roll and hit the gas the moment his own light turned green. He'd read that two thousand cars were stolen annually in the ghettos of South LA. In some ways driving a hacked-out VW was a good thing. Sweat began to pour down his chest.

The graffiti sprayed on the side of a cheap motel threatened to kill any

Blood caught on Crips' turf. A more legitimate sign mounted on the front of the building alleged rooms could be rented by the week, by the day, or by the hour. A homeless lady wearing a puffy gray coat, despite the sweltering heat, mumbled to herself as she pushed a shopping cart past a man who was curled up on the sidewalk sleeping. Matthew guessed the cart contained all her worldly goods, which seemed to consist of a wad of rags, a few bottles and cans, a hubcap, and a blanket. Moped, or whatever his name was, should come down here before pontificating on the overindulgence of America.

Matthew spotted the sign he was looking for and pulled up in front of the store with his engine idling, debating on whether or not to go inside. He didn't want to sell the ring; he wanted to see it on Layla's finger. For one brief moment, when she'd called him her fiancé, he'd almost thought it possible, but then had come the altercation with...OK, with Mohamed, followed by their terse conversation on the drive home and the fact that she'd missed last night's game. She hadn't even been polite enough to return his last few calls, though she might have been busy. Still, he didn't need Daniel to interpret the handwriting on the wall. The ring was just tying up money.

He looked up at the sign. "Fast Cash Jewelry Buyers." It wasn't where he'd purchased the ring. The man he bought it from had been very clear about that. No returns—no exceptions.

"But what if she doesn't like it?"

The man had an answer. "Take it to Fast Cash. They buy all kinda jewelry, no questions asked." And to the idea that they might not give him as much as he paid, the man with a cigar in his mouth had quipped, "Are you kiddin'? I sell stuff so cheap, I've had customers buy from me just so they could turn around and sell it to Fast Cash for a profit. Anyway, your girl ain't gonna wanna give this baby back. You're only payin' a thou, but this beauty's worth at least five. Just look at the color and the way it sparkles. Trust me, that's one fine rock you got there."

He'd wanted to believe the man, so he'd taken the ring and prayed for the best. He'd never know whether Layla liked it or not. She hadn't even *looked* at it. She hadn't rejected the ring; she'd rejected *him*.

There was a tapping on his window. He flinched and glanced up to see a large black face staring at him. The eyes were bulging white orbs and the lips purple and hard. Why so much hostility? There had to be hundreds of blacks at the church he attended, and he'd never found fault with a single one, but here everyone seemed to be in a state of nonstop aggression.

The man brought his fist up and made a circular motion, indicating he wanted Matthew to roll down the window. He obliged, but let the glass down only a quarter of the way. His heart was thumping so hard he was sure it could be seen rippling his shirt. Beads of sweat lined his forehead. The car lurched. He glanced at his rearview mirror. Another black youth was jumping up and down on his rear bumper, rocking the car. He tried to maintain control of his voice. "Yes... uh, can I help you?"

"Yo, man, this is a no-parking zone. You blockin' our action. Unless you be a Crip, you gotta move this piece." The man's biceps were the size of footballs, and his chest was as big as a wheelbarrow, leading Matthew to believe he'd spent time in the pen with nothing to do but work at making his already massive body even bigger. He wasn't smiling.

"Sorry, I didn't see a sign. No problem, OK? Ask your friend to get off my bumper and I'll move."

Another young man stepped in front of the car, folding his sleeveless arms to block the way. His head was a mop of dreadlocks. Half a dozen chains of different lengths and styles were looped around his neck, one of them bearing a peace symbol; another, a cross.

The spokesman placed his hands on the car just above the rim of the door. He looked like he was about to roll the car over onto its side. "I didn't say there was a sign. I said you blockin' our action, dig? Say, what you messin' on our turf for anyway, huh, bean? You got some jewelry you gonna sell my man inside?"

"Huh? Uh, no, I don't have anything to sell."

"What that lump in yo pocket? Maybe you should let me see what you got. I can give you a solid estimate of what it's worth, dig?" He snapped his fingers, thick as sausages, and held his palm out like he expected Matthew to plop the ring into his hand.

"No, I already told you I don't…" Matthew was praying God would forgive him this one small lie and protect him, and the ring, from harm.

"Hey, JoJo, look!" The kid standing on his bumper stopped rocking and pointed across the street at someone who quickly took off running toward the projects. The three boys ran after him. The one with the chains slipped a pistol from his waistband and popped off a few shots, *pow, pow, pow!*

Matthew didn't wait to see if the person they were chasing was hit. He stomped on the gas, his wheels throwing up dust as he raced down the street. He didn't stop looking over his shoulder until he was back on the Santa Monica Freeway, heading for home.

He took it as a sign. Maybe God didn't want him to sell the ring.

CHAPTER 14

EVENING SUN FILTERED THROUGH the Sequoias, spilling shards of light onto pools of dark water. The scene was pristine, a grove of redwoods that had probably stood for more than a thousand years. Mohamed sat drinking it in. The others had left at the end of a long day, but he'd decided to stay and take a walk before heading back. The misty trail wound its way through ferns and trees laden with mist to a stream that at times seemed to gurgle and at other times to roar as it cascaded over the rocks on its way to the sea.

He stopped to recline on a granite shelf, listening to the pounding of the water as it crashed over the edge. Yawning, he rubbed his arms, enjoying the potpourri of smells: the musk of the tall trees, the humus of the rich soil, and the briny tang of the ocean. The rumble of the falls seemed to relax his tension like a massage. In the distance, light shimmered on the water. He could see the deep green spreading for miles into the horizon.

He picked up a stone and tossed it with a *kerplunk* into a pool below, the purple-blue surface forming concentric rings as the stone broke water. Minus the seventy virgins, this was paradise. The ocean breeze channeling up the valley rippled his hair. He combed his scalp with his fingers and scratched his neatly trimmed goatee.

He'd been in Big Sur for two days of intense planning and preparation. It was the first time he'd had a chance to relax.

The meeting had been held in a cabin that looked as rustic as it was old. Long, squared timbers formed its walls, with caulking to block the wind and a shake roof overhead to keep out rain. Judging from the racks of antlers nailed to the porch outside, Mohamed assumed the house was originally built for a hunter. A single rock fireplace served to heat the interior. The thick dank fog that usually blanketed the area was known to produce a chill, but this was September, the end of summer, so the fireplace remained unlit as Sheikh Omar, Abdu, and Amre sat down with him at a split-log table to review the plans for the upcoming wedding.

Mohamed began by briefing them on his many meetings with Allie Rodashan. He was able to report how they'd determined the wedding list, making sure as many politicians as possible were invited, not to mention, of course, the president himself. The appropriate news coverage had been secured, ensuring the wedding would be billed as the event of the season. Allie and Mike were the darlings of the media. They played the beauty-from-ashes story of the recently widowed vice president and his soon-to-be blushing bride for all it was worth. It was just the kind of pulp romance Americans loved to read.

The men seated around the table were avowed terrorists, committed to raising the banner of Islam over the United States. Sheikh Omar, in a long robe and beaded headdress, sat directly across from Mohamed. The other men, one on his right and one on his left, were Abdu and Amre, two of Sheikh Omar's highly trained security personnel, always in the background wherever he went and sworn to protect him with their lives. They were first to volunteer for the mission. Both men were also bearded: one, gray and neatly trimmed; the other, a salt and pepper mat of scraggly strands. The man with the kempt beard was draped in a loose-fitting *abaya,* while the other man wore faded blue denims and a plaid flannel shirt. Both men had turbans on their heads.

They had been searching for the perfect plan, which they now believed Allah had delivered to them. Mohamed didn't consider himself to be a terrorist, but he was a devout Muslim and, if called upon, would do what was asked.

"What's the matter, my brother? Your face looks like that of a cat drowning in water." Amre slapped Mohamed on the back. "This will be our most glorious day."

Abdu sat back, a frown revealing his displeasure. His eyes shifted to

Sheikh Omar. "Are you sure your boy is up to this? A chain can only be as strong as its weakest link."

Sheikh Omar opened his large, leather-bound copy of the Quran and began reading aloud: "'Verily those who were swearing allegiance to you, were indeed swearing allegiance to Allah: the Hand of Allah was over their hands: then any one who violates His oath, does so to the harm of his own soul, and any one who fulfils what he has covenanted with Allah,—Allah will soon grant him a great Reward.' Surah 48, verse 10."

He closed the book. "What about this, Mohamed? Do you waver from your commitment? When I left Egypt, you were my most promising pupil. I felt you were destined for greatness, but I too have noticed how silent you have become when your heart should be filled with joy. I convinced myself you were ready. Was I wrong?"

Mohamed shook his head. "No, not wrong. My father gave his life as a martyr. And my uncle, in his own way, has done even more. It's just that my training is in law. Entertaining Miss Rodashan could be done by anyone, and it's taking time from my studies. I don't want to jeopardize my education. I'm sure you'll need me a lot more after Mike is in office than you need me now."

The sheikh stroked his beard. "Ah, this is your concern. I assure you, your role is vital. Allie is young and can be influenced much better by someone of her own generation. It is imperative that you gain her confidence so that when the time comes, she will be ready. Is that so much to ask—that you be your charming self and earn her trust?"

Mohamed nodded, but remained unsmiling.

Omar's eyelids fluttered. "Your role is crucial. I need to know we can count on you. If not, you already know too much, and I'm afraid we'll have to kill you."

The heavy silence in the room lasted only a moment. Sheikh Omar's face broke into a grin as he burst out laughing. Amre shoved Mohamed's shoulder playfully, and Abdu got up and smacked him on the back.

"Gotcha!" Omar chortled, using the back of his hand to wipe spittle from his beard.

Mohamed smiled, attempting to join in, but a part of him wondered whether it really *was* a joke. "No, you can count me in. The blood of my father and my uncle runs in my veins. I won't let you down."

Omar leaned back, folding his hands over his stomach. "This is a divine appointment, Mohamed. Never before have we been granted such an opportunity. My heart sings with joy to hear that you are with us and to know your years of training are about to bear fruit. I have been in touch with Sayyid, and I know he is pleased as well."

Mohamed stared out over the ocean, mesmerized by the endless bounty of blue. Translucent green waves furled into whitecaps that came crashing down on the shore in endless sequence. His homeland boasted places of great beauty too, but none like this. Only the Almighty could have designed such a thing.

He clasped his hands behind his head and bent forward, using his elbows to touch his knees—left elbow to right knee, right elbow to left knee—one, two, three, *huf, huf, huf*…he needed to loosen the stiffness in his back.

What would become of Allie? The thought troubled him. He *had* become her confidant. More than that, he'd become her friend. He admired her and in a way was envious of what she and Mike shared. She was a fascinating woman—handsome, intelligent, keeping in step with the modern world without forsaking her roots—the kind of bride he'd want for himself if he ever found time for a relationship. His mind wandered back to Layla—*No!*—He tried to purge the thought. Left elbow to right knee, right elbow to left knee, one, two, three, *huf, huf, huf.*

Allie didn't know she was to manipulate her husband—at least not yet—but when the time came, she would do as told. She wouldn't have a choice. It was bound to cause a rift in their marriage. As the pressure to advance Islam grew, Mike would begin to suspect his wife had married him more for his power than for his love. Would they stay together and ride it out even when the love bubble burst and he discovered he was being used?

It was a risk Omar seemed willing to take, though Mohamed warned several times that a breakdown of the marriage would bring to an end the entire plan. It would do no good to have Mike as president if Allie were not there to steer him in the right direction.

Mohamed stopped, out of breath, *uh-huh, uh-huh, uh-huh.* He sat up, wiping his sleeve across his brow. A squirrel scurried up the trunk of a nearby tree and out onto a branch, chattering at Mohamed. *Do not worry, my little friend. You will not be hurt.*

It had been nearly two years since Mohamed had landed in America. He'd been inserted into the master of laws program at Stanford, a logical transition since he'd already completed studies in Islamic law at Al-Azhar. Now it fell to Islam to play a key role in bringing the world back to God—to Dar Al-Islam. The United States was a morass of sin, a place where women sold passion like a commodity, men flaunted their lust for other men, and children were exploited for profit—open, blatant, gross perversion. Things that, if judged under Sharia law, would result in death. Magazines purveyed nudity. Kids sold drugs. Millions of unborn lives were sacrificed to the gods of abortion. The unbridled greed, sex, and violence went on unabated.

Surely it was an abomination. The people of this supposedly "godly" nation sat by and not only permitted it, but they also celebrated the freedom that allowed it. Even those who outwardly criticized such behavior took vicarious pleasure in watching it on television—*Oh, that's disgusting, but we would never do that!* It was time to bring it to an end.

He was grateful for the role he'd been called to play, though his heart increased its rhythm whenever he thought about what they planned to do. His was not to question; his was to do the will of Allah, even if it meant the arrangement of something so repugnant as this wedding.

Mohamed turned to look back over his shoulder. The breeze from the waterfall tousled his hair; the collar of his polo shirt flapped against his cheek. He stretched, letting the warmth seep through his shirt into his skin. He wondered if the chill would ever leave his bones. It was something the Middle East had over the United States. The sunny climes of Southern California couldn't compare with a warm Arabian sun, but he had to get moving. It was a long drive back to Palo Alto. He sat up straight, squaring his shoulders, and pushed the palm of his hand into his lumbar. He looked at his watch. Tomorrow was Sunday. It was two hours home and four hours back to LA. He probably shouldn't—but he just couldn't seem to shake her from his mind.

CHAPTER 15

L AYLA RUBBED HER ARMS and stretched, yawning. Hanging around the library was no way to spend a Saturday evening, especially when she'd been invited to attend a choral presentation featuring as lead vocalist one of the girls in her dorm. She had called earlier but found Matthew wasn't home. By the time she reached him, the day was gone, so they'd agreed to meet at five. At least this way they'd probably end up going to dinner.

They needed to talk, though explaining why she'd missed last night's game would be hard when she didn't have a good reason. If it wasn't so important, she'd wait until tomorrow and tell him after church, but she couldn't hold it back any longer. The news was too good to keep.

She'd scanned the report a half-dozen times already and was now reading it again. She'd tried working on her assignments. A pile of textbooks lay on the table, two of them open next to her blue book of notes, but she couldn't concentrate. There was no point in reading microbiology when her mind was somewhere else. She looked at her watch. It was ten minutes after. He was late. She laid her palms flat on the table and drummed with her fingers. News such as this didn't deserve to be kept waiting.

Big news! No matter how many times she reviewed the report, it jolted her. It all seemed so impossible, and yet—it had to be true. Her chest pattered with excitement. *Where is he?* She looked at her watch again—he should have arrived fifteen minutes ago. She'd sent him a text message and he'd replied saying he'd be there.

She slipped the papers into a manila folder and extended her feet under the table, trying to relax. Her eyes roamed the aisles, one hardwood bookcase after another, seemingly going on forever. Sometimes, when she sat with all these volumes around her, she felt like she was surrounded by the wisdom of the ages. There were over eight million books in the system, the accumulation of man's learning—virtually everything known—placed on the shelves of one institution.

She rubbed her bare arms, smoothing the goose bumps—whether a consequence of her nervousness or the air conditioner, she couldn't say. How would Matthew take the news? She'd find out soon enough, though in retrospect, she was glad they were meeting in the library. Whatever his reaction, they'd have to keep their voices down. No talking allowed, let alone animated conversation.

She'd have to let Mohamed know too, but that was a bridge she could cross later. She thought about getting up. She needed to do something—*go to the washroom? Pace the floor? Find something to read?*—anything to keep her mind distracted and quell her nervous anticipation, but she forced herself to stay in her seat, rubbing her arms.

"Hey, Layla."

Matthew's voice startled her, even though he spoke in a hoarse whisper. She twitched involuntarily as she looked up, her lips clamped together in a frown of displeasure. Glancing at her watch, she gave him a silent rebuke.

He tossed his worn brown briefcase on the table and pulled out a chair, taking a seat across from her. "I know, I know, but you didn't give me much notice." He was wearing faded blue denims and sandals with a baggy T-shirt hanging loose from his shoulders. He crossed his arms and leaned back in his chair. His eyes were veined, and his jaw held the shadow of a day-old beard. It looked like he hadn't been getting enough sleep.

How appropriate. She had dressed for the occasion, putting on a pink twill skirt and white linen blouse. Her wavy dark hair fell around her shoulders—the way she knew he liked it—and the gold cross necklace was the one he'd given her for her birthday, not that he'd notice. She exhaled in a huff that suggested she still wasn't happy as she reached for the file, pulling it to her. His arriving late took the fun out of it, but she couldn't let his lack of enthusiasm diminish the importance of the information.

She removed a single sheet from the folder and slid it across the table.

"What's this?" Matthew picked it up. His eyes began a quick scan back and forth across the page. He set the sheet down and keeled his head to the side, his nostrils flaring as air escaped in a puff. "Where did you get this?"

"Told ya. So what do you think?" She caught an annoyed look from the student at the next table and lowered her voice. "It's proof positive you and Mohamed are brothers. And not just brothers, but identical twins. I don't know how it happened, but you can't argue with the facts. You two must somehow have been separated at birth back in Egypt."

Matthew shook his head, his lips pursed and his eyes barely slits revealing his aggravation, but he modulated his tone so as not to be overheard. "I don't recall your sampling my DNA. You had no business going behind my back on this, Layla. What'd you do, steal some of my hair?"

She nodded, short little jerks of her head that were barely perceptible. "Don't be mad. I had to, for your own good. Mohamed used my handkerchief, so I had what I needed from him. And you've used my brush; plenty of hair there. It was easy. My dad has connections with several labs, so I talked him into checking into it." She studied his face. "I don't understand why you aren't excited. Don't you see? It solves the mystery."

Matthew pushed the piece of paper back across the table. "It doesn't change a thing. There's nothing here I didn't already know. It's just that you did it without telling me. It's kind of an invasion of my privacy."

"You already knew?"

Matthew pulled his briefcase over, unbuckled the hasp, and withdrew an envelope. "I was going to let you read this. I had to dig it out. It was buried in a box stashed away with all my mother's effects." He reached across the table, handing the envelope to Layla. "It was filed with her last will and testament, to be delivered to me after she died."

Layla focused on the envelope, her eyes darkened. She lifted the flap, removed a letter, and unfolded it, her hand shaking slightly as she began to read:

Dearest Matthew.

My heart is heavy, because I know if you're reading this I'm no longer with you. There's something I need to tell you, something I've wanted to share with you for many years, but for one reason or another, the timing never seemed right. It's a story that began long ago…

* * * 🌙 * * *

"*Auuuugghhhh!*" Zainab screamed. "How much longer?"

"Not much, my sister. I think I see the head. You must push."

"If it doesn't happen soon, I'll die."

"You won't die, sister. See, there he is. Push!"

The newborn slid into Hoda's hands. She reached for a knife to sever the umbilical cord and stood with the crying baby in her arms. "A boy, a handsome strong boy, just as you predicted, Zainab. You have a son."

"*Ahhhhh!*" Zainab grabbed her friend's robe, squeezing till her knuckles turned white. "Shouldn't I feel better? *Auuuugghhh!*" She let go and grasped her belly.

"Try to relax, Zainab. The pain will pass." But when Hoda looked down, she gasped. A tiny hand was protruding from between Zainab's legs.

Zainab screamed again, and a second child entered the world. The boy didn't wait to be slapped. He immediately began to cry.

"What have we here?" Hoda handed the first child to Zainab as she leaned in to sever the cord of the second. "God has doubly blessed you, Zainab. You have twins." Hoda reached down and handed Zainab her second newborn.

Zainab tried to hold on to the squirming babies. She looked at the two little heads, each with a crop of black curly hair. A tear rolled down her cheek, followed by another. When there's no rain, that's when it pours. "This is not a blessing, Hoda. We can't afford to feed one child, let alone two. Khalaf won't let me keep them both. He'll give one to Sayyid. What am I going to do?"

Hoda knelt down beside the mattress. She reached in to help, cradling one of the boys in her arms, gently rocking him back and forth. "Why would you deny him? Khalaf's brother is childless and certainly a man of means." She tickled the newborn under the chin, cooing to quiet the child. Then she stood and stepped over to the pail, dipping a rag into the water to begin the washing. "You'll get to see your son often, and he'll be well cared for."

Zainab held her tongue, her eyes filling with water.

Hoda laid the freshly washed son at Zainab's breast, his skin soft and smooth against her, then picked up the second to clean him. Still holding the infant, she stood back, brooding over her friend's obvious lack of joy. "What's wrong, Zainab?"

"Oh, Hoda, Sayyid is evil. Sometimes he looks at me and…it's not right. He comes when Khalaf's away. Yesterday, he drove ninety kilometers to see how 'we' were doing, when he knew Khalaf had gone to look for work in Cairo. Sayyid refused to leave until I told him you were coming today."

Zainab nuzzled her nursing baby, then turned a tearful face to her friend. "Don't you see…he should bring Fatma. I…I don't know. Maybe I'm imagining it, but sometimes he looks at me and I fear for my life. You say you want me to be a Christian, but you must know Sayyid is a devout Muslim. My child would be raised to be like him."

Hoda turned and handed the freshly bathed child to Zainab. The water dripping on the dirt floor made spots in the dirt.

"You could do it, Hoda. You could take the child and raise him."

"Me?"

"How long before you leave for America?"

"Zainab, don't. My husband's company had a hard time accepting that he's bringing home a wife. How would he explain another person?"

"You're only here for another month. You can say the child is yours. Take him to America with you, Hoda, please. You can make him a Christian. Khalaf will never know."

Hoda hugged the child. The infant reached up and took hold of her finger as she brushed his cheek with her lips.

...and so I share this with you knowing, if you're reading it, I've gone home to be with Jesus. Your mother loved you, Matthew. She wrote often to ask how you were doing. I collected her letters so you can read them, but as you see, one day they stopped. The last one I received spoke of her conversion to Christ. I wrote back inviting her to visit. I couldn't bring myself to tell you, but I thought if she were here, then maybe you would understand. I even offered to pay her way, but she never responded. I don't know what became of her, but I fear the worst. All my attempts to reach her since have been unanswered. The letters are enclosed. Please read them for yourself. Know this, Matthew, you were not rejected by your mother. Her name was Zainab, and she loved you. She gave you up as an act of love.

And I've loved you too, so you've had the love of two mothers. A son to her by birth, but to me by life. You are doubly blessed.

Layla focused on Matthew again. There was sadness in her eyes, but it lasted only a second, then her face grew flushed and her gaze narrowed. "You mean to tell me you knew all along?" She caught another terse look from the annoyed student and leaned in, lowering her voice. "When I mentioned that you reminded me of someone, you knew you had a brother, but you never shared that information with me? You *lied* to me."

Matthew shook his head, his eyes communicating hurt. "I never lied to you, Layla," he said. "I only said I wasn't the person you thought I was. Look, you've got to understand that this whole thing has me really confused. Mohamed's been flirting with you since the day he arrived. OK, so I have a brother...doesn't mean I have to like him. He's the one you've thought about all these years. How am I supposed to handle that? First my mother chose him over me; now *you're* doing it too."

Matthew leaned in to take Layla's hand, but she yanked it back. "You've got to lose this guy, Layla. He's not good for you. He'll want you to be a Muslim and...and you can't. I've been reading the Quran. There's so little hope."

"This isn't about Mohamed, Matthew, not about the Quran, and not about Islam. This is about trust. You say you want to marry me, yet you insist on keeping secrets like I'm some...some kind of teenybopper spreading gossip. This is exactly what I meant when I said I don't feel like I know you."

"Layla, please..." Matthew reached out again.

"No, Matthew. Not until you see love means transparency. As long as you're holding things back, I can't commit to this relationship." Layla scooted her chair back and stood. She swept the report from the table, gathered her things in her arms, and walked away.

CHAPTER 16

CARS FILLED THE LOT in every direction as far as he could see. Mohamed closed the door and stood by his Lexus, unable to justify his actions. Something about the place made him uncomfortable, like he didn't belong. *Well—he didn't!* A thin veil of perspiration tickled his skin, his heart picking up speed. If he was going to do it, it had to be now! All he'd get from standing in the sun was underarms soaked in sweat.

He began weaving in and out between the bumpers, working his way toward the front of the squat one-story warehouse. The building had a plank façade with a large wooden cross mounted over the entry, transforming it into a church. Etched on the glass doors were the words "Greetings in the Name of Jesus," hooped like eyebrows over the outline of a fish.

Mohamed pushed on through, feeling instant relief from the air conditioning as he melded into the crowd, letting the flow carry him across the vestibule into the sanctuary. He took comfort in the throng of people; being surrounded by so many gave him anonymity.

He caught the musty smell of body odor wafting in the air and discreetly sniffed under his arm to make sure it wasn't him. *No, he was good.* He smiled. *Let the fools swelter in their car!* At least now he knew who was following him. *The blue sedan—has to be Abdu and Amre. Now that's justice. Let the stooges bake in the sun!* Imagine their pretending to leave ahead of him and then hiding like little squirrels until he passed by just so they could trail him here. At least they wouldn't follow him inside. They'd never darken the door of a Christian church. He brought his hand up to stroke his goatee. The bigger concern was finding a way of explaining the excursion to Omar.

He checked the last aisle, the one closest to the wall. He wanted a spot as far back as possible—the better to see without being seen. The row was already crowded with people. He began squeezing around and over the knees blocking his way. "Excuse me, excuse me," he muttered, stepping on toes until he reached the midpoint and found an empty seat.

Folding his arms, Mohamed sat stiffly, his head swiveling back and forth. There had to be at least three thousand people crammed into the room. In calling for directions, he'd learned the church offered three Sunday morning services. He'd chosen to attend the middle one. The first was too early. It wasn't likely she'd attend that one, and though for convenience sake he'd stayed in a nearby motel, he couldn't say he was fond of rising early either. But if he waited for the last one, there might not be enough time to have lunch with Layla and still make the drive back.

His eyes roamed the building hoping to spot her, but it was futile. There were just too many people. He should have stayed home. He couldn't be at all three services, and she'd failed to mention which one she planned to attend. Now he wished she hadn't invited him…or, better still, that he could have extricated her from his mind. But the fact was, he'd been thinking about her all week. Now he was here, trapped in a glut of people with no way out. Decisions made on the spur of the moment were usually foolhardy.

He continued scanning the crowd. So many people from so many backgrounds. The congregations of most mosques were composed of faces like his, warm as desert sand, with only a smattering of those that resembled goat cheese, but the faces here were as varied as pebbles by the sea. It troubled him to see many Arabs in the crowd—men, women, and children who should be worshiping in a mosque—joining the infidel in bowing to a false god.

This was all so different from anything he'd expected. He thought he'd see high vaulted ceilings, stained-glass windows, long wooden pews, a droning organ, and a white-faced milquetoast congregation. The priest would come out wearing vestments and make peculiar signs with his hands while reading prayers from a book, like he'd seen on TV. But this building had little to speak of in the way of ornate design. Except for the occasional bulletin board, cross, or wooden plaque engraved with a passage of Christian Scripture, the walls were bare. And the people filing out on stage were picking up electric guitars. One sat behind a set of drums and tapped a rim shot that echoed through the room, followed by a few *rat-tat-tats*. The murmuring of the crowd settled down as the band began to play. The guitar led off with an electrifying riff as the man's fingers spider-crawled up and down the neck of his instrument.

The people sprang to their feet. The songs ranged from foot-tapping, hand-clapping, adrenaline-pumping rock sonnets to tear-jerking, hand-raising, harmonious songs delivered in an attitude of praise. But it wasn't worship, at least not in his view. Worship was kneeling on a prayer rug and bowing down with hands outstretched and forehead touching the ground, reciting the mantras of Muhammad. Worship wasn't meant to be frivolous; it was the obeisance of a slave paid to his master.

The music was compelling, but Mohamed didn't sing. He didn't know the words, but even if he had, he would not have joined the refrain. He never sang. He considered leaving, but the knees of the parishioners on both sides buttressed him in. And there was still a hope of seeing Layla. He'd come so far; he had to give it a chance. Who was he to question the will of Allah? After years apart, separated by an ocean, they'd bumped into each other at a soccer match in LA. That had to be the hand of God.

The band members looped their guitars off their shoulders, setting them on stands, and stood back, yielding the platform to a pudgy man who wore jeans and an untucked shirt. He took out a well-worn Bible and began to read. The words appeared behind him on a giant overhead screen:

"'Why should I fear in the days of evil, when the iniquity at my heels surrounds me? Those who trust in their wealth and boast in the multitude of their riches, none of them can by any means redeem his brother, nor give to God a ransom for him—for the redemption of their souls is costly, and it shall cease forever—that he should continue to live eternally, and not see the Pit....But God will redeem my soul from power of the grave, for He shall receive me.' Psalm 49, a psalm of Korah."

Mohamed hadn't been paying attention but his ears pricked up. Had the man said he was reading from the Quran?

The pastor began to pace. "I'm sure there are times when every one of you has wished you had more money." He paused, turning toward the congregation. He held his Bible open in one hand while he raised the other. "You know how it goes: 'Oh, if only I had a lot of money, the things I could do.' But the psalmist tells us it wouldn't matter. There's one thing that you can't possibly do with all your wealth. All your money's not going to keep you out of the grave. And that's what he is telling us in this psalm."

Exactly! That's just what I was saying when that fool cut me off and started lecturing me about my car. He leaned in to pay closer attention.

"First of all, notice the inevitability of death. No matter who you are, there's one thing you're going to do: old, young, middle-aged, wealthy, poor, gifted, intelligent, dull, it doesn't matter; you are going to die. And there's nothing you can do to prevent that. The wise die, the foolish die, the senseless die, everybody dies.

"But death is not a cessation of life. You don't just cease to be; rather, you go somewhere. It's very important to remember that death isn't the end. Death just takes you someplace else.

"If you wonder what it's like, read Luke, chapter 16, the story of the rich man and Lazarus. The rich man probably had a glorious memorial service and was buried in a magnificent tomb, but none of that mattered because while his funeral procession was going on, he was already in hell." Looking down at his Bible again, the preacher read: "'And being in torments in Hades, he lifted up his eyes and saw Abraham afar off, and Lazarus in his bosom.' And this rich man called to Abraham and said, 'Have mercy on me, and send Lazarus that he may dip the tip of his finger in water and cool my tongue; for I am tormented in this flame.' Lazarus, you see, was a poor beggar who had to satisfy his hunger with crumbs from the rich man's table; only now he was in comfort, sharing a place with Abraham in paradise.

"And that's what happens after death. Death is not the end. You are born, you live, and you die. And when you die, you are destined to go somewhere. There's no avoiding that. There are only two options: one is horrible, and the other is beautiful beyond description."

In his seat, Mohamed relaxed. He was prepared to endure a barrage of heresy, but so far everything he heard lined up with the teachings of the Prophet—Allah's immense justice, his fairness regarding the poor, a place of eternal punishment, and a place of eternal reward.

"God is omniscient. He knows everything. The record is kept in heaven, a record of all our thoughts, all our deeds, all our sins, all our blasphemies, all our disobedience. It's all written down. And therefore, you have an indispensable need. That need is for someone who can redeem you, or to use the language of this psalm, someone who can pay a ransom for you."

The man had been walking back and forth, pacing the stage, making sure he addressed the entire congregation, but now he stopped, his gaze sweeping the room as though trying to make eye contact with everyone all at once.

"And why is that? Because God is holy. This is something I'm afraid we don't think about much. But God *is* holy. God is so holy, that even the seraphim surrounding His throne fly with two wings covering their eyes because His holiness is much too bright to look upon. And they cover their feet with their wings lest they dare to stand upon holy ground. God is holy, absolutely holy, flamingly holy. He cannot abide iniquity, cannot stand sin, and He sees sin in all of us.

"Therefore, what you need is a redeemer. Job recognized that need when he said in Job 9:33: 'Nor is there any mediator between us, who may lay his hand on us both.' But who is there that can actually touch both God and man? In order to put his hand on God, he would have to be God. And in order to put his hand on me, he would have to be a man, a human being. Where are you going to find someone like that?"

Mohamed shrank back in his seat, his jaw tightening as he folded his arms. *There it is. The heresy. Man can't be God. Only God is God! Muhammad wasn't God. He never claimed to be. Jesus wasn't either.* He looked down the aisle, once again resisting the urge to leave. He was there to find Layla, not God. But if it weren't for that, he'd be out of there.

The pastor trundled back and forth, continuing his rant while waving his Bible over his head: "There's only one answer, and that answer is Jesus Christ. Who is He? Well, the Scriptures say Jesus Christ is God Himself. He's God, the Son. He has always been coexistent with the Father, infinite, before time. In a mystery we don't understand, called the miracle of the Incarnation, God, the everlasting Son, entered our world as a human, as an innocent baby. Yet at the same time He was, and still is, God. Galatians 4:4 says, 'But when the fullness of time had come, God sent forth His Son, born of a woman,' and Colossians 2:9 adds, 'In Him dwells all the fullness of the Godhead bodily.'"

One thing about the guy, Mohamed thought, *he keeps them entertained. Look at him prancing around up there, practically dancing. He's got too much extra baggage for that kind of thing. He'll be lucky not to have a heart attack. Then he'll see who goes to paradise and who goes to hell.*

"But it says in Matthew 20:28, 'The Son of Man did not come to be served, but to serve, and to give His life a ransom for many.' Paul picks that up in First Timothy 2, where he says, 'For there is one God and one Mediator between God and men, the Man Christ Jesus, who gave Himself a ransom for all.' He didn't just pay the ransom; He Himself *was* the ransom. A ransom sufficient to satisfy God, who is holy.

"How did He do it? Through the eternal Spirit, He offered Himself, sinless as He was, to God. After living a perfect life for thirty-three years, He, of His own volition, allowed Himself to be put to death on the cross— probably one of the most agonizing of deaths. But He went there, and He went there voluntarily..."

Mohamed's eyes probed the audience, sweeping up one row and down the next. The idea was absurd. He should be home studying. If he *did* see her, she'd probably be sitting with Matthew. He couldn't shake the image from his head—Layla and the infidel—hand in hand! *Bahh! He* was the man she was supposed to be with. The boyfriend was an impostor.

The pastor slowed his pace and turned to face the crowd, exhaling a sigh before continuing on. "And then came six grueling hours when all creation was forsaken and darkness covered the earth. I think it's fortunate this period isn't described in Scripture, because I don't know how anyone could express it in words. But during those hours He hung on the cross, we are told God Almighty, His Father, poured out all His anger, all His wrath, all His disapproval of all the sin committed from Adam right on till the end of the age. God poured all that punishment upon Jesus—who never sinned—to pay for all the sins of the world. To pay a ransom—the *King's* ransom.

"Jesus hung there in excruciating pain, paying the price for our sin, the righteous for the unrighteous, the godly for the ungodly. But before He could do that, something had to take place. That is, God the Father had to say to His Son, 'It's enough. I'm satisfied; the debt is paid.' Then and only then could Jesus cry out, 'It is finished.' And then go through death, burial, and descent into Hades.

"The ransom was paid, and every sin was covered—all of it—without exception. And so now there is forgiveness."

The pastor swung his Bible around and looked right into the heart of the crowd.

"I don't know you. I don't know what evil deeds you may have done or might be thinking of doing, but I can tell you this, through the blood of the Lord Jesus Christ, you can be forgiven."

Mohamed felt the man's eyes boring holes in his forehead. He could almost see the smoke rise and smell his flesh burning. He clenched his jaw and gripped the sides of his chair, hanging on.

"I'm telling you God can save *anybody* through Jesus Christ. And not only that, He can make you righteous—that righteous life of Jesus Christ. His righteousness is applied to me, and if you're a Christian, that righteousness is applied to you. So God sees you now, not as you are; He sees you covered with the righteousness of Jesus Christ, and that's why He can take you to glory."

The pastor closed his Bible, folding it in front of him as he looked down, carefully considering the words he was about to say. He stood in the center of a spotlight that rimmed his head and shoulders, and when he looked up, lifting his eyes to the rafters, the effect was of heaven shrouding him in a beam of light. His lips quivered. It was clear he was praying. He brought his eyes down again and leveled them at the crowd.

"The irony is, even though Christ paid your ransom, you can still perish. You have to accept what Christ did for you. You have to acknowledge three things: First, you have to believe that God is God and determine to worship only Him. Second, you have to believe that Jesus Christ is the Son of God and that He died to pay for your sins and cover the debt you owe. And finally, you have to believe that if you call on Him, He will save you. It doesn't matter what words you use, but you need to say something like this, and you need to mean it: 'God, You created me, and I've sinned against You. I'm asking You to forgive me because Your Son, Jesus, took the punishment I deserve upon Himself. And I'm asking Jesus Christ to come into my life, right now, and become my Lord and Savior.' When you decide to take that step and mean it from your heart, you pass from death to eternal life. You're saved!"

The man on the stage sighed, letting his shoulders slump, a gesture symbolizing he'd released his burden. He closed his eyes and bowed his head. "Father, You see us, You know us, and if there are those who are not saved, You know them too..."

The service was winding down. Now with everyone closing their eyes, Mohamed saw his chance. He pushed back against his seat, raising himself to see over the people's heads. He scanned the audience, stopping only when he saw a head of glossy black hair, but there were too many. It was pointless. He slid back down.

The preacher droned on: "I pray You would convict them of their sin and their need for a Savior, and indeed, make them restless until they find their rest in You. Help them to receive Your Son as Lord. In the mighty and powerful name of Jesus we pray. Amen."

Mohamed let out his breath and relaxed, thinking the service was over, but tensed when the minister started talking again. He looked at his watch. *Doesn't he ever stop?*

"I'm going to call our worship team back up, and if you feel you want to accept the ransom provided by Jesus, while they're playing, please just get out of your seat and come down front, and we'll pray with you and give you a Bible so you can learn more."

The band picked up their instruments and began to play. The crowd rose to its feet, the music loud but somehow solemn, as it flowed from the speakers. Mohamed glanced around, still hoping to spot Layla. People were pushing by him, flooding the aisle. Dozens, *no*, nearly a hundred were surrounding the stage, some standing, others dropping to their knees.

Mohamed stood his ground, narrowing his eyes, his teeth grinding. A God who redeemed man. Were it only so… But Jesus never died on the cross. Judas was the one Allah punished. Allah had them switch places. He was the final judge of everything. Each man had to account for his own sin.

Then and there, Mohamed redoubled his commitment to his mission. The lies had to stop.

He made one last attempt to find Layla and failed, then turned to make his way down the row, knowing everyone would think he was going forward. *Sorry to disappoint.* Instead, he turned the opposite way and fled out the door.

The sun slammed him in the face as he stepped outside, momentarily blinding him. He lifted his hand to shield his eyes. It had grown warmer, but he welcomed the heat. He was born for it. And if he wasn't going to see Layla, a little sweat didn't matter.

He climbed into his car and closed the door, feeling the perspiration trickling down his chest. His hands were slick. He slipped his key into the ignition. Why was he breathing so hard? He cranked the engine and sat back. *Ouch!* The leather was hot. He pulled himself forward, clinging to the wheel.

The preacher's words rang in his head. *Enough of that…* He clamped his lips together tightly. He would wait until the people came out. Maybe he could still catch a glimpse of her. But he would not go back inside that place—*not ever!*

CHAPTER 17

THE AIR WAS HOT and smelled of exhaust. Mohamed sat in the parking lot, studying the people as they pressed through the bumper-to-bumper line of cars that blocked his way. He'd stayed till the end of the service, and even until the beginning of the next service, but still no Layla.

He dialed up the air conditioner and eased into the fray, leaning forward to avoid sweating against the hot leather. The shirt he wore was a Hawaiian print of tan and green palm trees on a dark blue background. It was a casual but classy look he'd spent the previous evening shopping for, though by the time he checked into his motel, Wal-Mart was the only store he could find that was still open. Not exactly high-end fashion, but she wouldn't see the labels. His khaki pants were crisply pressed, and he wore boat shoes with no socks. He'd stood in front of the mirror admiring the ensemble, wondering what she'd think of him in a turban and *abaya*, while assuring himself he was *not* on the slippery slope of Western vanity. He just wanted to look nice—for *her*.

Once more he scanned the faces of the people driving toward the church, the last of those arriving, but still no Layla. He checked his rear-view mirror. If the blue car were there, it was buried somewhere in the line of traffic. It was too much to hope they'd given up and gone home.

His stomach tightened, feeling queasy. Some of what the preacher said made sense, but most of it was bunk.

The car in front of him stopped abruptly. He slammed on his brakes, raising his fist to pound the horn, but he refrained, his hand poised over the wheel. The fault was his. He needed to watch what he was doing. He relaxed, gripping the wheel with both hands.

He'd come to the church wanting to find common ground upon which he and Layla could build a foundation. All he'd found so far was shifting sand. A just God would not make one man bear the sin of the whole human race. Each man had to do his own righteous acts to earn the favor of God.

He shifted uneasily, belching to ease his discomfort. He hadn't had breakfast, not even a coffee. There was no reason for an upset stomach. Blame the preacher—enough deceit, lies, and subterfuge to make anyone edgy. Praise be to Allah, Islam would soon reign supreme even in the United States of America!

The car wasn't cooling fast enough. He pressed the button and rolled the window down to let in some air, but the fumes from the parking lot were worse than the heat, adding to his nausea. A brown blanket draped the mountains. The hills that formed the LA Basin were a giant wall, trapping the smog to keep it smoldering over the city.

Whew! Only a few cars from the exit, his foot hit the brake as traffic stopped. Sweat rolled down his cheek. A police officer was monitoring the flow of those exiting and those coming in, but the line of cars still crept forward one inch at a time.

The inside air was cooler now. He closed the window and brought his hand to rest on his stomach, then tightened his abdomen, releasing the pent-up gas as he exhaled. Leaving the parking lot, he turned right, heading up Wilshire Boulevard, the map laid out in his mind: *north on the 405 to the 5 and north to Palo Alto.* The sun behind the haze looked like a bauble of tarnished brass. *What a waste of time.*

The world was a crazy place—so many different people, so many different ways of approaching the same God. But only one way was right. If only they could see...but Satan had blinded their eyes. He gripped the wheel, pushing himself back hard against his seat.

There is no God but Allah, and Muhammad is his messenger. There is no God but Allah, and Muhammad is his messenger. There is no God but Allah, and Muhammad is his messenger. It bore repeating. There would be no peace on Earth until all men worshiped the one true God.

He checked his rearview mirror, his foot heavy on the gas in an effort to shorten the time it took to get home. *Oh, for the love of... unbelievable!* The sun's glare made it difficult to be sure, but the car was the same size and shape. It looked like he was being followed—*again.*

What's with these guys? Whatever Omar said, they weren't there for his protection. It was a matter of trust. But it didn't make sense. All of a sudden they were doubting him. *Why?* He hadn't done anything—he pushed off the wheel, bouncing back in the seat, air puffing from his nose as he exhaled a silent laugh—except maybe drive five hours to attend a Christian church and attempt to see a girl he'd been told to avoid. He wasn't surprised to see the car's blinker come on or that it followed him into the left lane.

The sign read Ventura Highway 101. He had an idea. He checked the traffic on his right. The move would require perfect timing. The Burbank Boulevard exit was just ahead. He waited until almost the last possible second. Then, without using his blinker, he squeezed one lane to the right. The driver behind him leaned on his horn, *hauuunnnnnnk*, but braked to let him in. Without waiting, he did it again, jamming himself between two more cars to land in the right lane, and then pulled off at the exit without a second to spare. Unable to get over in time, the blue car zoomed on by.

At the bottom of the ramp he checked his gas gauge and found he was down to a quarter of a tank. The sign of a Chevron station rose into the muggy sky a block down the road.

He pulled in, noting the price—his personal pet peeve. You could fly a plane in Egypt cheaper than what it cost to drive a car in the United States! He took consolation in knowing he didn't have to pay the bill. In spite of his other flaws, when it came to money, Sayyid was good to him. He eased his foot off the pedal and slowed to a stop in front of the pumps.

They would know he was headed for home. They'd probably pull to the side and wait for him to pass by again, but they'd be waiting a long time. He paid for his gas at the kiosk and started the car, pulling out of the station. He had a plan. He stopped at the curb and looked left. As he started to move into the street he felt a thump against the side of his car.

Swinging his head around, he noticed the shadowy form of something—or someone—falling, and he slammed on the brakes. He looked again but didn't see anything. His heart was thumping. Maybe it was his imagination. Maybe he should just drive on.

No, that wouldn't do. He put the car in park. They'd find him; the station had his credit card receipt. The last thing he needed was a visit from the police.

He got out and went around to the right front bumper. There on the asphalt lay a man, staring up at the sky. For a second Mohamed thought he was dead, but then he blinked. He knelt down beside the man. "Hey, I, ah...you all right?"

The elderly gentleman didn't respond. He appeared dazed, like he couldn't quite grasp what was going on. He blinked again and nodded. He tried lifting himself but groaned in pain.

Mohamed's eyes widened. He reached out to restrain him. "Hey, hey, stay there; don't move! We'll call an ambulance and get you to a hospital," and realized as he said it that the last thing he wanted was an ambulance with an attending policeman, asking a lot of questions and filling out reports.

The old man seemed undeterred and struggled to get up. Mohamed had no choice but to help him to his feet.

He cradled his elbow, wobbling in his tweed coat and sneakers. "It's my arm," he said in a guttural tone, like his throat was full of marbles. "Probably bruised, but I don't think it's broken. Be stiff in the morning, though." The man had a gray thatch of receding hair and blue eyes that seemed to reflect the sun's light. He grimaced as he swung his arm. "Yeah, I'm pretty sure it's not broken."

Mohamed's mind was churning. This was definitely not good. He needed to get home, but now he'd have to wait until they called the police, took each other's name, and notified his insurance company. "I, um, listen, if you need to see a doctor or want to be dropped at a hospital or something, just say so. I'll cover the bill. But I, uh, I don't really want to put this through my insurance unless I absolutely have to."

The man's eyes lit with understanding. "You'd rather we don't involve the police?"

Mohamed tensed. He took a step back, shaken by the man's intuition.

The old guy *seemed* OK. It was time to wish him well and take off running. "Well, I...I mean, I don't want to involve the insurance company. You know how it is; my rates are so high already. But they always require a police report, so, yes, I guess I'd rather not call them either. That is, as long as you're not hurt..."

The old man looked like he was feeling better by the second, though he kept testing his arm. He took a deep breath. "Nope, no bruising on the inside. I think I'm fine. It wasn't really your fault. I got distracted by the pigeons. I feed them, you see." He reached into his pocket and removed a plastic baggie, half full of yellow corn. "They follow me when I leave. I was watching *them* instead of where I was going."

Only a few feet away, a dozen pigeons were walking in circles and bobbing their heads. Several more, roosting on a curbside bench, were cooing softly. Mohamed hadn't noticed them before. "*Al hamdullah*," he muttered under his breath.

"Thanks be to God, indeed."

Mohamed shifted his glance to the shorter man, his eyes narrowing. "You speak Arabic?"

"I grew up in Israel. My father had a business that employed Palestinians. Their children were my friends. I had to learn the language just to be included." The man reached around and, with his good hand, rubbed the back of his head. "I seem to have lost my *yarmulke*. It must've come off when I fell." He turned, bending to look under the car. "There it is, behind the wheel. Think you could get it for me?"

Mohamed hesitated. Upsetting the man might lead to his filing a police report, but the idea of scrounging in the dirt to retrieve the infidel's hat...he succumbed to the lesser of the two evils. He stooped down to pull the skullcap from beneath the car, pinching it between two fingers like it was filled with lice. He handed it to the man and took a step back so he could wipe his hands on his pants.

"*Toda Raba. Shalom.* If you'll help me to a phone, I'll call a cab. I'm feeling a little too shaken to walk. But don't worry, my friend; no one needs to know of this."

"Someone's bound to see you're hurt."

"*Oy vey*, I'm an old man. Sometimes I fall. So what?"

Mohamed hesitated. He didn't want to touch the man again. He'd helped him get up, but that was before...then he wondered why it made any difference. The old man was nice...but so were cows, and no one worried about killing a cow when they had to eat. He took the man's arm, offended, but trying not to be. The pigeons circled around, bobbing their heads and cooing as Mohamed escorted the old man to a phone booth and parked him there, realizing for the first time that his own indigestion had abated.

"You sure you're all right?"

The old man reached out with his palm open. Mohamed gritted his teeth, but he shook the hand. Now they were bonded in friendship. *O you who believe! take not the Jews and the Christians for your friends and protectors: they are but friends and protectors to each other. And he amongst you that turns to them for friendship is of them.* That's what Surah 5:51 said. He found himself in the awkward position of being smitten by a Christian and befriended by a Jew. Today a church, tomorrow a synagogue. *Da-aeh-da!* What was happening to him? He pretended to scratch his back as he wiped his hand on his shirt.

"I came to America twenty-three years ago," the man said. "I came to get an education, to learn my father's trade and look for ways to improve it. But he died a year after I got here, and at his funeral, I decided it wasn't the kind of life I wanted for myself. I gave the business to the Palestinian families who worked for him and set out on a quest to find what was missing in my life, and ultimately I found it! So I'm still here and I'm still learning..." He smiled for the first time since the accident. "And why have *you* come? I think maybe God has you on a quest too."

Mohamed stared at the man, blinking. It was a statement, not a question. Either way, he was not prepared to deal with the issue. Not here. Not now. And definitely *not* with this infidel.

The man reached into his coat and withdrew a small red pamphlet. He held it for a moment, thinking, then handed it to Mohamed. "This changed my life," he said. "You asked if there was anything you could do for me. I do have one request. Read the little book, and wherever your journey takes you, go with God."

He turned, fishing in his pocket for a few coins, and reached for the phone.

CHAPTER 18

MOHAMED WAS FEELING PRETTY good about himself as he cruised up the freeway. The quiet hum of the Lexus and its smooth air-conditioned ride relaxed him. He took a deep breath, snuggling back into the rich leather upholstery. It was the first time he'd felt calm since pulling into the church and realizing by the sheer number of cars that he was on a fool's errand. The old man wasn't hurt. *Al hamdullah*, thanks be to God!

And he'd ditched the blue car. In all likelihood they were lurking somewhere north of his exit, waiting for him to pass by so they could tail him again. Not a chance. They'd see the Sahara freeze over first! To elude them, he'd gone in the opposite direction, back to the Ventura Highway, and crossed over. It was a nice day for a drive, and though it would take longer, he'd decided to take the coastal route. Anything was better than looking in his mirror and seeing *them* again.

He curled his hand. Scrubbing his palm with his fingers, he examined it for germs before wiping it on his pants. He wished he could stop just long enough to wash. He'd touched an unclean thing. But he'd already filled the car with gas, and he was beyond the point of being hungry. He didn't need any more delays, so it would have to wait.

It took him three hours to reach San Luis Obispo but only two seconds to make the decision. He veered left off 101 onto the Pacific Coast Highway. He'd made this drive before. Route 101 would get him home faster, but the water breaking on the rocks was a siren's call. The hills and forests of the coastlands were his beacon. The ocean off to his left rolled in a boundless synergy of water, earth, and sky.

At a scenic lookout, Mohamed pulled over and climbed out of the car, looking down the vertical face of rock as it spilled into the sea. Waves raging with whitecaps battered the seawall, trying to break it down, hammering it over and over again.

With the wind whipping his hair and the horizon seemingly infinite and blue, his mind slipped into thoughts about eternity. Would he ever know such rest? It seemed strange that he could leave the nauseous smog back in LA, lose the pressure of the persistent blue car, settle into the luxury of the Lexus's supple leather interior, and feel totally relaxed but not at peace. Peace was something different, and it eluded him.

He knew what it was. It was what they were planning to do. In spite of all his training, something deep inside told him it was wrong. He had tried to keep it buried, but it kept worming its way to the surface again, *and again, and again.* The tormentor's prongs. Ethics 101: the end does *not* justify the means. Not *that* many would die. A minimal loss of life would achieve a greater good, but the justification wasn't enough to assuage his nagging guilt. *The end does not justify the means.* What would Layla think?

He climbed into his car, shutting the door on the wind, and sat for a moment in silence, the only sound the *tink, tink, tinking* of the engine's cooling. He scooped his hair back with his fingers, reached for the key, and cranked the ignition. The Lexus fishtailed, spitting up gravel as he hit the gas and plunged back into traffic.

The horizon was a ribbon of blue, and the musky scent of redwoods filled the air. He rolled down his window, drinking it in. The trees to his right loomed skyward, pointing to dappled clouds laced with sun. He hadn't seen the blue car since leaving Van Nuys. He could only wonder at the tongue-lashing they'd receive from Omar.

By the time Mohamed pulled his car down the long dirt drive leading to the cabin, the sun was large and yellow on the horizon—right back where he'd started twenty-four hours ago. The thousand-year-old redwoods spread their branches overhead, shading him from the light. He rolled to a stop in the clearing, the sun pouring like butterscotch syrup on the ground. He clicked the seat belt free and flung it away, arching his back to smooth out the kinks, his arms braced behind his head and his fists closed tight. He let go, exhaling with a sigh. It was only a slight detour, just a few hours from home. He would continue the drive later.

He sat for a moment looking out through dusty glass that glared in the late afternoon sun. Jews hated Muslims, but he hadn't seen hatred in the old Jew's eyes. He looked again at the pamphlet beside him on the seat. "The Gospel According to John." He knew little about Christianity, but he knew enough to know that the word *gospel* was Christian. *A Jew who passed a Christian book to a Muslim?*

He needed to talk to Omar. The goal of Islam was to bring Christianity and Judaism under subjection to Allah. Having influence in the White House would certainly further that end, but he couldn't help wishing there were some other way. He'd heard it said: "Muslims love death the way Christians love life," implying that Muslims were strong and Christians were weak, but by what measure was death given such honor? The men who died would go straight to hell. Wouldn't it be better to keep them alive so they could learn and convert? There were mosques throughout North America, and their congregations grew steadily. If they waited long enough, they could end up conquering America through sheer numbers alone. *No!* He had to purge any thoughts of sympathy. A jihadist with a conscience was weak. He had to be strong!

Dust swirled around the cuff of his slacks as he opened the car door and planted his foot on soft ground composed of a redwood loam that had settled for over a thousand years. He reached down, swiping the leg of his pants, and climbed out. His push-button remote chirped as he popped the trunk lid and went to the back to remove his sports tote. The bag was made of red leather, an expensive indulgence that held three soccer balls and had pockets for his sweats, his shoes, and his competition jersey. A good workout was the best way to clear his mind.

He quickly changed clothes, then removed two of the balls and moved into a clearing. Once in the zone, there would be no room for distraction; he had to focus.

He tossed one into the air, then the other, and began a routine he'd developed as a child playing with socks full of Egyptian sand. He'd mastered the art of keeping one ball in the air, but anyone could do that. Circus clowns and other juggling acts aside, as far as he knew he was the only one who practiced with two balls.

He bounced one off his knee while the other was played off a heel. Keeping both balls in the air, each propelled by a different limb, took his full concentration. It was a great exercise. *Heel, head, knee, toe.* It took knowing where the ball would be before it arrived. When at his best, he was able to step into a zone where the only thing he saw was the rotation of the balls, like planets in space whirling around him in slow motion.

After about fifteen minutes, he let one of the balls drop to the ground and kicked it, aiming for a small crevice in the trunk of a nearby tree. The ball disappeared into the fissure, followed by the other ball. *Bang on! Score!* He was the best.

He sighed and took a breath. He had to convince Layla to join him. He walked over and got down on his hands and knees, scooping the balls out again, then got up, dusting redwood loam from his shorts. He drop-kicked a ball at another tree this time, aiming at a limb calculated to return the ball to his arms. *Bingo!* He had to find a way to convince her that her aim was wide of the goal. He tossed the balls aside and went back to the car to retrieve the old Jew's pamphlet.

He carried the little booklet out to the edge of a cliff overlooking the ocean and sat down to watch the red sun's descent into the brackish waters of the Pacific. He'd meditated on this rock before, a ledge at the edge of eternity, old as time itself. Sitting on something so timeless and immovable came with a profound sense of being close to God.

The only thing missing was someone to share it with. *Layla.* The idea of sitting here together, watching the sun bedding down for the night and seeing the stars click on, one by one, like tiny lights in the sky... but *no*, he shouldn't allow himself to indulge such thoughts. She'd once asked if they were meant to be married. It was a foolhardy idea, and even more hopeless now than it was then.

The only marriage on his horizon was that of Mike and Allie. The date was set and the invitations were out, giving the gossip rags grist for the paper mill. The presses had spun a fairy-tale wedding that seemed to increase in grandiose proportion with every new edition. The flurry of activity hadn't ceased. Senators and congressmen from both ends of the political spectrum had confirmed they would attend.

The sun was slipping into the sea. Soon he wouldn't have enough light to read. He opened the pamphlet, the pages looking rosy in the glow of the crimson sky. He began to read.

"In the beginning was the Word, and the Word was with God, and the Word was God.... And the Word became flesh and dwelt among us, and we beheld His glory, the glory as of the only begotten of the Father, full of grace and truth.... "

He put the pamphlet down, niggled by the audacity of the author. The man had the nerve to suggest that the Word, the one Islam recognized as the Messiah of Israel, was the Creator of everything. It was blasphemy— *but* perhaps he could use it to help Layla recognize the book's fallacy. *Only Allah creates.*

He watched the giant fireball of the sun disappear into the ocean, remaining until it became too dark to read. Groves of redwoods surrounded him, birds twittering in their boughs. God's creation, and it was marvelous. He'd had opportunity to visit Yosemite and stand amazed beneath the polished granite faces with their white waterfalls and mirrored lakes. He'd seen the red arched rocks of the painted deserts too, not to mention the golden plains of wheat—the breadbasket of the nation if not the world.

Again he wondered why Allah would create such beauty in this enclave of Christian heresy and plant the poor beleaguered people of Islam in such a barren land.

Egypt had its own beauty, to be sure, but nothing that compared with what he'd seen since coming to America. Even the cities were beautiful. Tall towers of glass and steel reaching to the sky, with homes sprawling into the suburban landscape for miles. Just about everyone owned a house with two or three cars in the driveway. People played with computers and cell phones like toys. The average person could reach into their pocket at any time and find enough change to buy a plethora of life's frivolities. Most of the animals ate better than the people in the town where he was born.

Allah had prospered this people, but their riches had made them weak, and that was their downfall, he reminded himself. Their lust for self-gratification had driven them into every kind of heinous activity—drugs, alcohol, adultery, homosexuality, pedophilia...there was no end to their disrespect for the laws of God. But that was about to change. *Inshallah! As God wills. There is no God but Allah, and Muhammad is his prophet.* To bring about the will of God—that's what he was bound by solemn oath to do.

Omar's school in the desert, Mohamed's fifteenth year

A semicircle of twelve teenaged students surrounded a bearded man dressed in a clerical robe. They had been reading from the Quran. The imam raised his hand and pointed at Mohamed. "Recite for me Surah 6:124."

Mohamed didn't hesitate. "When there comes to them a Sign from Allah, they say: 'We shall not believe until we receive one exactly like those received by Allah's Messengers.' Allah knows best where and how to carry out His mission. Soon will the wicked be overtaken by humiliation before Allah, and a severe punishment, for all their plots."

"Very good." The imam stood and the students followed, rising to their feet, but no one moved beyond that. The imam began to pace, his hands folded behind his back. "What do we know of God?"

"There is no God but Allah, and Muhammad is his prophet," the students chanted in unison.

"And who is the enemy that must be destroyed?"

"The enemy is Satan. All who serve Allah will join the jihad to destroy Satan."

"And what is our goal? What is our purpose?"

"Death to America, the great Satan, and to the lesser Satan, Israel! Death to America, the great Satan, and to the lesser Satan, Israel! Death to America, the great Satan, and to the lesser Satan, Israel!"

The imam spun around, looking each student in the eye, one at a time.

"You are the hope and future of Islam. Each of you has been chosen for a special purpose that Allah will reveal in his time. You will be leaders, some of you in finance, some in industry, others in education, but all of you will serve to the glory of Allah. And, if necessary, even unto death.

"You must be the best in body, mind, and spirit. Today we have exercised the mind and spirit. Now we must exercise the body. Mahir, as team captain I challenge you to use all of your mental, physical, and spiritual capacity to defeat the yellow team. Ahmed, I challenge you as team captain to use all of your mental, spiritual, and physical ability to defeat the blue team. May the will of Allah be done. There is no God but Allah, and Muhammad is his prophet."

The imam puckered his mouth and raised his bearded chin, staring at Mohamed. "Stay for a minute, Mohamed. The rest of you are dismissed."

One after another the students moved to the door, barely reaching the threshold before taking off running. Mohamed shuffled his feet, antsy to be playing soccer.

The imam placed a hand on Mohamed's shoulder, curbing his impatience. He was both a cleric and an educator, having once been a professor at Al-Azhar but now commissioned to handle a special project—the nurturing of twelve future leaders. His charge was to train a specific group of elite students in the ways of Western society so they could be inserted into European and American communities and bring about change from within.

He dropped his hand but kept his attention focused on Mohamed. "How are you coming with your English?"

"*Koyaes.*"

"In English, please."

"Yes, sorry…good, I think."

The imam paced with his hands behind his back. "I want you to speak English from now on, even when you're playing. Your friends have learned enough to understand you."

"*Mesh fahem!* I mean, I don't understand."

"You must make English your mother tongue. You must be able to speak it so fluently no one would mistake you for an Egyptian."

"But I am Egyptian."

"Yes, and of that you can be proud. For many years the brotherhood of nations has despised Egypt because our foolish government refuses to enforce Sharia law. They see us as weak and unworthy of Dar Al-Islam. But when America falls at the hand of Egypt, they will know we also serve the one true God. I trust you will be instrumental in bringing this about. To achieve such a goal, however, requires that you speak English without an accent." The cleric stepped back and regarded Mohamed solemnly. "To ensure your success, I have hired a tutor for you, an American, who will teach you to not only speak but to think in English, and also enlighten you concerning Western nuances and clichés. From now on, you are to speak English only. I will explain this to the others. They in turn will speak only English to you."

"What you ask is hard, but I will try."

"You will do more than try. You will succeed."

CHAPTER 19

MOHAMED MOVED THROUGH THE purple twilight, careful not to stumble on a rock or trip over a fallen branch as he made his way to the car. He used his remote to pop the trunk lid, the light spilling onto the ground and helping him to see. He reached in, taking his soccer bag by the handle, and brought it out, planting it at his feet. The sweat he'd worked up during his exercise was already dry, but the material still clung to his skin as he pulled his jersey over his head. He took a towel and wiped himself off. His Hawaiian shirt and khakis lay neatly folded on the carpeted floor. Working quickly, he slipped them on.

Picking up his leather sports bag, he tossed it back into the trunk, slamming the lid, but it popped up, nearly clipping his chin. He slammed it again. It didn't latch. He stooped down, peering under the lid. The handle of his sports bag was caught on the locking mechanism. *Grrrrr! Stupid!* He yanked the bag from the car and examined the once smooth handle, rubbing it with his thumb. The dye was scraped and the leather torn, a brand-new, three-hundred-dollar extravagance ruined! Tossing the bag back into the trunk, he banged the lid down, pounding on it with his fist, daring it to open again.

He huffed around to the driver's side of the car and slid in behind the wheel, yanking the door shut as he fired up the engine and threw the car into reverse. Jamming his foot down on the pedal and cranking the wheel to the left, he spun the car around, raising a cloud of dirt before coming to a stop in the opposite direction. The trees, ferns, rocks, and portion of road contained within the tunnel of his headlights were all he could see. He revved the engine again, then stomped on the gas and, with wheels spinning, raced full bore down the dirt driveway, his shock absorbers taking a pounding from the washboard in the road.

The angst compressed inside him felt like a spring about to explode. It wasn't the flaw in his sports bag—*stupid bag*—it was the book. The pamphlet was mixed with just enough truth to sound plausible. The problem was Layla believed it, and he didn't have time to convince her otherwise.

He drove the winding miles of coastal redwoods as though hoping to fly over a cliff. That would, at least, put an end to the annoying questions in his head. The trees zoomed by in a blur until he stomped on the brakes at the intersection to the main road and sat tapping the steering wheel with his thumbs, waiting for the stream of headlights to pass before hopping onto the Pacific Coast Highway. The sun had fallen off the edge of the earth, dragging his picturesque view into the shadows. The tall trees were dark silhouettes against an azure sky and the ocean a ribbon of purple, visible only where a faint stream of light still burnished the horizon.

Mohamed beat his fist against the wheel. *Ahhhh, stupid!* He'd forgotten his soccer balls. At dusk he'd left his sanctuary on the rock, but determined to finish the book and be done with it, he'd relocated to the cabin, collecting the balls on the way just so he *wouldn't* forget and leave them there. *Stupid, stupid, stupid!* That's what he got for his heterodoxy. If ever the devil wrote something to tempt men from the truth, this was it!

He glanced at the document tossed carelessly on the passenger seat, its curled red cover looking purple in the dim light. He'd thought to trash it but couldn't. Others had access to the cabin. Questions would be raised if they found Christian literature in their Muslim retreat. So there it was, sitting right beside him. He would examine it further, just to make sure he hadn't misunderstood.

He'd been disappointed not to find the glaring examples of error he was looking for. There was nothing to convince Layla her beliefs were foolish, nothing black or white he could point to and say, "See, that proves the whole thing's false." Instead, every word was a shade of gray, believable if you stood on one side of the fence, implausible if you stood on the other. The book presented the story one way, Islamic tradition another.

Moonlight flooded the inside of the car. Mohamed glanced over at the little book. The pamphlet claimed Isa came to give men life. *Why are Muslim mothers so willing to sacrifice their sons to God?* Christians had it the other way around. Christians said God sacrificed His Son for man. So far, he hadn't been able to find where Isa instructed His followers to kill themselves, or anyone else, to further His teachings. The Isa of America only showered His people with blessing.

Mohamed clenched his jaw, his hands twisting the steering wheel. *What is truth?* The question of the Roman procurator. He reached up, rubbing his ear as he inclined his head. The moon was on the rise. He observed its soft glow through the windshield—a sign from Allah! Mohamed took a deep breath and exhaled, trying to relax. *What is truth? Allah, grant me the ability to show Layla before it's too late.*

Behold! The Lamb of God who takes away the sins of the world! What? No, no, no, no, no! Salvation comes by prayer, fasting, and almsgiving— there is no God but Allah, and Muhammad is his prophet. There is no God but Allah, and Muhammad is his prophet. There is no God but Allah, and Muhammad is his prophet. His eyes rolled up, staring once again at the dusty moon...

Whispers of the Nile, twelve years earlier

Mohamed stared out across the dark surface of the water, the moon's white reflection rolling on the ripples that lapped against the shore. Layla took his hand, pulling him with her.

He resisted, holding his place. He didn't like the river, especially at night, with insects buzzing and amphibious creatures waiting to swallow him whole.

"Come on." Layla turned and scooped a handful of water, splashing it at him. He lurched forward, trying to grab her arm, but she squealed, pulling back, and ran in deeper. "*Hee, hee, hee,* can't catch me."

Mohamed stood knee-deep, unwilling to move. He couldn't swim, even if he were made of cork. "Come back here."

She stopped, spinning around to face him. "*Ooohhh,* the mud's so soft. Try squishing it between your toes. It tickles! Try it!"

Mohamed twisted his feet back and forth until they were buried in pasty soil. What was so good about that?

"Let's play hide-and-seek." Layla took off toward the marsh, her fingers leaving trails in the waist-deep water, her body breaking the current.

"We can't play hide-and-seek. There's nowhere to hide."

Layla flattened her hands, putting her palms together like she was preparing to dive. "What if I go underwater? Would you be able to find me there?"

"Don't! You're going to get wet."

Layla turned and sloshed farther down the beach, staying within the flow.

"Where are you going now?" Mohamed followed, but he remained in the shallows where the water only came up to his knees.

"To hide from you." Layla entered the marsh, pushing the reeds aside until she disappeared into the tall tubular growth.

"Come back, Layla. Don't go in there. Come on!"

"Come on yourself. You have to find me."

Mohamed didn't move. He stared at the growth into which Layla had disappeared, hoping to see a flicker of her blouse, trying to follow the sound of her voice, but she was gone. He moved to the edge of the reeds but didn't enter.

"See if you can find me," she teased.

"I can't."

"Why not?"

"Snakes like to hide in there."

"I'm not afraid of snakes. Come...find me."

Mohamed took a tentative step forward, and then another. He stepped on a small creature and jerked his foot back, but it was only a stone. He looked behind him. He was surrounded by tall swamp grass. The shoreline had disappeared from view.

"I'm over here."

He turned to follow Layla's voice, along with the splashing of water and the rustling of the reeds. Layla was on the move.

"*Hee, hee, hee,* can't find me."

Mohamed turned at the sound, now coming from behind him. The moon's light was bright enough to see detail even in the dark shadows of the marsh, but Layla remained invisible.

"Come on, Layla. I don't like this game. Let's go. My father will be looking for me." He waited for an answer, but…nothing. Water sloshed around his legs. All along the shore, frogs were calling. He turned, scanning the tall grass for signs of movement. "Layla?"

"Gotcha!" Layla jumped up behind him, causing him to jerk back and catch his foot on a clod of mud. He spilled into the wash, sinking beneath the water, his arms thrashing.

Layla grabbed his hand and pulled him to his feet. He stood, dripping wet, scraping the water from his arms. She was giggling.

"Not funny, Layla."

She covered her mouth with her hand. "Sorry. I didn't mean to scare you."

"I—I wasn't scared."

"Here, let me help you." Layla tugged her shirt over her head, leaving only her camisole, then used the shirt as a towel to dry his arms and mop his head. He took her hand, her body against his, their eyes locked on each other, their hearts beating as one—and for a moment it seemed as though time stood still.

"Mohaaamed! Mohaaaaamed!"

Layla pushed him away, her eyes wide, reflecting the moon's light.

"*Shhh!* It's my father." Mohamed crouched, ducking behind the reeds. "I told you he'd come looking for me. Put your shirt on and keep quiet. We can't be seen together."

"Mohamed!"

"I'm here, Father."

"Who is with you? I hear voices."

Mohamed raised a finger to his lips. "No one. I'm alone." He stooped over and whispered in Layla's ear. "Stay here until we're gone."

Layla nodded and sank slowly into the water, out of sight.

Mohamed turned and began sloshing through the river to the shore. He stepped onto the muddy beach. His father was standing there in his long dark *abaya*. Silhouetted by the moon, his turban looked like a mushroom sprouting from his head.

"What were you doing?" he asked.

"Bathing. I did not want others to see me, so I hid in the reeds." Mohamed wrapped his arms over his chest and shivered.

"It would be helpful if, the next time you want to bathe, you removed your clothing first." His father took him by the shoulder and turned him toward home. "You should not be out so late by yourself," he said, but Mohamed wasn't listening. He was looking over his shoulder, trying to catch a final glimpse of Layla.

Mohamed leaned back with his hand drumming the steering wheel and looked through the dusty glass at a dirty moon. That moment, stamped indelibly on his memory, had been one of the happiest of his life. At the time, he would not have thought it possible, but a mere six months later his father would be dead, Layla gone, and his life changed forever. *Why, Father? Why?*

CHAPTER 20

THE COASTLINE FADED FROM VIEW, absorbed into the darkness that comes when the world turns away from the sun. Mohamed cut over at Pebble Beach, hopping on 156 to intercept 101, the silhouettes of the rugged cliffs and tall trees giving way to a barrage of electronic lights. He was just outside San Jose, the new mainstay of commercial America. Row upon row of advertisements were stacked on top of each other like a deck of neon playing cards—Taco Bell, Shell, McDonald's—all soliciting his money. He pulled off the highway to get gas and a quick bite to eat.

The burger stand was near another twenty-four-hour Wal-Mart. He pushed the last bite of sesame seed bun into a mouth with bulging cheeks and wiped his hands on a paper napkin so he could start the car. A little all-purpose glue, maybe a little red dye, and he'd have his soccer bag looking good as new.

The lights were garishly bright, the aisles deserted on a Sunday night. He wound his way through the displays of merchandise. So many gadgets. A veritable wonderland of technological toys. If he hadn't memorized the Quran, he might be seduced by it all, but he knew the truth: "The Unbelievers spend their wealth to hinder men from the path of Allah, and so will they continue to spend; but in the end they will have only regrets and sighs; at length they will be overcome: and the Unbelievers will be gathered together to Hell." Surah 8, verse 36.

Mohamed made his way to the hardware department, amazed the store would be open on a Sunday night. No one thought of shopping like this in

Egypt. Where did people get the money? He walked past row after row of blankets, window coverings, throw rugs and carpets, coffeepots, blenders and juice makers, dishware and flatware, pots and pans, gardening tools, patio sets, and more. There were enough dresses, pants, shirts, and shoes to clothe an entire village. The most extreme form of excess.

He shook his head, tilting it to the right, trying not to let it bother him. The United States had so much, his village so little. Given the choice, he would choose America, but that was just temptation—*wasn't it?* Perhaps under Sharia law, they could avoid the pitfalls that made America the den of iniquity it had become, while still maintaining its prosperity. *No, that was compromise.*

In the hardware section, he scanned the aisle for glue, but stumbled across something even better—duct tape in every conceivable color. He picked up a roll and tried to imagine the shade. It looked like a perfect match. If he cut it just right, he could fit a piece in between the seams, covering the gash so no one could tell the difference. *Duct tape in red.* Anything anyone could possibly want under one roof.

On his way to the checkout counter, he stumbled upon another section of merchandise—*books.* He slipped down the aisle scanning the titles and, *yes*, there it was, just as he'd thought. *Holy Bible.* Another thing you wouldn't find in an Egyptian store. He thumbed through the first few pages to the Table of Contents, just to make sure the book contained the section called "John," the one he'd already read. Upon verifying that it was there, he picked up the Bible and held it to his chest with the same hand that held the tape. If he placed it facedown on the counter, no one would know what it was.

He walked to the checkout stand and waited in line, chiding himself for buying a Bible, though he had justification. Layla's so-called boyfriend—he didn't believe for a minute the man was her fiancé—had accepted the challenge. *Fiancé, or fool?* It was laughable. He'd seen the look on the man's face when Layla announced that they were engaged. If they were getting married, someone had forgotten to tell the prospective groom.

The clerk at the counter took his money, eyeing him with a curiosity that suggested he was either lost or confused. *Mind your own business, lady. What do I look like, a terrorist?* He smiled to himself and walked out with the bag under his arm. He would read the New Testament, whatever that was, and keep his end of the bargain, but only because Matthew—*Matthew?*

Mohamed pulled the box from the bag and removed the lid as he walked. Opening the Bible, he thumbed to the Table of Contents again. There! He was right. One of the sections was called "Matthew." No wonder the man was so twisted—well, *Matthew* had agreed to read the Quran—and the truth would prevail. But then, he was Mohamed, and he was reading the Bible. *Go figure.*

Convincing Layla of Islam's supremacy would be difficult, but he was determined not to lose her again, even if it meant reading the whole Bible. And if that didn't work, maybe he'd have to force her against her will—as Sayyid had his mother—for her own good.

Mohamed's thirteenth birthday, estate of Sayyid El Taher

He finished eating the slice of *basboussa* and licked the syrupy cake from his fingers, nodding to show his appreciation. It was his birthday, and the servants had gathered to give him gifts, but once again his heart was heavy with his mother's absence, and no amount of sweet cakes or brightly wrapped presents were sufficient to make him smile. She was away on one of her trips, traveling the world, or so he was told. He wanted her to be happy, but he could not imagine her in London, Paris, Cologne, or anywhere else without him. She hadn't even said good-bye before she left, nor had he received a call or a letter, not even a postcard. He was determined, on this day, to find out why.

He approached his uncle's private office with caution. Sayyid had blessed him with the hospitality of his home. Mohamed was considered a son. He should be grateful and unquestioning, but he needed to know. He pushed the door back slowly but it squeaked, alerting his uncle to the intrusion. The desk was huge, but the man's body concealed most of it. Only the drawers on either side could be seen. Mohamed thought Sayyid looked bigger each time he came home for a visit.

His uncle looked up and turned away from his writing, twisting his head around to acknowledge his nephew. "Yes, Mohamed, what is it?"

Mohamed tried to speak, but words failed him. The only conversation his uncle abided had to be conducted in the most concise way possible. Babbling, storytelling, and gossip were to be shunned.

"Yes? Speak up, boy. A question unspoken cannot be answered."

"Yes, sir. It's about my mother, sir. It...it's my birthday, and..."

His uncle frowned, the folds of his chin almost swallowing his mouth, but he nodded. "How old are you?"

"I turn thirteen today."

His uncle continued nodding, his jowls waddling. "Thirteen is the year the boy becomes a man. I guess you're old enough to know." He paused, but for only a moment. "You will not see your mother again."

Mohamed suppressed a gasp. "Isn't she ever coming home? Has she left us for good, then?"

"Your mother..." Sayyid squirmed in his seat, his excessive weight causing the chair to squeak. "Your mother is dead."

"Dead? But I—"

Sayyid raised a pudgy hand, silencing Mohamed's rebuttal. "Yes, I know. I wanted to protect you, but as you pointed out, you are now a man, capable of bearing the truth. Now, is that all? If you'll excuse me, I have work to do."

Sayyid swiveled in his chair, turning back to his writing again, and Mohamed, seeing he had been dismissed, shuffled out the door.

CHAPTER 21

L AYLA PULLED INTO A visitor parking space in front of the condo-minium, her headlights sweeping the grass. She opened the door a crack, activating the interior light, and checked the address on the building again. *This is the place. Sweet.* She folded the slip of paper and shoved it back into her purse, feeling goose bumps rise on her arms in a rush of nervous anticipation. Easing herself from the car, she stood for a moment, wondering how she'd get in. All she could do was try. *Lord, give me strength.* She closed the door, took a breath, and began walking.

The front of the building was designed to look old. An arched doorway, laid with two different colors of brick, the keystone and quoin a lighter shade, lent character to an otherwise flat façade. Lampposts with brass coach lamps bordered the curved walkway, illuminating her steps.

The evening was warm and smelled of night-blooming jasmine as she moved along the path, but still she rubbed her arms, feeling a slight chill. The lawn to the side of the walk spread out like a park, but owing to the darkness, she could see only far enough to know it was well manicured and filled with shrubs and trees.

Light streamed from the vestibule, painting the glass bright yellow. She paused to look at her reflection. She'd worn her olive suit because she'd been told it made her eyes sparkle with flecks of green. Her hair fell long and wavy, the way Matthew liked it best. She pulled it around front and scrunched it just to give it an extra bit of curl. She didn't consider herself beautiful, but she wanted Mohamed to see her at her best—though she really shouldn't care. Her heart belonged to Matthew. Didn't it?

She reached for the handle and pulled. The door opened without resistance. *Past the first hurdle*, she thought as she stepped inside.

A concierge desk was stationed along the far wall but was unmanned. She stood for a moment, taking in her surroundings. The walls were shades of rose and peach, with framed paintings tastefully filling the empty spaces—like the one behind the ebony grand piano. Two cushy leather chairs and a sofa flanked an ornate coffee table, graced with several oversized picture books. The furnishings were grouped in front of a marble fireplace. Elevators on the far wall, plated in brass, required a card reader. Access was for residents only. *Pretty upscale for a student*, she thought, and for the first time since seeing his Lexus parked in front of Las Brisas, Layla found herself wondering where Mohamed got his money.

She looked around, hoping to find someone to assist her, but the lobby was vacant. A tall lectern with an open book stood beside a table with a fern, a wall-mounted phone above. She walked over to the table and began turning pages. The book contained a guest register and in the front, under plastic sleeves, a list of residents along with their apartment numbers. She ran her finger down the list of names—*Taber, Taggart*, there it is, *Taher, M., Apt. 314.*

Glancing at her watch, she saw it was already 9:42. She'd planned to arrive by six, hopefully to join him for dinner, but was delayed when Matthew insisted on taking her to lunch after the morning worship service. She couldn't beg off without his becoming suspicious and asking a lot of questions. And she didn't want him talking her out of it or persuading her to let him tag along. Not this time. This was something she had to do on her own. It was now or never. Her heart began to race.

She picked up the phone and punched in 314. What if he wasn't home? She should have called ahead to let him know she was coming, but if they'd talked, she would have been tempted to tell him the news over the phone and...

"Hello?"

A woman's voice? "Hello, ah, who's this?"

"Who are *you*?"

"Sorry, I must have the wrong apartment. I thought this was the residence of Mohamed El Taher."

"It is. He's not here. Can I help you?"

"That...that's all right, thank you." Layla placed the phone back in its cradle and brought her hand over her heart, trying to catch her breath. Six hours of nonstop driving for *this*? She swallowed the lump in her throat. So Mohamed had a girlfriend, so what? She had Matthew. Mohamed's private life was none of her business. She just wanted him to know he had a brother. She blinked back the burning in her eyes, picked up her purse, and headed for the door.

Mohamed was back on the freeway, sailing past condos and apartments on the left and more stores on his right, looking for the exit that led to the home of Omar Muhsin. It was late, but Omar would be up. He doubted the man ever slept. There were always visitors at his house, usually students learning about Islam, but not more than two or three at a time. Omar discouraged large gatherings in order to be discreet. The proselytes would sit in the living room discussing the Quran, or kneel on prayer rugs practicing submission, or read books on theology taken from the library.

He pulled into the drive, climbed out, and headed for the door. He didn't bother to knock; he was entering a mosque where all were welcome. He scanned the room. A few shoeless people were kneeling, their foreheads touching the rug, all of them wearing Western dress, which wasn't unusual. Several dough-white faces betrayed their Christian heritage. He doubted the recent converts knew enough Arabic to recite from the Quran.

But he had to give them credit; they were more faithful than he. His studies, the university's soccer program, and the time he was forced to spend with the vice president's betrothed—all interfered with his keeping a regular routine of prayer. He could only hope Allah would understand and be forgiving. As a student, he'd been in submission five times a day, crawling out of bed to pray before sunrise, and again at noon, then around three thirty, once more after sunset, and finally, at nine thirty in the evening. It was required, and lest anyone forget, imams sang the call to prayer from loudspeakers mounted on tall minarets.

An interloper—another pasty white American—came through the door, paused to remove his shoes, and brushed by Mohamed with a prayer rug rolled under his arm. *Good man.* The supplicant was forbidden to touch the ground while praying; it was unclean. The rug provided separation, keeping him undefiled.

Mohamed listened to see if the new recruit knew what he was doing. The young man stood and recited *"Allah Akbar"* along with two short surahs from the Quran spoken in Arabic. *Not bad.* He knelt with his hands on his knees and praised the greatness of Allah, and then did it again. Rising to his feet he stood for a moment and then went down on his knees once more, his hands and forehead touching the floor. The entire procedure was repeated twice before the supplicant withdrew. Omar had taught him well.

Mohamed felt a burn of nostalgia in his chest, but things were different in the United States. Imams weren't free to pace around minarets calling the faithful to submission, so exceptions were made. The busy American workday wasn't conducive to formal prayer.

He turned, looking over his shoulder, and then spun around to head down the hall. Omar wasn't lecturing in the mosque where he'd hoped to find him. Instead, after scoping out a few other rooms, he found Professor Muhsin in the kitchen, pouring a cup of tea and conversing with a student. He was dressed in his role as a host, in contemporary street clothes, though his hollow cheeks and shadowy eyes made him look more like a famine survivor than a bearded academic.

"You grace us at this late hour?" Omar asked, breaking off his conversation to address Mohamed.

"Got a minute?"

Omar shrugged and, waving off wisps of steam, took a sip of his tea. He placed the cup on the saucer and set it on the counter, then excused himself and led Mohamed to his private study, closing the door behind them. It was a place other guests rarely saw. Omar motioned Mohamed to a chair and took a seat behind his desk, folding his hands like a steeple in front of his mouth. "So, why are you here?"

Mohamed nodded, knowing his question might be misunderstood, but forged ahead because he had to ask. "You know me. You practically raised me as a child, and you continue to mentor me even now. Please don't misconstrue what I'm about to say." He paused, waiting for Omar to acknowledge him. The imam dipped his head forward and blinked approvingly.

"I've been thinking about something, not questioning, just thinking, but I was wondering what we hope to gain by attacking America's political system. Maybe it would be enough to just defeat Christendom. Isn't there another way to establish the supremacy of Islam without killing a bunch of innocent people?"

Omar's lips thinned, losing their color. He raised his jaw slightly and placed his hands on the table. Then leaning to the side, he slid open a drawer and pulled out an envelope from which he removed several sheets of paper.

Mohamed shuffled his feet as Omar slid the e-mails across the desk.

"I warned you about the danger of making new friends. They're causing you to question what you have learned. The devil is crafty. He likes to seduce us by making us feel sorry for those he loves."

Mohamed didn't acknowledge the documents. He'd seen them before. "You've got it all wrong. I'm not feeling sorry for anyone. It's just that centuries have passed, and Christians still win people to their cause without bloodshed. Why can't we do the same? Why do we have to force people into submission?"

Omar began stroking his beard. "Mohamed, have you lived here these many years and not seen for yourself all the abominations these so-called *innocent* people engage in? Is nothing sacred to you? The president of this country is a fornicator and a drunk, a Jew-lover who will pour money into Israel so they can torture more of our people. Do you really think he's *innocent*? We are predestined to bring reformation to America. This is where God's justice is needed most. Need I quote the Prophet?

"'Therefore, when you meet the Unbelievers in fight, smite at their necks; at length, when you have thoroughly subdued them, bind a bond firmly on them: thereafter is the time for either generosity or ransom: until the war lays down its burdens.'

"The words of the Messenger, may he be forever blessed. Do you dare question Allah?"

"No, of course not. It's just that Allah's will cannot be altered. Our families are five times larger than Christian families. We could outgrow them by procreation alone. But more than that, new converts are coming to Islam every day. Look how many come to your house just to be taught. Given another hundred years, there will only be one religion. Why must we force it now?"

Omar collected the papers with the accusing photographs and slid them back into the envelope, returning them to his drawer. He leaned back in his chair. "You stay away from these people. I'm not asking. That's an order."

Mohamed kept his face flat, void of expression. He leaned forward, placing his elbows on his knees, clasping his hands in front of him. "First of all, I don't take orders from you. We are in this together. I'm glad to be part of it, but what I do, I do of my own free will. As for these so-called friends, you can do whatever you want with the man, but the girl is mine. I claim her for Allah. I intend to make her my wife."

The imam shook his head. "Ah, so the child grows to be a man. Good! This shows strength. But I question your choice. She is a Christian."

"Islam permits me to marry a follower of the Book."

"And if she refuses?"

"She won't. We're destined to be married, one way or another. Perhaps it's as you say, the will of Allah must be done."

Mohamed sat back, considering the words he'd just spoken. Were he and Layla *destined* to be married? If so, Allah needed to change her heart.

CHAPTER 22

MOHAMED PULLED HIMSELF FROM his silver Lexus and stretched, pressing his hand into his lumbar to ease the ache in his back. Underground parking, with its cement walls that echoed his footsteps and artificial light from somewhere above, always reminded him of the tombs of Egyptian pharaohs, the shiny cars stored for their amusement in the afterlife. It even smelled dank. He leaned in to retrieve the Bible and the pamphlet but removed the duct tape from the bag and tossed it back on the seat. He'd deal with fixing his sports tote later.

His leather shoes clapped against the cement as he trudged through the lot toward the elevator, glad to finally be home. All he needed was a hot shower, and he'd fall into bed and be asleep before his head hit the pillow. He slipped his access card into the slot and poked the button. No response. He poked it again and again—*come on, come on*—and stood back when he heard the *ding*, waiting for the doors to open.

The door slid closed as he leaned against the wall, the bag with the Bible held against his chest, feeling the tension of the day jittering under his skin. That would be the last time he'd run a fool's errand. He yawned. It had been a long drive, and all he had to show for it was wear and tear on his car, a sore back, and more questions than answers. He shook his head.

The car stopped at floor three, sounding another *ding* as the doors opened. Mohamed pushed off the wall and exited left, dragging his angular frame down the hall. He fished in his pocket for his key and slid it into the lock.

"Oh! You're finally home!" Allie set aside the book she'd been reading and rose from the couch, the tips of her dark hair burnished yellow in the light of the lamp.

Mohamed straightened himself, feigning composure, though the shock of finding someone in his apartment had his heart pounding hard enough to drive nails. "What are you doing here? Who let you in?" He swung around to drop his keys on the letter table by the door.

"Sorry to surprise you, but I needed to talk to someone, and the more I thought about it, the more I knew it had to be you. I hope you're not mad."

"No, of course not, but how did you get in?"

She looked down, her toe sweeping the carpet. "Well," she said, "as the fiancée of the vice president of the United States, I'm not without some influence. The man downstairs recognized me. I told him I was supposed to meet with you—about the wedding and all that—but I rang your apartment and you weren't at home, so I just assumed you were running late. I offered to wait in the lobby, but he insisted on letting me in."

Her mouth held a smile, but her eyes revealed pain. Mohamed started to set his package down, but changed his mind. He went to the kitchen, opened a cupboard, and placed the plastic bag on the top shelf behind the boxes of cereal and crackers. He returned to the living room holding a glass of water. "So, to what do I owe the pleasure? What brings you here?"

"I don't know. I probably shouldn't be. I was about to give up, but I kept thinking you would be home any minute. I guess the minutes turned into hours." She feigned a laugh. "But at least you're here now."

Mohamed turned and walked to the coffee table, setting his glass down. "Where's Mike?" he said, eyeing her curiously. She was wearing tight slacks that rode low enough on her hips to expose her belly button and a low-cut cotton shirt that revealed the roundness of her bosom. Far from traditional Muslim attire. Her hair was parted on the side and bobbed around the neck with long bangs that swept across her forehead, accentuating her sultry Arabian eyes. Her lips were full and red.

But the comeliness of her face seemed to fade as she considered his question. Her expression grew distant and glazed. She looked away. "I don't know how to bring this up, because when I say it out loud, it sounds crazy."

"What?"

Her gaze met his again. Her eyes were dark and full of questions. "All right, but understand that this is hard for me. Please don't think I'm paranoid. I'm not. The thing is, my parents are acting weird." She turned and sat on the couch, pulling a pillow into her lap. "When Mike first asked for my hand in marriage, you should have seen my father's eyes light up. There was no doubt that he approved, which was unusual to say the least. We may not observe strict Sharia law, but we are Muslims, and for a woman to marry outside the faith is strictly forbidden."

She tossed the pillow aside and rose, pacing before him. "That's what was so neat. My father chose my happiness over tradition. He appeared to be overjoyed. My mother even started making wedding plans, asking Mike if we'd set a date, where the wedding would be held, how many would attend. I was embarrassed, but he took it well. We agreed not to say anything outside the immediate family until we could arrange the engagement party and make our intentions public." Allie settled back onto the couch, her face wrinkling as tears welled in her eyes. She reached for her purse and found a tissue.

Mohamed sat down beside her, placing his arm around her shoulder and pulling her head onto his shoulder as she began to cry. "Hey, there, what's wrong? What happened? Did you and Mike have a fight?"

He could feel her body quivering against his chest. She let out a muffled, "No, it's not that," and brought her head up, tears running down her cheeks. She sniffed, wiped her nose with her tissue, and took a calming breath.

She leaned forward with her elbows on her knees. "It's my parents...we had a huge fight. They've been acting so strange lately. I...I finally couldn't take it anymore. I just had to know what was going on. At first they denied anything was wrong, but I could see they were upset about something, so I kept pushing. Finally my father exploded and said this marriage was wrong, that I should be marrying a Muslim. He said he was calling off the wedding!"

Mohamed leaned back, guilt rising over the part he'd played in ruining her life, but perhaps this time it was for the best. Allie's parents were reacting to the pressure put on them by Omar. The plan had always been to use the Muslim Brotherhood as a threat. Omar had met with Allie's parents and explained how, in order to ensure the safety of their families still living in Egypt, they were expected to see that their daughter influenced the vice president on certain issues, particularly regarding policies that favored Arab nations over Israel. While he would have assured them what he asked was for the benefit of not only Muslims in America but also believers worldwide, the veiled threat that harm might come to their loved ones should they refuse to cooperate was bound to have shaken them. But if Allie could be persuaded to call off the wedding, it would ruin Omar's plans.

"I don't know, maybe they're right," he ventured. "Living with someone who doesn't understand our ways would be hard on a marriage."

Allie jumped up and spun around, her fists clenched and her eyes blazing. "No! Don't you say that! Don't you dare! I love him. I told my parents I intended to marry him whether they tried to call it off or not. I thought...I thought you would understand." She softened her voice. "I thought you were my friend." She brought the tissue to her face and began sobbing again.

Mohamed stood, taking her in his arms. She was shuddering, her warm breath on his neck coming in gulps.

"Oh, Mohamed, it's so hard. I love my parents, but I won't let them ruin the best thing that's ever happened to me. I can't. I just can't, you understand?" She lifted her head and looked into his eyes.

He nodded. "Yes, I understand."

She sighed, laying her head on his shoulder. "I guess that's why I'm here. I just wanted someone to talk to, and I thought of you. I know it's just about the wedding and stuff, but you always listen." She gave his waist an affectionate squeeze, then let go and reached for her purse to retrieve another tissue.

She began dabbing her eyes as she turned to face him. "Oh, I forgot to tell you. While you were out, a young lady dropped by. I didn't catch her name, but she seemed surprised to find me here. I hope I haven't put you in an awkward position, but if you must explain, please don't mention my name. I had to sneak out to avoid being followed by the Secret Service, and now I'll have to..."

But Mohamed was no longer listening. *A young lady...Layla? No.* She was four hundred miles away, *but*...had they really crossed paths in the night? Mohamed's heart was thudding in his chest. He'd have to come up with a way to explain, but that was a problem for another day. Right now he had to find a way of convincing Allie to call off the wedding without sending her into hysterics.

CHAPTER 23

ATTHEW SAT IN THE waiting room staring at a magazine, thumbing through its pages without stopping to read. The doctor's office had scheduled the appointment, saying only that his tests were back but refusing to give him the results over the phone. He looked at his watch. He had arrived on time, but that was forty-five minutes ago.

His stomach tightened. No news wasn't necessarily *good* news. He turned another page, then glanced around the room: fourteen metal chairs with thin cushions, positioned around three walls with a dozen other waiting patients, all nervously shuffling through the well-worn magazines. The color of the room was pale yellow, as barren as sand, devoid of pictures or other comforting distractions.

A lady behind a counter walled off by glass finished a call, cradled her phone, and came around front. "Mr. Mulberry, the doctor will see you now. Please, follow me."

She led him down the hall and opened a door on her left, then stood aside so Matthew could enter. She took his file, slipped it into a clear plastic holder on the door, and closed the door behind her, leaving him sitting there alone to consider worst-case scenarios.

The fact that Dr. Michaels catered to lower-income patients was obvious. Most of those in the waiting room were either men with blue-collar work boots and motorcycle tattoos, or welfare women with two or three children. None of them looked like they could afford to pay, which explained the sparse environment, and Matthew was one of them. His friend, the

141

good doctor, might waive his part of the bill, but the laboratory wouldn't, and the tests he'd ordered were expensive.

Matthew looked around, his hands gripping the sides of the chair. A padded mat and pillow lay atop a metal examination table with a two-door cabinet beneath. A small writing desk piled with paper stood in the corner under a lamp, and a poster on the wall displayed a skeletal diagram that revealed the positions of internal organs, along with the logo of a pharmaceutical company.

He began fidgeting, pushing back the cuticles of his fingers with his thumb. The suspense was killing him. He felt his stomach roll. He pushed himself up in his seat, extending his legs, but it did little to relieve his apprehension. When *he* became a doctor, he wouldn't make his patients wait for critical news—*ever!* What if he had cancer...or diabetes? Diabetes could cause light-headedness. He wanted to see Dr. Michaels and get it over with.

He wasn't going to die. God wouldn't do that to him...but what if He did? He'd given it a lot of thought over the past week, more than he should. Worrying about something before it happened was a waste of time. Everyone died sooner or later. His friend Gerard was killed by a drunk motorist while riding his bike. A person never knew when his time was up.

He was ready, if it came to that. Secure in his faith, he knew where he was going. Christ would usher him to glory. He'd miss growing old with Layla, the children they'd have, and the fulfillment of his dream to do missionary work. He shook his head. Silly to fret over what he'd miss on Earth when heaven was so much better. But why would God introduce him to his brother, only to separate them again? OK, he could have been nicer about it. It was Mohamed, not Moped—maybe God was punishing him for being rude.

Lord, I can do a whole lot more for You if You just give me a little more time... Oh, for crying out loud; he was probably working himself up over nothing. It was probably something simple, something he could control with medication. If he had diabetes, he'd have to take insulin the rest of his life—that wasn't so bad—but he didn't have the right symptoms:

loss of weight, insatiable thirst, frequent urination, though low blood sugar would account for his passing out.

Dr. Michaels entered, holding the file. "Hey, Matthew, how's it going?"

"Good. They tell me you got the results. Don't keep me in suspense. What's the prognosis?"

The doctor pulled a chair back from his writing desk, turned it toward Matthew, and sat down. "I don't want to make light of this," he said. "Your MRI revealed something significant, and I'm afraid there's not much we can do about it, at least not for the moment. You've got an aneurysm located in the region of the corpus callosum. I'm not a surgeon, but that's a hard place to get at. I don't think there's much chance we can operate."

Matthew felt relieved. "A brain aneurysm? That doesn't sound so bad. There are treatments for that, aren't there? I can keep it under control, right?"

The doctor shrugged. "I hope so. There are actually several things we can try. Let's just take it one step at a time. Aneurysms are funny things. Sometimes people live for years and never have a problem. Then again, sometimes something happens, and a person we thought was doing fine doesn't make it. The truth is, we just don't know. But we can hope…"

"Hope? Why hope? I'm good with this. God isn't going to take me out of the game. It's just a little bubble on the brain. What we have to do is pray."

"Yes, we do," the doctor said, but he remained unsmiling. "Matthew, I'm not going to beat around the bush. You've got a serious case. The bubble's quite large, and the walls of your arteries are extremely thin. It appears there may be leakage too, which could account for your headaches. We can try to shrink the aneurysm, but there's no way of knowing ahead of time if it's going to work. And there are more tests we need to do first."

He paused, waiting to make sure he had Matthew's attention. "I have to have your full cooperation on this. Until we find out for certain what we're dealing with, you have to stop playing soccer. One bad bump to the head and it could be game over."

CHAPTER 24

CLOUDS HAD FORMED ALONG the coast. A spattering of rain dotted Mohamed's windshield as he pulled into a parking space a half block down from Las Brisas. He glanced to the side, where his soccer ball sat in a plastic shopping bag on the passenger seat. He was probably crazy for bringing it, but he hated to go anywhere without at least one ball. He never knew when an unexpected delay might have him sitting around doing nothing, and he could use the time for practice.

The wind whipped his hair as he climbed from the car. He closed the door on the white Grand Prix. Not a bad car, just not his. He'd determined not to make the seven-hour drive this time. Instead, he'd hopped a sky cab between San Francisco International and John Wayne Airport in Orange County, where he rented a car and drove the few short miles to the restaurant.

He looked around, making sure there weren't any other cars pulling into spaces nearby. Raindrops spotted his coat, the wind flicking his lapels. Maybe he was just being paranoid, but then again, maybe not. With any luck, he'd lost anyone who might be following him before he boarded the plane.

He felt the salty spray of the ocean on his face, a different feel, finer and softer than the rain. The sound of the surf pounding the shore met his ears, the smell of musty seaweed saturating the air. There was tranquility in the coolness, but he still couldn't help wishing for a sun-drenched day as he strolled through the gray mist, fine grains of sand crunching beneath the soles of his shoes. The path was bordered by palm trees, leafy shrubs, and gardens of roses dappled with rain.

An attractive Spanish girl, with dark chocolate eyes and her hair banded in a ponytail, seated him by the window. It was too cool to sit out on the patio as they'd done before. Mohamed looked around the restaurant, his gaze lingering on each face, but only for a moment. He'd used every precaution to make sure he wasn't tailed, but he wasn't taking chances. He smiled. Ditching Omar's stooges in Van Nuys felt good, but they'd be even more vigilant now.

A man seated toward the back of the restaurant kept looking at him. In the shadows his complexion appeared to be dark, but he was fat and bald and seemed more Indian than Arab, though that didn't mean much. Pakistan was full of Muslims. Still, he didn't seem the type.

Just about everyone else in the room was white Anglo-Saxon. Mohamed unrolled his napkin, removing his spoon, knife, and fork, and spread the napkin in his lap. A server approached and poured a glass of water. He thanked her, explained he was waiting for someone, and ordered a cup of tea. He glanced at his watch, fiddling with the band.

It would be a moment of truth. He'd felt the chill in her voice when he called, not cold, like: "What do *you* want?" just detached: "You want to get together? I suppose so. Whatever," which in some ways was a good thing because it suggested she probably *had* been at his door the other night. If so, she had every right to be hurt.

He'd make appropriate excuses. The trick was how to bring it up without asking outright, which he wanted to avoid, if possible. If she denied it, she'd be left wondering why he thought she was there. If she admitted it, he'd have to explain Allie. The best excuse he'd come up with so far was that Allie—*ah*, he had to remember not to use her name—was just a hapless friend who needed someone to talk to.

He'd spent the entire week trying to reach the ill-fated fiancée—getting her to call off the wedding was as much for her own good as it was for his—but she'd made herself scarce. He'd tried calling and sending e-mails; he'd even gone to her door and explained to her mother how important it was that she contact him, but she wasn't making herself available.

He had to be careful—expressing too much interest might raise questions from Mike, though Mike knew Mohamed was helping her plan the wedding, so stopping by for a visit shouldn't seem strange. Maybe his attempts to contact her had spooked her into thinking he was trying to pursue a relationship. Or maybe she was too embarrassed by her behavior to face him again. Whatever the reason, she wasn't taking his calls, and the longer she waited, the harder it would be to get her to break off her engagement. The guests were already sending their RSVPs.

He looked at his watch again. *Come on, Layla.*

The hardest part was rationalizing his desire to break rank. He'd wrestled with it night after sleepless night. He had everything to gain by just letting go, but he couldn't help himself. What they were doing was wrong, and he had to try and stop it. It didn't matter that it was for the good of Islam; his makeup didn't include mass murder.

As a student he'd had the opportunity to tour another school, one camouflaged under nets and tarps and hidden in the high deserts of Iraq, where kids were taught to become soldiers. Perhaps if he'd been trained there, things would be different. But he had attended a school of civility, with a group of students destined to become educators, lawyers, and politicians. They played with soccer balls while the others played with guns.

He looked out the window, drumming his fingers on the table. The clouds continued to build, the day turning chilly. If Layla didn't arrive soon, she'd probably arrive wet.

His dilemma continued to vex him. It wasn't a question of loyalty. He was as committed to the future of the Dar Al-Islam as anyone. Christians and Jews had to come under subjection. The justice of Allah required it. He was simply opposed to the method they'd chosen. Conversion by force was not true conversion.

He wasn't alone in his thinking. The vast majority of Muslims in the United States held the opinion that the three dominant religions could mutually coexist, not the least of which was the soon-to-be vice president's wife. She would be furious to know her wedding was a Trojan horse, a contrivance they planned to use to assemble politicians from both parties outside the high security of their government buildings.

And boy, had they responded! Omar's scheme was brilliant. Threaten the parents of the vice president's fiancée to ensure their cooperation. Have an insider—in this case, himself—persuade the bride to invite as many members of both legislative bodies as possible. Position the story in the newspapers as a must-do event. (The politicians had to say yes; to decline would be an insult to Arab people everywhere.) Make sure a Jewish caterer handled the reception—so they could take the blame. Have *special* guests—Abdu and Amre—spike the champagne with a colorless, odorless, tasteless poison and sit back as, one by one, half the Congress dropped dead, beginning, of course, with the president, whose propensity for alcohol was a well-established fact.

The world would be in shock. Blame the dirty Jews for exacting revenge on the executive office for a perceived shift in foreign policy. With the vice president married to a Muslim, it was bound to happen. Only their reprisal would fail, because the vice president and his new wife would be unharmed—Muslim law forbade the drinking of alcohol, and Mike was off the bottle since coming out of rehab after nearly drowning himself in rum during his year of depression. Assuming his new role as president, Mike would step in and take charge, declaring a state of national emergency, and assume wartime powers as commander in chief. And when the dust settled, foreign policy would change as revulsion over what the Jews had done increased and Mike came under the influence of his beautiful young wife. The perfect coup d'état.

Mohamed stared out the window at the ever-darkening clouds. Lightning pulsed over the ocean. The fact that it was a foolproof plan did not deter him from wanting to thwart it. People shouldn't have to die. There had to be a better way. But so far he hadn't been able to reach Allie. If he couldn't get her to call off the wedding, it would likely move forward as planned. *Inshallah*—as God wills.

He checked the time again. Only a few minutes had passed since the last time he looked. *Come on, Layla. I don't have all day.* Laguna Beach was a long way from Westwood. He hadn't known that the first time he'd invited her out. Maybe she was lost. He'd asked her to meet him here for two reasons: one, because most of the clientele were upscale white folk—anyone of ethnic origin would stand out, making it much easier for him to spot anyone who might have followed him; and two, because she *supposedly* knew the location of this restaurant. It was the same place they'd met before.

Too bad they couldn't use the patio, but it was already becoming wet with rain. At least he was seated along the glass wall with an ocean view. Almost as good. About the only thing missing was the cry of the seagulls and the ocean's roar—and the sun.

He glanced toward the door. After staring out the window for a few minutes, the interior of the restaurant looked dark, making the approaching couple appear in silhouette. It couldn't be her, unless…Mohamed tilted his head to the side.

With her hand at shoulder height, fingers curled, Layla waved at him. He had asked *her* to lunch, *not Matthew*. Were they inseparable, this woman and her shadow? Was she incapable of doing anything by herself?

"Hello, Mohamed. Sorry we're late."

Matthew waited until Layla was comfortable in her chair before seating himself across the table from Mohamed.

"Matthew was on time, but I was running late, so don't blame him." Layla took her napkin and unfolded it in her lap.

"No bother," Mohamed intoned. But it did bother him. He didn't think there were spies watching, but if he had to explain, having lunch with Layla wouldn't pose a problem. He'd already stated his intention to make her his wife. But he had agreed to lose Matthew, and *that* was nonnegotiable.

He glanced at the man sitting across the table from him. Looking at a living mirror was creepy. It felt like someone cloned him while he was asleep. The boy could use a shave, but at least he was dressing better. He was still wearing denims, but the blue shirt and tan jacket were an improvement, though vastly inferior to the new camel coat he himself wore. "Have trouble finding a place to park?"

Layla shook her head. "No, not really. We found a spot only one or two spaces down." There was nothing in her answer that suggested discontent, but she wasn't smiling. She reached for her purse and withdrew an envelope, laying it on the table. "I have news," she said. "Matthew already knows. In that envelope are the results of a test I asked my father to do on samples of yours and Matthew's DNA. It's absolute proof that you and he are brothers."

Mohamed kept his face expressionless. He glanced at Matthew, but his nemesis was as stoic as he himself. He blinked once and picked up the envelope. The type in the corner read, "Uno Scientific Laboratories." He slipped it into his inside coat pocket.

"Aren't you going to read it?"

"What for? You think I'd believe some laboratory rat? They can say anything they want; it still won't make this man my brother."

Matthew frowned slightly but otherwise kept his face deadpan, observing the conversation without comment.

Layla picked up her menu and looked at it. "Have you ordered?"

Mohamed shook his head. Inwardly he was happy to see her, but outwardly he was festering. Bringing Matthew again was rude; suggesting they were brothers, an affront. He picked up his own menu, hiding behind it as he considered the gloomy prospect.

Layla lay her menu down and began staring at Mohamed. It took a few seconds, but he finally felt her gaze and lowered his menu also. "What?"

"You seriously wouldn't believe a scientific test that conclusively proves Matthew is your brother? And not just your brother, but your identical twin? Matthew doesn't have a problem with it. He even has a letter from his adoptive mother, explaining it to him. Show him the letter, Matthew."

Matthew fidgeted, twisting in his seat. He pulled his foot up over his knee, playing with the cuff of his jeans. "I didn't bring the letter," he said, not looking at her.

Layla raised an eyebrow. "Didn't bring it?"

Matthew shrugged. "Why would I? You've got the report."

"I wouldn't believe it anyway," Mohamed said. "I don't know what you two are trying to pull, but I know this man could not be my brother. My father was a martyr. He gave his life for Allah. He would not have a son who's a Christian. You're both Christians. I can't believe anything either of you says. All Christians are liars."

Matthew uncrossed his leg and leaned forward. "Your mother, and I guess mine too, was secretly a Christian. I'd be careful who I called a liar. And if our father killed himself in a suicide bombing, it makes him a murderer, not a martyr."

"Watch your mouth!"

Diners at other tables turned their heads, gawking at the raised voices.

"When a man straps explosives to his chest and goes out to kill other people, he becomes a weapon. That's homicide, not suicide."

Mohamed leaped from his seat, diving across the table to send his water glass toppling as he tried to catch Matthew by the throat. But Matthew tipped back out of his reach. For a moment he teetered, his arms flailing, trying to catch his balance, but the momentum was too great. He toppled over backward and sprawled on the floor. Layla jumped up to keep the water from pouring into her lap.

Mohamed came around and stood over Matthew with fists clenched. His face and eyes were red, his lips quivering. He glanced at Layla and then at Matthew again. "All Christians are liars!" he said again, and stormed out.

Layla watched him go. Another attempt at reconciliation, another disaster. Part of her wanted to chase after him but, no, he was out of control. He wouldn't be open to reason until he calmed down. Murmurs rose from the restaurant's patrons as they strained to see what had happened.

A waiter rushed over, and only then did Layla notice: Matthew's eyes were closed. He wasn't stirring. She gasped and knelt at his side, tapping him lightly on the cheek, tugging at his shoulder. No response.

She snapped at the waiter. "Don't just stand there; do something! Call an ambulance! Can't you see he's unconscious?"

CHAPTER 25

LIGHTNING SPARKED, ILLUMINATING DENSE caverns in the sky, the dark clouds billowing like pads of steel wool. Thunder rattled the windows of the stores along the street. Mohamed found himself standing in the middle of a torrential downpour. He couldn't go back inside, and his car was parked more than a block away. He had no choice but to run.

He started to sprint but halted at the sight of a VW Bug parked at the curb. He raised a hand to block the rain. It was the kind of car Layla's boyfriend said he drove and the only one nearby. An audacious yellow.

Mohamed ground his teeth. *Augggggggh.* With a quick look over his shoulder to ensure he was alone, he grabbed the car's antenna, bending it back and forth until it snapped off in his hand. Twisting it, he folded it into an accordion of wire and threw it on the ground, stomping on it until it was flat. He turned and ran down the street, his brown loafers splashing through puddles.

He was well up the road before he realized he wasn't looking for his Lexus. He spun around, scanning makes and models. The white Pontiac was a dozen cars behind him. *Stupid!* He stood there, a fully clothed man looking like he'd just crawled out of the ocean, his new camel coat turned from a fine buff brown to a dark wet matte. He started backtracking, squeezing his fingers into the wet pocket of his pants to retrieve the keys, but when he pulled his hand out, the pocket came with it, sending coins scattering into the street. *Forget it,* he thought, aiming the wireless key-fob. He heard the *woop-woop* of the door unlocking and stepped in a puddle deep enough to bury his shoe. He yanked his foot back, but it was too late; water had already soaked through his sock. *Auggggggh!*

He reached for the handle, flinging the door open, and quickly dropped inside. His hair was plastered to the sides of his face, his goatee dripping. Water from his wet clothes seeped onto the fabric of the seats. *So what?* It was a rental. He sat looking beyond the shrubbery at the horizon. There was no longer a distinction between land and sea. The ocean bled seamlessly into the sky, creating a giant wall of gray. Palm trees whipped back and forth in the wind.

He grabbed the steering wheel, gripping it so tightly that his knuckles turned white. *Grrrrr.* He pulled himself forward and pushed back, pounding against the seat again and again and again, hating himself for being such a coward, afraid of everything: afraid of losing Layla, afraid of his uncle, afraid of dying, afraid of blood. Why had he run? What if he *did* have a brother? So what? *No*, his mother would have said something. He'd always been an only child.

He peeled back his coat and reached into his pocket for the envelope, holding it by the corner. His hands were wet, but the coat's inner lining had kept the paper dry. Reaching over, he wiped his fingers on the fabric of the other seat. He pinched the letter out and flicked it open.

The logo at the top read, "Uno Scientific Laboratories." He scanned the page until he found what he was looking for: "Sibling Probability 100%. Identical Match." He tossed the letter onto the dash.

His coat was drenched. He rolled it off his shoulders, pulling on the sleeves, but it was wet and stuck to him like paste. Too late to think about staying dry. He opened the door and stepped out onto the asphalt, tugging at the cuff to drag the coat from his arm. A $350 fashion statement he'd bought just to impress Layla—now ruined. She of all people should know he was an only child. What kind of scam were they trying to pull? They'd probably submitted two samples of the same DNA.

He wadded up his coat and tossed it into the car, then reached down to remove his shoes, one at a time, dropping them onto the seat. Next, he peeled off his socks. It was still raining, but the deluge had passed. The drops continued to pelt his head, but he no longer felt like he was standing under a waterfall.

Mohamed leaned inside to retrieve the lone soccer ball. Hopping back onto the sidewalk, he kicked the ball in the direction of the restaurant and took off running. And when he caught up with it, kicked it again—and again. *Déjà vu.* The exhumation of a day he'd buried long ago...

Mohamed's thirteenth birthday, estate of Sayyid El Taher

"She's dead?" Mohamed collapsed against the wall. *Dead? How?* He felt like the wind had been knocked out of him, like his internal organs had been ripped from his body, leaving an empty shell. *How?* She was in Europe, traveling across the continent on vacation. What happened? Images formed: a plane crashing and bursting into flames; a car racing down the autobahn spinning out of control; a suicide bombing in a hotel, leaving no survivors. *When?* Why hadn't Sayyid told him? He had a right to know.

He turned around, stumbling to his bedroom, and stood at the door, leaning on the frame for support. His prayer rug was neatly rolled and sitting in the chair. His bed had been made by the servants. Right in the center of the bedspread, positioned like a stuffed toy between the pillows, was a brand-new soccer ball. It was more of a tradition than a present. His uncle gave him many gifts, but each year on his birthday he always received a brand-new ball.

Biting his lower lip, he stepped onto the bed, drawing his foot back to strike. The ball slammed against the wall, vibrating the pictures, one of which fell to the floor, sending shards of glass clattering across the tiles. He clenched his fists and ground his teeth. *Grrrrrr! Why, why, why? Allah most merciful, why? Wasn't my father enough? Why do you take my mother also?*

The response wasn't audible. It came more like a thought planted in his head. *Why do you blame Allah for what your uncle has done?* He felt his skin prickling.

It was her fault. You can't become an infidel without paying with your life. She betrayed Allah.

He jumped off the bed and kicked the ball again, bouncing it off a different wall, and repeated the process. He kicked it again…and again.

The voice of his uncle thundered down the hall. "Mohamed! What are you doing?"

Mohamed scooped the ball up and ran from the room, passing the kitchen where the servants were preparing the evening meal, their heads bobbing to watch as he rushed by, mindful that he'd just learned of his mother's fate. In the dining room he passed Sami, his uncle's oldest and most trusted servant, his wizened eyes drooping with sorrow. Out the door and into the yard he fled, holding the ball under his arm as he ran barefoot to the end of the lane and turned right onto the road. He threw the ball down and kicked it and ran after it, kicking it again, running down the road with puffs of yellow dust at his heels, the ball spinning fiercely in front of him.

He did not feel the hot wash of his tears, though they blurred his vision. But if asked, he'd say he never cried. Tears were for boys. Today he was a man. He focused on the ball, giving it his total concentration. When he was running, he was numb to the outside world. There was nothing but the ball and the search for a net in which to score. But there were no nets, so he just kept running.

Time passed in irrelevant seconds. It came almost as a surprise when he found himself standing at the edge of the Nile, a place he often used for practice. The rough bank offered a test worthy of his skill; the tufts of grass and washed-out sluices made control of the ball difficult, but it was an obstacle course he had mastered.

He began sweeping the ball around his feet, then popped it up to his elbow, and then to his head, down to his other elbow, and back down to his feet—working through a routine he'd practiced over and over again.

He settled into a rhythm, keeping his mind occupied with the ball's journey, always knowing where it would be one second before it arrived. He was in the prime of his youth, possessing a natural stamina. Even so, his limbs finally began to fatigue. With no strength left to continue and when he could no longer hold the ball aloft, he collapsed onto the shore and lay on his side, curled into a fetal position like a pile of laundry left on the floor for cleaning.

The tears broke again, but he attempted to choke them back. He sat up, wiping his eyes, and then stood. His uncle must not see him cry. Tears were for the weak. The ball was at his feet, a southern breeze in his favor. He kicked the ball out over the water as hard as he could and watched as it was carried upstream by the wind. It went farther than he'd ever kicked a ball before. He giggled. Then he ran for the water and dove under the surface and stood, but it was only up to his waist.

He walked out into the deep, paddling with his hands until the water reached his neck, and then his mouth, and then covered his head. He would drown himself and join his father in paradise. Enveloped by water, with cheeks ballooning and arms extended, he looked up through the green soup and saw a light swirling above. A hand reached out to take him, but he pushed himself back—just a log with a limb probing downward.

He was floating somewhere between heaven and Earth, trapped in the netherworld. But then his lungs exploded, releasing his pent-up oxygen, and he began to thrash until he found himself bobbing on the surface again. The current was towing him deeper into the river. He could no longer feel the bottom, and he didn't know how to swim. The waves churned around his head. He was taking on water in gulps, windmilling his arms but losing strength and doing more to sink himself than stay afloat.

Something bumped his head. He turned and grabbed on. It was his soccer ball. He pulled it into his chest, clinging to it for dear life. Already depleted, his arms cried out in pain, but he refused to let go. The river carried him farther downstream.

How many kilometers he traveled or how much time passed, he couldn't say. Most of the ride felt like a dream, a state between the real and the surreal, with the sun pounding on his head and water spewing from his mouth. It took him by surprise to suddenly realize his heels were dragging the bottom. He prodded the silt with his toe and found it accommodated him. Holding the ball at arm's length, he tried to stand. With his head tilted back, his chin stayed above water—but just barely. The current continued clawing at him, but he pushed away and tiptoed toward the shore, one slow step at a time, until the water around him receded and he fell on an exposed bar of land, exhausted. He flopped over, staring up at the sky, coughing up water.

Where exactly it happened he didn't know—the mind works in funny ways—but during the stupor of his ride, he'd somehow come to a conclusion. He didn't know how he'd do it, nor did he know when, but in his heart he knew.

Someday he would kill his uncle.

That day never came, but as he ran his ball up the street, dripping wet, he thought about it once again—and the cowardice that had preserved his uncle's life.

He was passing in front of the restaurant when the door opened unexpectedly. A man in a business suit stepped out and raised an umbrella, glancing at Mohamed like he thought it strange someone would run by, kicking a soccer ball in thoroughly soaked clothes with bare feet. For a moment, Mohamed felt alarm, but it passed when he realized it wasn't Layla or her boyfriend. What was he thinking coming this way again?

The restaurant was perched on a cliff overlooking the ocean, but the south side rolled off toward the beach. He was running downhill, the ball rolling faster and faster until it reached the sand below. Lightning brightened the clouds over the ocean. He could feel the thunder shaking the ground. Perhaps another downpour was coming, but he no longer cared.

He reached the boardwalk, scooped up his ball, and hopped down onto the sand. The soft white grains were now dingy and wet. He drop-kicked the ball out toward the waves. Save for a few scrounging seagulls, the beach was empty. He went into his drill, oblivious to everything around him except the ball. Sand, water, and sky all melded into the routine of his practice.

He heard a siren on the road above, even saw the flashing lights as an ambulance pulled to the curb, but he kept them in the periphery of his mind. He turned toward the water and kicked his ball into the surf. After a few minutes a wave tossed it back, sending it skittering up on the hard wet sand. He ran across the beach, skipping over clumps of seaweed while splashing through the waves as they rolled up on the shore, his ball in front of him one minute and carried out on the tide the next. He waited for its return and scooped it into his arms, then ran into the water, diving headlong into a wave, breaking the surface. As the tide pulled back, he felt himself being dragged into the sea. Today he would die.

He was bobbing on the waves, clinging tight to his ball, but the ocean was not a river and the tide not a current. The force pulling him now had more power than any he had experienced as a child. He began kicking his feet while clinging to the ball, afraid of dying—forever a coward. A white-capped wave came rolling up from behind, catching him in its curl. The ball acted like a buoy, keeping him afloat as the wave carried him to shore. He caught his footing and staggered up on the beach, out of breath, covered head to foot with a mat of heavy wet sand. He put the ball down and kicked it again, then ran after it.

"One, two, three, lift!" The paramedics hefted Matthew's unconscious body onto the gurney. A man in a white nylon coat with a shoulder patch bearing a red caduceus checked his vital signs while his partner held smelling salts under his nose.

Tears washed Layla's face. She held Matthew's hand. "Matthew! Wake up; please wake up. Matthew, *please!*"

One of the emergency technicians tapped Layla on the shoulder, indicating that she needed to step back. When she complied, he took over, rolling the gurney to the door. Stepping outside, he opened an umbrella to shield Matthew from the rain as his partner pushed the gurney to the waiting van. They opened the back of the ambulance and slid Matthew inside.

Layla started to get in, but the man raised his hand, preventing her. "Sorry, no riders. Insurance doesn't allow it."

She backed up. "But I came with him. I don't have a car. Where are you taking him?"

The man shook his head. "South Coast Medical," he said as he closed the door. The ambulance pulled away from the curb with a *whoop whoop* and lights flashing, leaving Layla standing on the crest of a hill overlooking Laguna's main beach.

A lone figure down by the waterfront caught her eye. Some crazy fool kicking a ball in the rain. *Is that Mohamed? What's he doing?* She didn't have time to find out. She rushed back into the restaurant to get her purse. She had to call a cab.

CHAPTER 26

LAYLA PACED, WALKING THE corridor from one end to the other and back again. She looked down the hall, a place bustling with nurses and doctors and patients being taxied about in wheelchairs or hitching rides on adjustable rolling beds. There was nothing wrong with the hospital. It seemed to have all the right equipment and facilities, and procedures were aggressively maintained; it's just that it was the *wrong* hospital. She needed to get Matthew back to UCLA Med, where he could be looked after by colleagues and friends.

Staying here meant she had to miss classes; there was no way she could commute. Her hair splayed on the polished linoleum as she bent over to touch her toes, stretching her stiff muscles. Only the tingling in her nerves, the rush that came from anxiety, and the two cups of coffee she drank between fitful hours of sleeping in a chair kept her awake.

She stood upright, placing her hands on her waist as she leaned back and, with her hair hanging behind her, rotated her shoulders and hips. The hospital should provide beds for visitors. She'd been there all night and knew as little now as she did when they'd first brought Matthew in.

She turned and began her vigil, marching down the hall, past the waiting area to the nurses' station, and back. The ladies in their cotton blues behind the counter refused to tell her anything. The most she'd been able to find out was that Matthew was in intensive care and not allowed to have visitors. Beyond that, they could say little else. She wasn't a relative, and friends weren't privy to patient information.

Worry consumed her. He'd blacked out twice recently, and for no good reason. This wasn't about being hit on the soccer field or falling off a chair. Those things happened every day. Most people got up and shrugged them off. No, there was more going on. If he was fine, they'd say so and she'd be with him, sitting beside him and holding his hand to bring him comfort. Something was seriously wrong.

Mohamed sat at his computer searching travel sites for airline tickets. He purchased not one but three—one in his own name and one in Layla's—round-trip to Mexico for a special flight he planned for the two of them to take later—and one to fly him back to LA now so he could see Layla this afternoon.

The clock was ticking. He was unable to contact Allie, and the wedding was less than two weeks away. If it was really going to happen, he needed to get Layla someplace safe. Let her read about the tragedy in the newspapers, how the Jews had killed the president because his administration dared to extend an olive branch to Muslims. The media would be sucked into believing it. There was precedent. Anwar al-Sadat, a Muslim, had been killed for making friendly overtures to Israel. Tit for tat. Layla would buy it, as would the rest of the world—*but the annihilation of an entire government?*

In the aftermath the Feds would temporarily lock down the borders and cancel all international flights, making sure the assassins didn't escape, and maybe his short weekend with Layla would turn into a full week together. She wouldn't be able to return until the dust settled.

He stared at the phone. The question was, would she even talk to him? He hadn't exactly shown her his best side—but that was Matthew's fault, goading him like that. He reached out, then hesitated in indecision. His hand fell short, plopping on the table. He began tapping his fingers. She deserved better—*but he'd already purchased the tickets.* He felt his uncle's hand on his shoulder, a phantom whisper in his ear: "Women were made for the pleasure of men, my son, not the other way around." He picked up the phone and dialed.

· · · 🌙 · · ·

The sound startled Layla. She bolted upright in her seat, eyes wide. *What!* She must have dozed off. She'd only sat down to rest for a moment. She heard it again. Her hands swept the cushion for her phone. The muffled chirping was coming from her purse. She fumbled with the bag, trying to get it open, her heart accelerating. Her fingers wrapped around keys, cosmetics, a checkbook, wallet, and tissues until they found the rude device. "Hello...hello?"

"Layla?"

"Matthew?"

"Ah, no, sorry, it's Mohamed."

She froze, letting seconds pass, not sure what to say.

"Did I catch you at a bad time?"

She wanted to say she'd been at the hospital for the past twenty-four hours, waiting to find out what was wrong with his brother, and that he needed to be there too. He was Matthew's only living relative. The hospital would provide *him* with information, but she'd already decided not to do that. Their jealousy of each other was fierce. If he came, it would likely be to gloat. And if he acted poorly, it might further tarnish her view of him. She was still trying to rationalize the girl in his apartment. "No, I'm good. What's up?"

"Listen, ah, I was just calling to apologize. I behaved badly. Sorry if I embarrassed you. I didn't mean to make a scene."

Layla stretched and yawned, then leaned over and removed a few clips from her purse. She held her phone under her chin while she pinned up her hair. "Yes, you certainly did that...." She paused, trying to discern whether his tone revealed smugness or sincerity.

"I know, and there's really no excuse. It's just that...that this whole thing is really upsetting, and I guess I overreacted. But the idea that I have a brother I never knew...I just don't know what do to with that."

Layla wrestled with a rebellious lock of hair, pinning it back. "Well, for starters, you need to simmer down long enough to listen. Your brother has a letter explaining how it happened. It's a story you need to hear." There was a pause on the line. She looked around at the others who, like herself, were awaiting news about someone they loved. Several were dozing; some were reading magazines. Two tykes played with a plastic car on the carpet.

"Maybe...but I can't face him right now. Something gets into me and...maybe you and I...I mean if we could meet for dinner, you could explain. But it would have to be just the two of us. I know Matthew's your fiancé, so that makes me your future brother-in-law. It should be OK. At least give me this. You and I have a history. This whole thing about me having an identical twin, some kind of clone who's stepped in to take my place...that's pretty hard to take. Know what I mean?"

Layla finished fixing her hair, patting it down as she looked into the window of the nurses' station. What a mess. She shouldn't. She was engaged to Matthew, well, *almost*, and already she'd abused his trust once, driving halfway up the state to see Mohamed without letting him know. But Matthew was incapacitated, and she *did* need to eat, and Mohamed deserved to know the truth. "I think so. Are you still in town, in Orange County, I mean? Because if you are, I'm free this evening."

"Tell me when and where, and I'll be there."

"OK, how about the same place as before? But this time you have to promise to stay calm."

"What do you mean?"

"Just promise."

"OK, I promise. As long as you come *alone*, there won't be a problem."

"All right then, six o'clock at Las Brisas?" She grimaced as she said it, wondering if she had enough time.

Layla snapped her phone closed and slipped it into her purse, groaning. She had exactly three hours to get ready. Her hair was piled on her head in a rat's nest; she was wearing yesterday's clothes and hadn't brought a change; her makeup bag was at home, and her eyes were ringed from lack of sleep. *How do I get myself into these things?*

CHAPTER 27

HIS LAUGHTER WAS INFECTIOUS. Layla reached up to rub her cheeks, suddenly realizing they hurt. She couldn't remember when she'd laughed so hard or felt so good. The room, along with all the people in it—hostess, servers, and patrons—had vanished. She and Mohamed were in a bubble unto themselves, safely ensconced behind an invisible barrier that separated them from the rest of the world. His dark eyes glittered as she reached for a glass of water.

"You were such a character," she said, setting the glass down. Her brunette hair fell around both sides of her neck, lying on her bare shoulders in thick waves. Her brand-new sundress, deep red and sleeveless, made her olive complexion glow, and her red lips matched her fingernails—the complete ensemble purchased on the fly while she held her cab at the curb and raced from one store to the next. Yesterday's dress was in a plastic bag with the hostess, a favor she negotiated after taking a sponge bath and changing in the restaurant's ladies' room.

"You remember the man who used to sell falafels from a cart in front of the small grocery where we used to hang out, the *ba aal*? The guy who said I had to pay for the camel ride?" She looked down, slicing off a bite of broiled chicken breast, scraping aside the topping of tomatoes, avocados, and queso fresco.

"The old guy ripped you off. But it was worth it. You were so scared. I thought you were going to cry."

"Was not!"

"You were too. You were screaming, 'Put me down, put me down!' You had everyone laughing so hard. What a show! The old guy kept saying his camel liked you because he wouldn't kneel so you could get off. Remember that? He was threatening to take you with him." Mohamed took a bite of his filet, followed by a mouthful of garlic potatoes.

Layla set her fork down and wiped her fingers on the linen in her lap. "So, why do you suppose that old guy took my money when the man who owned the camel was giving rides for free?"

"Beats me." Mohamed wiped his mouth and reached for his water. "All I know is I paid him back the next day. Remember?"

"How could I not? You let his chickens go. He was chasing them from one end of the street to the other."

"Yeah, but do you remember what else I did?"

"You took two pita slices and filled them with his beans and herbs, and we had free falafels."

Mohamed stroked his goatee. "Fair trade. It didn't cost him any more than what he charged you for the camel ride. Best falafels I ever ate too."

Layla smiled. "Oh, we did have some good times, didn't we?" She released a sigh, her eyes growing pensive. "Walking along the Nile with that huge orange sun warming our backs...the water so blue."

"The water was green."

"No, it was definitely *blue*. I thought it would never end."

"Ever think about going back?"

"Where, to Egypt?" Her smile faded as she shook her head. "No, never. I couldn't."

"Why not? It's your home. It's where you were born. Wouldn't you like to see it again?"

Layla began playing with her napkin. "We had to leave," she said, not looking up. "They would have murdered my parents if we'd stayed. What kind of country does that? Lets its citizens kill anyone who doesn't believe in Islam."

"They don't kill anyone for *not* believing. Your father was proselytizing. He broke the law. That's where he messed up."

"But what kind of country does that? My dad was only sharing what he believes."

Mohamed's face was flat, the laughter gone from his lips. He looked beyond the table as though seeing the other people in the restaurant for the first time, but his gaze quickly returned to Layla. "What if your version of truth is wrong? I read part of your Bible. Your Jesus seems like a nice man, even a prophet, but Muhammad came after Him. Anything Muhammad has to say supersedes the words of Jesus because he brought a later revelation. What makes you think Jesus had the final word?"

Layla nodded, leaning in, her fingers gripping the edge of the table. "Really? You already started reading? What part?"

"The part called 'John.' Answer the question."

She smiled, excited by the challenge. "Because Jesus *is* the Word. Even Islam teaches that. Besides, He's the only one who proved He was who He said He was. He fulfilled all the prophecies written about Him. And on top of that, He did the kind of miracles only God could do, like rising from the dead. Muhammad didn't do anything like that."

"We don't believe Isa died. The only reason He was seen after the Crucifixion was that Judas took His place on the cross in order to pay for his sin of betrayal."

Layla shoved her plate aside and folded her forearms on the table, leaning further in. "That's just plain silly. Look at the historical record. When Christ was arrested, all His disciples were frightened and ran away. They were afraid they'd be taken and killed too. Peter even denied knowing Him. But after the Resurrection, every one of His disciples, except maybe John, became a martyr. They all died because they claimed to have seen Jesus alive after His crucifixion. If Judas had been on that cross, it's a sure bet they'd know it. They wouldn't have allowed themselves to be killed if they knew Christ's resurrection was a hoax."

Mohamed skewed his head to the side. "Lots of people die to prove their loyalty to a cause. People die for Allah every day."

Layla sat back, pulling on a lock of hair, twisting it with her fingers. "It's not the same, and you know it. Jesus's disciples didn't kill themselves. They stood for what they believed, and it cost them their lives. They were killed because they wouldn't renounce what they saw. The ones you call martyrs are just people bent on taking their own lives, usually killing a lot of other people in the process."

Mohamed sat back, pursing his lips.

She watched him tap the table with his fingers, withholding comment. She may not have convinced him, but he was resigning himself to withdraw before the argument became heated. She almost felt sorry for him.

He slipped a hand into his coat and withdrew an envelope, laying it on the table.

"What's this?"

"You once said if I wanted to marry you, I had to become a Christian. I'm not ready for that, but I won't close the door. Here's what I propose. This envelope contains two airline tickets to Puerto Vallarta. I've booked resort reservations for the weekend after next. You and I need to get away from all this." His fingers made a discreet sweeping gesture. "This is your home turf, so you have the advantage. If we were in Egypt, the advantage would be mine. What I propose is we establish a base in neutral territory and continue our discussion. Just for a weekend, the two of us. We can walk along the beach, have some fun together, just like old times, and I'll give you a chance to convince me you're right."

Layla frowned.

"Separate rooms, of course."

She slowly shook her head. "It's not just that, Mohamed. Did you forget I'm engaged?"

"You don't love him. You just thought you did, because you thought he was me. Go through with marrying him, and you'll spend the rest of your life wondering if you married the wrong man. Spend the weekend with me, Layla, just as friends. Then you'll be sure. Even *he* deserves that."

"I...I don't know. Are you admitting he's your brother? We still need to talk about that. I haven't even had a chance to tell you how it happened. And there's something else. It's something I've been trying to bring up all night, but—"

Mohamed's phone rang. He raised his finger, cutting her off as he flicked it open to read the display. "Sorry, but I have to take this. I'll only be a moment." Mohamed stood and, sliding back his chair, turned and walked away.

Layla sat for a moment, the air conditioning in the room giving her a sudden chill. She crossed her arms, rubbing her bare shoulders as she tried to understand what she was feeling. She *did* love Matthew, at least part of her did—but she loved Mohamed too. Still, she couldn't *marry* Mohamed—not unless…well, unless he became a Christian. Maybe the weekend wasn't such a bad idea. He'd promised to let her share the gospel, and they'd be staying in separate rooms—*what was she thinking?* Matthew was in the hospital! How could she even consider running off with his brother? If Mohamed had known what happened, he would never have asked.

She needed to tell him. She just had to figure out how. *Lord, please give me the words.* She didn't want Mohamed to think it was his fault. Matthew hadn't blacked out because he'd fallen off his chair. There was more going on…

She looked up and saw Mohamed outside on the patio, talking on his phone. He was animated, pacing back and forth with one hand waving around excitedly. She'd tell him as soon as he got back. But as for running off with him, Matthew would have to be out of the hospital and on his feet for her to consider such a thing. She needed time to make him understand it was in his own best interest. If she married him while secretly harboring feelings for Mohamed, they'd both be miserable.

Mohamed was standing with his back to the glass. He was wearing the same white coat he'd worn the first time they'd had lunch together. It made him seem so…so *suave.* She rubbed the goose bumps on her arms. The late evening sun was yellow and looked warm on his shoulders. She scooted her chair back and stood. If she hurried, she could make it to the ladies' room, freshen up, and be back before he finished his call.

She leaned toward the mirror, smoothing a fresh coat of lipstick with her finger. Straightening herself, she slipped the tube into her purse and brought up her hand to fluff her hair. She was pleased with what she saw.

She was no beauty queen or Hollywood star, but God had been kind. Her long, straight nose wasn't as small as she would have liked, and her face lacked the contoured cheekbones of her mother, but her eyes were dark and sultry. She placed her hand on her hip and, with an exaggerated flair, batted her long lashes. *Dark and alluring.* She giggled, twisting sideways to look back over her shoulder, the line of her sundress accenting her small derriere. At least her slender figure made her appear tall and statuesque, though she was five foot seven, which wasn't all *that* tall.

Facing the mirror again, she patted down a flyaway strand of hair. She always felt her wavy tresses were her finest feature, cascading like streams of dark water. Tossing her hair back over her shoulder, she returned to the dining area. The table was empty, and someone had cleared the plates and left a bill. Mohamed was still outside on the patio.

Her body quivered. She blamed the air conditioning but knew it was more than that. Matthew didn't make her feel like this. What was it about Mohamed? They were identical in every way. Was it the history they'd shared, or was it something deeper?

The sun on the patio looked inviting and would lessen the chill. Mohamed was standing near the door, but the deck was big enough for her to wait at a distance until he finished his call. She wouldn't invade his privacy. She stepped outside into the most glorious display of evening sun, pausing just long enough to stretch, feeling her chill dissolve in the warmth that caressed her skin.

He was speaking in Arabic, but she understood. And even though his voice was low, she really couldn't help overhearing.

"Yes, I assure you everything is in place. Yes, I did see they'd upped the estimates. Far more people responded than we'd originally planned…yes, I know that means more dead. We didn't anticipate so many wanting to come but…I told you, I'm committed, no turning back, that's why I'm here. *Allah Akbar.* The Great Satan must fall…"

Layla reached for the door and slipped quietly back into the restaurant.

. . . ☽ . . .

Mohamed snapped his phone closed and dropped it into his inside coat pocket. It was imperative he get Layla out of the country…and *soon*. A scattering of clouds refracted the sun's light, splitting it into a display of prismatic color—rose and magenta, yellow and orange, purple and blue. The sunset was perfect, the palms waving in a gentle breeze, the sky fair and warm. He would find Layla and suggest a walk along the beach.

The room appeared dark as he stepped into its dim interior again. He sauntered between tables filled with guests enjoying the evening repast until he spotted her, the most beautiful woman on earth, standing by the door. She was holding her purse and a plastic shopping bag.

"I've already paid the bill and called a cab," she said. "The driver is waiting outside. Sorry to rush off like this, but I'm not feeling well. I just wanted to say good-bye." She extended her hand, making sure Mohamed knew she wasn't inviting a kiss.

CHAPTER 28

THE PLANE HIT AN air pocket and bounced, leaving Mohamed's stomach on the ceiling. The small sky taxi wasn't like the jumbo jet he'd arrived in from Egypt. Then his uncle had spared no expense in seeing to his comfort. He had enjoyed lounge-chair seating, dined on five-star cuisine, and watched a selection of new-release movies, everything but alcoholic beverages. As a good Muslim, he abstained from strong drink.

But this was a no-frills flight, with knees-in-your-face spacing between the seats, and he was glad it was almost over. People were leaning against the wall, straining to look out their portholes at the lights of the approaching city, but Mohamed didn't bother.

"*Ouch!*" he exclaimed as the plane took another bounce. The whole plane seemed to be shaking apart. Wouldn't *that* be ironic. Running off to woo Layla, only to be killed before being able to tell her how he felt. The paper napkin filled with his writing was still in his hand. He unfolded it and read the scribbled words: *You are the sun on the water, a star in the nighttime sky. You are my morning, my evening, the sum of my every thought, the air I breathe...* Such drivel. He wadded it up.

What was he supposed to think? One minute, she'd been all smiles and laughter; the next, downright morose. Was it his invitation? Had he been too presumptuous, too forward? A devout Muslim girl wouldn't run off with the brother of her fiancé before her wedding—but Layla was a *Christian*. American girls did things like that all the time. She'd hesitated, but she hadn't said no. Maybe she *had* become sick. Who could say? All he knew was one minute he was planning a romantic stroll on the beach, and the next she was gone. There was nothing left to do but return to the airport and catch the next flight out.

The plane bounced again, and they were on the ground. At least the short commuter flight carried fewer people. He wouldn't have to wait long to deplane, and with no customs lines to stand in and no luggage to collect, he should be able to make it home without delay.

He thought about writing Layla a letter. Maybe he could express on paper the feelings he couldn't seem to put into words when they were together. Or maybe he should just wait until Mexico. The complications of their past, the differences in their beliefs, his fear of being usurped by a brother he didn't know—all of this could be resolved if she'd just agree to accept his invitation. They just needed more time to talk.

Walking briskly through the terminal, on his way to the parking lot to retrieve his car, his phone chirped. *What now?* He was anxious to get home so he could start writing the letter he was composing in his head. He flipped his phone open and saw someone had left him a message. He scrolled through the menu, hoping it was Layla, but the voice mail was from Omar, urging him to call immediately.

He stopped, rolled his eyes, and dropped his phone into his pocket. Living a double life was hard, to say the least. But Omar's place was only a half-hour drive from the airport, and since it was on his way home, he decided it would be better just to stop by. There were other things they needed to discuss.

Mohamed entered the house just as the intercom announced the nine o'clock call to prayer. Omar had the recording on a timer set to play five times a day, drawing the faithful to submission. Supplicants were expected to drop what they were doing and assemble in the mosque at the sound of Omar's voice chanting the *azan*, but Mohamed ignored it. He would pray in his own time, alone, not with a bunch of neophyte pilgrims still learning the routine. He couldn't recite his prayers standing next to someone who was butchering the language in such a way as to make it almost unintelligible.

Omar always returned to his study to put his rug away after prayer, so Mohamed decided to wait for him there. A large globe, three feet in diameter, sat on the floor to his right. A transparent red film had been carefully applied to all countries already part of the Dar Al-Islam. Standing over the globe gave one the sense of being like God, able to look down on the earth and evaluate man's exploits and accomplishments. You could spin the sphere on its axis, arbitrarily point your finger at a country, and if you deemed it sinful, isolate it for judgment. Mohamed imagined someone splashing a glass of water on the globe, instantly flooding four continents, or lighting a match under it to unleash the fires of hell, or thumping it with their fist to watch the tiny little people run from the earthquake—a magnitude nine on the Richter scale—and all in a matter of seconds.

Mohamed smiled. It probably wasn't a bad analogy. If Allah wasn't interested in doing it himself, they'd do it for him. It was time to shake the people up!

Omar entered the room, pausing to place his rolled rug on two pegs that protruded from the wall. He folded his hands and stopped in front of Mohamed, letting out a sigh. He was wearing clerical garb: a long robe that hung down to his sandals, an *emma* on his head. His long thin fingers lifted his robe as he took a seat opposite Mohamed—not the one behind his desk, the position of authority he usually assumed, but facing Mohamed as an equal.

Omar placed his hands on the arms of the chair, lowering his chin to peer at Mohamed over his reading glasses. His long beard lay in his lap as he slouched. His expression was particularly dour.

Mohamed squirmed in his seat. Seeing Omar in the role of imam always dredged up memories of his youth. "You wanted to see me?" he asked.

Omar raised his hand, palm up, like a holy man bestowing a blessing. "My door is always open."

"Yes, I know, but I also know you're a busy man and your time is valuable, so I wouldn't be here if it wasn't important." Mohamed waited, twisting in his seat as the imam's dark eyes studied him.

"This is about the girl, isn't it? You know I'm determined to marry her.

I'm sorry if this disappoints you. I know she's a Christian. I've wrestled with this, and I have prayed, and I am fully convinced she is to be my wife. She'll live by the Quran; I'll see to that."

He paused, but Omar remained silent, his hands folded in his lap.

"What is it then? All the arrangements are in place. Abdu hired a well-established Zionist to do the catering, and Amre will hide what's left of the chemicals they used in his shop where they'll be found by the FBI. You yourself instructed both Abdu and Amre on how to conceal the tiny packets in their bodies, and in any event, security will be scanning for guns and knives, not for powder, so everything should go smoothly. Since we have to keep ourselves above suspicion, which is why you and I aren't invited to the wedding, I've decided to take a short vacation. I'm going down to Mexico, and I'm taking the girl with me. I don't want her here when all this happens. Far better to be in a hotel watching the news as it breaks on television. Of course, you can always reach me if needed, but…"

Omar was shaking his head. His hand finally came up to interrupt Mohamed's discourse. "All in good time, my brother, all in good time. You have done well, but right now there's a more pressing matter that requires our attention." Omar stood and went to his desk, retrieving a sheet of paper, which he turned and handed to Mohamed.

It was an e-mail written in Arabic. Mohamed began to scan the page, picking up significant phrases:

"…He is close to death. The doctor says it's only a matter of time, days if not hours. There's no chance he will recover; the cancer has spread too far. He wishes to see Mohamed to bless him one last time before he passes into the arms of Allah…"

"I received this within the last hour," Omar said. "I know how hard this must be for you. You were just saying how everything is ready, and now this…it's a shame Sayyid won't be around to see it. I know it was his heart. A great tragedy. No one knew he was even sick. As you can see, you must return home immediately.

"I took the liberty of purchasing an airline ticket for you. Your plane leaves at midnight. That's less than three hours. I suggest you go home and pack and head directly to the airport."

CHAPTER 29

THE FLIGHT WAS BUMPY, but Mohamed had just survived turbulent weather in a commuter prop job, so riding out the storm in a 747 was a piece of cake. He reached up to tweak the air vent and adjust the light so he could see better as he thumbed through the pages of his in-flight magazine. He was settling into the boredom. It was a long ten-hour ride to Heathrow in London, followed by a two-hour layover and then another five-hour flight to Cairo. His stomach rose to his throat as the plane hit another gust of wind. At least he was riding a big bird. It was shaky, but it didn't feel like the fuselage was coming apart.

He only wished they'd peddle faster. Seventeen hours of plane and airport time, followed by a three-hour drive, was too long. It wasn't that he was afraid his uncle would die before he got there; it was that he was afraid his uncle wouldn't die soon enough. The interior lights flickered as the plane rocked from side to side. He had to get back in time to save Layla. The wedding was less than two weeks away. If his uncle lingered, it might prevent him from being there when she needed him most.

He turned another page and smiled at the obvious solution. *As Allah is faithful, I will do what I must.* It might just be the answer to his prayers, a chance to bring about Sayyid's demise on his own. He could see his hands wrapped around his uncle's throat, the old man's eyes growing dim as the lamp of his life was extinguished by the boy he thought was weak—the boy whose mother he had killed. Revenge was sweet.

But the idea also terrified him. Sayyid was a large man—and severe—a man not prone to suffering foolishness. A knife would be easier. Just one quick thrust. And he knew exactly which one to use—the gold-handled dagger with the sheath of jewels and that wicked crescent blade. Sayyid kept it in a glass case under lock and key as part of his collection. Mohamed had never had the courage to touch it before—*but with Sayyid bedridden?* His uncle loved bringing the bejeweled weapon out and showing it to his guests, telling them the story of the fifth-century *jinn* whose name it bore. He used it to impress them, a symbol of his wealth. It would be justice to die with it buried in his gut, the perfect way to bring his vanity to an end. Just slip the fine steel blade into that fat belly and....

But perhaps he should wait until his uncle blessed him first.

El Taher estate, eight years earlier

He was running along the shoreline, the waters of the Nile shimmering yellow in the afternoon light, the sky an azure shield over his head. The hot Egyptian sun scorched the earth, scalding his bare feet when he stood still, but that only provided him with incentive to keep moving. The ball was in front of him, spinning like a top, bouncing off mounds of dirt and tufts of grass, making progress a challenge. Getting through the maze took agility, but it was a fine way to hone his skill.

He looked up, distracted by a cloud of dust looming on the horizon. A car was speeding down the road toward the house. Sayyid was home.

Mohamed scooped up his ball and ran off across the field of freshly harvested beets, timing it so he'd be there when the car arrived. He skipped over trenches saturated with water, his feet squishing in the mud. The ball was tucked under his arm. He'd lost interest in his practice, no longer mindful of keeping the ball spinning ahead of him on the ground.

He slowed at the entry to the yard, careful not to trample Sami's roses. The black Mercedes rolled to a stop in front of the house, crunching the gravel driveway under its wheels. Mohamed waited as his uncle climbed from the back, his portly bottom barely able to squeeze through the door, even with the help of Sami, who took him by the hand. The driver stayed behind the wheel with the engine idling until Sami finished removing the luggage and carrying it into the house. His uncle stood watching as the car rolled around the corner to be parked under the shade of the canopy around back.

Mohamed stepped forward tentatively. "Uncle," he said, nodding respectfully. "I'm pleased you are home." He held the ball tightly under his arm.

Sayyid stared at him blankly, then nodded in return and started for the house. Mohamed fell in behind.

"Uncle, I need to ask you something."

Sayyid, now filling the threshold, turned to place his hand on the door-post, looking down. "Your feet are filthy. Go wash them before coming inside. Have you been playing soccer? Why are you not doing your studies? Have you memorized the eighth surah yet?"

Mohamed nodded. "Yes, Uncle."

"Repeat verse sixty-five."

"'O Messenger! rouse the Believers to the fight. If there are twenty amongst you, patient and persevering, they will vanquish two hundred: if a hundred, they will vanquish a thousand of the Unbelievers: for these are a people without understanding.'"

Sayyid turned to enter the house without responding.

"Wait!"

His uncle stopped, his face skewed with mounting displeasure. He was wheezing heavily. "What?"

Mohamed dropped his gaze, his courage fleeting. He drew an arc in the dirt with his toe. "I need to know if you're coming to the match on Saturday."

"What? You're mumbling. Stand up straight and speak clearly." His uncle frowned, waiting.

"I gave you a note from Sheikh Omar. He needs to know how many parents are coming. It's the match he arranged with the high school in Cairo. El Sheikh wants us to see what it's like playing against a team we don't know. You're the only one he hasn't heard from."

Sayyid's bushy brows furrowed. "So, Sheikh Omar sent you to deliver this message? This is how he sees to your education, by having you play soccer? Tell El Sheikh, no, I will not be attending this preposterous event."

"But...I thought you liked my soccer."

"What? Whatever gave you that idea? It is Sheikh Omar who likes your soccer. I think the whole body, mind, and spirit thing is absurd. Besides, I don't have time for such trivialities. Go wash your feet, and then come inside and memorize another surah. If you have time for soccer, you have time to study."

Mohamed stood looking down at the ball in his arms, fighting to control the burning in his eyes.

"Well, what are you waiting for? Go! You must never forget you are the slave of Allah. You exist for only one purpose—to do his bidding."

Something tugged at Mohamed's thoughts, something he'd read and questioned at the time but brushed aside in hopes of considering it another day. As he recalled, the pamphlet said men had the right to become the sons of God—not slaves. *Sons?*

The plane rocked. He stood, taking hold of the seat to keep from stumbling. It felt good to stretch his legs, though they'd only been in the air an hour. His grip tightened on the headrest as they slammed into an updraft. He hadn't looked at his ticket. He'd assumed he'd be flying first class, but upon boarding, the flight attendant had pointed down the aisle—*way* down the aisle—to a seat near the back. *Thank you, Omar.* Though in all fairness, it was probably the best El Sheikh could manage at the last minute. The next flight wouldn't leave until seven in the morning and would arrive seven hours later than the flight he was on. At least he had an aisle seat and an empty place between himself and the spiky-haired boy by the window playing computer games.

Mohamed opened the overhead compartment, holding on with his feet spread apart for balance, as he unzipped his bag. It was buried toward the bottom, but it wasn't hard to find. He withdrew the Bible. He'd promised to read it.

Ducking back under the compartment, he slid into his seat again and opened the book to "Matthew"—the section bearing his brother's name. He'd have to ask Sayyid about that *before* he killed him. *The book of the genealogy of Jesus Christ, the son of David, the son of Abraham.* Might as well start from the beginning. Seventeen hours might just be enough time to do it.

Al hamdullah, he was home! Waves of heat roiled up from the asphalt, but it was a warmth that welcomed him in a way he couldn't explain. The California sun just wasn't hot enough to warm his bones. Mohamed made his way to the curb, rolling his carry-on luggage behind. As an Egyptian citizen with nothing to declare, he'd made it through customs quickly. It felt good to speak Arabic again.

He raised his hand to hail the first taxi he saw. He might have rented a car, but he was anxious to get home. Filling out the paperwork would take time, and he didn't need a vehicle; his uncle had several he could use. His lungs welcomed the warm air. *Sobhan Allah*—Praise God—it was wonderful! He looked at his watch, noting his rumpled sleeve. It was just after three. He'd have to get his uncle's servants to clean and press his clothes for him.

He settled into the back of a small black-and-white taxi. The driver, a short gaunt man wearing a red fez, hustled the luggage onto the seat beside Mohamed and jumped in front to drive. He craned his neck around and began haggling the price, mistakenly thinking his passenger wanted transportation to downtown Cairo. Mohamed explained that his destination was a farm just outside Assyut. The man thought for a moment and, after assessing the cut of Mohamed's clothes, named a price so outrageous Mohamed opened the door and started to get out. The cabbie began a rapid-fire negotiation and ultimately lowered his fee to a more reasonable level, though he still insisted Mohamed cover his trip both ways because, as the driver pointed out, he would have to return without a fare.

Mohamed tried to stretch his legs so he could relax, but there was no room—376 kilometers with his knees tucked under his chin—and that after seventeen hours in a plane! He'd thought about traveling by rail, but he was too restless to wait. He didn't know the schedule and disdained the idea of having to loiter in the station until the train arrived. Besides, the trip took five hours, and if this camel jockey was worth half the money he was asking, he'd have him there in three.

He wrinkled his nose. The inside of the cab smelled of a thousand sweaty bodies—or maybe it was just him. His skin itched, his back ached, and he could feel an abrasive coating when he scraped his tongue against his teeth. But he was hours from being able to do anything about it, so he settled in and tried to enjoy the ride. His father had crossed the desert by camel. That had to be worse than this.

He swung his arm over the back of the seat, tilting his head to the side as he stroked his goatee. His father had given his life for Allah. Isa gave His life for men. *Aaaahhh*, he needed to rid himself of such unprofitable thoughts. He was asking too many questions. He grabbed his bag and unzipped it. The Bible was on top, within easy reach. The cabbie had his eyes on the road. Mohamed wavered, then changed his mind and zipped the bag closed again, lacing his fingers over his stomach. He closed his eyes and took a deep breath, but the passage wouldn't leave his head.

Isa said love your enemies; do good to those who hate you. He said the thief had come to kill and destroy, but He had come to give men life. In one place He'd left a town called Samaria, and when two of His followers begged Him to rain fire down upon the people who'd mistreated Him, He told them they were possessed of a different spirit. Isa said He had come not to destroy men's lives but to save them. *Father, forgive them, for they do not know what they do.* So foreign to the instructions Mohamed had been given. It defied practically everything he knew.

His father was a good man, kind and gentle—and courageous. He'd sacrificed his life for Allah, but Mohamed wasn't that brave. The service he would perform would require the lives of others, but not his own. *Aauuuggh! Fool.* Reading the Bible was feeding his already festering doubts. He should probably burn it the first chance he got.

He'd better find his uncle either already dead or standing at death's door, waiting to be pushed through. If Mohamed didn't have the strength to kill him before, where would he get it now? *Love your enemies, do good to those who hate you...*

Foolishness! He leaned his head against the window. They were passing through another village, virtually identical to all the others, a hodgepodge of buildings made of yellow clay. Sheep bleated and children played. It was like being thrust back a thousand years. America was blessed, there was no denying that, but was it because they served a different God?

He felt the heat on his face as he closed his eyes and drifted off to sleep.

His head bounced against the window, jolting him awake. *Flap, flap, flap, flap, flap.* The driver pulled to the side, catching Mohamed's eye in the rearview mirror.

"Ah, it is only a tire. Do not worry; I have a spare. You stay here. It will only take a moment to fix." The driver jumped from the cab, leaving Mohamed to swelter in the back of a tiny tin oven, baking in the sun.

CHAPTER 30

L AYLA LOOKED AT HER watch—11:00 a.m. The sun streaming in through broken clouds spoke of a fair autumn day, one of those made for riding bikes through the park or lying in the grass watching butterflies dance, without a care in the world. It might as well have been raining. She'd been up half the night sitting in the hospital, waiting for word on Matthew. She had to return to Westwood soon, but she couldn't bear to leave him alone, and she didn't have transportation.

Matthew's car was still parked at Las Brisas. She had seen it when she'd met Mohamed for dinner and prayed it wouldn't be towed. She couldn't move it—she didn't have the key—which meant she faced taking a bus. But she'd rather just ride back with Matthew when they released him—*if* they ever did! At the least, she wished they'd tell her what was wrong so she could determine a course of action.

Curled up in a chair, she'd been unable to sleep comfortably, which left her wrestling half the night with what to do about Mohamed. Every time she came to a decision, she talked herself out of it. At first light, she retreated to the hospital cafeteria to get a bran muffin and a cup of tea. After encouraging the nursing staff to please call her cell phone if there was any change, she walked to a nearby Internet café. And now she sat waffling over her decision.

She couldn't just ignore what she'd heard—but what if she'd misunderstood? She tried, but she couldn't quite bring herself to believe Mohamed would be mixed up in something so awful. She'd called him half a dozen times, willing to hear an explanation, but the phone message said he couldn't be reached, which meant his phone was either turned off or he was out of range. What if he was off doing something unthinkable? What if she waited until it was too late? *I know that means more dead...I'm committed, no turning back...The Great Satan must fall.* She knew who the "Great Satan" was. To the radical, the Great Satan was America. She *had* to report this to the authorities. The information was just too suspect to ignore.

She sat down at the computer and googled the Web site of Homeland Security. Matthew had called Mohamed a terrorist. Of course, he was just trying to provoke her—but it was like he *knew*.

The page loaded, but it was a jumble of information about cases being worked on and those already solved. She scanned the screen, looking for some way to leave a tip. The hollow ache in her chest made her question her actions. She must have misunderstood. Perhaps, but not likely.

She clicked on the words, "Contact Us." A phone number was listed, but she didn't want to talk to anyone. There had to be a way to make this less personal. She scrolled down until she saw the "Report Incidents" link. She clicked on it, trying to keep her fingers from trembling. The link took her to a site for the FBI. The banner read: "Suspected Criminal or Terror Activity." Mohamed was mischievous—at least he had been as a boy—but was he *really* a terrorist?

She recalled the incident with the falafel vendor and the way Mohamed had laughed when she'd questioned him about it over lunch. The man had stood at his cart outside the *ba aal* and lied, telling her if she wanted to ride the camel, she had to pay. He'd taken her money, smiled with a mouth full of brown teeth, and pointed his long-handled spoon. "Go tell the man to give you a ride," he'd said, withholding the fact that the rides were being offered for free.

Mohamed had been incensed. The next day, while the vendor was inside buying cigarettes, Mohamed had let his chickens out of their pen. The man had limped out of the store with his hands raised, nattering so fast he couldn't be understood. He'd hobbled around, trying to get his birds back, chasing them from one end of the street to the other while Mohamed stuffed two falafels, handing one to Layla and taking one for himself. They ran around the building and hid behind a stack of wood crates, giggling between delicious bites.

Mohamed called it justice, and perhaps it was, but she also remembered how, once they'd stopped laughing, he'd felt sorry for the man. Watching him drag his game leg around was pathetic. He wasn't able to catch the fugitive fowl. The poor man had a family to feed too.

Mohamed had burped and patted his stomach, showing his satisfaction, but he'd run off to help the man and ended up catching every last escapee, making sure each one was safely back in the cage. The man was so grateful that he offered Mohamed free falafels for a week.

Layla sat back, dropping her hand from the keyboard. A character, yes, but a terrorist? *I know that means more dead…The Great Satan must fall.* His words haunted her. What was she supposed to do? She looked up. *Lord, I need wisdom here.* Please help me decide. She stared at the link, "Online Report to FBI Tips." She held the mouse in her hand, tapped the plastic shell with her finger…then clicked.

The page requested her name, address, phone number, and a description of the suspected activity. She started to type, but then froze with her fingers curled over the keyboard. They were asking for *personal* information. Would he find out she'd betrayed him? What if they arrested him? Would he be held indefinitely—guilty until proven innocent? What if they needed her to testify at his trial about what she'd heard? Could she live with that? She blocked her name and backspaced, erasing it.

Maybe she should call and ask if there was some way to leave an anonymous tip. She picked up her cell phone, snapping it open as she clicked back two pages to get the number. She entered it, saw it on the display, but held her thumb over the call button, hesitating. *Please, Lord, help me do the right thing.* She pressed the key, looking around. Other people might hear her. She snapped her phone shut, interrupting the recorded message that had begun to play.

Layla walked from the Internet café down the Pacific Coast Highway toward the hospital, the doldrums of the sky in keeping with her mood. She stopped to listen to the surf pounding the shore at Aliso Beach. There was something about the thunderous *whoosh* and *gurgle* of the waves bubbling up on the sand that spoke to her confused mind. The clouds had rolled in, making the weather dreary, definitely not designed for sunbathing, and though she couldn't explain the appeal in words, she responded. She needed to find a place of contemplation. She needed a place to pray.

She removed her shoes. Hooking the heel straps around her finger, she made her way out across the sand toward a formation of rocks at the base of the seawall. Houses were perched atop the cliff, their view of the Pacific unobstructed. Homes of the rich and famous. Mohamed was right about one thing. America was self-indulgent. The money used to purchase one of those houses could feed an entire village like the one she'd grown up in.

Her dress was flapping in the wind. She was still wearing the outfit she'd bought so she'd look nice for Mohamed, but she also had on the light jacket she'd worn the day before. And even then she felt a chill.

Her hair swirled around her face. She scooped it behind her, twisting it into a rope, and held it against her neck. Pinning it up would be futile; there was too much wind. She waited until the foamy water pulled back and then, before another swell could build, scrambled onto the shelf. A wave was cresting, rolling in toward the rocks. She scrambled to move away, hopping from stone to stone until she was out of reach. Over her shoulder, she saw the wave split apart on the barrier, sending a spray into the air that a second later crashed at her feet.

Layla made her way to an outcrop of sandy stone and sat down. She was ruining her new dress, but she had the other one. She could always change again. A loose strand of hair caught in her mouth, but she plucked it out and combed her fingers through her tresses, considering once again how much she needed a shampoo and a bath...but for the moment she was stuck in Orange County without a place to stay. She didn't want to leave until she knew the doctor's prognosis. Would he tell her? She had to get Matthew back to UCLA.

The waves were breaking on the rocks, throwing misty gloves of white spray into the air. So many changes in such a short period of time. Two weeks ago she had been a medical student, happy to be earning her degree and following in her father's footsteps. She would spend her life helping others the way he had done, only from the safe shores of the good old U.S.A.

Matthew would have been part of her life somehow, though she'd had reservations about marrying him even before Mohamed appeared on the scene—*Lord, please, I really need You to tell me what to do.* She'd proved the two were brothers, causing one to lash out in anger and the other to be rushed to the hospital. Doubts about the sincerity of her love for Matthew were being played against the feelings she still had for Mohamed, though she wanted to discourage those feelings; she now questioned whether things were as they appeared to be—*is he really some kind of terrorist?* Her logic was at war with her emotions, and her emotions were winning. Otherwise, she would have made the call.

She looked at her watch. One o'clock. She had to be getting back to the hospital. *Lord, what would You have me do?*

She got up and dusted off her dress, but the dampness from the rock only smeared the dirt. *Ohhhhh!* What she wouldn't give for a washing machine and a shower. A wave was retreating, pulling back from the shore. Seeing her chance, she hopped from one rock down to the next until she stood in the sand again. She held her hair in one hand and her shoes in the other as she made her way up the beach to the road. The hospital was another mile down the Coast Highway, and that was at least a half-hour walk.

The nurses' station was its usual flurry of activity. Layla waited at the counter for the lady whose dark skin glowed like polished ebony to finish a phone conversation. The person on the other end of the line was in no hurry to get off. The nurse looked up and gave an apologetic shrug. Layla smiled weakly. She'd done nothing but wait since coming to this hospital.

The nurse finally put the phone down and caught Layla's eye. "Where have *you* been?" she challenged. Her tone was anxious, her bright red fingernails tapping the counter with excitement.

"Where have I been?"

"Looky here, girl, your boyfriend's been awake for hours and hasn't stopped asking about you for one minute. Now you get yourself in there and tell him you're all right and put his mind at rest."

Layla shook her head. "But...why didn't you call me? I left my number. Someone was supposed to call."

The smile dissolved from the nurse's face. "They didn't call you? I'm sure they did. I know they tried. Everyone's been looking for you."

Layla slipped her hand into the pocket of her jacket, producing the pink cellular device. "My phone never rang—not once. I've got it right here. Never mind. Where is he? Can I see him?"

The black lady pointed down the hall. "Sure, honey; straight down the corridor to the elevator, and then..."

Layla meandered through the hospital maze, dazed, avoiding wheel-chair traffic and the man mopping the floor. Her heart was speeding now, a jumble of anxiety and apprehension. She paused just outside the open door but far enough back to remain out of sight. On the other side of that threshold was her boyfriend, a man she had recently called her fiancé, and yet somehow she dreaded taking the next step. She should be rushing in with arms open wide, overjoyed at his being released from the hospital. Instead, she hesitated. Love was about being sure, and she was anything *but*. There were too many unanswered questions, too many conflicting emotions.

Matthew always claimed it was love at first sight. She called it the hand of God, but then, up until a few days ago, she'd thought he was Mohamed...

Ronald Reagan Medical Center, UCLA, one year ago

It was midway through a coronary bypass, and they were huddled around the surgeon in the OR. The retractors were holding, but a clamp slipped and blood spurted into the air.

"Get that!" the surgeon yelled, but his cardiologist was checking the patient's blood pressure, the perfusionist was operating the heart-lung machine, the anesthesiologist was monitoring the sedative, and his surgical nurse had turned to place a scalpel on the tray.

Matthew jumped in and, though procedures prohibited fledgling students from assisting, clamped the artery, cutting off the flow of blood. The doctor angled his head slightly to see who it was and went back to work without a word.

Only after the final sutures were in and the students out of the OR did the doctor finally turn to him and say, "Nice work in there. That kind of quick thinking is what we like to see. Saves lives." He peeled his latex gloves from his hands and walked away, leaving Matthew standing there with his mouth hanging open.

"Can you believe that?" Matthew asked, turning to the student standing beside him as he pulled down his mask.

Layla's eyes widened. She was staring into a face she hadn't expected to see. She reached behind her to untie her own mask, letting it fall away, and pulled her paper cap from her head. Her long hair fell loose in a wavy ponytail behind her.

Matthew took one look at those dark, exotic eyes and in his cocky, over-confident way said, "I don't know what you're doing later on, but if you're not busy, how 'bout marrying me?"

That was the beginning, and no matter how confused she was, she would be sorry to see it end. And that's why she dreaded taking the next step. She had rebuked Matthew for being jealous when—though she wanted to deny it—his suspicions were justified. Her heart had been wrongly swayed. If she were smart, she'd crawl in on her hands and knees, beg his forgiveness, accept his proposal of marriage, and get on with her life. Perhaps the thing that troubled her most was her inability to do just that.

She inhaled slowly, trying to quiet her heart. What if he greeted her with a smile and a warm hug, like nothing had happened when she knew it had? How should she react to *that*? *Please, Lord, help!* She needed strength and the right words to say. Matthew deserved better than a woman who couldn't make up her mind. Still, how could she choose one brother over the other when, in almost every respect, they were identical?

The one glaring exception was the God they served. Matthew loved the only true God. Mohamed worshiped Allah. That should disqualify him from the start. *God, please.* She drew in a deep, steadying breath and stepped tentatively into the room.

Matthew sat on the side of his bed, fully dressed. He looked up, acknowledging her as she entered, but didn't break into a smile. Nor did he get up and walk over to offer her a hug.

He knows. "Hi, Matthew. You're looking good. How are you feeling?" Layla stood her ground. She crossed her arms, feeling awkward.

Matthew's lips puckered, but he nodded. "I'm fine."

There was a silence neither seemed willing to break. Layla's gaze drifted from Matthew to the window. His room actually overlooked the ocean. *A room with a view.* But the instruments, the heart monitor, and IV were standard protocol. This wasn't intensive care. He must have been moved. She summoned the courage to speak first. "You ready to go? I can drive you home, but we'll have to get your car. It's still parked at the restaurant."

"Where were you?"

"What do you mean?"

Matthew stood, pausing for a moment to get his bearings, then went over to the closet for his coat. He slipped his arms into the sleeves, keeping his back to Layla as he swung the jacket over his shoulders. "Don't play dumb. I come out of a coma I've been in for forty-eight hours. I ask about you, but they say you've gone. I call your cell phone, but you don't answer..."

"Matthew, let's not get into this now." Layla reached for her phone. Maybe she had it switched off.

He turned around, tugging his shirtsleeves down around his wrists. "Nice dress. What happened to the one you were wearing?"

She shook her head. "Nothing. I just needed something clean."

He made an ingratiating face, his lips puckering into something closer to a smirk than a smile. "Yeah, real clean. Looks like you've been rollin' in the hay in that one."

She tucked her phone to her breast, looking back over her shoulder at her derriere. She reached to dust herself off again. "Matthew, I—"

"You what? You were too busy to make sure I'm all right, too busy to even call? Must have been something, or someone, awfully important. You were with *him*, weren't you?"

She flicked the phone open. *Oh, no.* She held out the flamingo pink device so Matthew could see. "Look, my battery's dead. The hospital tried to call too. I just went for a walk, that's all. I'm sorry, Matthew. I should have been here, but let's not argue. Can't we just go?"

"Go? Oh, absolutely. Let's just…go!" Matthew swept past Layla, marching out of the room and down the hall without looking back to see if she was coming.

Layla closed her eyes and sighed. It had begun. She turned and followed.

Matthew's oxidized yellow Volkswagen pulled to the curb in front of Layla's apartment. The last time they'd made the trip back from Orange County, Matthew was at the wheel, with Layla pretending to be asleep. This time she'd taxied him. Out the window a webby coastal gray covered the LA Basin, adding to the sober mood in the car. Neither had said a word the entire trip. It niggled Matthew that they hadn't been able to play music, but someone had smashed his antenna while he was in the hospital.

He sat looking through the streaked glass as a hazy sun broke through the clouds, glaring into his eyes. The doctor had sternly warned him not to drive, so he'd been more than willing to let Layla take over when she'd volunteered, though he'd refrained from telling her about his aneurysm or that his condition was unstable. Now he would have to risk driving himself home alone.

Layla turned off the engine and sat back, folding her arms.

Matthew struggled to straighten himself and twisted in his seat to face her. It was time to break the long silence. "Just tell it to me straight. Were you with Moped or not?"

"Matthew, don't call him that, not even in jest. He's your brother. We've driven all this way, and you haven't even told me what's wrong with you. What did the doctor say?"

"The doctor says I'm fine—not that it matters to you."

Layla placed one hand on the wheel, bringing her shoulder around to lean against the door. "How do you expect me to respond to a comment like that? You know it matters to me. Quit acting like a baby and tell me what the doctor said."

Matthew cocked his head to one side. "I told you he said I'm fine. I just passed out, no big deal. He may want to run a few more tests, and he wants me to lay off soccer for a while, but there's no real concern."

"Oh, Matthew. No more soccer? That must be hard on you."

"It's not the end of the world. I'll be out for only a few games. If he doesn't come up with a good reason to keep me out by then, I'm putting myself back in, regardless of what he says. OK, I answered your question. Now you answer mine."

Layla reached out to cup her hand over Matthew's. "I *was* with Mohamed," she said, squeezing his hand gently, but he jerked it back. "They wouldn't let me see you because, like you said, you were in a coma. He asked me to dinner, and I agreed because I wanted to see him alone—not to discuss anything private, but just that you two are so hostile toward each other. But there's nothing going on between us. All we did was talk, and then I came back to the hospital and spent a second night sleeping in a chair."

Her brow creased, stressing her sincerity. "I *was* with you the whole time, Matthew. I was only gone the hour I met with Mohamed and then this morning when I went for a walk. The doctor wouldn't tell me anything, and I was so worried, I had to get out and get a breath of fresh air to clear my head. I walked down to the beach to be alone and pray; that's all. That's how I got my dress dirty. Please don't be mad..."

Matthew opened the car door, letting it swing wide. He brought his foot out, planting it on the curb, and craned his head back around to look at

Layla. "I'm not mad," he said, "but I do have some things to think about." He swallowed the pit in his throat. Reaching for the door, he pulled himself from the car and stood with his hands in his hip pockets.

Layla got out of the driver's seat and came around to meet him. "Walk me to the door," she said.

Matthew held out his hand, waiting for her to deposit his keys.

"They're in the ignition."

"Some other time," he said. He sidestepped Layla and shuffled around the back bumper to climb in on the driver's side.

He cranked the engine to a start, clutched into first, and with the gearbox grinding, squealed away.

"Matthew!"

Matthew didn't leave because he was trying to be rude or obnoxious. He left because he didn't want her to see him cry. He pulled around the corner, pounding the steering wheel with his fist. *Why, God? Why are You doing this to me?* A tear rolled down one cheek and clung to his chin, then another. *She's my girl. I had her first. I don't understand. Are You really planning to kill me? I'm not ready to die, God, hear me? I'm not ready. I can't even tell her what's wrong with me. She's not gonna marry someone whose head could explode any minute, and if I don't tell her... Why are You doing this, Lord? What did I ever do to You?*

CHAPTER 31

THE SUN BURNED LIKE a welder's arc, cutting a white hole in the sky. OK, maybe the Egyptian sun wasn't *always* so nice. Mohamed mopped his forehead and glanced at his watch as the driver turned into the gates of the walled mansion. It was already seven. The trip had taken longer than anticipated. The flat tire had caused a half-hour delay that ruined his clothes. His shirt had become soaked with sweat and his hands and pants streaked with black tire marks. He almost regretted rolling up his sleeves to assist the driver.

The man had seemed embarrassed to accept help from his customer and kept insisting Mohamed wait in the car, but with the air conditioner off, the inside of the cab was unbearable. He had to get outside where there was air to breathe, and the little man was struggling to lift the tire from the trunk. At least they didn't have to suffer an invasion of desert crawlers; even the scorpions had sought the shade of the rocks.

Mohamed stretched as they pulled to a stop in front of his uncle's house. He reached into his pocket to pay the driver but had only credit cards and American currency, and the man refused both. Mohamed explained he'd have to find someone inside to give the man his money.

Sami, the oldest of his uncle's *khadem—How old was he now? Had to be at least eighty—*met him at the door. The servant's dark brown face was even more wrinkled than Mohamed remembered, and he was far more stooped, making him appear shorter, though he'd never been a man of great height. His toothless grin exposed rows of brownish pink gums. He spread his arms wide, embracing the prodigal.

"*Wahashteny, Ostaz* Mohamed. I missed you. Haj will be overjoyed you are here!" He stooped, picking up Mohamed's bag to carry it inside.

The horn from the taxi sounded. Mohamed reached out to catch the servant's arm. "The man still needs to be paid," he said.

Sami bowed and rushed into the house, returning a few seconds later with a fistful of Egyptian pounds. Thirty-five years of service to Sayyid had earned him oversight of the household budget. He handed the wad of bills to the cab driver without counting, knowing it was enough. The driver sat in his cab tabulating his fare and grinned as he quickly realized he'd received considerably more than the agreed-upon price.

"Haj has been asking for you," Sami said, using Sayyid's title rather than his name to show respect.

The smell of dried fruits, dates, and incense filled Mohamed with memories. He had long ago realized that he was one of the privileged. When most considered themselves fortunate to receive a small cake on their birthday, he was given lavish gifts—like the red bicycle with shiny chrome fenders he never rode because he preferred running with a soccer ball at his feet. But he had also borne the loss of his mother, waiting month after month for her return while suffering Sayyid's lie.

"I'll take your bag to your room," Sami said. "You must go directly to Haj. He is…" The old man shook his head sadly. "There is not much time. He left instructions for you to go in even if he's sleeping. He is determined not to die until he sees you."

Mohamed watched Sami trundle the small travel bag down the hall, his spindly brown legs protruding from his robe, his bare feet pattering against the hard tiles. Oddly, he would feel more regret when Sami died than he felt about the imminent death of his uncle.

He paused at the threshold of the main room, taking in the familiar surroundings: the posh rugs, the walls hung with his uncle's collection of antique Arabian swords, the land beyond the open window stretching all the way to the Nile with date palms, pomegranate trees, and acre after acre of crops. Soon it would all be his. But he didn't want it.

Sami's words from long ago echoed in his ears: *Be patient with him.*

Your uncle loves you. It is just hard for him to show it. The warmth he felt when Sami wiped his eyes—that's what he wanted. It was the only thing of value. He would leave it all to Sami. The only thing he cared about now was having Layla at his side. He could no longer imagine living in this world without her.

He found his uncle's bedroom at the far end of the hall. Sami had disappeared into the room where Mohamed knew he would spend the next few days.

Outside the door, he hesitated, trying to quiet his apprehension. What was there to fear? The man was dying. Mohamed squared his shoulders, standing erect. The door was slightly ajar. He brought his hand up and pushed until it opened wide.

His uncle lay under blankets embroidered with leafy Arabic designs. Mohamed eased over, not willing to disturb the dying—no matter what Sami said. *Allah all merciful!* The man was a shell of his former self, like a giant vacuum had sucked the life out of him. Most of his hair was gone, and what little remained was as bent and limp as dead grass. His skin was stretched over his skull, and his face was sallow under his bearded cheeks. He looked mummified—a skeleton with rotted flesh clinging to it. It was the cancer, of course; cancer had a way of eating one alive—*but in so little time?* A year ago Sayyid had come to California for a visit. Mohamed had noticed, but not mentioned, his uncle's loss of weight. It looked good on him—*but this?* He wondered if Sayyid had known even back then.

Sayyid's eyes began to flutter and then popped open. They rolled back and forth like he might be wondering where he was and then came to rest on Mohamed. His face brightened, his chapped lips forming a weak smile.

"I knew you would come," he said.

Mohamed nodded. The voice that once made him tremble had been reduced to a hoarse whisper. His uncle flopped an arm over, extending it toward a chair. "Please, have a seat." The breath escaping his lips seemed shallow.

Mohamed looked around. A chair of elaborate French provincial design stood in the corner. He picked it up, carried it to the bed, and sat down. He thought he saw his uncle nod, a mere lifting of the chin.

"You look good, my son." Sayyid took another halting breath, staring up at the ceiling. "You have done well. I've heard much about your accomplishments... reports that encourage me greatly. I wish I could be around to see your success, but it appears Allah wishes that I receive my reward. I called you home"—he rolled his head to the side, fixing his gaze on Mohamed—"not to watch an old man die, but to admonish you. It has come to me that your heart"—*uh, uuuh,* he struggled to breathe—"is softening toward the Americans."

Mohamed felt his fingers tighten around the edge of the chair, but he didn't respond. What could he say? He wasn't prepared to acknowledge or deny such a statement. He waited for his uncle to continue.

"This must not be so." Sayyid raised his head slightly, his voice stronger now. "Our neighbors laugh at us. Egypt is weak, they say. Our government has chosen the way of the Western world." He coughed and then wheezed, pausing long enough to gather strength. "We are not weak," he continued. "We possess a superior cunning and intelligence. You must not forsake your task, Mohamed. If this woman stands in your way, she must be removed."

Woman? "What are you saying, Uncle? If you are referring to the virgin I've been seeing, her name is Layla, and she's just as Egyptian as you and I and..."

"Is she not *Masehia*? Is she not Christian?" Sayyid's eyes narrowed, revealing the spirit of rage Mohamed had known as a child.

He drew in his breath, carefully considering his answer. "She is a person of the Book, Uncle. Under Sharia law, the very law you say we must observe, I'm entitled to take her as a wife."

Sayyid tried to raise himself but fell back against the pillows, though he rallied strength enough to reach out and grasp Mohamed's arm. He glared at his nephew, his eyes dark and burning. "Do not play the fool with me. You cannot hope to unite the nation if your own house is divided."

Mohamed didn't recoil. The bony fingers clutching his arm felt odd but not threatening. He held his uncle's gaze. "She will convert. I will see to that."

Sayyid relaxed his grip, letting go to tuck his hand under his beard. His fingers massaged his neck. "You're a bigger fool than I thought. Alas, it is the curse of our family, for I too was seduced. Nonetheless, I cannot permit you to be beguiled the way I was. You must end the curse."

Sayyid closed his eyes, and in the silence that filled the room, Mohamed began to wonder if his uncle had fallen asleep. He leaned forward, listening to the quiet rumble of his uncle's chest, but Sayyid's eyes popped open, causing Mohamed to reel back.

"I have decided you must bring me the head of your mother..."

"My moth—"

"You must prove once and for all that no woman can come between you and the will of Allah. When you go to your room, you will find that your passport has been removed from your luggage. I have had it put away for...safekeeping. You will not be permitted to return to America until you bring me Zainab's head...and if you do not...I have instructed Sheikh Omar to set the plan in motion without you."

"But...but my mother's dead."

Sayyid fluffed his beard and pulled his blankets up under his chin, his eyes once again fixed on the ceiling. "Sadly, I loved your mother too much. It is my curse to have kept her alive all these years."

"But you said she was dead!"

"A necessary deception. Your mother refused to recant her Christian faith, as I'm sure your girlfriend will also do. Sheikh Omar and I were determined to keep her from poisoning you with her lies...and we wanted to keep your mind focused on your training. You will not be able to convert this girlfriend of yours. El Sheikh told me this many years ago, but alas, I did not listen.

"Now I say it to you. I have decided you must pass this one final test. You must remove the head of your mother and bring it to me before I die. I want to look into those eyes one last time…I want her to know the fallacy of believing in a God who cannot save.

"Now go." He waved his hand in dismissal. "I'm too weak to argue with you. We will speak more of this tomorrow…after I have had time to rest."

CHAPTER 32

I T WAS 3:00 A.M., and Mohamed couldn't sleep. He lay on his bed with his hands behind his head, staring into the darkness. The blue-gray light from the open window was enough for him to make out shapes and shadows, leading him to believe it was almost dawn. But it was still early. This time he would say his prayers. Maybe all this was happening because Allah was displeased with his unfaithfulness.

He got up and walked to the window. The musty smell of the river greeted him, the sound of crickets and frogs drumming the air. A startled mouse scurried away from the wall, leaving tracks in the moonlit sand. He couldn't do it. His uncle should have known better than to ask. How could he think killing someone—*anyone*—was right? Sayyid needed to read the Bible. Perhaps Mohamed could point him to the verse that said unrepentant murderers didn't merit eternal life.

They were talking about his *mother*. He'd spent most of his childhood hating her for abandoning him and then, after he learned she was dead, hating himself for having hated her—and now to be told that she was still alive and he was to *kill* her? His head was throbbing. It was too much to take in.

The rows of date palms along the drive were bristling in the breeze, the stars flickering in the sky. It was a perfect night. Any other time he'd be praising Allah for his goodness. He turned back from the window, gazing into the room's dark core. So what? What difference did it make? If she hadn't converted to Christianity, she wouldn't have been taken from him, so in a way she *had* abandoned him. He *could* kill her. Sharia law allowed it. No! Sharia law *demanded* it. She had blasphemed Allah. She was a stranger, a person he didn't know. What made killing her any different from killing senators and congressmen? They had families, with children who loved them…

His stomach tightened. His hands were heavy. He brought them up, examining his fingers in the moon's pale light. They looked cold and dead, but were they the hands of a killer? Could they really shed blood? What if he didn't have it in him? Sayyid was right. He was weak. He wasn't trained to kill. He'd toured *that* youth camp. He'd watched the kids line up with swords to hack the heads off straw infidels. It required desensitization. You had to believe you weren't killing people. You had to be convinced you were killing bugs or rodents, things so disgusting they had to be exterminated for the good of man. It wasn't a skill he possessed.

He'd do it in a heartbeat if Allah required it of him, but Allah wasn't the one who was asking—it was his uncle. Allah held sway over life and death. He didn't need help. If he wanted someone dead, they'd be dead. But none of that mattered because Mohamed didn't have a choice. Sayyid *was* the law.

Mohamed tried to imagine what it might be like. He'd have to pull a mask down over his face so his mother couldn't see him. And even with that, he'd have to do it from behind. He couldn't stand having her look at him, even if she didn't recognize her executioner. What if he just closed his eyes, raised the sword above his head, and struck her down? Would her head roll across the floor, or would it wallow in a pool of blood? Would her eyes stare up at him, blinking in death?

Would he feel loss? Would he feel anything at all? As far as he was concerned, she was already dead. If she were suddenly removed from the planet, would she be missed? It appeared that no one but Sayyid, and maybe Sheikh Omar, knew she was even alive. She was an infidel, not worthy to live…but if so, what did that make Layla?

He began to pace, his skin feeling tight and prickly. He didn't have a choice. His uncle had the power to keep him there indefinitely. Mohamed had gone through his things, and, as promised, his passport was missing.

If he didn't follow through, Sayyid would call friends in high places and make sure he never left the country again—*ever*! Good-bye, Layla!

It was probably Sayyid who'd put El Sheikh up to spying on him, and it was very likely that someone was tracking him here too. He moved to the window and peered into the darkness. The black silhouettes of the palms and the fields beyond were visible in the moon's light, but he saw little else. If someone *was* out there, they were undetectable.

The idea of killing a helpless woman—his mother or any other—was disgusting. If he was destined to never see Layla again, it should be for killing Sayyid, not for refusing to kill his mother—*Allah, give me strength*. He had dreamed of it. The number of times he'd sat in his room with his door closed, devising a plan, were too many to count. It was time to bring justice. Besides, it wasn't like he'd really be committing murder. The man was practically dead.

His heart fluttered. He'd lived in the West too long. He had become soft.

He left his room, moving as stealthily as possible, sidling past his uncle's door and down the hall to his office. He'd seen Sayyid hide the key in his desk. He didn't need the knife. His uncle was so weak a child could strangle him, *but*—he slid back the drawer—the knife was backup in case he was wrong. The key was just where he expected to find it. He pinched the ring with his fingers and cupped it in his hand as he slid the drawer closed again.

He entered the hall, remaining close to the wall with his finger lightly touching it to guide him until he reached the living room. The couch—a French provincial design with an embroidered back and high swan-neck arms—clipped his thigh as he tried to slip by, *ouufffff!* Its wooden legs scraped against the floor.

He stopped, looking over his shoulder to see if anyone had heard. The room remained still. The glass case was just ahead, mirroring the moon's light. He stepped forward and inserted the key, raising the lid to remove the antique dagger. The blade was sheathed, the jewels on the gold handle glinting. The weapon felt strangely heavy in his hand. He gripped the dagger and silently closed the case. Hopefully, he wouldn't need to use it.

Without windows, the hall was darker than the living room. He moved more slowly, stepping lightly to keep his leather soles from clapping on the ceramic tiles. He paused just outside Sayyid's door to gather courage. His heart was beating loud enough to be heard through the wall—*thump, thump, thump, thump, thump.* He brought the hand with the knife up, pressing the hilt against his chest, trying to regulate the pace. Droplets formed on his brow. He could do this. He had to. It was either Sayyid or his mother—*or Layla.*

He smiled, his mustache moist with beads of perspiration. Sayyid said he was too weak to kill; he was about to prove him wrong. Mohamed raised the knife to wipe his sleeve across his brow. He had to stop his hands from shaking. He lowered his weapon, but the curved blade hooked his belt, jerking the dagger from his hand. It clattered to the floor.

Oh! He looked for the blade, but it had vanished. He took off running. When he reached the kitchen, he realized he should have gone to his room and ducked under the covers, but it was too late. He fled out the door.

Mohamed sat on the crest of a hill overlooking the Nile, with the sun rising over his shoulder and turning the water bloodred. He wrapped his arms around his knees as he stared out at the horizon. He couldn't do his uncle's bidding. And if that meant staying here and never seeing Layla again, *Inshallah*—as God wills, though he was in no position to barter with God since he'd missed *fajr*, his sunrise prayers—*again.*

He had to be getting back. The servants routinely rose at dawn to prepare meals and launder clothes. They would be up and about by now. He needed to bathe. If Sayyid confronted him about the knife, he'd say he'd taken it to slay his mother but had decided he couldn't go through with it. He'd thrown it down and gone out to pray.

His stomach rolled, empty as a rag wrung dry. His body felt like one big itch. He stood, looking at the crimson belt of the Nile as it cut across the Egyptian plain. Sayyid's crops could be seen stretching for miles in both directions. His uncle had done well for himself. He arched his back and rubbed his arms. Aside from a few catnaps on the plane and in the taxi, he'd been awake almost thirty hours.

He entered the house as quietly as possible, but there was no way to go down the hall without passing the kitchen. Would the knife still be on the floor where he'd dropped it? He veered around the coffee table with its gold-roped legs and ochre-marbled top, to check the glass case. The jeweled dagger had been returned to its place and the box closed and locked.

Heads turned as he passed the kitchen. "*Sabah el kheer, Ostaz* Mohamed"—good morning. Mohamed nodded but didn't respond. It was likely the servants thought he'd been to the mosque and was returning from *fajr*.

Steam rose in the bathroom. Mohamed scrubbed the grit from his skin. By the time he'd toweled off and dressed in the clean outfit Sami had pressed and laid out for him, he felt much better. He emerged from the bathroom a new man. His thoughts were focused. He could see clearly now that he'd overreacted. The way to reach Sayyid was through reason. He needed to use dialogue, not deadly force.

Perhaps Allah could tell him what to say to his uncle. He took his rug, the same one he'd used as a child, and spread it on the floor facing east and then removed his shoes. Better late than never. "*Allah Akbar.*" He recited his surahs and went down on the rug with his hands on his knees. The Christian Bible said death was an enemy—

Stop! He was doing it again. He had to purge his mind of impure thoughts. Christian ideas stifled the worship of Allah. But that's how he felt. Death certainly wasn't his friend. Christ the Messiah said He died that all might live.

Auugggh! He covered his ears with his hands. *Stop it, stop it, stop it!* He got up and sat on the edge of his bed, burying his face in his hands. He was weak—and a coward! He stood. *No*, those were his uncle's lies. His stomach growled. He needed food.

He entered the kitchen, where the smell of eggs, meats, and cheese greeted him. Suddenly he realized he was famished. Sami and two female servants he hadn't seen before were busy preparing the day's meals. Sami was wearing a tightly wrapped turban. He smiled, showing his mouthful of brownish gums.

"*Wahashteny*, I missed you, Mr. Mohamed. Please, the dining room is ready. Sit, sit. I will bring everything."

The display looked wonderful, a full course of his favorites. Mohamed grabbed slices of fruits, cheeses, breads, and meats off the trays and wolfed them down, not waiting to swallow one bite before taking another. He sat back and finished his meal with a cup of tea. The room was bright and, with the distraction of the servants to keep his mind off his decision, somewhat cheery.

He laid his napkin on the table. Sami entered with another tray of breads and meats and set the plate on the table. "*Bel hana wel shefa*"—enjoy.

"Oh, Sami, no, I couldn't possibly." Mohamed placed a hand on his stomach and burped to make his point. "I'm stuffed. What I'd like to do right now is see my uncle. Is he awake?"

Sami raised his hands with his palms up, shrugging his shoulders. "I do not know. He has not summoned me. I thought it wise to let him rest. I'm sure he did not sleep well last night with the excitement of your arrival."

Mohamed nodded. He left the kitchen, walking down the hall to his uncle's room. Sayyid had wanted to see him last night just to drop a bombshell. It was only fair to awaken him this morning to deliver a bombshell of his own. His heart was *thud, thud, thudding* against the walls of his chest.

He closed his fist and, with his knuckle extended, tapped lightly on the door. He waited a second to be acknowledged, but the room remained quiet. He knocked again, louder this time. He leaned his ear toward the door. *Nothing.* He pushed it open and entered, forcing himself not to be afraid—*fear is a place I no longer choose to go.*

Sayyid appeared to be asleep. Didn't matter. Mohamed was determined to say what needed to be said. He reached down to tap his uncle's arm but pulled back. Even without touching the cold skin, he knew—his uncle was dead.

El Taher estate, nine years earlier

Mohamed was glad to be home. He'd walked the two kilometers from the bus stop at the edge of the village, keeping his ball at his feet, not running, but controlling the ball nonetheless. Had his uncle known he was coming, he would have had a car waiting, but Sheikh Omar had dismissed the class a day early, saying something about meetings to attend and that the students were free to leave or stay overnight as they chose. Ramadan would begin in a few days; they were expected to be home. Most called someone to come for them, but Mohamed took the bus, just as he always did. He saw no reason to change. Sayyid wasn't likely to be there anyway.

He scuffed the dust as he traipsed down the road, leaving a yellow coating on his shoes. The house, set back behind the low wall that surrounded the yard, was a flurry of activity. Two or three men stood in front holding guns in their hands, their shoulders heavy with belts of ammunition. Others were loading crates into a van.

Mohamed grabbed his ball and trotted around the side, entering through the kitchen. He set his ball down and scooped a handful of *goz* and *loz* from a bowl and a few *balah* from the tray on the sink. Voices were coming from the living room. Tilting his head back, he poured the nuts and seeds into his mouth as he stepped closer, curious to see what was going on.

Wood boxes were stacked on the floor. A few bottles and bowls sat haphazardly on the coffee table. A camera mounted on a tripod stood ready to document the event. Mohamed bit down on a date. The substance was as sweet as sugar on his tongue.

In the middle of the room stood a bearded man wearing a vest. He extended his arms on both sides as a second man made adjustments to some kind of harness. Short lengths of pipe, with a wire running across the top to link them together, were positioned vertically around his chest. The wire continued up his arm to a device with a button the man held in his hand.

Sayyid stood to the side, observing. His back was to Mohamed, his huge body blocking most of the room from view. He brought a hand to his chin. "That looks fine," he said. "Take his picture and get him into the van, and then get the rest of these boxes out of here."

Mohamed turned and slipped out the door. He ran around the back of the house into the field, trampling the cane underfoot. Sayyid would be angered by his flagrant disregard for the value of the crops, but he didn't care. Hot tears washed his face as he spit out the remainder of a date that had become bitter in his mouth.

It may have been someone else, but in his mind he'd witnessed his father preparing to die.

Mohamed stared at the shell from which Sayyid had somehow been removed. Where had the life gone? When the body was alive, Mohamed feared it and wanted it dead, but now it was gone and all he felt was pity. But he also saw justice. Had this man lived another day, he would have killed again, beginning with Mohamed's mother. For all his faults, he had served Allah well. Now Allah would receive his soul into paradise with open arms, a welcome friend of the Muslim Brotherhood, upholder of the creed: "Allah is our objective. The Messenger is our leader. Quran is our law. Jihad is our way. Dying in the way of Allah is our highest hope."

Mohamed stared into the vacuous eyes of his departed uncle. Why did God reward men for death? Why not for life? Perhaps in that one thing, the Christian way was better. He leaned over and whispered, *"Allah Akbar"*— Allah is great, first in Sayyid's right ear and then in his left. He straightened himself. Folding his hands in front of him, he turned around. There stood Sami, ever faithful.

"Do not worry, Mr. Mohamed, we knew this time would come. Everything is ready."

Sami left the room and a few minutes later returned with a man who walked slowly, carrying a bowl of water. Mohamed stepped to the side. The body had to be cleansed for burial. The man leaned over, stuffing Sayyid's nose, ears, and mouth with cotton, then stripped the clothes from the body so he could wash it head to toe.

Four men came in carrying a long, unvarnished box. They set it down, moved a respectful distance back, and remained huddled in a group, waiting. Sami's efficiency amazed Mohamed. Nothing was left to the last minute; everything had been arranged in advance. The man doing the cleansing finished toweling Sayyid and nodded to the others, who stepped forward, lifting the body so it could be wrapped in linen. The pallbearers were bearded men, dressed in long *abayas* with flat-topped caps circling their heads. Together they hefted Sayyid's body into the box. A year ago they couldn't have managed it without help, but now it seemed they were lifting a sack of dry bones.

They said nothing as each took hold of a corner and lifted the box onto their shoulders to carry it from the room. They were followed by the man with the washing bowl. Mohamed and Sami fell in behind. The troop shuffled down the hall and out the front door into the bright morning sun. An old pickup was parked in the driveway. The men loaded the box containing Sayyid's body into the back.

Mohamed gazed out across the yard. A crowd was gathering on the other side of the wall. Fifty or more of Sayyid's workers lined the streets. Two of the men got into the truck's cab, and two climbed into the rear. He heard the engine turn over, and with a *clunk* and a *clank*, the truck started down the drive.

Sami appeared at the door, holding a ring of keys. "These start your uncle's car. Yours now, I think. Sorry, but there is no driver. He was fired when Haj became no longer able to travel. Here. The truck will wait for you. You must follow it to the mosque."

Mohamed nodded, taking the keys. It wasn't necessary that he attend, but it was expected. He felt the weariness in his bones. What he needed to be doing was searching for his mother.

"Come with me," he said to Sami.

"No, Mr. Mohamed, I will walk. See, everybody walks," Sami said, extending his hand toward the people in the street.

Mohamed shook his head. "I want you with me. I don't want to be alone."

Sami nodded, but his wrinkled face held a frown. He stepped inside to get a pair of sandals.

Mohamed forced himself around back where the car was parked under a canopy. The vehicle was new, but it looked like it hadn't been washed in months. Dust layered the shiny black lacquer, making it appear dull and old. Mohamed climbed in, flicked on the air, and drove the car around to the side of the house to pick up his *khadem*.

As he climbed in, the old man's eyes were bright as a child with a new toy. "This is the first time I've been in a car such as this," Sami said, patting the seat.

The people parted to let them through. The car rolled into the street and pulled up behind the truck. An arm shot out the window and waved. The vehicle began moving forward. Mohamed had to wonder if Sami wasn't right. Maybe he should have walked; at such a pace it would take forever to reach their destination. The throng of people fell in behind, and the funeral procession began the slow, two-kilometer march to the mosque.

Built on the northwest corner of an intersection bordering three properties, the mosque served the farm community, giving the laborers a place to perform their daily *Salawat*. The local imam, Sheikh Mustafa, was waiting. A runner had raced ahead to inform him that Sayyid El Taher was dead.

Mohamed could see the imam standing at the entrance, watching the procession slowly moving his way. Dozens of people gathered in front of the building, the crowd milling about the vehicles. Sheikh Mustafa stepped back inside. Sayyid's family and friends had been notified, so the funeral could proceed without delay. The idea was to get the body into the grave as quickly as possible; the time for mourning would come later. Mohamed looked around. It was a small mosque. There wasn't enough room for so many people.

He made his way through the assembly, leading the men who carried the box. Sheikh Mustafa instructed them to bring the casket inside as far as possible, but though the people were jammed in tight, some were still obliged to remain outside.

El Sheikh had the men drape the coffin in a green shroud embroidered with gold thread. The crowd settled down so he could begin his prayer. Unlike the pomp and ceremony that attended Western funerals, Muslim burials were simple affairs that generally occurred without respect to the individual's status or station in life. Sheikh Mustafa prayed over the head of Sayyid while all those who were in attendance stood at his feet, and that was it.

The men raised the box onto their shoulders and carried it out. The burying place was a family site where several generations were already entombed. The box was set down at the base of the sepulchre and the lid removed. Reaching in, they lifted the linen-wrapped corpse from the wooden crate. The container was only meant for transportation and was now set aside to be used the next time someone died.

The tomb was aboveground. The mound had been built to contain the remains of several family members. They placed Sayyid's body inside, where the bones of his father and mother were already laid. The remains of Fatma, Sayyid's first wife, were also there.

Up until last night, Mohamed thought his mother had been placed there too. But if his uncle's deathbed confession proved to be right, she was alive. The problem was—where?

CHAPTER 33

A LONE PELICAN FLEW BY, a silhouette on a shimmering red sky. Layla watched as the bird landed on a rock surrounded by water and raised its head to ingest the fish it had caught. Waves crashed with a thunderous roar, only to be sucked back with a *whoosh*, leaving the shoreline bejeweled with fingernail shells sparkling in the crimson light of the dying sun.

She shivered, wrapping her arms around her shoulders. Tendrils of hair, whipped by the onshore wind, furled around her face. The sun was slumping into the Pacific. She inhaled the salty brine, the smell of washed-up seaweed, crustaceans, and decomposed fish. She had come to seek solace, hoping the Lord would tell her what to do. She hadn't heard from either Mohamed or Matthew. She knew Matthew was hurting. He had to have sensed her withdrawal. It grieved her to know that, while she never intended it, her words and actions were the cause of his pain. She wished he would call and allow her to explain but feared if she took the initiative and called him, he might misunderstand her intentions. Any encouragement now would only deepen his wounds later.

She *had* tried to reach Mohamed, but she assured herself it wasn't to pursue romance. She just wanted clarification of the conversation she'd overheard. She was still conflicted over not contacting the FBI, but she couldn't bring herself to do it, not without approaching him first. It was only fair. But every time she called, she got the same voice message: *The party you are trying to reach is either unavailable or out of the service area.*

It appeared Mohamed had fallen off the map. Another wave crashed onto the shore, scattering seagulls in its wake.

The sun was swallowed by the ocean and the light faded, taking with it all residue of warmth. She pulled her sweater in tight, picked up her purse, and stood, looking out over the vast expanse of rolling green. "Lord, only You know what's going on with Matthew and Mohamed, so I'm asking that You watch over them and bring healing and reconciliation into their lives. Please help Matthew not to be angry with me. You know I didn't mean to hurt him, but You're the one who brought Mohamed here, so what do I do now? And it looks like Mohamed is gone too...maybe I've lost them both. O God, please work on Mohamed so that he comes to know You. That's all I ask."

Layla stepped down off the shelf of rock and made her way up the beach. Scavenger gulls cried and took flight as she passed, but they landed again only a few feet away, continuing their search for morsels left by the daily invasion of tourists. In the distance, on the other side of the beach, she could see Las Brisas perched on a cliff, its windows filled with light. A crowd of happy-hour clientele milled about the patio with drinks in hand. It looked charming and romantic. She could imagine herself and Mohamed there, arm in arm, watching the sun as it set over the ocean, but it wasn't to be. The thought made her melancholy. They had met there three times, and each rendezvous had ended in misunderstanding and regret.

She passed under the lee of the Laguna Beach Hotel. The building was a monument to the grand old days, when the rich and affluent visited the tiny tourist town to celebrate their wealth and good fortune. Those were the days of shiny chauffeur-driven Rolls-Royces, filled with movie stars wrapped in furs. Today the tourists were more modest, usually families from Midwest suburbia, a mom and dad with three kids in tow, returning from a day at Disneyland. She stepped off the beach onto the sidewalk, the sand crunching under her feet.

The intersection of Forest Avenue and the Coast Highway was usually a glut of traffic, but this evening it seemed unusually quiet. She leaned into the lamppost and pressed the pedestrian button, waiting until the light turned green before crossing.

216

The stores featured random displays of bric-a-brac and fine art, along with clothing and accessories. She stopped to look in a window at a purse stitched with tiny shells and caught a flicker of movement from the corner of her eye. But when she turned to see what it was, the street was empty. She shook her head and pulled her own purse up onto her shoulder. The seventy-nine-dollar price tag on the one in the store window was *way* too much.

Cars were usually parked on the street, angled toward the storefronts, but most of them had moved on. She'd forgotten that the shops closed early on weeknights. A shadow flickered, giving her a start. The lights were out and the dark glass a reflective mirror. Suddenly a man appeared at the window. She jerked back. *Silly.* It was just the store owner slipping a "Closed" sign onto the sill before walking away.

The street was dark and not nearly so inviting as it had been earlier when it was bustling with people. The traffic was so thick, she'd had to park several blocks away. She stopped, pausing to look at herself in another window. Someone ducked into the shadows behind her, or was it her imagination? She turned. "Mohamed? Is that you?" Her voice sounded strange in the broken silence.

A car turned the corner, catching her in its yellow beams. She spun around and began walking down the street faster. Laguna Beach was known for its art and upscale stores, but it did have its seedier side. During the sixties it had been invaded by hippies who followed their guru, Dr. Timothy Leary, in storming the gates of paradise with a subculture of drugs, flower power, and free love. She could feel the residual influence even now.

She increased her pace, not because she really believed she was being followed—that was absurd—but because it was cold. She clutched her arms, massaging away the goose bumps. Thinking she heard footsteps behind her, she stopped, bracing herself, and turned around, but no one was there. *This is silly.* She had to get a grip, yet she couldn't shake the feeling that she was experiencing some kind of premonition. She passed a small café, where people were clustered around tall tables sipping coffee. A welcome relief. It was good not to feel alone. She picked up her pace, turning right at Glenneyre Street. She was parked just down the block.

As she approached the lot, she spotted her car, one of only a few remaining. Her purse fell from her shoulder and caught on her forearm as she crossed the street, fishing for her keys. She heard the sound of someone's feet on the pavement behind her and tossed a glance over her shoulder. It was a man in a business suit—short cropped hair, clean-shaven—probably on his way home from a hard day's work. Certainly not someone to be afraid of. Her car and the shelter it provided were just ahead.

A sigh escaped her lips as she reached out to slip her key into the lock. She saw a reflection in the car window... *uuhhh!* The man was standing behind her! She started to turn. The lights of the car beside her popped on, and the engine sprang to life. She raised her hand; *ohhhhhh,* a pair of arms clamped around her, holding her tight. The man's warm breath was fetid, a mingling of fish and onions.

Layla tried to push herself away. She was fighting to scream, but a hand covered her mouth. She recognized another smell—ether. She struggled again, but her strength failed. Her body went limp as she passed out.

CHAPTER 34

MOHAMED DROVE HIS UNCLE'S Mercedes like a spear flying across the desert—not unusual in Egypt where it seemed the speed laws were made to be broken—but Mohamed was driving in a particular frenzy. He was anxious to find his mother. The shock of realizing she might be still alive was foremost in his mind. He should have insisted Sayyid tell him where she was *before* he died. Now he had to find her without help. He'd interviewed every household servant and every laborer in the field but had come up blank. He'd searched every room in his uncle's estate, even the barns where livestock and crops were stored, but to no avail.

The questions had begun with Sami, who looked at him like he'd lost his mind. The old man's face bunched up like a child about to cry. "You need not look for her, *Ostaz* Mohamed; she will not be found." The search should have ended right there. If Sami didn't know where she was, no one did.

Now he was at a complete loss. For all he knew, his mother was being held captive in another country. Sayyid originally said she'd gone to Europe. Maybe he wasn't lying—*at least about that.* But his uncle wanted her head, and he wouldn't have expected Mohamed to smuggle it across international borders. Airports routinely X-rayed baggage. No, he must have meant she was being kept nearby.

He swerved and jerked the wheel back. He'd been driving on the shoulder again. He shook his head and slapped his cheeks. He had to stay awake. The last time he'd been on this stretch of road he was with his mother, holding her hand. They'd been picked up by a man delivering produce to Minya—a truckload of melons that Sayyid had subsequently destroyed.

. . . ☽ . . .

Minya, Egypt—twelve years earlier

The shed provided little shelter, but it was better than sleeping in the street. Zainab wrapped her *galabia* around Mohamed, drawing him to her bosom to keep him warm. He stirred and blinked his eyes open. The grayness around him told him that morning was fast approaching. He felt his mother's head move, heard her whispered prayer. "Isa, please, can You not save? If You choose not to protect me, at least take care of my son."

"What did you say, Mother?"

She wrapped her arms more tightly around him. "Nothing, just rest. We have a long way to go."

A mouse skittered by, disturbing a piece of aluminum flashing, the sound magnified by the morning stillness.

"Mother?"

"Yes, Mohamed."

"Where are we going?"

She hesitated. "There are bad men out there," she said. "Your father listened to them when he should not have. I refuse to submit to their ways, and this makes them angry. If they catch us, they will take you from me, and—I want you to promise me something, Mohamed—if something should ever happen to me, promise me you won't become like them. Promise me?"

"I promise."

She nuzzled her chin against his hair. "My prayer for you is that someday you will know Isa."

• • •   🌙   • • •

Mohamed ground his teeth, his hands squeezing the steering wheel. A thousand times more than a thousand, he'd regretted calling out to Sayyid. But he'd been a child; how could he have known? It was time to make restitution. Sayyid was dead. He would find his mother and bring her back.

The dust plumed up behind his tires as he squealed around another bend, his wheels sliding on the sand swept across the road by the wind. He rubbed his eyes, trying desperately to stay awake.

At least he'd recovered his missing passport. He'd asked Sami about that too. "Your uncle asked me to remove it for safekeeping," the old man had said. Sami had run off and returned a few minutes later, passport in hand. "This is your house now, so now I serve you." He smiled his big toothless grin, lifting his hands with his palms turned up.

The long shadows disappeared as the earth rolled away from the sun and covered itself with a blanket of dusk. Evening was already upon him, and he still hadn't slept—*was this day two or three?* He looked up through the sunroof at the murky sky and shouted, "Allah...God...whoever You are, tell me where she is!"

He'd looked everywhere he could think of, and now, even though it was a long shot—one that could cost him several hours of valuable time if he were wrong—he was screaming toward the town of his birth. He didn't even know if anyone still lived there or if the village still existed. He hadn't been there in more than a dozen years.

The small blip on the surface of the desert grew into a bump, then a cube, and then broke apart and became a pattern of small rectangles, forming the town's silhouette. He pulled off the highway onto a dirt road, refusing to slow down, even though the beam of his headlights revealed he was bouncing over sand knolls and rain troughs, pounding his shock absorbers into scrap metal. The levee of an irrigation ditch was off to his right, but he couldn't tell if it contained water.

He wasn't sure he'd even recognize the place. He slowed as he pulled onto the main road. It looked like several new additions had been built, but it was the same village, still alive, though some of the landmarks he'd expected to see were missing.

Then he saw it, the small *ba aal* where the villagers bought groceries. Layla had shared a good part of what her mother gave her, buying him ice cream and chocolate bars there.

He pulled the car in front of his old house, the dust swirling up around his fenders. The place appeared to be abandoned. Killing the engine, he stepped out and closed his eyes, trying to quell the thumping in his chest while containing an urge to rush in and rescue his mother. He wasn't sure he was ready to see her. What would he say? Of course, there was a good chance she wasn't even there; after all, the house might be occupied by someone else now.

He stood on the terrace and knocked. The door creaked open. He stuck his head in, looking around. The place was deserted. It was foolish to have come. Sayyid wouldn't try to keep someone here; escape would be too easy. He walked into the main living space, puzzled by how small the room actually was. He knew he hadn't lived in a mansion, but his childhood memories had conjured up something larger than this. He could almost reach out and touch both walls at the same time.

He had only the light of the moon, but it was enough to see that the place was in shambles. He felt the pressure of the past thirty-six hours weighing on his shoulders. He hadn't slept, not really slept, in all that time. He stood in the room where he'd stayed as a boy, leaned his back against the wall, and slid down into the dirt. Sayyid had to be keeping his mother in Asyut, or Cairo, or some other big city where she'd never be found.

His shoulders began to heave, the tears pouring down his cheeks. He wrapped his arms around his legs, burying his face in his knees, and collapsed onto his side.

He couldn't say when he fell asleep. He couldn't say for certain he actually *was* asleep. In the darkness he saw a motion picture of himself, projected on the rough surface of the mud brick wall. He was standing in the shallows of the Nile with a line of men and women waiting to be washed by him, but they seemed nervous, like they were afraid.

He woke with a start and staggered outside into the cool night air. Clouds covered the moon like a pile of silver boulders, but there was enough light to see. He leaned over with his hands on his knees, catching his breath. He shouldn't have fallen asleep. He had to resume his search. He shook his head, trying to focus. Where else could he look? He stumbled forward, feeling the ache in his body. *Ohhhoooooooo*. That's what he got for sleeping on the ground. His back was a mess.

The dream troubled him…people wanting to be washed in the Nile? He turned and saw the river shimmering in the moon's light. He put a foot forward, then another, not sure if he was heading for the water or just walking off his aches and pains. The moon found a portal in the clouds and seemed to be guiding his way.

Three small feluccas stood at the river's edge, leaning over at an angle, their sails removed for the night. He kicked off his shoes and socks, watching as the moon danced on the water, reminding him of lemon slices swirling in a glass of cold tea. In a daze, he righted the outermost boat and began pushing it back into the eddies of water. It was foolishness. He had no oar, no sail, and he didn't know how to swim, but he kept sliding the boat back until it was free of the shore, floating in the river. He set the vessel adrift and climbed in, lying on his back to look up at the moon.

He folded his hands over his stomach and laughed. His lack of sleep was driving him mad. He sat up, pulling his legs in to brush the silt from between his toes. His pants were wet to the knees. The gentle rocking was like a cradle. His eyes started to droop, the lids sliding down like evening shades on a window. He felt like lying back and falling asleep, but he forced his eyes open. He leaned over the side, splashing water on his face, and saw the reflection of the clouds on the broken water, slipping along the side of the boat like the petals of a white rose.

The moon swirled and changed shape as it rolled on the river. Suddenly he was blinded by its brightness. He raised his hand to block the light. *What?*

When he looked at the water again, he saw the clouds had taken the form of a man, or was it a man on a horse? The rider raised a sword: *"Ask, and it will be given to you; seek, and you will find; knock, and it will be opened to you."* The image was soft and indistinct, the motion of the water too rapid to make out detail—but the voice? Were the words inside his head or coming from somewhere else?

The white horse! Now he knew where Sayyid was keeping his mother.

CHAPTER 35

IGH NOON ON THE desert. The sun bounced off the earth in waves of corrugated heat, making the building on the horizon appear soft and indistinct. Mohamed rolled slowly down the lane, too slow to even raise dust, and brought the car to a stop in front of the palace. He'd taxed the engine getting there, but now, with date palms shading him and his air conditioner running full tilt, he hesitated, reluctant to leave the car's placid interior. This had to be the place. But what if it wasn't? The vision—or at least the voice—had said: "The white horse," though he might have imagined it. Or perhaps his lack of sleep had made him delusional.

He leaned in to switch off the ignition. He had about a minute before it became too hot to stay inside. The edifice loomed in front of him. It was the perfect hideaway, a shrine built for Sayyid's precious horse—the glorious house of Prince. That horse had been bought with blood money, a curse to the man who possessed it. Or so his mother had said.

Thirty kilometers off the main road and nestled in the desert, the land had been expropriated, though Sayyid preferred to say its former owner had gratefully transferred the title to him as penitence. The man had been caught living with a woman to whom he was not married. Allah, in return, had graciously spared his life and sent him away. The woman, who in pleading her case claimed her former husband had been abusive, was not so fortunate. Her adulterous bones were to be found somewhere in the desert. Only Allah knew where.

Sayyid was happy to take possession. He'd always coveted the property. It was a place of beauty, an oasis in a barren land. The seventy palm trees had been planted by the previous owner, but it was the natural spring that gave them life, an ever-replenishing source of water.

In front of Mohamed stood a stable as beautiful as any mosque, but built for a horse. He shook his head. Sayyid would not have tolerated such hypocrisy from anyone else. Animals were not to be worshiped. Islam rejected the evils of Egyptian pharaohs who made gods of birds and beasts. Rather, they rightly chose to follow the Law of Moses: "You shall not make for yourself a carved image, or any likeness of anything that is in heaven above, or that is in the earth beneath, or that is in the water under the earth." Pictures of men or beasts—be they insects, mammals, reptiles, birds, or fish—weren't to be found in places of Islamic worship, not even on the rugs upon which they knelt. A shrine like this, built for an animal, was pushing the limits.

He stepped from the car, the rhythm of his heart increasing at the prospect of what he might find. Ceramic tiles and Arabic patterns surrounded the exterior of the building. It may have been built for a horse, but it was still a place of worship, even if Sayyid had summarily executed the object of his devotion.

A desert oasis, eleven years earlier

The sun had not yet topped the horizon when Mohamed finished his morning prayers and, hoping to catch a few minutes of extra sleep, lay down, placing his head back on the pillow.

"Prayers start the day, Mohamed. Get dressed. I have something to show you." Sayyid stood at the threshold of his room, his massive bulk filling the doorway.

Mohamed rolled his legs off the bed and sat up, rubbing his eyes. "What?"

"You'll see. Sami has a meal prepared. Eat something, and be at the car in fifteen minutes."

They drove into a sun that looked large and red as a pomegranate as it rose over the desert. The driver wore dark shades to shield his eyes against the glare. Mohamed sat beside his uncle, uncomfortable with the weight of Sayyid's body squeezing him against the door.

They pulled up in a cloud of dust that settled like the drawing back of a curtain as they climbed from the car. In that moment Mohamed got his first look at the palace. The tiles gleamed in the morning light, obscuring their design, but in his mind, it was the Taj Mahal. It was the most beautiful thing he'd ever seen.

"Well, what do you think?" His uncle stood beside him wearing his royal regalia, the turban and sash of a sultan.

Mohamed looked down, scuffing the dirt with his toe. "It is very nice, Father."

"Very nice? Stand up straight, Son." Sayyid spread his arms out in front of him. "This is the work of a master builder. This is the palace of a prince."

A man with a humble *galabia* hanging to his knees led a horse by a leather strap. He held the tether close to the horse's mouth, giving the animal little room to negotiate, thus keeping it under tight control. He circled the inside of the fence, bringing the stallion up beside a tier of three steps. The horse was already saddled and ready as Sayyid crossed the paddock, tapping his leg with an English riding whip. The trainer held the animal still while Sayyid climbed the stairs and mounted the pristine white steed. He took the reins and laid them against the stallion's neck, turning the animal away. The horse pranced just the way Mohamed remembered seeing it a year earlier.

Sayyid managed to maintain his balance with one hand on the pummel and the other holding the reins as he tried to hold the horse in check. "Open the gate. We're going out for a ride."

The man did as he was told, lifting and pulling the gate back. Sayyid let the horse prance, its hoofs high-stepping in anticipation of a run. They reached the opening, and he gave the animal a sharp kick to the ribs, but as he did, Mohamed heard a *sssssppffffff* and caught a quick movement. A horned viper sat coiled, ready to strike. The horse reared back, pitching

Sayyid to the ground. His uncle struggled to his feet as the horse retreated, circling the inside of the fence, leaving Sayyid at the snake's mercy. "Do something!" he screamed at the trainer.

The trainer grabbed a rake and poked it at the viper. It sprang but hit the wood prongs and fell, twisting to the ground. Rolling to its belly, it quickly slithered off.

Sayyid turned and, looking rather foolish, waddled into the barn, returning with a rifle in his hands. Mohamed thought he was going after the snake, but instead he pointed his weapon at the stallion's head and pulled the trigger. The crack echoed off the nearby hills.

"That will be the last time you ever throw me!" Smoke was still wafting from the barrel as Sayyid tossed the rifle to the ground. He turned, glaring at the trainer. "Get that carcass out of here and get off my property. You're fired!"

Mohamed had to wonder if his uncle ever regretted that temper of his. He scanned the side of the building. The living quarters for the caretaker, the man Sayyid fired the day he shot the horse, were attached, just as he remembered.

Mohamed approached, cupping his hands to his mouth. "Mother, Mother, are you there?" The windows had been boarded up and the door padlocked. He knocked softly at first, and then more loudly. "Mother?" He stopped with his hand mid-stroke. *Ask, and it will be given to you; seek, and you will find; knock, and it will be opened to you.* He had asked, he had sought, and now he was knocking. He resumed rapping and put his ear against the wood, but he didn't receive an answer.

He flipped the padlock upside down, examining it. There wasn't any dust clinging to the brass, not like he'd expect to see if it had been hanging there all those years without being opened. He stepped back. There was no point in trying to smash the lock—better to pry the hasp from the wood. All he needed was the right tool.

He went around to the front of the stable. It too had been secured, only its brass lock was tarnished and dirt-encrusted. He walked the entire circumference, letting his hand ride along the smooth tiles, noting the intricate detail in their design—the work of a master craftsman. The window around back was covered with slats, but there was a gap between two of the boards. He squeezed his fingers into the narrow slit and began pulling and pushing, back and forth, until the plank worked loose and the nails on one side gave way. *Ahhhhhhgggh!*

He bent the board back and, by twisting, ripped it from the frame. The window was now exposed. The glass shattered as he smashed it with the board. He spent a few minutes clearing the shards away. He had an opening, but not yet big enough to crawl through. He looked around, found a stone the size of his fist, and reached in, hammering the backside of the other boards until they came loose and fell to the ground.

Making sure the windowsill was free of broken glass, he shimmied into the opening and slipped through to the other side, extending his hands to block his fall. He rolled into a sitting position and caught his breath. Specks of dust floated on the beam of light streaming through the window. It took a minute for his eyes to adjust. He tried peering into the darkness.

"Mother? Is anybody here?" His voice was louder than he intended. It occurred to him he might be committing a crime. Then he realized what Sami said was true; he was Sayyid's only surviving heir. Everything now belonged to him.

The floor was littered with straw. He got up, dusting himself off. Something in the air seemed out of place, a strange acrid smell. Probably ancient horse droppings. He looked around. He needed an iron tool strong enough to pry a hasp from a door.

A few old tires were stacked against one wall, and a decaying pickup truck sat just inside the main door like it had been driven inside and forgotten. One of the stalls held a few harnesses made of leather. They had tether rings, but nothing with the right shape or enough strength to pry metal. *There!* A pitchfork on the ground along the back wall! He walked over and picked it up. Tools used by Egyptian farmers were often made of wood, but his uncle—rich man that he was—had purchased an iron implement. *Good! It just might work.* He walked back to the window and tossed the pitchfork through the opening.

He looked around one last time, making sure he hadn't missed anything. The truck sat in the dim light like a shadow against the wall. He checked the truck's bed, but except for straw and a worn tire, it was empty. Pulling open a side door, he poked around until he found what he was looking for, a tire iron. It was angled on the end with the lug wrench, but the other end, made to remove a tire from its rim, was flat. *Perfect!* With the tire iron in hand, he started for the window again, picking up an upended box along the way and carrying it with him. He placed the box under the window, stepped up on it, and climbed out.

Perspiration rolled down the sides of his face as he made his way around to the front of the barn. He drew a sleeve across his forehead. The dark hair of his goatee glistened.

Paint was peeling from the door of the former caretaker's residence, but the wood appeared to have strength. He wedged the flat end of the tire iron behind the hasp. Using it as a lever, he pried it forward. The screws on one side pulled out, and it fell away. Easier than he thought. He twisted it aside and pushed the door back to enter. It was a single room with a sink, stove, and toilet at one end, and a bed at the other. On the bed was a body.

He sidled over, his heart thumping hard enough to hurt as it banged against the walls of his chest. Fearing the worst, he kept his eyes turned away, refusing to look until he had to. He sipped in a breath, glanced over, and then released it with a sigh of relief. The face attached to the unconscious body wasn't his mother's—and yet, strangely, it *was*, but not the woman he remembered. The face was pale, the lips chapped and white. The cheeks were sunken, and dark caves filled the sockets of the skull where eyes should have been—she looked dead.

"Mother?" He reached out and touched her hand. It was warm and pliable. His stomach refluxed. He twisted around, thinking he was about to vomit, but he brought his hand to his mouth and swallowed hard. His face felt flushed, prickles of sweat beading his forehead. *What have they done?* His face was sizzling. He stooped over, bracing his hands on his knees, and breathed deeply. This was his *mother*. He waited until the reaction passed and then straightened, still taking his breath in gulps. *How could they?*

When he felt strong enough to face her, he turned around, reaching to take hold of the iron bands that encircled her ankles. Her legs were thin as reeds. His eyes followed the chain to where it was linked to a metal ring that was bolted to the floor. It was long enough for her to walk to the other end of the room, where she could fix herself something to eat or use the toilet, but she wouldn't get farther than that.

He went to the cupboard and opened it, but it was empty. He began cranking the handles of the tap. They *screeched* like dry metal, but with a *spit*, *sputter*, and *splatter*, a flow erupted. At least there was water from the spring. He didn't know how long his uncle had been bedridden, but it was apparent his mother hadn't eaten in all that time. She was starving to death.

He had to get her chains off, but without a key, he couldn't remove them from her ankles. He went back outside to get the tire iron.

There was no way to wedge the flat edge under the bracket. It was bolted tightly to the floor. He ran the steel rod through the ring and leaned back, pulling the handle forward, and then dropped it back, rocking the ring until it started to come loose. It would have been harder if the wood used for flooring hadn't been old, but his testosterone was churning, and with his sweat continuing to pour, the ring gave way. He took the chain and coiled it around his arm as he moved back to his mother. With the weight of the chain borne on his right arm, he slipped his hands under her shoulders and knees and lifted her to his chest. Then he turned and carried her out to the car.

Mohamed pulled into the driveway of the estate with Zainab lying against his shoulder. He'd tried to prop her up, but she kept sliding to the side, so he finally gave up and let her be. The car rolled to a stop in front of the house. He held his mother as he leaned forward to kill the engine. Of all the incredibly evil things his uncle had ever done, this had to be the worst.

He sat Zainab up and, after making sure she was steady, got out and went around to her side, where he gathered her into his arms. Without the weight of her fetters, she felt light as a feather. But he had to bring the chain along too. He held her close, leaning in to rope the links around his hand. When he had it coiled, he turned around—and there stood Sami.

"Mr. Mohamed!" he exclaimed. His eyes were wide with questions.

Mohamed didn't respond. He marched past Sami, carrying Zainab into the house and going straight to his uncle's bedroom to lay her on the bed. The servants would have changed the sheets and cleansed the entire house by now. His mother moaned. Her eyes opened slightly, fluttering, but she expelled her breath and passed out again.

Sami followed Mohamed in. "Is this your mother I see? I am so sorry, Mr. Mohamed. I could not know. We were told she was dead."

Mohamed turned around. "So was I, Sami. So was I." He went to the armoire, pulling his uncle's wardrobe out one piece at a time, going through the pockets.

"What is it you seek, Mr. Mohamed? Perhaps I can help."

"My uncle was holding my mother a prisoner. I want the key to those chains."

"Ah." Sami rushed from the room and came back holding a ring of keys. "These he kept by the door. I believe they lock the house as well as...ah...other things." He held them out.

Mohamed tried inserting a key that appeared to be the right size, but it wouldn't fit. He tried another, going through the keys one at a time until he found one that slid into the cylinder. He gave it a twist, and the manacle popped open.

Zainab's ankles were bruised and swollen. Their blackish-purple color defied the description of skin. Mohamed flung the chain and shackles away, sending them clanking across the tiles.

Sami had disappeared but was now back again, holding a bowl of warm water. He knelt beside the bed and began gently washing Zainab's face and hands, but after a few minutes, he glanced toward the door and stood. "Please, Mr. Mohamed, I have asked the women to attend to your mother, if this is all right?"

Mohamed nodded. He passed the two veiled women and left the room, closing the door behind him. To bathe Zainab would require they remove her clothing. Mohamed waited outside with Sami. The old Egyptian's face was always wrinkled, the folds of his skin hanging down, giving him an uncharacteristic frown, but now he looked especially dour.

Mohamed began unbuttoning his shirt. "Sami, I want you to get a doctor over here right away. I don't care how you do it; just get him here fast. In the meantime, get some food into my mother. Give her broth if she can't chew, but make her eat something. She needs nourishment."

Sami nodded but didn't move. He kept his head bowed, shifting his weight from one foot to the other.

"What is it, Sami?"

The old servant's shoulders teetered back and forth as he rocked from one foot to the other. He folded his arms, still looking down. "Ah, Mr. Mohamed, I know something you may find unpleasant, and I fear that I should be the one to bring this to you."

"Sami, I just found my mother alive. I doubt you could say anything to upset me right now. Go on. What is it?"

"It's just that...all you see around you should be yours, but..."

"But what, Sami?"

"I was witness when your uncle married your mother. It was not something she wanted. They held a knife to her throat and told her what to say, so perhaps it can still be annulled. Your uncle wanted your mother as his wife, not as a mistress, and the papers were signed and witnessed by me and are in the safe in your father's library. Legally, that makes her his heir also, which means you will have to share all this"—he paused, his hand sweeping the room—"with her."

Mohamed wadded his shirt in a ball, smiling at the irony. He hadn't told Sami yet, but he had to leave, and probably on the next flight out. As far as he knew, things were moving forward in the United States, and he might not be back for a month, or maybe more. And—*may the will of Allah be done*—he still had to rescue Layla.

"Tell me something, Sami."

"Yes, of course. Out from my eyes for you, Mr. Mohamed."

"I used to get a new soccer ball every year on my birthday. It was never wrapped, always just sitting on my bed. Where did it come from?"

Sami locked his hands behind his back, lowering his eyes.

"My uncle told me he didn't approve of my playing soccer. A waste of time, he called it."

Sami rocked back on his heels. His head was bowed, but he looked up from under his eyelids and smiled sheepishly. "A gift is still a gift even if one does not know the giver. Is this not true?"

Mohamed nodded. "So be it," he said, "and thank you. You've always been a faithful friend. As for my mother, she can have it all. Just make sure she is nursed back to health."

CHAPTER 36

THE BOWL OF SPAGHETTI sat in front of Matthew, uneaten. He picked up his spoon and brought it to his mouth but hesitated. The saucy, out-of-a-can meal fit his budget, but there probably wasn't much nourishment to be gained from starchy pasta and tomato sauce, so what was the point? The spoon fell away, tipping sideways over the bowl. He watched the little tomato-covered noodles slide down and wiggle back into the tomato goop—*plop, plop, plop*. He couldn't eat. Not as long as Layla refused to return his calls.

He looked at his watch. He'd placed the last call less than an hour ago, but a lot could change in an hour. He found the redial button with his thumb. One ring...*two*...*three*...he snapped the lid closed, cutting the connection. He tightened his grip around the small cellular device. She was avoiding him—*again!* He'd waited two days before calling, giving her ample time to seek his forgiveness, but she was too callous for that. He shook his head, grinding his teeth. Only whatever vestige of sanity remained kept him from throwing the blasted phone against the wall.

He'd made more than a dozen calls and left three separate messages, starting with a friendly, "Hi, Layla. I think we need to talk. Give me a call," but progressing to, "What's the matter? What have I done? Please don't avoid me," delivered in a voice of desperation. She hadn't returned a single one.

His lunch sat drying in front of him, the tomato paste growing crusty along the edge of the bowl. He set the phone down, tapping the case with his forefinger. He'd spent half a day skipping classes, lurking in places she was known to frequent, but she hadn't shown. And it wasn't because she was sick either, because when he'd called the dorm, her roommates said she wasn't there, not that she wasn't feeling well and couldn't come to the phone.

He didn't need a mirror to know his eyes were red; he could feel them stinging. He continued tapping with his finger, then wiped his cheeks with the back of his hand. The burning in his chest was real—not manufactured, not pretend—the real deal, a tangible feeling that consumed his soul. If she'd only let him explain, he'd tell her why he'd been acting so weird. He'd apologize and let her know what he'd been going through. It wasn't easy knowing at any moment he could die. He didn't expect her to marry him—not now. He was a ticking time bomb, as likely to drop dead on the way down the aisle as any other time.

Pulling himself from his chair, he reached for the bowl and made his way to the sink. He scooped the pasty goo into the shopping-bag-lined receptacle under the counter and, reaching for the faucet, set the bowl in the sink and filled it with water. She didn't love him anyway. Her refusal to return his calls was proof of that. If he could get it together long enough, if he could face her without breaking down, he'd release her. He wiped his hands on the towel hanging over the oven handle and went to find his satchel. He needed a pen and something to write on.

The hands on the clock over the breakfast nook ticked off an hour before he was through. Balls of wadded-up paper were piled on the table, a plethora of false starts with muddled words. He sat back to read his final rendition, pleased with himself for going through the exercise. He'd found the writing therapeutic, giving him the ability to express what he was feeling in a nonthreatening environment, free of objection, criticism, or heated discussion. Line by line he read, satisfied he'd carefully considered what needed to be said and how it might be received. He folded the paper and sealed it in an envelope, flopping it over so he could address the other side. He leaned back and tapped the rigid paper against the palm of his hand, then tucked it into his inside coat pocket. Maybe he wouldn't even send it. Now that he could air his thoughts without sounding harsh, he had a better chance of explaining himself in person.

. . . 🌙 . . .

Matthew pulled up in front of Layla's apartment, his dusty yellow Volkswagen *screeeeching* as he applied the brakes. *If the mountain wouldn't come to Muhammad, Muhammad would go to the mountain.* He smiled at the irony. The mountain had probably already found Mohamed waiting with open arms. He laughed, shaking his head as he climbed from the car.

The crisp fall air was energizing as he made his way up the walk. All things considered, he was feeling good. A car beeped its horn as it raced by with a jock hanging out the window. "Hey, Matthew, Bruins rock!"

Matthew spun around in time to see one of his teammates in varsity leathers extend his arms, with his fingers spread in a victory *V*. He gave a half wave in acknowledgment and turned back toward the door, facing the sober reality of why he was there. Even if she didn't want to see him, he had to try. He stepped up onto the porch and knocked, waited, and then knocked again. The door was opened by a blue-eyed college preppy. Her blonde ponytail hung over one shoulder, and she had a fuzzy pink sweatband around her head.

He faltered for a moment. "Is Layla in?" but the words felt foolish leaving his mouth. If he were her boyfriend, he should know.

The coed shook her head, her ponytail swinging from side to side. "Nope, haven't seen her." The television was blaring behind her. She looked back like she didn't want to miss out on some important part of a soap opera plot. She was wearing a pair of black tights that exposed her belly button and a yellow halter top with no bra, leaving little to be imagined.

Matthew averted his eyes and ducked his head, peering around her slim waist into the room. "You sure?"

The girl looked askance. "Hey, what are you doing?"

Matthew was standing on his toes, trying to see over her shoulder.

"You don't believe me?" She stepped back, pulling the door open wide. "Go ahead, see for yourself."

"Thanks," he said.

"I haven't seen her in days," she called over her shoulder as he swept by. The cadence from the TV was deafening.

Matthew went to Layla's room. He'd been there before, most recently to help her move in a new dresser. Little, if anything, had changed. It was a sparse environment. She wasn't one for hanging posters on the walls, and *clutter* and *mess* were words she'd excised from her vocabulary. It was just one of many things he loved about her—a place for everything and everything in its place. Her clothes were either hung or put away. The bed had the appearance of having never been slept in. Every ruffle was symmetrically furled, like it belonged in a store window display. A small writing table had neatly stacked papers and books. It looked ready to use except...he walked over and ran his finger across its surface. *Dust!* Layla never allowed dust to accumulate.

He hurried into the living room. The coed was doing some kind of aerobic exercise in front of the TV. On the screen, a man in a black leotard was leading a group of ladies through the steps, *one, two, three, turn and one, two*...

"You said you haven't seen her in days?"

"That's right." The girl didn't stop; she kicked her leg up and clapped her hands under her thigh, *one, two, three, and*...

"She doesn't answer her cell. What would you do if you had to reach her?"

The girl shrugged, still jumping and breathing hard, her forehead moist with perspiration.

"And you're not worried?"

"Worried? *Uh-huh, uh-huh,* what for? Half the girls in the dorm spend more time, *uh-huh,* at their boyfriends' place than they do here. *One, two, three, step*...it's not my job to keep tabs on them."

Matthew shook his head. "If she comes back, would you have her call me?" He spun around and marched out the door.

He was halfway across town when it dawned on him where Layla might be. He reached for his phone and flipped it open, an idea forming. She'd given him her parents' number in case of an emergency.

"Hi, this is Matthew. Remember me? We had dinner the last time you were in town visiting your daughter." He grimaced.

The response was hesitant, but it wasn't anything he didn't expect. "Yes…certainly. It's nice to hear from you, Matthew. What can I do for you?"

"I was just wondering if Layla was there."

"Here? No, she's in school."

"Have you heard from her recently?"

"No. Should I have? She usually only calls on weekends. Is everything all right?"

"Uh, yeah, sure, everything's fine. I was just trying to reach her, that's all, but it's not important. You don't have to tell her I called. I'll catch up with her tomorrow. 'Bye." Matthew snapped the phone shut, his heart pounding. Talk about leaving a bad impression.

There was one other person he could try, but he didn't have the number. He dialed information and had the automated operator put him through. *The person you are trying to reach is either unavailable or out of the service area.* His brother wasn't answering his phone either. They were probably together. She always answered her phone—unless she was with someone and didn't want to be disturbed. She must be with Mohamed…they'd been gone for days.

Matthew gripped the steering wheel, his knuckles turning white, then took a breath and tried to relax. The ache was back in his chest, his eyes starting to burn—*sometimes loving means letting go.* He spotted a mailbox up ahead and pulled to the side. It was time to send the letter.

CHAPTER 37

THE CLOUDS SPARKED LIKE strobes popping behind puffs of cotton. Mohamed leaned his head toward the window, his breath fogging the glass. The plane was passing through layers of stratocumulus coming in on descent to San Francisco. It had been another rough ride with the turbulent weather knocking out the lights and killing the movie. He adjusted his headphones and tuned to another channel. He couldn't find anything worth listening to, but he was determined to pipe something into his head. He'd been punished by his thoughts long enough.

With a four-hour stopover in Paris, the return trip had taken twenty-one hours. Four hours wasted sitting in a terminal with nothing to do but mull over his life and where it was taking him. His newly purchased Bible provided some diversion. He was determined to read it once more before getting back, but inevitably he'd come to a part where it contradicted something he'd been taught, and, becoming uneasy, he'd closed it again, which left him sitting in a stiff airport chair reading the same newspaper for the umpteenth time.

The plane shuddered, making a tempest of the coffee in his cup. It was one thing to plow through thunderheads that buckled the aircraft in the wind, a mere bodily discomfort, but what troubled him was the turbulence in his soul.

He looked at his watch—the countdown had begun. The wedding of Mike and Allie was a week away, and along with it one of the most heinous mass murders ever conceived. He had to get Layla out of the country. He wanted to believe he was doing it for her, but the more he thought about it, the more he realized he had to do it just as much for himself. He didn't want to be around to watch the debacle—innocent men grappling with their ties, their eyes bugging out, the look on their faces revealing they knew they were about to die. His stomach rolled, making him feel queasy. If he were forced to witness the event, he knew he'd vomit.

"Sir?"

Not only did he want to avoid being there when it happened, he wanted to wash his hands of the whole thing. But he was in too deep and there was no way out. If he tried, Allah would send him to hell. He didn't relish the thought of having someone pour boiling water down his throat or having his skin flame-broiled until it seared off, only to have new skin stitched on so it could be burned off again.

"Sir!"

"Huh?"

A flight attendant reached out to take the cup from his hand. "Please fasten your seat belt and bring your seat to an upright position. We're preparing to land."

He pushed the button that brought the seat up straight, then struggled with the belt, grimacing as he snapped the latch. At least he was riding first class again. He hadn't been able to get a flight out until the following day, which had frustrated him at the time but later turned out to his advantage. It had given him a few extra hours with his mother and time to rummage through his uncle's things.

Mohamed's investigation—noon, previous day

He was sitting at the desk in Sayyid's office, shuffling through a stack of photos when Sami walked in.

"You will need money for your trip, will you not?" his uncle's *khadem* asked.

"Money's something you never have enough of," Mohamed replied without looking up. He was distracted by the pictures in his hand. Each showed a different man with a band of explosives strapped to his chest. He stared at a photograph of a young boy who couldn't have been more than sixteen. His eyes seemed to be begging the photographer for help, his young face a portrait of terror. "Uh...why do you ask?"

"Because you could not pay the taxi man. I think perhaps I can help."

"Uh huh." No doubt these people were weapons in Islam's war against Israel. He half expected to see a picture of his father, but it wasn't there.

Sami shuffled over to the bookshelves and removed several volumes, stacking them on a chair. Behind, set into the wall, was a safe. Sami started spinning the dial.

"Haj instructed me to open this only in the case of extreme emergency. I think it is OK now."

Mohamed got out of his chair and eased up behind Sami. The small balding man came up to his chin. With a click of the lock, the safe door swung out to reveal bundles of rubber-banded bills. Mohamed removed a stack, fanning through it with his thumb. Hundred-pound notes! He reached in again, riffling through the stacks to remove one that was green—U.S. hundred-dollar bills worth five times as much. There had to be ten thousand dollars in there, not to mention property deeds and investment portfolios.

The little man backed out from under Mohamed's arm, beaming a wide toothless grin.

"Sami, you never cease to amaze me," Mohamed said.

The doctor had arrived that afternoon and announced that Zainab's chief medical issues were severe malnutrition and a serious infection where the skin had been rubbed raw by the ankle chains, but given good care, she would recover—Allah be praised! After binding her shins with bandages and ointment, he inserted a drip tube into her wrist and began a program of intravenous feeding.

Early the next morning Mohamed and Sami entered the room to find her lying in bed with her eyes open, staring at the ceiling. She was cognizant enough to know she was free—just the absence of her chains told her that—and the intravenous tube told her she was under a doctor's care.

Tears exploded from her eyes when Sami explained how her son had found and rescued her.

Mohamed sat on the edge of the bed, holding his mother's skeletal hand. Except for the dark shadows that circled her eyes, her face lacked color, and when she spoke her lips cracked, revealing tiny fissures of blood.

They sat looking at each other, their eyes raining a storm. "Don't be angry with your uncle," she said. "Sayyid loved you, but he wanted a son of his own. He thought Fatma was barren, but..." Zainab lowered her eyes modestly, "*she* wasn't the problem."

Then she recounted her never-ending nightmare, how she'd lived more than a dozen years in the darkness, sweltering in a steamy prison, afraid every night of rats nibbling her toes, terrified each day of hearing the car that meant Sayyid had come to force himself on her again. He beat her, he said, for refusing to disavow her Christian beliefs, but his anger suggested it was because she'd failed to give him a child.

She ran her fingers down Mohamed's cheek, wiping the tears from his mouth with her thumb. "Sometimes he would tell me about you. He wanted me to know what a good Muslim you'd become, but I prayed for you..." Her voice trailed off as though afraid to ask whether her prayers had been answered. "Oh, Moh, you are so beautiful." She held his face with both hands, her eyes locked on his. "You must find it in your heart to forgive. Did you know he once gave me a Bible?" She smiled, her lips quivering ever so slightly. "I read it every day, and it made me want to live. I memorized what I could, praise God, because one day Sayyid lost his temper and took it back. But I thank God that I was able keep it as long as I did. And I forgave Sayyid. No one is so bad they're beyond God's love. My Isa, He died so that your sins, and mine, *and* Sayyid's, could be forgiven. Hear me? You must forgive, or you will not be forgiven."

Mohamed held her in his arms, feeling the bones poking through her skin. It was like holding a bird. If he held too tight, she would be crushed, but if he let go, she might fly away and never return. So many tears streamed down their cheeks that when they finally pulled apart, wet streaks stained their garments.

• • • 🌙 • • •

As they passed through the clouds at five thousand feet, Mohamed considered his only regret. He'd refrained from telling his mother that he knew about Matthew. She was frail, still recovering from her ordeal. He wasn't sure what such a shock might do to her system. It was a flimsy excuse, and he knew it. The truth was, he was jealous and wanted to keep his mother to himself, especially since he didn't know what the outcome of the next few weeks might be. The brothers might never speak to each other again.

Saying good-bye was the most difficult thing he'd ever done, but he had no choice. He had to return—*had to*—or risk losing Layla. The irony didn't escape him that the only two people he loved were both Christians. *Da-aeh-da!* What's with that?

The flight attendant was making sure all trays and seatbacks were up and all baggage stowed in the overhead compartments. Not a bad-looking woman. Two weeks ago he might have flashed her a killer smile to see where it would lead, but not now. He desperately wanted Layla in his life. In Egypt, he might get away with forcing the issue. There was little outcry when a Christian disappeared. But what would he gain? Layla would become to him what his mother was to Sayyid: a hostage, a prisoner, a...a...a, dare he even think it—*a sex slave*—but that was perversion of the worst kind.

His uncle was insane. And here *he* was, on a mission to fulfill his uncle's dream. He had to wonder, as they cruised on a landing pattern at two thousand feet heading into San Francisco, just how much like his uncle he had become.

He couldn't make Layla love him any more than Sayyid could command his mother's love. And he couldn't force her to convert. His eyes rolled to the ceiling. *You can't force people to love You, God.* It was a conundrum. The only two people *he* loved were, according to Islam, both infidels deserving death. He had saved his mother. Would he be able to save Layla also?

The ground moved closer, the roofs of houses and buildings looming larger. The grass was a blur, then lines on the asphalt screamed by like a picket fence. He felt the bounce as they touched down.

. . . ☽ . . .

Mohamed paid the parking attendant and rolled into the street, clicking on his windshield wipers. He always felt a little melancholy when it rained. Drawing in a deep breath, he tried to relax, settling into the embrace of the cushy seat.

Forget that. He reached for his phone to call Layla. He had to let her know where he'd been in case she'd tried to reach him and somehow in the same breath convince her to run off with him to Mexico. Once there, away from all outside influence, they'd be able to resolve their differences. He'd seen enough similarity in what they believed to find common ground.

And he'd seen Jesus, the way He appeared in the last book of the Bible, though Mohamed was sure He'd been sent by Allah. Allah could use whomever he wanted to deliver a message. It didn't mean Muhammad wasn't the greatest prophet. Maybe he and Layla could just agree to disagree and leave it at that. Or maybe they'd decide to live in Mexico the rest of their lives.

The rain pelted his car. *Heaven's tears.* It had to be done now. He dialed her number. The phone rang three times. When it was finally answered, the shock of hearing a man's voice at the other end of the line made him grip his phone so hard he nearly cracked its housing.

"Hello, Mohamed. *Wahash tena.* We missed you."

"Omar? What gives? I was calling my girlfriend." Mohamed drew the phone back to look at the caller ID display, realizing El Sheikh must have done the same thing. His display showed he was connected to Layla's number. "What are you doing with her phone?"

"My condolences on the fate of your uncle, may Allah grant him mercy. I assume since you're here you succeeded in carrying out his wishes."

"OK, you knew about that, fine…but what about Layla?"

"We have the girl. Do you not now see why this cannot work? Say the word, and she will no longer be a concern."

"No! I…"

"I thought not. Love makes fools of all men. Do not worry; I have personally arranged for her transportation out of the country, just as you requested. She will be returned to you as soon as your mission is complete."

Mohamed sucked in his breath—*Oh, no! Not this, not now!* He exhaled slowly, determined to keep Omar from sensing his apprehension. "Good, excellent, good. So, where is she?"

"You must focus on your mission. We will take care of the girl. There is much to be done and little time remaining."

"Yes, of course, I know, but I should probably talk to her. I imagine she's terrified. I can assure her everything's going to be fine. She trusts me."

"I'm sorry, Mohamed, that is impossible."

"Impossible?"

"She has become a liability. While checking her phone, we discovered the number for Homeland Security on her list of recent calls. In fact, she made a call to them soon after you left. And your number was also called, an odd coincidence that cannot be ignored. We think she's providing the FBI with information. We must make sure there is no further communication."

"Layla would never…"

"Doesn't matter. You're our link to Allie, and through her, the president. The role you play is vital. Your lust for this woman is a distraction. We need you to focus. All this will soon be over. Once the new administration is established, your friend will be returned to you. Then you can do with her as you wish. But until then, you just focus on your mission…and leave the woman to us."

Chapter 38

Mohamed's feet were dragging on the carpet. He tossed his keys on the table by the door and dumped his bag in the foyer, plopping on the sofa with his cell phone still in hand. His head fell back on the cushion as he rolled his eyes up to the ceiling, his stomach in a knot.

This was the second time his actions had put someone he loved in jeopardy. He had to find Layla—and without it taking twelve years—but once again it was a moot point because he didn't know where to look. Even if he did, what was he supposed to do, kick down the door and go in with guns blazing? Other than negotiation, he had no way of getting her back, and he couldn't negotiate because he had nothing to trade.

Only a few days ago his mother needed to be found—*Ask, and it will be given to you; seek, and you will find; knock, and it will be opened to you.* "OK, God, Allah, Supreme Being, whatever, I'm asking." For all he knew, she was already on her way out of the country. He might never see her again.

He looked at the phone in his hand and tossed it on the coffee table. It slid across the wood surface, bounced off a copy of the Quran, and narrowly missed falling to the floor on the other side. He brought his hands up, holding his head, and swept his fingers through his hair. At least she was safe. They'd use her to keep him focused on the goal, but she wouldn't be hurt. They needed her as leverage. As long as they could threaten him by implying harm might come to her, he'd be under their control.

He considered the only other option. He could stand up to them and refuse to cooperate, turning his back on everything he believed, and become a traitor to Islam. His mother would love him, and so would Layla, but he'd fall under the judgment of Allah. He grimaced. They would kill Layla and then come after him. *Why?* Why were they so ready to kill in the name of God?

It wasn't supposed to be that way. Allah was the giver of life. As long as men observed the five pillars of the faith: the *shahadah*—the testimony that there was no God but Allah and that Muhammad was his messenger; the *salah*—the requirement to pray five times a day, facing the Kaaba in Makkah; the *zakah*—the giving of alms; the *swam*—or ritual fasting; and the *hajj*—the pilgrimage during the month of Dhu al-Hijjah to the city of Makkah, they could earn eternal reward, and Allah would grant them life. But you never knew for sure. Allah, on that final day, could also decide you hadn't done enough to merit such favor.

Now it dawned on Mohamed that if he turned on Islam, his own God would want him dead, and the people of his God, his so-called *friends*, would carry out the order. What kind of God sanctioned crimes like that?

And what about this other God, the One who said He loved man so much He gave His Son to die for everyone's sin so that by believing on His name, they might have eternal life? He had to admit, that kind of God was beginning to make sense.

He leaned forward, slid his copy of the Quran over, and started reading the passages he'd marked to justify what they were about to do.

"Those who reject Our Signs, We shall soon cast into the Fire: as often as their skins are roasted through, We shall change them for fresh skins, that they may taste the penalty: for Allah is Exalted in Power, Wise." *Surah 4, verse 56.*

"If you gain the mastery over them in war, disperse, with them, those who follow them, that they may remember." *Surah 8, verse 57.*

"Therefore, when you meet the Unbelievers in fight, smite at their necks; at length, when you have thoroughly subdued them, bind a bond firmly on them: thereafter is the time for either generosity or ransom: until the war lays down its burdens. Thus are you commanded: but if it had been Allah's

Will, He could have exacted retribution from them Himself; but He lets you fight in order to test you, some with others." *Surah 47, verse 4.*

Mohamed closed the book, biting his lip. Isa had said, "I have come that they may have life, and that they may have it more abundantly." He'd memorized the entire Quran and couldn't remember a single verse about loving your enemies or being kind to those who mistreated you. He pulled himself up, went to the foyer, and, kneeling down, unzipped his carry-on bag to retrieve his Bible. He'd read where it said men should go into the world preaching the gospel, not wielding a sword. There was nothing about forcing men into submission.

He walked back to the couch, thumbing through the pages to find a verse he'd marked. In his brief reading he'd discovered this Book claimed that God *was* love. He'd memorized more than one hundred names for Allah, and not one of them referred to him as loving. *There*, he found it... in the part called First John, chapter 4, verse 8: "He who does not love does not know God, for God *is* love."

Either the Bible was in gross error, or... but the Dar Al-Harb, the territory of war, was designated to bring about Dar Al-Islam, one world under God. How could that be wrong? And how was he supposed to know which was right? The Quran talked mostly about judgment and death, the Bible about blessings and life. If he had to choose one over the other, he'd choose life, but if he chose the God of the Bible, it would lead to his death. He was trapped in a paradox.

There was one other thing. Being reunited with his mother and Layla had made him feel something—*pain, hope, joy.* All he'd felt before was numbness. Those two Christian women actually had him smiling again—for the first time since he was a child. That didn't mean Muslim people weren't good. He knew countless Muslims who were decent, hardworking, peace-loving people, but he'd joined the wrong Muslim camp, because the people in his circle of friends rarely smiled. It was deemed inappropriate. The work of Allah was too serious.

He made a decision. He chose to smile. He held the Bible over his head and looked up. "Jesus, if You are the giver of life, then I choose You!"

Mohamed sat down grinning, wondering why. There was certainly nothing to grin about. He was still tangled in a plot to kill the president, one which, if he tried to extricate himself, would lead to his death. But he felt light-headed, almost giddy, and couldn't help it.

He picked up his phone and crossed the room as he flipped it open. His heart started to pound. He could only hope they would take him seriously. He pushed 411 and got an operator.

"Please, I need the number of the FBI in San Francisco."

A few seconds later a recorded voice gave him the number. He waited, tapping his foot on the carpet as he accepted the option to be automatically connected and, after explaining to the receptionist that he had information about a group who was planning an act of terror against the United States, was put through to a man who answered right away: "Special Agent Ambrose Barnes."

Mohamed began pacing. "Please don't make the mistake of discounting what I'm about to say. This isn't some kind of crank call. This is deadly serious. I have information about a plot to assassinate the president of the United States. These people mean business. I'm convinced they have the ability to execute their plan, and you've got less than a week to stop it from happening. I can give you names, the timing, even the location, but…"

"Whoa, slow down. First, who are you, and how do I know your information is reliable? Like you said, we get a lot of crank—"

"I can guarantee the accuracy of the information 100 percent, but before I let you know who I am, I need some assurances. Your investigation will no doubt uncover my name. I make no denial, since I've been involved in this from the beginning. I expect complete immunity, but if you arrest my cohorts and I'm the only one you leave alone, my life will be forfeit. They'll issue a *fatwa* in my name, and I'll be dead before the ink dries on the paper. I want written guarantees of two things: one, that you'll provide me and, if she'll agree to it, the girl I hope to marry with new identities and relocate us someplace where it's safe, and two, that I'll never have to testify before the courts. I don't want my name to appear on documents of any kind. If you can agree to this, I'll tell you everything I know."

There was a pause. Agent Barnes cleared his throat. "*Uhhummm*, I think it's doable, as long as what you say checks out. Still, it's not my decision to make. That has to come from the bureau chief. He's in a meeting right now but should be out shortly. Call this number again in one hour, and I'll let you know where we stand."

It was a weird feeling. Mohamed had just betrayed his God, along with most of the friends he'd made since coming to America, not to mention those back home. Yet, rather than feeling uncomfortable, he actually felt good. He started to smile, slipping the phone into the holster on his belt. That didn't diminish the fact that what he'd done might cost him his life.

He needed to pray. And, assuming he'd just converted, though he couldn't say he had since he wasn't sure *how* it was supposed to be done, he needed to know how to pray. It was obvious Christians didn't prostrate themselves or use prayer rugs or stick to certain times of the day. That would take some getting used to. The pastor of the church Layla attended spoke to God like a friend. That's what he'd been doing too, so far, and it seemed to work. All he could do was try, and he knew where he had to be.

He walked outside, poked his finger through the ring of his keys, and twirled them around, still smiling. His car, one beautiful Lexus shining like a polished jewel, was parked on the street.

The sun broke through the clouds, pouring down rays that looked like the wings of angels. He felt the warmth on his face. He hopped off the curb, feeling like he didn't have a care in the world. Pointing his remote, he heard the locks electronically release. The inside of the car was warm, soothing his fatigued muscles. He sat for a moment, looking out the window. A rainbow of the most brilliant hues of blue, magenta, orange, and gold formed over the park, hitting the ground just behind the trees.

God—the God of Muslims and Christians and Jews alike—the God who spoke through visions and dreams, would reveal to him how to find Layla. He didn't know how he knew it—but he knew. *Ask, and it will be given to you; seek, and you will find; knock, and it will be opened to you.* He slipped the key into the ignition and checked his rearview mirror.

A car pulled up behind him, a tiny yellow Volkswagen. He recognized the driver immediately.

CHAPTER 39

THE SUN SLIPPED BEHIND the clouds, drawing a curtain of shadow over the day. Mohamed pursed his lips, his face growing hard. He'd been enjoying a first-rate high, the ecstasy of a child bouncing on balloons or swinging out over the water on a rope, a rush of carefree excitement he couldn't put into words. But it was his, and he didn't want to share it.

The door opened, and Matthew climbed out of the car. Mohamed turned his eyes away, staring out the window. The clouds were the same, but they'd lost their golden lining, and the rainbow, along with the angel's wings, had disappeared, *but*... For a moment he thought he saw a rider on a white horse, then the image faded, scattered by the wind as fast as it came. Just cloud formations. If he wasn't careful, he'd start seeing Jesus in everything.

Matthew squeezed between the bumpers of the beat-up yellow Volkswagen and the shiny new pearl-gray Lexus. He came around to the passenger side and stooped over, looking in with his hand pressed against the glass. Reaching for the handle, he pulled the door open and slid inside without saying a word. He sat, staring straight ahead.

Mohamed scowled. "Now's not a good time, my brother. I've got a lot on my mind."

Matthew's head fell back against the headrest. "Imagine that," he said. He stared out the window a moment longer, then his head rolled to the side. His bloodshot eyes were puffy and held a watery glaze. He was wearing the same corduroy jacket he'd worn before, only now it was badly wrinkled. It looked like he hadn't slept in days. "Where is she?" he asked.

Mohamed looked away, his mouth forming a pout. He stuck his tongue into the side of his cheek and drummed the steering wheel with his fingers.

"Where's Layla? What have you done with her?"

Mohamed tweaked his head to the side. "I haven't done anything with Layla," he said, making sure Matthew felt the bite.

"You two ran off together. Don't you think I know that?"

Mohamed's eyes glanced to the side, glaring at his brother. "What are you talking about?"

"I'm talking about you and Layla and whatever little affair you're having. She's *my* girl."

"Matthew, I don't have time for this. Get out. I have to be somewhere."

"Not until you tell me where she is. I've been calling her for days, but she doesn't answer. And I've been calling you and you haven't answered, and that tells me whatever's going on, you two are in it together."

Mohamed shook his head. "What's with the goatee?"

Matthew's hand went up to his chin, rubbing the new growth.

"If you grew that to look like me, it won't work." He skewed his head to the left, squinting.

Matthew tilted his head to the right so, though neither saw it, they looked like a mirror image of each other, an exact copy, with everything on the opposite side. "Get real. I didn't grow anything. I just haven't bothered to shave."

Mohamed creased his mouth, his lips compressed. "Look, Matthew, if I knew where Layla was, I'd tell you. The reason you haven't been able to reach me is that I've been out of the country, back in Egypt. My plane only landed an hour ago."

"Egypt?"

Mohamed grabbed his goatee, stroking it, as he looked out the window. No horse and rider, no voice telling him what to do, just clouds of gray.

He turned toward Matthew. "Our uncle died a few days ago, OK? He was your father's brother and the one responsible for his death, so take it from me, you were better off *not* knowing him. I went home to set his affairs in order. That's all it was. I came straight here from the airport."

Matthew seemed to relax. He turned, sinking farther into the seat, then raised his head, gazing out the window at Mohamed's condo. "Is she in there?"

"Who?"

"You know who. Layla. I assume she went with you?" he snapped.

Mohamed's eyebrows furrowed. "No, Layla was not with me. And I don't know where she is. Now if you don't mind, I have someplace to go." He reached across his brother's lap to open the passenger door, but Matthew caught his wrist. Their eyes locked, glaring at each other. Their jaws were clenched.

Matthew relaxed his grip and took a breath. "Did you see my...our mother?"

Mohamed sighed. "It's a long story, Matthew.

CHAPTER 40

THE ROAD WOUND ITS way into a Pacific grove, cutting through a fog so dense it hid the mammoth trees that had stood guarding the coast for a thousand years. Mohamed rolled down his window, listening for the sounds of the ocean. He heard a whitewater steam cascading over smooth stones. It channeled under logs covered with moss, barreling down through ferns and blackberry brambles in its mad dash to the ocean.

"You're saying my fiancée's being held by a bunch of suicidal maniacs?"

Mohamed rolled his window up again, rebuffing the moist air. He picked up his cell phone and keyed in a number. "That's exactly what I'm saying. Excuse me." He gave his brother a sidelong glance. The hard lines of his twin's face had softened, and a faint smile played on his lips. Matthew was probably storing the confession for future reference. That's what *he'd* do if the situation were reversed.

He'd held nothing back—except the part about his conversion, which he kept to himself because he wasn't quite sure what to make of it yet. He'd given Matthew plenty of ammunition to shoot him down. Layla and the terrorist—a match made in heaven, or…Matthew would bury him, but that wasn't important. They had to find Layla and get her to safety. That's what mattered. She could decide for herself after that. If she were smart, she'd opt for Matthew—same good looks without all the duplicity. It didn't matter, as long as she was happy. He grimaced. Maybe he could convince Layla that's how he felt, but he'd never convince himself.

"Mr. Barnes?…Yeah, it's me." Mohamed said, not bothering to explain to Matthew. "OK, but this has to be done in person. I don't want anything recorded... Now? No, I'm down in Big Sur. I'd never get back in time...Tomorrow morning then...OK, see you."

He snapped his phone shut, putting it away. Matthew was staring at him. "I'm taking everything to the FBI first thing tomorrow," he said.

Mohamed kept his eyes fixed on the road as silence settled into the car. He could probably guess what his brother was thinking, but either Matthew didn't know what to say, or he was too stunned to reply.

The road meandered up the valley, deeper into the primeval forest. With the rolling fog, Mohamed was driving more slowly than he liked. He felt an urgency he couldn't explain. He needed to be alone so Jesus could appear and tell him where to find Layla. And he didn't need distractions.

He braked for a turn that came up too suddenly. That was another problem. He was drawn to this spot for its beauty—it helped him feel the presence of God—but the fog was so thick he couldn't see a thing. There wouldn't be much of a view.

"And you don't have any idea where she is?"

The sound of his brother's voice jolted him from his thoughts. He nodded at the glove compartment. "Try in there."

Matthew leaned in to pop the button. The box fell open. Inside were a car service manual and one other item. He pulled it out. It was a map of the United States.

"Open it."

Matthew angled his head to the side, his lips compressed, but he unfolded the creases, spreading the entire map across the dash.

"What do you see?"

"I see the United States of America. What do you think I see?"

"Well...that's where she could be. We have mosques and cell groups in every part of the country. There are any number of people who would take Layla in without question and keep her until otherwise instructed. She could be anywhere."

Silence returned to the car and stayed with them for the next few miles.

It was like the fog that surrounded them had dampened not only the forest but also their conversation. Mohamed wondered what this brother was thinking. It probably wasn't good, but that didn't matter; he deserved it, though he'd honestly believed what he was doing was right. No, that wasn't true. He'd believed the idea—preparing the world to serve God—was just, but he'd had trouble with the method all along. The plan involved killing innocent people, and now the one he wanted to protect from the fallout was in more danger than anyone else. The FBI might stop the wedding and save the lives of the president, members of Congress, and all the invited guests, but it still wouldn't save Layla. She was beyond their reach. He wouldn't be able to live with himself if she died because of him.

It surprised him how calm his brother seemed. He would have expected Matthew to harangue him with accusations and threats. Instead, his head was propped against the headrest and his eyes were closed like he was either sleeping—*or praying*. But then, he had to admit he was pretty calm himself, considering the situation. Maybe it was because they were now both trusting the same God.

"You know what I think?" Matthew said, his eyelids still drooping.

Mohamed didn't respond. He was focused on the road, piloting their vehicle through dense clouds that prevented him from seeing more than a few feet ahead.

"I think it's all about legalism. Your Quran reads a lot like the Hebrew Scriptures, the Old Testament, where God gave the people certain commandments, knowing they wouldn't be able to keep them but also knowing once they acknowledged their failings, He'd send them a Savior. Paul, one of the guys God used to write the New Testament, called it the law of sin and death." He rolled his head to the side as if waiting for a response, but none came. Mohamed kept his eyes fastened on the road.

"That's what I see in Islam, whether it's killing an unbeliever, or wiping out a nation, or stoning someone who commits adultery, or even just trying to adhere to a strict set of rules so when you die God will let you in—it's pretty much the same stuff the Hebrews practiced. But Paul said Christ came to free us from the law. No one has ever lived without breaking one of the commandments, except Jesus, of course. He came to get rid of all that.

Then five hundred years later, Islam comes along and, déjà vu, everyone's under the law again. Back to the same-ol', same-ol', still trying be good enough to earn our way to heaven without any hope of doing it."

Mohamed took in a deep breath and let it out slowly. "Matthew?" he said.

Matthew rolled his head to the side. "Yeah, bro."

"What would you say if I told you I think I've become a Christian?"

Matthew eyes widened. "No way," he said. "What do you mean, you *think*?"

Mohamed kept his hands on the wheel, but he shrugged. "There's something I left out when I told you the story about finding our mother. I couldn't find her on my own. The prophet Jesus told me where she was."

"No kidding. For real?"

Mohamed skewed his head to the side. "I don't know much about your religion. I only know your Holy Book says it's all about who you believe in, and I've decided to believe in Jesus, so I guess that makes me a Christian."

"You bet it does, bro!" A smile spread across Matthew's lips. "You bet it does."

They pulled off the road onto the dirt drive leading to the cabin. The gate was closed, but that wasn't unusual—only Mohamed knew he hadn't closed it. The last time he was there he'd been riled by the pamphlet. He'd left in such a funk he'd ignored security and raced by the gate, leaving it hanging open. Someone else had to have been there.

Water dripped off the limbs of the trees overhead, *tap, tap, tap.* "You wanna get that?" Mohamed said, raising his chin to indicate the pipe and wire blockade.

Matthew climbed out and approached the gate. A padlock secured the hasp. He flipped the lock up so Mohamed could see.

Mohamed nodded and eased himself out, the low clouds circling his feet as he made his way to the gate. He used his key, slipping it into the padlock and twisted, but the mechanism didn't open. *What? Locked out? No way.* He had as much right to be there as anyone. He huffed back to his car and popped the trunk. The lid felt cold and wet to his touch. He thought about his mother. This car had a tire iron too. He marched back and pried the hasp free, leaving it dangling from the post. He nodded at Matthew.

Matthew lifted the gate, the fog wrapping him in a gray shroud as he walked it back. Mohamed climbed into the car and pulled up next to him so he could get in.

They rolled slowly, bouncing over the potholes and washboards. Mohamed lowered his window, hoping to get a whiff of the ocean. The air, mixed with the smell of stale water, moss, and rotted wood, seeped in. The giant sequoias, looking eerie with the vaporous mist swirling around their roots, dwarfed the car. A rush of black wings startled them as a crow flew in front of their windshield. Mohamed slammed on the brakes, causing Matthew to jerk forward. He slid the car into reverse and, looking over his shoulder, backed up until they were around a bend.

"What's going on?"

"There's a van parked in front of the cabin. I saw it through the trees."

"So?"

The smell of a wood fire wafted through the air. Mohamed looked at his brother. "I didn't think they'd be so stupid. They've got Layla in there. I'd bet on it. I can't believe they'd bring her here."

Matthew reached for the door.

"Wait! You can't go in there. They'll be armed. Let me handle it. I'm one of them. They trust me. You need to get out of the car and hide nearby. If Layla's in there, and I see an opportunity, I'll bring her out. But if I'm confronted"—Mohamed reached for his belt—"here, take my cell phone. I added the FBI number to my address book. If you hear the sound of gunfire or see anything suspicious, call and get them here fast."

"Shouldn't we do that now?"

"Definitely not. We don't know for sure Layla's in there. It could turn out to be nothing. Bringing in the FBI now would only tip them off and cause everyone to go underground."

Matthew pulled himself from the car, slipping out of his wrinkled corduroy jacket. He tossed it on the seat. "It's new," he said. "I don't want it getting dirty."

He leaned back in, resting his weight against the doorframe as he peered into Mohamed's eyes. "Did you mean it? About being a Christian, I mean."

Mohamed hesitated, not sure about what to say. He nodded.

"Then I think we should pray."

CHAPTER 41

THE CAR PULLED AWAY, disappearing into the mist like a bug caught in a spiderweb.

Matthew held his place until Mohamed was out of sight and then took off through the woods, chasing after him. He couldn't just sit and wait. His feet scuffed through the wet leaves. He imagined his brother carrying Layla out of the cabin, her arms locked around his neck as she batted her long eyelashes saying, "*Myyyyyy hero,*" with an exaggerated sigh. But that wasn't the point. Brother or not, the man was an admitted terrorist, and that wasn't a foundation upon which to build trust. His alleged change of heart was good news—great news, in fact—but it didn't mean his cronies in the cabin couldn't turn him back to the dark side.

Matthew bounded forward, leaping from one rock to the next, trying to stay off broken branches that might snap and make noise. He bumped into a sapling. The water shaken from its limbs fell on his neck, running cold and wet down his back. Even if he'd wanted to wait, there was nowhere to sit. Every rock and fallen tree was covered with a damp green moss, and he wasn't anxious to get wetter than he already was. He stopped atop a boulder, peering through the gray soup, trying to locate the cabin. But all he could see were the trunks of the shadowy trees a few feet ahead. He looked at his watch. By his estimation, he had about fifteen minutes to save Layla.

He hopped down and continued plowing through the woods, brushing against droplet-laden ferns that painted his pants with streaks of water. So much for keeping dry. He still couldn't see the cabin. He had to get a better view. He stepped up on another rock and hopped down to find himself standing in a clearing, totally exposed. He backed up, ducking behind a tree. The silver Lexus was just ahead, stopped in front of a rustic hunter's shack with smoke streaming from its chimney. Mohamed was climbing out of the car. He went around back and popped open the trunk, reaching in to remove a bulky red bag, which he set on the ground as he quietly closed the lid. *Now what's he got in there?* The thing looked big enough to hold several weapons. Was he planning an armed assault?

Mohamed stooped over and snatched the bag up, heading for the cabin. The crossbeam of the porch sported a dozen pair of antlers. He didn't bother being subtle as he clomped across the century-old boards. Taking hold of the knob, he threw the door open.

Two men jumped up from a game of chess, upsetting the pieces, toppling the king, knight, and bishop to the floor. An automatic weapon was lying across the lap of one of the men, who fumbled to recover it. The other set his cup down and used his fingers to flick spilled tea from his *abaya*.

For a moment, Mohamed was taken aback, then he smiled, nodding at each in turn. "Abdu, Amre, *salam*! I didn't recognize you at first." Mohamed brought a hand up to rub his goatee. "You guys look good without your beards, very becoming."

Amre brought the gun up and cradled it in his arm, making sure Mohamed saw it. "It is a necessary evil. We must look like the other guests at the wedding." He wore faded blue denims and a blue plaid flannel shirt. His right eye began to twitch. Mohamed had seen the tic before, but only when the man was nervous.

"We did not expect you," Abdu said, still wiping the tea from his robe. He looked strange wearing an *abaya* and turban, but with a clean-shaven face. "Why are you here?"

Mohamed glanced around the room, nodding. The fire burned brightly. Several logs were stacked on the hearth ready to be used as fuel, the floor in front of the fireplace overspread with soot and ashes. Arab newspapers littered the furniture. Draped over the arms of one chair were two suits, along with belts and ties and polished shoes—their disguises for the coming event. One of the suits was brand-new, still wrapped in plastic. Judging from the clutter, it was obvious the men had been here several days, which only meant Layla was here too. "I guess I could ask the same of you."

Their eyes darted back and forth, questioning each other, but Abdu spoke first. "We are here to organize the final details of the wedding," he said.

If they were making plans, there wasn't any evidence of it. A plate of cheese, fruits, and cold meats sat on the table along with a carafe of tea, but no maps or diagrams. And why the gun?

"By yourselves? Wouldn't you think El Sheikh or I should be involved? I think we'd want to know about any last-minute changes." He smiled and winked. "Come on, guys, I know what's going on. You're down here on vacation." Mohamed set his bag down. "Don't worry, I won't say anything. Everyone likes to get away every now and then. Truth be known, that's why I'm here."

The two men exchanged furtive glances but didn't respond.

"I was on my way to Frisco to do a final inspection of our staging area, and I remembered I'd left a couple of soccer balls here, so I thought I'd stop by and pick them up and maybe take a few hours off just to relax. It's bound to get hectic from here on in. Who knows when we'll get another chance, know what I mean? But this weather, can you believe it? What happened to our sun?" He walked to the table and stood between the two men, separating them. "Food! I'm starved." He slipped a slice of cheese into his mouth and turned around. "Sorry to spoil your game." His eyes flicked from one to the other. He reached for a grape, stuffing it in with the cheese.

Matthew waited until Mohamed was inside, then determined a course of action. They probably had Layla locked in one of the bedrooms, and if Mohamed was now persona non grata, they'd try to prevent him from seeing her. He stepped into the forest and moved back until the cabin was no longer visible through the fog. There was abundant foliage to keep him hidden, but it was hard hopping from one blind to the next while making sure he stayed out of sight.

The tree would work better. A giant sequoia lay on its side, running uphill parallel to the cabin. Its root system radiated out like the burst of a black star, with the massive trunk burned hollow on one side as though hit by lightning. He grabbed a root stem and pulled himself forward. The concave area was big as a house. You could put a bed, table, and chairs in there and still have room to move about, but he didn't have time to play Robinson Crusoe. He looked up. The top of the trunk was well over his head. All he had to do was go around to the other side and stay behind the tree as he followed it up the slope.

He was moving quickly, but every time his foot snagged a twig or sent loose gravel sliding down the hill, he stopped. Might as well shoot off a cannon. It'd be a miracle if they didn't hear.

He'd traveled a hundred feet before the tree became too narrow to shield him. Stooping, he went a bit farther and found a place low enough to crawl over. The branches gave him something to hold on to as he pulled himself up and then slid down on the other side. Now he was above the cabin and behind it. He turned, looking through the breaking fog on a cedar shake roof, strewn with pine needles. Smoke swirled up from the chimney. The rear of the building, which he assumed was the bedroom, had a window on the left, but nothing along the back. He wouldn't be seen if he made his way straight down.

He started sidestepping, scooting one foot ahead of the other, thankful the blanket of leaves created a soft cushion under his feet. Kicking loose gravel down the side of the hill would make too much noise. *Aaa-yikes!* He stopped abruptly, teetering at the edge of a solid granite wall, a shower of pine needles, leaves, and dirt spilling over the sheer ten-foot drop. He regained his balance. *Rats!* He'd have to go around. If he followed the precipice to the left, he'd end up on the side with the windows. He had no choice but to go to the right. He walked along the edge, thanking God for catching him before he stumbled over the cliff.

Mohamed sat at the table and picked up the fallen chess pieces, placing them back on the board. He shuffled everything around, setting the game up for play. He looked at Abdu. "Anyone up for a match?" he said. He wasn't good at chess, but he needed to do something to get these boys to relax, and the best way to do that was to provide a distraction. If he could catch them off guard, maybe he'd have a chance to grab the gun.

Amre stood by the closed door that led to the bedroom, cradling his assault rifle. The quivering of his eye let Mohamed know he had something to hide. He held his ground, refusing to fall for the "Hey, ol' buddy, let's sit down and play a game" routine.

Abdu, on the other hand, pulled back a chair and, lifting his robe, took the seat opposite him. Mohamed continued setting the pieces in place. "I guess this is kind of like what we're trying to make happen here, isn't it? I mean, we got Queen Allie here"—he set the queen in place—"and King Mike, ready to put the boot to King Bob and Queen Rachel." Smiling, he took the black king and flicked it, knocking down the white king and queen. "Not bad, huh?" Abdu didn't smile, nor did Amre. "Hey, come on, guys. What's the matter, no sense of humor? You guys have to lighten up. All work and no play makes for a very dull day."

Abdu picked up the two fallen pieces, setting them aright. "We can play a match, if you like, but I warn you, I'm very good at this."

Mohamed stared into the fire and rolled his eyes. *Brother, what have I gotten myself into?*

Matthew hid behind a tree. At least he was back on level ground with the cabin just a dozen feet away. He brought his head out to peek around the trunk. All he had to do was cross a few yards of open space, twenty feet at most. His heart was pounding. This was where it got tricky. The window was around the corner. If he wanted to see what was in that room, he had to chance being exposed. He could only hope Mohamed had the undivided attention of those inside.

He took off running, his feet padding the ground, going for the goal. He pulled up short and stopped, flipping around, back against the wall, hands feeling the moist wood, chest thumping. It was all a bit much, like he was part of some B-grade movie, but the throbbing of his heart told him it was real.

He slowly brought his head far enough out to peek around the corner. The fog seemed lighter than before, but it was still too thick to know for certain there wasn't somebody lurking around guarding the house from the outside. He had to trust God. *Please, Lord.* Sometimes faith was spelled r-i-s-k. He went for it, tucking into a crouch as he inched his way over to the window, stopping just beneath the sill.

He was breathing hard, not because he was out of breath, but because of the way his heart was hammering in his chest. If he raised himself up, would there be someone with a gun on the other side, waiting to blow his head off? He moved to the side, out from beneath the sill, and slowly stood with his back still flat against the wall. His hand was trembling. He stared at it, then reached out and waved it in front of the window. *Nothing.*

Slowly he peered around the bottom corner. The lights were out. He didn't see anyone. He cupped his hands and pressed his face to the screen, trying to peer in. The room was dark and the screen dirty. He could taste the century-old dust. A bed and a dresser were visible, but they were mere silhouettes. But—it did appear that someone was lying on the bed. The longer he stared, the clearer the image became. It had to be Layla.

The window was open, presumably to let in fresh air, but a screen blocked the opening. He scratched it with his finger, making a rasping sound.

"*Pssst,* Layla! Layla, wake up!"

She didn't move. *Must be sedated.*

There was a small hole in the wire mesh. He pushed his finger in and wiggled it around, making the gap bigger. The old fly screen gave way easily as he started pulling it from the frame, one rusty staple at a time. He was sure every sound he made could be heard by those on the other side of the door. He didn't have a plan, but he couldn't leave Layla there. Hopefully he'd be able to wake her and get her out before anyone knew she was gone.

"And that's checkmate," Abdu said. "Perhaps you should stick to soccer. You're worse than Amre."

Mohamed smiled, conceding defeat. He picked up the carafe, but it was empty. "And your manners are worse than my chess. You didn't even offer me tea." He got up and headed to the sink but stopped and put the flask down on the counter without turning on the water. "Forget it," he said, turning around. "I have to be going." He moved toward the bedroom, but Abdu jumped up to intercept him.

"I am sorry if it seems we've been rude. This was not our intent."

"Excuse me. I need to get something before I go. I left two soccer balls in the bedroom the last time I was here. I don't like losing them. They're expensive." Mohamed tipped his head toward the soccer bag he'd left on the floor by the door.

Abdu's hand came up flat against Mohamed's chest. "Amre will get them for you."

But Mohamed shook his head. "No bother. I know where they are."

"You question my hospitality and then refuse my help? No, my brother, I must insist." He looked over his shoulder at his partner. "Amre, please, take care of this for our guest."

Amre smiled thinly. He turned and opened the door, but only wide enough to slip inside, then closed it again.

Abdu kept his hand up, holding Mohamed at bay, but his head turned at the sound of muffled voices, a thump against the wall, and what sounded like a scuffle coming from inside the room. The gun went off, *puftt, puftt, puftt,* followed by the sound of shattering glass.

Abdu spun on his heel, followed by Mohamed, who was standing on his tiptoes to see over the man's shoulder as the door flew open.

Broken pieces of window covered the floor, and bullet holes striated the wall. Amre was standing, feet apart, his weapon pointed at a man sprawled on the floor.

Matthew rolled over and sat up, rubbing his head. Mohamed could see Layla stretched out on the bed. Matthew struggled to his feet and stood facing the man with his hands raised.

Amre spun around, pointing his gun at Mohamed.

"Two of you? What trick is this?"

CHAPTER 42

AMRE'S HEAD FLICKED BACK and forth, looking from Matthew to Mohamed and back to Matthew. "Who are you?" He brought his automatic weapon around, pointing it at Mohamed, and took two steps back, motioning with his eyes. "Over there, please," he said.

Mohamed's heart leaped to his throat. He raised his hands defensively. He didn't know one gun from another, but he didn't question that Amre was capable of using the weapon or that a few short bursts would turn him into confetti. Tiny beads of sweat broke out on his forehead. "Didn't your mother ever teach you not to play with guns?" he said. He turned and began backing up, but one of the balls he'd come to fetch was behind him, causing him to almost trip. He kicked it with his heel and continued backing away from Amre and Abdu.

"You will show me identification," the militant barked, keeping one hand under the barrel of his weapon and the other around the stock with his finger on the trigger.

Mohamed stopped and reached into his vest pocket, slowly removing his wallet. He spoke in Arabic to prevent Matthew from understanding. "You know who I am. I'm Mohamed El Taher, servant of Allah Most High and Muhammad his Messenger." He reached out, trying to keep from trembling as he handed the wallet to Abdu, whose hand was stretched out waiting to receive it. "Be careful, my brother. If anything happens to me, you will be accountable. I suggest you put that gun down. No, wait!" Mohamed tipped his head to the right. "Keep this man covered. He's an impostor."

Abdu shuffled through the wallet, examining the driver's license and student ID. He looked at Matthew and held his hand out again. "Where is your wallet?"

Matthew shook his head. "Sorry, friend, I don't have it on me." He shrugged his shoulders, keeping his hands raised in front of him. "It's in my coat, and I left my coat in the car, but if you can wait a minute, I'll get it for you." He took a step forward.

"Stay where you are!" Amre screamed.

"I told you he's a fake," Mohamed said. "Grab him!"

Both men now focused their attention on Matthew. Mohamed did a quick assessment. He'd left two balls in the room. The one he'd just kicked was at his brother's feet. The other was behind him. He continued backing away, still following Amre's instruction, and didn't stop until the second ball was by his toe. With his hands raised he wiggled a finger, catching his brother's eye. He glanced down at Matthew's feet and then brought his eyes up, nodding imperceptibly. Both Abdu and Amre caught the movement, but Matthew coughed, bringing their eyes back to him. In a motion quick as a blink, Mohamed used his instep to swipe the ball, striking it hard, and with practiced precision scored a direct hit to the side of Amre's face.

The man had no time to duck. His hands flew up, still holding the weapon as he stumbled backward, off balance, *puftt, puftt, puftt, puftt,* sending rounds into the ceiling. Abdu stepped back to keep from being shot, giving Matthew time to launch the other ball into his stomach.

Mohamed leaped forward, grabbing the rifle by the barrel as he kicked Amre in the groin, doubling him over. He wrenched the weapon from his hands and swung the butt of the gun down hard, hitting Amre between the shoulder blades, forcing him to the ground.

Abdu was clutching his stomach, trying to regain his wind. Matthew did a pirouette, sweeping a foot under the man's legs, knocking him to the floor alongside Amre.

Mohamed took a step back, aiming the gun at both men. "Who said soccer's a noncontact sport?" He grinned and, with the automatic tucked under one arm, turned and gave Matthew a high five—*Yes!*—which, as they brought their arms down, led to a natural embrace. They let go and stood back, looking at each other, their heads angled curiously, then burst out laughing.

Mohamed inclined his head the other way and Matthew followed suit. They laughed again. "I saw you do that in the restaurant. That's when I knew you were my brother," Mohamed said. "Man, I hated that."

"Layla noticed it too," Matthew chimed in, still high on laughter. "She told me about it, but I didn't believe her."

They tried choking back their amusement but couldn't. Mohamed covered his mouth, but they kept staring like they were seeing each other for the first time. Matthew drew his fingers across his lips, wiping spittle from his new goatee. "I hate your guts," he said, and they both started chortling again, but he raised his hand. "No, wait a minute. I mean I hated you for stealing Layla, but what I wanted to say is, I can see why she likes you. You're one good-looking dude."

Mohamed spit and spurted and burbled, and they laughed until they were teary-eyed and their sides ached.

It was all Mohamed could do to keep from doubling over and losing control of the gun, but out of the corner of his eye, he caught Amre pulling his feet in, crouching like a cat ready to pounce. He turned and fired a short burst into the floor. "Please don't move. I'd hate to have to shoot you."

And in that moment he realized that even if the police came right then and arrested these two, he was as good as dead. The American judicial system was eminently fair. It would be a long time before they came to trial as they wound their way though the legal maze of petitions, discoveries, motions, and other manufactured loopholes too numerous to count. The word would get out—*Mohamed El Taher has betrayed us*—and a price would be put on his head. The best he could hope for was a relocation program, but as long as they continued looking, he'd eventually be found. There were just too many sympathetic eyes and ears in America.

He looked at his brother. At least Layla would be in good hands. She couldn't ask for a better man.

"Keep them covered," Matthew said. "I'll get something to tie them up." He turned and circled the two, giving them wide berth as he exited to the other room.

Mohamed was still chuckling. How can a man laugh, holding a gun?

But the thought made him chortle even more. He took a breath, the air fluttering in his lungs. He felt positively giddy.

His attention drifted to his captives—not a more dour-looking duo on the planet. That's what he used to be like, all narrow-eyed and pinch-lipped with no smile. It's what he noticed most about the change he was experiencing. He was laughing again, not the evil *ha, ha-now-I've-gotcha* laugh, but a genuine, belly-busting happiness that came from joy unspeakable. Now where was that from? *Oh, yeah.* The Book. That's how the Bible described knowing Jesus. *Whoopee, I'm saved! Whatever in the world that means!*

He smiled at his one-time friends, now turned foes. *Love your enemies, do good to those who hate you.* "Come on, guys, you look like you're sucking lemons. Lighten up. At least you're only going to jail for kidnapping. It's a lot better than murder."

The side of Amre's face was sporting a large red welt. He pursed his lips, glaring. Abdu tucked his chin into his robe but raised his eyes, his pupils rolling up under his eyelids. "Those who reject Faith and do wrong,—Allah will not forgive them nor guide them to any way—except the way of Hell, to dwell therein for ever…"

"Yeah, yeah, Surah 4, 168 and 169. I know that one. Fact is, I know them all. Ever read the one that says Allah roasts people in hell for their entertainment? Yeah, that one's in there too. And one that talks about burning people's skin off and then replacing it with new skin to burn it off again, and making people drink boiling water. Used to make me wonder what kind of God would do that. I mean, come on, a just punishment's one thing, but taking pleasure in torturing people? When I watch that kind of stuff on TV, I call it sadistic."

"You blaspheme."

"Do I? Don't you ever wonder what kind of God encourages his followers to lie and cheat and kill in his name but never talks about loving, just threatens to toss you into hell if you tick him off?" He looked over his shoulder, tilting his head at Layla. "Here you are; you've got this innocent girl who's never done anything to you, yet I have no doubt, if you didn't get what you wanted from me, you would've killed her and done it with a smile on your face like you were doing God a favor. What kind of God do you serve? You really need to look at the Bible. The *God* in there brings life and love, and…and joy…"

Matthew stepped back into the room, empty-handed. "I couldn't find anything."

Mohamed nodded. "Doesn't surprise me. This place is only used for meetings." He looked around and then remembered the roll of duct tape he'd bought to repair his soccer bag. "I think I have something in the car," he said. "Here, watch them for me." He handed Matthew the weapon.

Matthew looked over his shoulder, tilting his head to the right. "Take Layla with you. We have to get her to a hospital as soon as possible."

Mohamed glanced over. Layla's unconscious body was stretched out on the bed—*because of him*. She looked radiant. If it were possible, and he Prince Charming, he'd awaken her with a kiss. His mother said forgiveness was of God. Maybe so, and maybe Layla *could* forgive him, but he'd be a long time forgiving himself.

He leaned over, slipping his hands under her legs and shoulders to lift her into his arms. Holding her close to his chest, he felt the soft beat of her heart. Her skin was smooth, her body warm, but he squelched his desire. He'd have to relocate and virtually disappear as soon as he received his new identity. And she couldn't come with him—not now—not with a price on his head.

He turned and raised his chin toward his brother. "I did this to her," he said. The atmosphere of merriment had vanished.

Matthew nodded. "Just get her in the car."

Mohamed started for the door.

It was a subtle gesture, the hand moving so slowly that neither Matthew nor Mohamed, distracted as they were with Layla, noticed. Abdu slipped his hand into his robe and removed something small, round and gray. He brought his hands together like he was about to pray and screamed, "*Allah Akbar!*" and pulled his hands apart, letting the object fall. The grenade went skittering across the floor.

It happened so fast Matthew had but a second to think. He tucked the gun to his chest and dove on the explosive. "Go!" he screamed.

Mohamed lunged for the exit.

A flash of light bounced off the wall of fog. A second later Mohamed heard the sound. The explosion blew the door off its hinges, sending it slamming into his back, knocking him to the ground, with the door covering and protecting him and Layla from the falling carnage.

He tried to breathe, but the air was stuck in his lungs. He looked out from under the door and saw objects raining down around him, but the scene was strangely quiet. There was a droning in his ears, though he knew instinctively that the bits and pieces of things hitting the ground were making noise. He coughed, expelling the trapped air from his lungs, and sucked in. His breathing came in gasps as he tried lifting himself to take his weight off Layla. He slid the door to the side, shifting it off his back, and struggled to raise himself, but he teetered to the side and fell over. Bringing his legs up, he pushed himself into a crouch and sat back with his hands on his knees, still trying to regain his breath.

The roof of his car was crushed flat under the weight of a square log. He reached for Layla, but she was too far away. His hand dropped to his thigh. He turned around, falling on his backside facing the other way. His whole body screamed in pain.

The cabin looked like a pile of Lincoln Logs. The square beams had separated and lay askew, and the roof was entirely gone. The row of antlers lay upturned, like claws vainly grasping the air. Smoke rose from a pile of rubble that once was a chimney. A few small fires burned in the yard. One consumed the remains of a turban. His sports bag was ripped in half, lying face up, a red clamshell with a ball nestled inside like a pearl. Mohamed's chest swelled and deflated, his shoulders heaving as his body shook with sobs. *Matthew? Nooooooooo!*

Two men in dark suits appeared out of the smoke and fog. Mohamed gave them a fleeting glance, but the light hurt his eyes. He kept his head down, seeing only their legs and their shiny black shoes as they shuffled through the debris, but he faintly heard their movements and what sounded like muffled conversation. One stooped down, taking Layla's wrist in his hand, feeling for a pulse.

CHAPTER 43

LAYLA'S EYES FLUTTERED FOR a moment, then opened but immediately closed again, and then opened in a squint. She brought her hands up to explore the blanket and felt the bandage on her wrist with a needle affixed to a tube. Lifting the covers, she saw she was wearing pajamas.

She rolled her head in the direction of the light. A breeze was coming through the open window. She heard a bird, *cheer-cheeralee*, a robin perhaps. She tried to focus through watery eyes. To her right a bouquet floated over the nightstand like a blush of indistinct pastel colors. She rolled her head back, staring at the ceiling, blinking to clear her vision. She could see the dotted pattern of the acoustic tiles coming into focus, her sight returning. The overhead light had a white plastic grill covering a bank of fluorescent tubes. She blinked again, gathering more detail with each passing second.

She tried lifting herself on her elbows but settled onto her pillow again, too weak to hold herself up. The colors caught her eye, a vase of flowers with a card attached. She relaxed. OK, she was in a hospital. If the flowers didn't give it away, the stainless steel tray on wheels did, that and the crank attached to her bed. The question was, how did she get here?

Ooooh, her head hurt. The light was blinking on and off, or was that just the throbbing? She closed her eyes, trying to remember. She'd been in Laguna; she remembered the rolling whitecaps breaking on the shore and the seagulls crying for food, and the store windows and hearing the sound of footsteps, and then...did somebody grab her from behind? There was a smell, *like ether*; she was fighting, clawing at the hand holding a rag over her nose. She couldn't breathe. Everything after that was fuzzy.

She tried raising herself again and this time, in spite of the pounding in her head, found the strength. Her mother was asleep, slumped in a chair with a magazine open in her lap. Layla smiled softly, laying her head back down. She needed another minute to collect her thoughts. Her folks must have hopped on a plane and flown all the way out from Arizona just to be with her. How serious *was* this?

She rolled her head to the side. The digital letters of the clock on the nightstand said 8:01. *What day is it? How long have I been here?* Her lungs felt sore and heavy. Maybe she'd been in a car accident. Maybe the man she saw holding something to her face was trying to sedate her. She jerked her legs up, wiggling her toes, making sure they hadn't anesthetized her and amputated a leg to extricate her from a wrecked car. It felt like she'd been crushed. She took a deep breath, ignoring the ache in her chest, and held it, then let it out, trying to breathe normally.

A nurse stood at the door, her face the color of pecans breaking into a glossy white smile. She walked over and took Layla's hand, placing her fingers on her wrist as she shook a thermometer.

"You are conscious again. This is good. I must take your temperature now." Without waiting to be acknowledged, the nurse slipped a thermometer into Layla's mouth and grabbed her arm, extending and clamping it under her own as she wrapped it in an inflatable bladder. The uniform she wore was standard hospital white, but her head was covered with a black *khimar*, the traditional scarf of Islamic women.

The disturbance roused Layla's mother. She stretched and sat up, the magazine in her lap sliding to the floor. She reached for it as the nurse began squeezing the pump, filling the bladder with air to tighten it around Layla's arm. "You have a boyfriend, yes? I know he's stopped to ask for you. He is very famous."

"*Umm-hum,*" Layla nodded, keeping her mouth closed. *A local soccer boy, hardly famous.*

The nurse released the air, taking a count, which she recorded on her clipboard. Then she removed the thermometer and logged its reading as well. "I am glad he stopped those butchers. They give Muslims a bad name."

Layla's mother stood behind the nurse, waiting for a chance to speak but polite enough not to interrupt.

"Your vitals are normal," the nurse said. "This will be good news for the doctor." She smiled, her round almond cheeks glowing. She unzipped the Velcro fastener and removed the monitor, laying it on the clipboard against her chest.

"What happened?"

The nurse turned, looking over her shoulder at the woman standing behind her, and then back at Layla. "I will let your mother explain. The doctor will come soon." She smiled again and turned, her rubber-soled sneakers squeaking on the waxed linoleum as she rustled out the door.

Layla's mother took her hand and sat on the edge of the bed. "How are you feeling?"

Maybe it was the drugs they had her on, or the fact that her eyes had not yet fully adjusted to being awake, but her mother looked like an angel, or at least someone with a shining aura. She appeared to be surrounded by light. Her perfect teeth held a lustrous smile. Though she had dark Egyptian features and her silver hair was wrapped in a bun, her beauty, more than anything else, was expressed in an air of calm assurance. Layla knew that her mother would have prayed the whole time she was here.

She brought a hand up to rub her head. "Terrible. I feel like I've been hit by a truck. Where's Dad?"

"He'll be along in a minute. He just went downstairs to get me a tea."

Layla nodded, squeezing her mother's hand. "So, what happened? How'd I get here?"

"Well, that's a difficult question," her mother said. "That boyfriend of yours, Matthew..."

"How is Matthew?"

"Oh, he's all right, but he's sure got some kind of a story to tell. I gather you knew he had a brother, supposedly an identical twin, and if I'm putting the pieces together correctly, someone you used to play with as a child, that boy Mohamed. You remember him? I knew his mother. Your father had her over a few times and tried to teach her about Jesus, but it was a real surprise to learn she had another son. She never said a word."

Layla struggled to get up. Her mother reached out to assist. She stood, taking Layla's arm, helping her to a sitting position. "There, is that better?" She fluffed the pillow behind her daughter's back, and turning, went to get her chair, dragging it over so she could sit down.

Layla nodded, pushing on the mattress to make herself more comfortable. "It was a surprise to everyone. I asked Dad to do a DNA screen and"—she leaned forward, adjusting her pillow—"we only received verification a few days ago. Apparently Matthew and Mohamed were separated at birth."

"I wonder what became of their mother. She was so close to coming to the Lord, but something must have happened. Did you know her son was part of a terrorist organization?"

Layla didn't say anything. She remained still, though the tempo of her heart increased. She waited for her mother to continue.

"The FBI had him under surveillance. There was some kind of plot to blow up something, some bank or government building, something or other. All I know is, it went sour, and your very own Matthew is a hero."

Layla shook her head. "What do you mean?"

Her mother looked down, searching for something. She leaned over and scooped a newspaper from the floor, handing it to Layla. The headline read: "Terrorist Plot Foiled in Battle of Yin and Yang."

Yin and yang? Equal but opposing forces? Good and evil? She recognized the photo of Matthew taken from his university ID. They'd probably acquired the photo of Mohamed the same way. Layla set the paper aside, preferring to hear the explanation from her mother.

"This Mohamed fellow," she said, her finger tapping the picture of the man with a goatee, "kidnapped you. I don't know why, but he and a couple of other thugs held you captive in Big Sur. They had you locked in a cabin in some remote part of the woods. That's why you've been out so long. They kept injecting you with Pentothal to keep you sedated."

Layla reached for the paper, looking at it again. Two brothers, so much alike, and yet so different. She shook her head. "Kidnapped...why?"

Her mother patted her hand reassuringly. "I'm not sure we'll ever know. Matthew thinks his brother was obsessed with the idea of having you for himself. He thinks he wanted to take you back to Egypt and was planning to force you to marry him, but he was involved in a plot to destroy a lot of American assets, and he had to do that first. Only Matthew found out about it. He followed his brother and called the FBI. That's why everyone's calling him a hero. He went to get you and was carrying you out when the whole place just blew up. The FBI says they were trying to make a bomb. Praise God, if you'd been in there just a few more minutes..."

A tear started to build in her mother's eye. She reached over to pull a lock of Layla's hair over her shoulder, combing it through her fingers. "You're going to have to take it easy. Matthew landed right on top of you. No broken bones, but the doctor says you'll be sore for a while."

Layla placed a hand on her chest, taking a breath, and then let it slide to the bed. "Yes, I feel that. It hurts just to breathe. So, what happened to the other one, the brother?"

"Oh, he's dead, thank goodness. I don't mean to speak ill of anyone, but he would have destroyed many lives. I guess the Lord gave him a taste of his own medicine. It's Matthew I feel sorry for. He's been in to see you several times. The flowers are from him," she said, lifting her chin to indicate the bouquet on the nightstand.

Layla glanced over and nodded. She pushed herself back so she could lie down, grimacing as her head found the pillow. She turned her face away, her eyes watering, blurring the vase of flowers. "You'll have to excuse me, Mom. I'm feeling kind of tired. I think I need to rest."

CHAPTER 44

THE ROOM FELT AS cold and dank as the inside of an aquarium. Mohamed rubbed his arms, looking at the two-way mirror. The people on the other side were like tourists watching the gyrations of a rare aquatic species. He shifted in his seat—it was impossible to get comfortable in a folding metal chair—answering the same questions asked a dozen different ways for about the hundredth time.

He sat across from Ambrose Barnes, his FBI contact, who with pencil in hand and digital recorder at his elbow, took his statement. Mohamed made sure the recording device was turned off, but he couldn't be certain there weren't bugs around the room, picking up his voice and sending it somewhere else. He had only Ambrose's word for that. By prior agreement his name would not be entered into the record, though his written deposition would be read at the trial. He was viewed strictly as an informant.

Only now was it revealed to him how close he'd come to spending the rest of his life in jail. Unbeknownst to him, the FBI had been watching him for some time. They knew about his relationship with Sheikh Omar. It turned out Omar had been under observation for several years. They weren't fooled by his quiet professor act. A single complaint by an undergraduate claiming his Eastern lit teacher, Omar Muhsin, was trying to draw him into a radical form of militant Islam had brought the outwardly timid academic under scrutiny. There were long-range listening devices and cameras positioned around his property, recording every conversation that took place outside the house and the face of every visitor who came and went. Mohamed's gravitating there after arriving in the States had raised flags on several fronts.

And, *oh, yeah,* the pesky blue car—that was theirs too. They knew Mohamed thought Omar was having him followed, so they didn't bother being discreet. Sowing seeds of distrust worked in their favor. They were on him all the way, so when he called and told them he was in Big Sur, they already knew. They just looked at each other, smiled, and followed the GPS locater they'd mounted under the chassis of his car as he led them right to the cabin. They'd crossed the culvert onto a neighboring property, hidden the blue sedan beneath the boughs of a giant sequoia, and walked in. They were concealed behind rocks and ferns, deep in the woods, with their high-powered binoculars trained on the cabin when it blew up. The entire fireworks show rained down around them while they sat with their arms folded over their heads. It was their quick response that enabled him to get Layla to the hospital without delay.

The FBI had helped him, and he thanked God for it; now it was his turn to help the FBI. The agency had followed Omar and Mohamed to the engagement party and had watched with great interest as Omar met with Allie's parents and Mohamed with Allie herself. They knew something was going to happen that involved the soon-to-be-wed vice president; they just didn't know what. The terrorists were careful in their planning, keeping their secrets to themselves. Intel analysts had lots of pieces, but they hadn't been able to fit them together to form a complete picture. That's what Mohamed brought them now: the key to the puzzle, the missing pieces.

Mohamed shifted, redistributing his weight in the chair. He considered himself fortunate to have come forward when he did—*the will of Allah?* Yes, in the sense that Allah is the Arabic word for God, but no, in the sense of it being His name. From now on, he would pray only to Jehovah God. And it *was* God's will. As a suspected terrorist, he most certainly would have been arrested and tried, and probably would have spent the rest of his life in prison.

Ambrose studied Mohamed with a look that suggested he appreciated the information but wasn't sure about letting an admitted terrorist back on the street. He was a big man, with biceps that looked like ham hocks, stenciled with a Navy SEAL tattoo. "As far as you're concerned, this is the best thing that could have happened."

Mohamed swiveled in the chair, crossing his legs, but he felt awkward trying to look relaxed when he was so tense. He brought his foot down and leaned forward, with his elbows resting on his knees and his hands clasped in front of him. "You're talking about the death of my brother."

Agent Barnes tossed his pencil down and sat back, extending his feet under the table. "I don't mean to sound callous. I know what it's like to lose family. I lost my older brother in Vietnam. It happens. You can't change it; you just gotta let go and get on with life. But in this case, it does give you the perfect cover. His wallet was in the coat we retrieved from the car, which you'll get as soon as we're done here. Your wallet, though damaged in the explosion, was intact enough to establish you as being inside, killed by the bomb you were trying to make. We fed that to the press. They took pictures of your wallet with your ID cards and everything, and that's how it was reported in the papers. You'll have to drop out of school, but that would be understandable given what you've been through."

Mohamed nodded. He rubbed the palm of his hand with his thumb, then straightened his arms and brought them down between his knees. There was only one problem—or maybe two. Layla would know. She'd seen the difference between him and Matthew from the very start. She knew him too well. Would she be able, or even *desire*, to forgive him?

The other issue was a bit more complex. He wasn't sure he wanted to stay in America. He rubbed his arms as if trying to convince himself it was too cold, but that wasn't it. In reality, the Egyptian sun was *too* hot. His mother needed him, and he wanted to comfort her, but that wasn't it either. She could always visit or come to live with him in the States.

No, the real problem was this seed of an idea that had taken root in his head and wouldn't stop growing. This new thing he was feeling, this happiness, the desire for life—whatever it was—was just too good to keep to himself. It needed to be shared. There were millions of people, the good decent ordinary citizens of Egypt, who needed to hear about Isa. He wanted to share the news with other Muslims.

He hadn't worked out the details. If he allowed himself to dwell on the problems, he'd never go. Returning to Egypt with an American passport saying he was Matthew Mulberry wouldn't make him safe. He was bound to be recognized sooner or later. He'd grown up there. But he refused to think about that. He'd given up his claim on life. He'd been bought with a price. There was a debt to repay. He should be lying in a grave beside Matthew, but he wasn't, or at the very least be rotting in a prison, but he wouldn't be doing that either. God had saved him now, and God would save him from whatever was to come.

He looked into Ambrose's small blue eyes. "We agree then. I have complete immunity, I'm never to appear to give testimony, and when I walk out of here, I become Matthew Mulberry, a free man."

"That's the deal. You're now a U.S. citizen. You were born in Egypt, but you grew up here. Your parents are deceased. You tell UCLA you're dropping out to get your head together. Everything fits like a glove. Stanford's been officially notified of the death of Mohamed El Taher. You just go live your life the way Matthew would have."

"What if I want to leave?"

Ambrose picked up his pencil and tapped his palm, squinting. "Leave? Why, where would you go?"

"I'm not sure, but I don't want to feel trapped. What if I want to see Canada or visit Europe? What I'm getting at is, the only difference between me and Matthew is our fingerprints. Even identical twins have different prints."

"No problem. We checked into that. Matthew didn't have an arrest record, and he wasn't fingerprinted at birth, nor was he fingerprinted when his parents brought him to the States as an infant. His prints aren't on file anywhere. Neither are yours. Next time you get fingerprinted for any reason, those prints become the fingerprints of Matthew Mulberry. You're him, lock, stock, and barrel; take it or leave it." Agent Barnes leaned in. "Look, it couldn't be any better. Everyone knows Matthew. We don't have to invent a whole new life and background."

Mohamed glanced at the mirror, wondering if any of those watching were able to empathize with his situation. He folded his arms and crossed his legs. His mother's life had been ruined, Layla was in the hospital,

Matthew was dead, and all because of decisions he had made. What kind of God could forgive that?

But there was Paul, that guy in the Bible who killed Christians. Jesus met him and turned *him* around. If Jesus could forgive Paul and even draft him into service, there was hope. *Happy is the man whose sins are forgiven.*

"Look, you weren't responsible for your brother's death." Ambrose broke in, as though reading his mind. "If you're telling the truth, you told him to wait for you in the woods. He made a choice and got himself killed. OK, I guess that makes him a hero, but the best thing you can do is go out and bring honor to his name by living right. He's sure not going to get it lying in a graveyard with your name on his tombstone. I know it's hard, but you only met each other a few weeks ago. You couldn't have been *too* close. Just let it go and move on."

Mohamed brought a hand up to rub his cheek, his skin feeling naked minus the goatee. He wasn't Matthew Mulberry; he was Mohamed El Taher, but perhaps, with the help of God, he *could* pull it off.

He squirmed, his seat feeling numb on the unpadded metal. Why God took Matthew, he might never know. The ways of God were mysterious and unknowable. Maybe there were windows in heaven. Maybe Matthew would look down and see his brother living the kind of life he himself would have lived and rejoice in the sacrifice he'd made. Maybe, *just maybe*, God would one day allow Matthew to pull the clouds of heaven apart—and let Mohamed see him smile.

CHAPTER 45

LAYLA STROLLED THROUGH THE cemetery, savoring the sun on her shoulders. It was a delicious autumn day, the kind you wake up to stretching your arms and saying, "*Yes!* It's good to be alive." The sky, following an overnight rain, was silken blue with fleecy white clouds balling up like wads of cotton in the sky. But more than anything else, it was the air she breathed that made everything seem right, clean fall air that filled her lungs with a desire for life. She took a deep luxurious breath, drinking in the smell of wet grass and roses.

Man's days on Earth were few, the brevity of life confirmed by the thousands of headstones surrounding her. Layla stepped lightly down the narrow path, staying between the markers so as not to intrude on those long since laid to rest. She had to wonder how many she'd see in glory and how many were reserved for the final day of judgment. She feared Mohamed was among the latter, and it added pain to her sorrow. It was bad enough they wouldn't be together in this life, but sadder still that she might not see him—*forever*.

I am the way, the truth, and the life. No one comes to the Father except through Me. That's what Christ said, and if Mohamed refused to believe it, he wouldn't be there. She felt a chill interrupt the warming of her soul, goose bumps rising on her skin. A tear escaped the corner of her eye and rolled slowly down her cheek.

In her hand she held a bouquet purchased at a neighborhood grocery. Mohamed wouldn't know what she paid for the flowers, and if he did, he wouldn't care. They'd spent so many hours hiding from the sun in the local *ba aal*, it seemed fitting.

She stopped, looking down upon the marker at her feet. Small bits of grass stuck to her black leather shoes. The simple rectangle was etched with the words, "M. El Taher. He gave his life for what he believed." However true, it was a less than heartwarming eulogy, but it would have to suffice. There wouldn't be a funeral. There was no one to invite.

She had tried to reach Matthew; she thought it proper to share this moment with him, but he hadn't returned her calls. She couldn't help it if he was hurting—*so was she*. She wanted him to understand—it wasn't her fault! Love wasn't a light switch to be flicked on and off. She couldn't marry him, knowing her love was misplaced, but she desperately wanted him as a friend. How could he, on the one hand, treat Mohamed like part of his family and have him buried in his own plot alongside his parents and, on the other, refuse to be there to pay his last respects? The explanation was probably in the letter, but she hadn't opened it yet. She should, but she knew whatever excuse he'd made, it wouldn't be good enough. He should have come.

She reached down and, holding her black leather purse to make sure it didn't slip from her arm, placed her gift on the polished stone, a bright spray of colorful roses. She'd tried to think of one color that symbolized his life, but in the end had settled for a rainbow. His life had so many facets. A tear rolled quietly down her cheek. She wiped it away with the back of her hand.

Now you've done it, Mohamed; you're making me cry. Her wet lips tried to smile but ended up in a flat line. *Why couldn't you wait? I would've…I don't know what I would've done, but not this…stupid, stupid, stupid. I thought we had something, at least a chance, and…did you have to go blow yourself up? You would have killed me too, you…you!* She felt like running off and hiding someplace where she'd never be found.

Mohamed sat less than ten yards away, watching from behind the tinted glass of a stretch limousine parked under the shade of a California oak.

His eyes were focused on Layla, praying she would understand. Was she crying? It *looked* like she was crying. She looked beautiful even in tears. She wore a dark shift that accentuated her slim waist, with a matching thin sweater to ward off the chill, and her hair was rolled in a bun that seemed to shine whenever she turned toward the light.

He drew in a breath, his whole body shuddering as he let it go. The flowers were nice, but it didn't mean she was mourning. They'd shared a special friendship as children; she'd bring flowers in remembrance of that. But she might also feel relief in knowing the man who'd kidnapped her was dead and in the ground. There was no way to be certain.

If ever he needed the help of God, it was now. *How do Christians pray?* His soul burned in his chest. He hated the deception, no matter how necessary.

Layla looked up, startled by the approach of a man wearing a black suit and thick dark sunglasses. "Sorry for the intrusion, miss." He pulled out a leather wallet and displayed a gold shield and eagle. The badge bore the words: *Federal Bureau of Investigation, U.S. Department of Justice.* "I'm Special Agent Barnes, with the FBI. There's someone who'd like to speak with you," he said, nodding toward the car. "I can't force you to come, it's strictly your choice, but you might want to hear what he has to say."

Layla looked at the car. She'd seen the black limo as she made her way across the lawn, but she took it for a hearse and hadn't given it a second thought. The windows were tinted, so she couldn't see who, if anyone, was inside.

"What's this about?" she asked, knowing full well the events of the past week necessitated inquiry by the FBI.

Barnes reached into his coat again and removed a sheet of paper along with a pen. "All your questions will be answered," he said, "but before we can say anything, I need you to sign a nondisclosure agreement, stating everything you hear will be held in strict confidence and that unauthorized release of this information is an indictable offense. Think about it carefully. Sometimes secrets are hard to keep." He unfolded the document, crinkling it in his meaty hands as he held it out. "There's an ongoing investigation into the death of the man buried here. My first priority is to make sure it isn't compromised."

Layla took the paper and gave it a once-over: "Writ of Binding Nondisclosure. I the undersigned …" Her name was spelled out next to a blank for her signature. She read the first few lines, skipped to the bottom, and signed.

Barnes opened the car door for Layla. The limousine was furnished like a room with two couches, each facing the other. Layla hesitated at the sight of Matthew sitting on the rear seat, looking toward the front with his hands folded in his lap. He gave her a tepid smile, but it quickly faded. She thought she'd be meeting someone from the FBI. She forced herself to step in, but chose to sit across from him on the opposite side. Agent Barnes closed the door behind her and remained outside.

"What's with all the cloak and dagger?" Layla pushed herself up in her seat, trying to get comfortable, tugging on her dress to smooth the material beneath her legs. "It's a bit much. Why couldn't you just meet me like I asked?" She squirmed again and looked up apologetically but unsmiling. "Sorry, I guess I should thank you for saving my life, but I haven't seen you since. Why haven't you returned my calls? It's like you're avoiding me. So, who's your new friend?" she said, looking out the window at the mastiff guard.

Mohamed followed her gaze. "I know how this must look," he said, "but please, hear me out. Not everything is as it appears. That grave over there has my name on it," he said, gazing out the window with eyes heavy and red. "But it's really Matthew who's buried there."

Layla's eyes widened, the color deepening in her cheeks. She leaned forward, staring hard at Mohamed's face. "What are you saying? You can't mean…"

Mohamed brought his head around to look at her and nodded. "Yes, I do. It was Matthew who was killed when that cabin blew up, not me"—his eyes welled and began to overflow—"but I had no part in your kidnapping. I knew nothing about it. We weren't making a bomb; we were plotting to kill the president. But I got called back to Egypt and…and something happened...and I met your Jesus, and then I knew I had to stop them, and...there's just so much..."

Mohamed tried to relate the story, including his part in the assassination plot and how he'd found his mother alive, but Layla, though she nodded to express her interest, for all intents and purposes was still hung up on the words, *I met your Jesus*. Her eyes were like floodgates broken open, her heart stammering in her chest. She pulled her purse up into her lap, scrambling for a tissue to blot her eyes.

Mohamed looked out the window again, his breath steaming the glass. "I had them use my first initial on the headstone...it's the same as Matthew's...and El Taher is our family name, so it's accurate. But I'm the one who should be there. In some ways it *is* me, at least the old me. I feel like a very real part of me has died, but the body buried there, that's Matthew's. *He's* the hero, Layla." He paused to swallow the lump in his throat. "Me, I...I don't know who or what I am." He brought his hand up, drawing a cross on the fogged glass with one finger.

He turned his head to face her again. His breath fluttered in his chest as he spoke. "I read something yesterday, a verse from the Christian Bible. It really shook me. 'Greater love has no one than this, than to lay down one's life for his friends.' My brother did that, just as Jesus did." The tears continued to flow, saturating his cheeks until they hung from his chin.

Layla wanted to reach out and wipe them away, but her vision was blurred by a flood of her own tears. She felt jittery, caught in that undefined place where love and hope and uncertainty and frustration and anger merge, creating a jumble of confused emotions. She didn't know which was causing the pain, only that her heart felt like it was on fire. She scrunched the wet tissue in her hand and looked up, blinking to keep her tears from spilling again. "So you're going to become Matthew; is that it? You're taking his identity, his name..."

Mohamed nodded. "'Greater love has no one than this, than to lay down one's life for his friends.' I can't get over that."

Layla tried to swallow, but a lump in her throat blocked the way. She wondered if her face was as wet as Mohamed's. She poked around in her purse, looking for another tissue, and found the letter she'd received earlier, bearing Matthew's return address. She'd presumed it to be full of excuses about why he hadn't returned her calls, either that or a soppy plea for her hand in marriage. She'd stuffed it into her purse, unopened. Now she took it out and sat holding it in her lap with her eyes closed, the tracks of her tears glistening in the window's light. She removed the single sheet of paper and began to read:

Dearest Layla,

Please forgive me if I've seemed a bit distant lately. I've had a lot on my mind. I know you haven't said it, and would probably deny it if I confronted you directly, but I know it's my brother you love, not me.

When you're with him, the light shines the way it once did when you were with me, but now when we're alone, the shadows grow ever longer. I know you never meant to hurt me, and I love you for that. Layla, I love everything about you, and I probably will until the day I die, but I have to let you go.

It's not that I'm a coward, or unwilling to fight for you. Lord knows I want to lash out and hurt someone, you, him, anyone within reach. "Hurt people hurt people," at least that's what they say, but what good would it do? I could beat him silly and it wouldn't change a thing. Besides: "The wrath of man does not produce the righteousness of God."

He's calling me home, Layla. I don't know when; it could be today, tomorrow, even ten or twenty years from now. All I know is my time on Earth is short. I've discovered I have a brain aneurysm. You know what that is. And in my case it's inoperable. My doctor says the walls of the bubble are exceptionally thin. I'm like a walking time bomb. I could explode at any moment. I can be doing something perfectly normal and all of a sudden start feeling light-headed and I wonder, *Am I hemorrhaging? Is it happening now?* That's why I've been passing out so much lately.

I guess the bottom line is, even if you were of a mind, it wouldn't be fair to ask you to marry someone with only a short time to live. You deserve better than that. So I'm calling off our engagement.

I love you, but someone else loves you too, and I think you love him.

Here's where I get my strength. The Twenty-third Psalm. "Yea, though I walk through the valley of the shadow of death, I will fear no evil, for You are with me; Your rod and Your staff, they comfort me. You prepare a table before me in the presence of my enemies. You anoint my head with oil; my cup runs over. Surely goodness and mercy shall follow me all the days of my life, and I will dwell in the house of the Lord forever."

Who knows, now that I've said it, I'll probably live to be a hundred. I may even outlive you, but however it plays, I want to ask you a favor. I'd be honored, Layla, regardless of when we get there, if you'd save your first dance in heaven—for me.

Love, with no strings attached,
Matthew

Layla crumpled the letter and looked away, another drop from her cheek hitting the now moist paper. She reached for the door, opening it to let herself out.

"Layla?"

Ambrose turned and gave her his hand, helping her step down. Mohamed followed, but she was already marching away. He hurried, taking two steps to her one until he was beside her, walking beneath the oaks, the light filtering through the branches and creating puzzles on the ground.

"Layla, I..."

"Don't...please, don't say anything." She dabbed her eyes with her tissue. Turning in the direction of the grave, she stood looking across a lawn festooned with flowers. "So that's Matthew?" she said, wiping her nose. "I feel awful. I've thought so many terrible things."

Mohamed puckered his lips, nodding. "He saved our lives."

Layla had her tissue out, but it came apart when she tried to unravel it to wipe her cheek. "I don't know, I'm...I'm so confused." She faced Mohamed again. "It's so much to process. I've been mourning your death for days, and...I have no reason to doubt you. You have to be telling the truth.

Matthew wouldn't tell me he was dead and then pretend to be you acting like himself. I know he loved me, but he'd never go that far. It's just that, I have to be sure..."

Mohamed took her by the shoulders and looked into her eyes. "I told you my story."

"Yes, but you could have told Matthew too."

Mohamed nodded. "Do you remember the last time we were together in Egypt, what you said to me?"

She looked up, shaking her head, her mouth wet, still dabbing her eyes. "Uh uh."

"You told me if I wanted to marry you, I had to become a Christian. And do you remember what you did?"

"I...I think so...I..."

But Mohamed cut her off, assuaging her doubt—*with a kiss*.

EPILOGUE

THE LITTLE FELUCCA PADDED back and forth, rocking on the current under the light of the moon. Mohamed pulled in the sail and dropped a bag of rocks over the side to anchor the boat, keeping it from drifting downriver. The sixteen-foot craft was the first purchase he'd made upon arriving back in Egypt, a flat-bottomed vessel with a triangular sail, made to accommodate only one or two people. It suited him fine, since most of the time he would be using it alone.

The moon poked through the cloud's silver lining, washing the small deck so he could see. He stooped over to pick up a short length of rope, his baggy sleeves sagging around his wrists. He was looking every bit the part of an Egyptian fisherman dressed in his *galabia*. The loose-fitting shirt hung down past his knees.

The boat creaked on the water. He folded the lateen over the yard, tying the canvas sail to prevent it from catching wind, though there was little chance of that on this particular night. The Nile lay calm and flat under the silver shining of the moon. Every time he slipped out onto the water he was reminded of stories he'd read in the Bible where Christ had called His disciples from mending their nets to follow Him. They would have used a mesh of strong cord, able to hold many fish, their vessels much like the boat he was standing in now. Christ had said He would make them fishers of men. That was the kind of fishing Mohamed wanted to do.

The clouds piled up one atop another except where the moon shone through like a beam of light cutting across his shoulder. The yard chafed against the mast, wood groaning against wood with the occasional clinking of an iron ring. Behind him, up and down the shore as far as the eye could see, were acres of cotton and beets and sugarcane. He turned, taking in the vast display of wealth it represented, the labors of his uncle now blessing his mother. And farther in, sitting on a rise above the floodplain, was Sayyid's former mansion, its windows filled with yellow light. It was a place he'd once called home but not a place he'd ever felt welcome.

Now his mother owned it all. Ever-faithful Sami had seen to that. At Mohamed's request, he had recovered the document that bore witness to the marriage. He'd even tracked down the imam that performed the ceremony and got him to confirm that Sayyid had married Zainab all those years ago. Zainab was now the rightful owner of everything Sayyid had once possessed.

She didn't want it. Her son was her reward. She had the house, food on the table, and a car, which she still hadn't learned to drive. The rest was excess. It had to be done quietly so as not to attract attention, but Mohamed's ministry—though now he called himself Matthew—would receive most of the profits from the farm. He prayed he would be worthy of his brother's name as he vowed to realize his dream. His father had abandoned him, choosing to give his life to destroy the lives of others. His brother had found him and had given his life, to save...he shuddered, struggling with the thought—*greater love has no one...*

The lights from the town, though dimmed by distance, winked on and off in the night. As far as the people of the village were concerned, he was dead. Zainab had framed both Arabic and English versions of the stories printed in the newspapers and had them hanging on her dining room walls. She had to; they showed pictures of Matthew, the son she had never known. But they also served to provide the meddlesome townspeople with an explanation. Her Islamic son had died in an attempt to destroy the Great Satan, but the Christian son, stolen from her as a child and raised in America, had survived and was now home.

Mohamed wouldn't be staying with her in the mansion. He was planning to share the Jesus he'd come to know. The more he remained out of sight, the better. He would occupy the small mud brick hovel he'd lived in as a child. Christ had appeared to him there.

Along the shore, crickets chirped and frogs croaked, breaking the still-ness of the night, but the air was calm and filled with the sweet aroma of the marsh. Mohamed hoisted the keel out of the river, the drain from the blade forming concentric rings on the dark blue water. An ancient Egyp-tian proverb said: "The one who voyages the Nile must have sails made of patience." *So true.* Tonight was one of those nights when movement down the river would be slow.

The moon passed in and out of the clouds; the air was warm, the evening still. He combed his fingers through his hair, scanning the coast. He'd spent many joyous hours holding Layla's hand as they wandered the shores, tramping through the reeds and building cities of silt and mud. She was in the United States, completing her medical degree. He was praying she'd one day join him in his quest and, like her father, minister to the needs of the impoverished peoples of Upper Egypt in hope of bringing them to Christ. He still felt warmed by her embrace...

"You told me if I wanted to marry you, I had to become a Christian. And do you remember what you did next?"

"I...I think so...I...

Mohamed cut her off, pulling her in to steal a kiss. Her arms circled him, and for a moment they shared an eternity, the bliss of heaven and all that was good on Earth, but Layla opened her eyes, breaking the spell. Her lips grew taut as she pushed him away.

"No...I can't. It's too soon."

Mohamed let his hands fall from her waist. "But I thought... "

"I do...but...but he was your brother, and I'm not even sure I know you anymore. Please, let's just give it some time. That's all I ask. Just a little time... "

And now he was here, and she was half a world away. Who knew if she'd be able to give up her comfortable life in the United States to endure the rigors of Egypt? The main thing was they were *both* seeking the will of the Lord. He had nothing to offer her, except maybe a small house made of yellow clay, and flowers from the newly planted garden in the front yard, and endless moonlit evenings sailing the Nile in a little wooden boat—not much perhaps, but it came with all the love one human being could give to another.

He shook his head, closing his eyes for a moment with a sigh, gathering strength. *Love*—it was the one thing Sayyid had denied him. You can't give what you don't possess. He might have given him power and the wealth this world has to offer, but it would have come with a chain. The bonds of his mother had lasted twelve years, but in all that time she was free. *Therefore if the Son makes you free, you shall be free indeed.*

Mohamed knelt down, gripping the rail to keep his balance against the boat's rocking as he leaned over the side to peer into the water. The veiled moon was softly diffused by the current's ebb and roll. Perhaps Jesus would reappear. If not tonight, someday soon. He would ride a white horse with His sword raised, coming for His own. That was His promise. Sayyid, and even his own father, had failed him—but they were just men. How much better to have a Father in heaven. How much better to be a son of *God*.

He gazed into the midnight blue of the river and saw the clouds part, revealing a reflection of himself—like a face with a look of approval smiling down on him from above. He tilted his head to the right and watched the image copy his move. They were exact opposites, yet somehow the same. He tilted his head the other way and chuckled, then rolled back onto the deck laughing, his heart free of all that once held it bound, laughing like the wind, the rain, and the sun when it shines, until tears streamed down his face—*oh, the love of Jesus!*—he was home, and he was *free*.

Other books by Keith Clemons

Angel in the Alley
These Little Ones
Above the Stars
If I Should Die

I found it so gripping I could not put it down. It's well written. It's an amazing book. I hope he does a lot of books like this. There's talent here. You've got to pick up this book.

—David Mainse
President of Crossroads Television and TV Host of
100 Huntley Street

It is refreshing to find a writer who aspires to a level of creative excellence. I highly recommend this book to everyone who can read. To those who cannot read, find a friend to read it to you.

—Paul A. Webb
Publisher and Chairman, Head to Head Ministries

Clever, brave, insightful, and compelling. This is one of those novels that demand to be read and demand to be discussed.

—Michael Coren
Author and Television Host of *Michael Coren Live*

Mr. Clemons has written a very moving novel, one in which you care about the characters and empathize with what they're going through.

—Virginia Boreland
The Christian Herald

A fascinating, attention-grabbing novel that deals with tough, real-life situations, examining the aftereffects of euthanasia on countless lives.

—Excerpt from a review in *Catholic Insight*